~~Re

The Oath

"... an all around good read, and a sobering one at that. Gaylon McCollough is a consummate story teller and he has produced a real thriller in *The Oath*—a yarn that could be ripped from today's newspapers. While The *Oath* is a fictional account of a classic struggle of good and evil, the story is inspired by current events in this nation and beyond. The reader is quickly drawn into this fast paced and well crafted thriller and once it has been picked up it is hard to put it down,

.... Dr. Thomas P. Rosandich, President,
United States Sports Academy

* * * * *

"*The Oath* isn't just a thriller; it presents an object lesson—grabs the reader's attention early and holds it through each page. Like the oaths that many of us have taken, it conveys a far deeper meaning. It reconnects us to our founders and the basis upon which freedom is built and preserved."

.... Lloyd Ketchum, U.S. Army, Retired,
CEO Liberating Technologies

* * * * *

"Truthfully frightening and eye opening... so much fact and truth written in this story of fiction...kept me glued to the book until completion."

.... Sharon Santurri, MPA, Accountant,
Former Political Consultant

* * * * *

"Astonishing facts woven into *The Oath* results in a spectacular story about the dangerous and secret Global Empire and its effect on Americans, past, present and future. This undoubtedly would make a blockbuster movie."

.... Terry D'Orazio, Owner, Community Printing, Inc.

* * * * *

"*The Oath* is an intriguing and timely book. Has the Cycle of Democracy run its course in these United States? Can a small group of intellectual elites and financiers orchestrate America's demise? Hard to stop reading and impossible to forget..."
.... Lou Vickery, Radio Host/Author

* * * * *

"*The Oath* tells the story of how one little man, only nine years old, becomes a great man impervious to the lure of power and money. Mason Edmonds embodies the heart and soul of a man about whom God surely must feel proud to call a son, wonderfully hand-crafted into His own image. A perfect sequel to McCollough's, *Let Us Make Man.*"
.... Dr. Karen Gold, Forensic Psychologist

* * * * *

" I found *The Oath* informative and interesting. People need to be reminded that we are 'one nation under God.' Readers will get insight into how our freedoms are being attacked and that we must all be vigilant, aware and involved."
.... Claudette Lessard, U.S. Navy, Retired, Sr. Chief, Clinical Administrator

* * * * *

"A fascinating story that will not let you lay down the book to the very end. Historical facts and trials and tribulations of individual characters are blended masterly, reminding us of situations that resemble the predicaments we are facing today. Read it; you will love it..."
.... Dietmar Schellenberg, PhD, Behavior Specialist

THE OATH

A Secret Operation Exposes a Conspiracy to Deliver America into the Hands of Her Archenemy, the Illuminati

By

E. GAYLON
McCOLLOUGH

Argus Enterprises International
North Carolina ***New Jersey

The Oath © 2010
All rights reserved by: Dr. E. Gaylon McCollough

No part of this book may be reproduced or transmitted in any form or by any means, graphic, electronic, or mechanical, including photocopying, recording, taping, or by any informational storage retrieval system without prior permission in writing from the publisher.

A-Argus Better Book Publishers, LLC

For information:
A-Argus Better Book Publishers, LLC
Post Office Box 914
Kernersville, North Carolina 27285
www.a-argusbooks.com

ISBN: 978-0-9845142-5-0
ISBN: 0-98945142-5-2

Cover designed by Bryan Lee

Printed in the United States of America

"Sometimes a story finds a storyteller rather than the other way around.[1]"

Never was the epigram truer than when President Mason L. Edmonds contacted this author.

---

[1] *Neverwas,* Joshua Michael Stern, Miramax Films, 2007

PROLOGUE

Although this is his story, I spoke with President Edmonds only once. He called me late one evening from the Oval Office and asked for my assistance in creating a historical narrative to expose "a treasonous conspiracy involving at least two branches of the U.S. government that had been conducting acts of political and fiscal terrorism," and that he and a group of patriots had investigated their activities. When the President mentioned unfamiliar terms, like *False Flag Operation, Emasculation Proclamation* and the *Rothschild Formula,* I detected an air of uneasiness in his voice. He would only say that there was a lot to report and little time to do it.

I listened intently, making notes, as the President spoke. He said that some of the nation's highest-ranking officials and members of the press were "no more than flag bearers for America's archenemy. Others were political assassins who were groomed to ensure the demise of democracy and capitalism worldwide."

The President also recommended that we meet to discuss the details of his memoirs. Due to his untimely death, we never got the chance to do so. I did the next best thing. I visited Fountainhead, a small ranch that Mason and Norene Edmonds named in honor of Ayn Rand's 1940's novel.

For three rather intensive weeks, I interviewed the former First Lady, taking her back to what she remembered about her late husband's family and childhood. I inquired about his teachers, instructors, heroes ... and enemies. The more I learned from each of these sources, the more certain I became that Dr. Edmonds and his Operation Annuit Coeptis (OAC) allies had, indeed, uncovered a deeply seated conspiracy and that President Edmonds expected me—with his wife's assistance—to expose the bitter truth: global reformists are orchestrating the demise of America.

If I was going to tell Mason Edmonds' story, I had to delve into his mind. I made every attempt to draw out what Norene Edmonds knew about her late husband's thoughts, accomplishments, fears, and failures. And with her blessings, I poured over his writings and lectures, including a small notebook that he kept in his right hip pocket. I was also privileged to review a private collection of diaries and unpublished essays that dated back to his childhood. Oval office audio and video recordings were made available to me by his successor, General Harold Purcell. I was given permission to interview Mason Edmonds' long-time executive assistant, Martha Shores. And I was shown the handwritten oath to which Mason Edmonds and his OAC colleagues once swore as they set out on a mission to expose the Illuminati's ever-stiffening grip on America's politicians and mainstream media.

Everything I could gather was used to construct a manuscript that takes readers into, what the late President recorded in one of his diaries as, "America's near death experience." It was then that I realized the gravity of the challenges that Dr. Edmonds faced when he was suddenly and unexpectedly elevated from Secretary of Health and Human Services into the Presidency. Because he was one Commander-in-Chief who could not be bought with money and/or favors, he became the prime target of America's archenemy: a clique of what has to be the most narcissistic, ruthless, and power-hungry personalities on the planet. The Inner Circle of this group of self-proclaimed overlords believes themselves to be descendants of the Annunaki or "sons of God" mentioned in Genesis 6:4 *("There were giants on the earth in those days; and also after that, when the sons of God came in unto the daughters of men, and they bore children to them, the same became mighty men which were of old, men of renown.")*

As you wind your way through each chapter of *The Oath,* bear in mind that though this is a novel. It personifies—in modern day terms—the ageless battle between Good and Evil. In that vein, the character I chose to call Mason Edmonds embodies the resilient spirit that has resided in freedom-loving, well-meaning citizens since the beginning of time. Like all children, he was influenced by those who mentored him, one of which was a maternal grandmother. A sagely, lucid ninety-nine-year old Laney Lambert told him, "At the time of creation, human beings were given dominion over the new world. Part of God's plan was to have us participate in creating a society here on Earth patterned after the one in Heaven.

"Man's purpose on this planet is really not as complicated as some would have you believe," Laney explained. "In fact, if you don't get bogged down in the distractions intentionally planted by the Devil's disciples, God's plan is quite simple—obey His commandments, tell the truth and treat others as you would want to be treated.

"The mysteries of life are intended to be solved", she added. "The answers have always been there. The one, true Ruler of the Universe has seen to it. Watch for—and recognize—the signs when they are revealed. Clues do not always come at once or on the brilliant light of day. The signs are many, like pieces of a puzzle. When pieced together, a clear picture or story emerges. What comes to light is often pretty; sometimes it is not. So, you must always be prepared to deal with both the good and bad that exist in this world and to make others cognizant of the dangers you've discovered."

In keeping with the advice offered by a wise grandmother, this novel is intended to plant seeds of inquiry and let each reader reach his or her own conclusions as to whether *The Oath* is fact, fiction or a sign of things yet to be unfurled.

A virtual treasure trove of ideas and ideals are woven into the pictorial edifice of the story's hero. Like him, the events, characters and places depicted in this novel are based upon ponderings, possibilities and probabilities as seen from this storyteller's perspective of past history and current events.

Vignettes set out in the early chapters are intended to demonstrate how the situations that people experience as children shape who they become as adults, when the fate of their world rests on their shoulders.

The odyssey that is Mason Edmonds' struggle against a secretive, invisible empire begins in a small southern community, appropriately named Prideville. The story could, however, originate anywhere in America and describe thousands, if not millions, of citizens and neighborhoods. The world of young Mason, his extended family, and community are introduced in early chapters to remind readers of how—in a single generation—the geopolitical world has changed. Sadly, much of the change that has occurred has not been for the betterment of humankind.

Before one can understand the 21st century version of the United States of America, or see what it might become, it is necessary to reflect on a bygone era that Margaret Mitchell appropriately described as having been swept away by the wind, in this case "Moriah, Conquering Wind," one of the many names attributed America's long-standing archenemy, The Order of The Illuminati.

As you peruse the pages of this novel, keep in mind that the chapter in history it depicts ends in the year 2012 A.D. Whether—as some have predicted—the world ends that same year, one thing is certain: more "change" is coming. America will be heading down one of two roads. It will either be returning to a free and independent republic ruled by auto-determination or continuing down its current path of destruction, as described in Alexander Tyler's "Cycles of Democracy." Without a revolutionary change of direction, America will likely become a puppet nation in an Orwellian-styled, One World Government ruled by self anointed gods of a New World Order.

Finally, you are urged not to set this book aside until you have read the Epilogue; for in it you'll get an up close and personal look at an incredible former First Lady, sworn to a noble cause—seeing that her late husband's revelations reach the masses. It is her way of ensuring that the conspiracy pieced together by her husband and his Operation Annuit Coeptis colleagues does not end up as dust, scattered into oblivion by the conquering winds of cataclysmic change.

E. Gaylon McCollough, MD, FACS

CHAPTER 1

It was July 4, 1952, a time in history when Americans were oblivious to the invisible enemy in their midst. While the vast majority of citizens were busy commemorating America's independence, the press was conspiring with founders of a New World Order to sell her into bondage.

If the U.S was to remain a society governed by fair and equitable laws, a diverse militia of patriots would need to arise and to make their voices heard. To turn back democracy's archenemy, men and women from all walks of life and every corner of the nation would have to come together proudly, and simply, as Americans. If—during the process of saving America—heroes emerged, they would come from seemingly ordinary people who responded to extraordinary times and circumstances.

Mason Lambert Edmonds embodied this kind of hero. He was an "old soul on a new mission," one that surely transcended time and space. Though there had been many, this assignment was to protect and defend the Constitution of the United States of America and its borders against "all enemies, foreign and domestic." On his way to the Oval Office, the son of Owen and Angela Edmonds would be reminded—once more—that the universe is filled with enemies of different orders, including those out to shackle the resolute human spirit and commandeer its sacred bond with God.

When the smoke from Armageddon's opening act finally clears, what kind of world will remain? Who will inherit it—the meek, masters of the meek, a healthy mix of both, or none of the above?

Six decades would pass before answers are forthcoming; but we are getting ahead of the story that I was asked to tell. First, let us look back, at the making of an unlikely President and get to know the people and places that shaped his character.

. . . .

Mason's father was a veteran of World War II. From hearing Owen share stories with other veterans, Mason was familiar with conventional warfare. However, the mounting siege that the lad would be called upon to foil as an adult was anything but conventional. The war for the heart and soul of America had long been declared—from realms unknown as well as from within borders that had intentionally been thrown open to the enemy's minions.

In years to come—and at the direction of America's archenemy—puppet administrations would encourage illegal immigration. The intent was to create numbers at ballot boxes. Generating such chaos fit the Illuminati's modus operandi. It is part of a greater plan designed to take control of the U.S. Part of the plan called for clouding Constitutional lines between lawful/unlawful and legal/illegal. Playing on the conscience of good and caring people with Judeo-Christian upbringings, the Illuminati could methodically break down all kinds of barriers that were erected by the founding fathers to protect America against this group. If it could become unlawful to identify and detain law-breakers, laws and law enforcement could be emasculated. New laws would be imposed and administered by overlords of a New World Order. With a migration invasion—and in keeping with Tyler's Law—ballot boxes would end up becoming weapons of mass destruction against the mightiest nation in Earth's history. It was an ingenious plan, long in developing.

Through clever wealth redistribution schemes, New World Order advocates intended to confiscate the resources and government of the U.S. As they had done in with Freemasonry, in Europe, Illuminati disciples would infiltrate one of the major political parties and promote their ghoulish agenda through the political process.

Owen Edmonds was a Freemason and knew of how a group of bankers and intellectuals had confiscated much of the Order in Europe. He and his fellow Masons had been warned that the same tactic would be tried in the U.S.

Descendents and recruited disciples of the original Illuminati on this side of the Atlantic were out to revise the U.S. Constitution. From past experiences, they knew that control could be gained and maintained by catering to a gullible, entitlement-seeking society. Recipients of redistributed wealth could be counted upon to vote for politicians who promised them what they wanted, even though what they wanted was wrong for the nation.

With shackles having been gently slipped around the nation's neck, in less than a generation, the U.S. and a new breed of slaves would be owned by an Illuminati-controlled World Government. Although the mainstream media knew about—and participated in—the plan to broker a broken America into the hands of a self-designated "supranational sovereignty," most of the people and organizations that could have prevented the transfer were *intentionally* uninformed and/or misled. This was, however, not the case in the Edmonds' household. Mason's parents and a wise grandmother were busy teaching truth to a boy eager to know it.

How can we be certain that the Illuminati's conspiracy was launched in 1952 and that the American people were kept in the dark? We can, because—according to Operation Annuit Coeptis files—four decades later, at a meeting of the Trilateral Commission, Illuminist David Rockefeller announced:

> "We are grateful to The Washington Post, New York Times, Time Magazine and other great publications whose directors have attended our meetings and [we have] respected their promises of discretion for almost forty years. It would have been impossible for us to develop our plan for the world if we had been subject to the bright lights of publicity

during those years. But, the world is now much more sophisticated and prepared to march towards a world government. The supranational sovereignty of an intellectual elite and world bankers is surely preferable to the national auto-determination practiced in past centuries."[2]

As Rockefeller and his fellow Illuminists conspired behind the veils of transparency, families like that of Owen and Angela Edmonds were going about the daily business of living.

The Edmonds' family circle was governed by simple rules: the even-handed laws of God and Man, the Ten Commandments, the Golden Rule, a pledge of allegiance to the Jeffersonian Constitution of the United States of America and the flag that stood for it.

In the minds of post World War II Americans there was no doubt that the founding fathers considered God's covenants as they created laws that would govern a new republic steadily rising out of a Western Hemisphere wilderness. The average American family was not aware of the fact that the architects of this new nation were aware of the freedoms that had been confiscated in Europe and intended for America to become—and remain—the standard bearer for democracy and capitalism.

. . . .

On Main Streets, post World War II America was characterized by a colonial sense of courage, patriotism, liberty, and abundance that among much of the population—and in keeping with Tyler's Cycles of Democracies—has since been replaced (in large part) with selfishness, apathy and dependence upon government.

In the 1950s, Americans believed that Providence had, indeed, favored their undertakings. An overwhelming majority took pride in the fact that—like a rat—the defeated

---

[2] *The Bilderbergers,* The Jeremiah Project, Vic Bilson, 2009

butcher of Nazi Germany retreated to a secret bunker and took the coward's way out. Rather than face his accusers, he took his own life. On the opposite side of the globe, imperialists perpetrators of the dastardly Sunday morning attack on Pearl Harbor had signed on to an unconditional surrender rather than be wiped off the face of the earth. It was a time of justified celebration. Independence had won the day against servitude. At least this is what the people were led to believe.

The post-war national debt was high; yet a loyal and unsuspecting public trusted all branches of government and the American free press to watch their backs and make prudent decisions on its behalf. Unfortunately, the people's trust was misplaced. Little did Americans know that a gang of conspirators, to whom the U.S. owed a lot of money—and with the knowledge of The Washington Post, New York Times, and Time magazine—were summarily dismantling the U.S. Constitution and the nation it under pinned. It was an all-out attack on each of the foundations that had been responsible for America's becoming a great nation. Taking directions from headquarters in Europe, Illuminati minions were going about banning the Ten Commandments, shelving the Golden Rule, lobbying to remove prayer in schools and planning to remove God from the Pledge of Allegiance, all for the purpose of establishing a new set of rules—New World Order rules—created by, and for, America's and God's archenemy.

This is the mystery-laden dramathon into which an "old soul" inhabiting the body of young Mason Edmonds was casted. His character was supported by people, spirits and philosophies that shaped the ideals for which he lived—and died—long before his mission was fulfilled.

CHAPTER 2

Billboards at the city limits displayed the greeting: "*Welcome to Prideville: an America-First Community.*"
Travelers taking Highway 98 through the quant southern community on the Fourth of July, in nineteen-fifty-two, learned that town officials and citizens took the sign's message seriously—perhaps too seriously, for some.

At precisely 11: 45 a.m. police barricades were placed at the city limits, bringing the flow of traffic in all directions to a halt. Beyond the barriers, a parade was about to begin.

Trying to escape the heat of the midday sun, stalled passengers abandoned non-air conditioned vehicles, sought out sprawling shade trees, and prayed for the faint gust of a rare summer breeze that might blow in from the Gulf of Mexico, just a few miles to the South.

In the distance, familiar sounds of John Philip Sousa's marches and fireworks enticed some of the stranded to join a sea of local flag-waving Americans, who lined Main Street in celebration of Independence Day. Though the day had been set aside to celebrate America's independence from one oppressive superpower, another was taking its place, one that was gently applying the shackles of bondage while making Americans *believe* that they were free.

By 1:00 p.m. the procession of marching bands, war heroes, and patriotic floats had turned south off Main Street. Barricades were removed and traffic began to inch forward. But, progress was short-lived. The crowd dispersed, returning to their respective homes to barbeque ribs or chicken on an open, outdoor grill.

Just east of town center, the highway was once again blocked, this time by a trans-generational squabble that had taken over a section of Main Street. Two unlikely participants were engaged in what appeared to be an emotionally charged tug-o-war.

Under different circumstances, horn-blowers and expletive-shouters might have exercised more tolerance or taken the time to realize that the younger of the two women was, actually, risking her life to save a mentally-impaired senior citizen.

"Please come back to the house with me, Mamma. We're going to cause a wreck ... or get run over!" Angela Edmonds exclaimed.

"Turn me loose, or I'll slap you," Laney Lambert scolded. "I've got to get home and take care of my children. They're all by themselves. Who are you anyway?"

"Mamma, I'm Angela—your daughter. There are no children at home. We're all grown up. You live in that house right over there with me," Angela said, pointing to the modest home on the south side of the street, much of which was built by her husband's own hands. "See that boy in the window—the one looking at us. He's your grandson, Mason. Today is his birthday."

Though physically removed from the action, eleven-year-old Mason Edmonds anxiously watched from the living room window of his home while his mother attempted to restrain and retrieve a bewildered grandmother and return her to safety.

"I don't believe you," Laney chided, still trying to pull free. Though she was approaching eighty, the wiry product of the Great Depression exhibited exceptional strength for a woman of her size and age. Recruiting every ounce of her genetically-instilled grit, she tugged against her daughter's younger – yet tiring arms, convinced that her children were home alone and needed her.

Losing ground with present tactics, Angela concluded that if she had any chance of convincing her mother to come out of the street and back to safety, she needed to try a different approach. If she could *re-direct* her mother's train of thought, perhaps she could gain control of an otherwise unmanageable situation. It had worked before.

"Mamma, it's too far to walk. I'll drive you home. Let's go back to the house and get your purse," Angela said."

"It's a long way. And my children will be afraid if I'm not home by dark," Laney responded. "Do you have a horse and wagon? I have a good one at home. Who did you say you are?"

"A good friend," Angela replied.

Having been assured that she was going to be taken to her waiting children, Laney's demeanor changed from resistance to compliance. She followed Angela to safety, ending what had been a trying and danger-ridden situation.

Along the way to the Edmonds' home, Angela continued to re-direct Laney's attention, pointing out the beautiful flower garden in full bloom in a neighbor's yard.

A single file of Army helicopters flew overhead. The choppers were returning to a nearby military base after participating in Prideville's Independence Day activities.

Raising her voice to overcome the puttering roar of the crafts' turbo engines, Angela said to her mother, "Those beautiful flowers remind me of the flowering bush in the front yard of your house." She was referring to a large Azalea plant that she had sprigged from a bloom given to her by Owen Edmonds on one of his Sunday afternoon courtship visits before the couple was married. Like the pair's devotion to each other and to each other's families, the sprig grew with each passing year.

As his mother and grandmother approached the house, Mason—dressed in red, white and blue for his birthday and that of his country—opened the door. Although he had missed the parade and Fourth of July festivities, he was glad to see that the incident involving two of the most important people in his life had ended well. It was not the first time he had witnessed such behavior. The occasions on which his beloved grandmother turned into a different person were becoming more frequent. And, he didn't understand why.

Once inside the house, Angela locked the door behind her and said, "Mamma, let's go to the piano and practice the songs we're going to sing in church on Sunday. Mason will sing with us."

"That's a good idea," Laney responded. "I like to sing and listen to you play the piano", once again remembering who Angela and Mason were. Angela, Laney and Mason went into the living room where an upright piano stood against an outside wall. It was a frequent gathering place. Laney loved music and seemed to respond favorably to the melodic notes played by her daughter. The sound of music seemed to provide a link between the past and present.

Angela was a natural-born entertainer. Many referred to her as a "look-alike" of the popular screen actress, Joan Crawford. While she was not a traditionally-trained musician, Angela played the piano for anyone who asked. If she heard the melody in her head, she could duplicate it on a keyboard. The colloquial way to describe her gift was that she "played by ear."

After hearing *Amazing Grace* and *The Old Rugged Cross*, Laney was content. Angela handed Laney a magazine and said, "Mother, look through this and see if you like anything in here."

Laney began to turn the same pages that she had examined hundreds of time, not remembering that she had seen them before. Still, she was content – at least for the moment.

Angela went into the adjoining room, closed the door and telephoned her doctor's office. Wallace Grimsley, a former grammar school classmate, had been the family's doctor since his return to Prideville upon completing medical school, some twenty years previously.

"Hello, doctor's office," the receptionist answered.

"Melba, this is Angela. I'm surprised that you answered, being the Fourth of July."

"Illness takes no holidays," Melba replied.

"Is Dr. Grimsley available? I need to speak to him if possible," Angela said.

"As a matter of fact, he's coming through the door now. He is just returning from the parade to see a couple of people suffering from heat prostration. It must be ninety-five in the shade," Melba replied.

"Hello, Angela, what can I do for you?" Dr. Grimsley asked.

"It's about my mother, Wallace," Angela replied. "Her outbursts and episodes of confusion are coming more frequently. It is getting harder to keep her from running away. Today, I found her in the middle of Main Street, trying to find her way to a home that she hasn't lived in for more than eighteen years. Is there anything I can give her to treat her confusion?"

"I wish there were," the doctor answered. "Once a patient develops *hardening of the arteries*, there is not much we can do. It's similar to the condition described by a Doctor Alzheimer called '*pre-senile dementia.*' But the disease described by Doctor Alzheimer occurs in younger people, most commonly women. Almost anything I would prescribe to keep her calm would compound her confusion and disorientation. Does she still recognize you?"

"Most of the time she does. But the times that she *doesn't know me* ... or Owen ... or Mason are getting more frequent."

"I was afraid of that. Is she eating?" the Doctor asked.

"When I remind her to eat, she does," Angela responded. "But, she's as thin as a rail. She's been like that for the past year."

"Angela, hold on for just a moment so that I can get Martha to take the temperature of a couple of patients and start pushing fluids. I'll be right back with you," the doctor said.

"The condition your mother has is one that we will all face one day, assuming we live long enough," Dr. Grimsley said when he returned to the phone. "Hopefully, medical research will discover some way to slow the process or make it more tolerable for patients and families alike. Sometimes, I wonder who is really in charge of medical research—which conditions they want to abolish and which ones serve their purpose. Right now, the only thing you can do is to try to keep your mother well-nourished and comfortable. Keep your doors locked in a way that she can't open them when you are not watching. I'm sorry that you have to resort to these measures but that's all the advice I can give you at this time," the doctor said.

"Thank you for taking my call," Angela replied. "It always helps to know that there's nothing to do for her other than what I am doing. If she knew how she sometimes acts, she would be embarrassed. Except for the periods of confusion, she is such a grand lady."

"I know," Dr. Grimsley replied. "I clearly remember how she was just a few years back."

"Sometimes, the things that come out of her mouth sound demonic, so cruel, so hateful," Angela said.

"Clearly, there are demons in this world," Dr Grimsley replied, "but your mother is not one of them. I don't think that there is an evil bone in her body. With dementia, patients often repeat what they heard from others, statements that were upsetting at the time and immediately suppressed. When the suppression mechanisms of the brain are no longer functioning properly, the words that were stored away come out, often as unfiltered outbursts."

"But, they are so hurtful," Angela interjected.

"They are not your Mother's words or thoughts. They were sewn by those who are sworn to spread evil throughout the world," the doctor said.

"That helps a lot," Angela responded, "I won't keep you any longer. I know that you need to take care of patients there in your office. Have a good day ... and Doc, thanks again for being there for us," Angela added.

"Always, It's what I was sworn to do, you know the Oath of Hippocrates," Dr. Grimsley replied. "Call me if you need me," he added, hanging up the phone.

"What did Dr. Grimsley say?" Mason asked his mother.

"He said that Granny has an incurable condition that comes with getting old and that her periods of confusion will only worsen with time."

"You mean that she's not going to get well?" Mason asked his mother.

"No, son, I'm afraid not."

"Is she going to die?" the lad asked.

"Granny is getting older by the year. In time, we will all die," Angela said. "But, we will have her memory with us always."

Angela could see the tears well up in her son's eyes. On the way to his room, Angela could hear him say, "That doesn't seem fair. It's just not fair. When I grow up, I'm going to use all the clues that she gave to me during our storytelling sessions to find a way to make people like Granny well."

Angela thought about her earlier conversation with long time friend and family physician. His reference to diseases "serving the purpose" of those in charge was baffling. "Who is in charge," she thought, "and what do those in charge plan to do with the rest of us?"

Though Angela would never know the answer to her question, her son would know it far too well.

But, today was a special day for her son and she, still, had to bake his birthday cake.

CHAPTER 3

Young Mason Edmonds' support system was broader than most. It was as if he had two families. In many ways, Mason was the son that his Aunt Cloe and Uncle Danley Littlejohn never had. Weekends, holidays, and summer vacations meant that Mason would go to the country. When the work around the farm was done, Danley and Mason went fishing or hunting. Evenings were often spent with neighbors.

In the country, storytelling was an art form practiced by the men of the house. Any excuse to have a gathering was seized. Barbeques, "peanut boilings" and sugar cane parties provided entertainment and a chance to break bread—or something edible—together.

In those days, houses were far apart. People often rode horses or horse driven wagons to social gatherings. Danley saddled Cricket, a gentle mare he had bought for Mason, and tied her to the back of a wagon pulled by Sol, the muscular gilding that Danley also used to work the fields on his farm. Rather than joining Danley and Cloe in the wagon, Mason rode behind it—on a well-restrained Cricket.

Those who didn't come in horse or mule-drawn wagons arrived in pickup trucks. Children sat on a homemade quilt in the open back of the truck. Though the dirt roads were bumpy, there were no car seats or belts ... or laws dictating restraints of any kind.

Children were told to sit still in the back of the truck ... and did as they were told. In 1952, discipline was not considered child abuse, but an expression of love and caring. Godfather of the "Hippie Generation," Dr. Benjamin Spock's, parenting and child rearing manual had not been published.

Sitting in the backyard around an open fire, over which hung a large black kettle filled with salt water and freshly uprooted and picked green peanuts or around an open pit over which a pig was stretched over a skewer, created great anticipation for the hungry crowd. Freshly cut stalks of sugar cane, carved into small slices provided appetizers during the long waits for the meat or nuts to cook. Conversations often focused on the ailments of those in attendance. In many respects the neighborhood events served as group therapy sessions. Like listening to country music, when one knows that others are having problems, it seems to ease their own pain—at least a bit.

After airing out physical ills, the conversationalists turned to discussing local and national politics. So as a child, Mason became versed in the kinds of things that grass root Americans worried about—health, making a living, and politics. He saw how the grassroots political system worked and the kinds of expectations placed on elected officials.

It was the responsibility of the host family to see that the County Commissioner attended these gatherings. By attending the precursors of town hall meetings, elected officials had to face and be directly accountable to their constituents. Doctors were always invited. Free medical advice would have been as welcomed in the 1950s as free healthcare was to become fifty years later.

In public gatherings, women generally did more listening than talking - at least in mixed company; however before her memory began to fail, Laney had been a great storyteller. As a widowed mother of seven children, she had a lot of experience with what the late great New York surgeon, Dr. John Conley, called "vocal painting," although Laney liked to call it "yarn-telling." And, she was always encouraged by the crowd to tell a tale or two.

Though the evening began with "yarn-telling," it invariably ended up with discussing politics. Word of mouth was how news traveled in the country. A politician verbalized his or her platform and received instructions on how to vote on issues directly from the people responsible for electing—and re-electing him. And, anytime politics was discussed, young Mason was all ears. He saw how important it was to those who cared for him to have a voice in the political arena.

He was particularly interested in the comments of an older gentleman who was only known to the community as "Dexter." There was a mystic surrounding Dexter. No one dared ask him for his real name. Forty-two years earlier, Dexter had worked at a private resort owned by financial mogul J.P. Morgan. The exclusive clubhouse was located on Jekyll Island, just off the Georgia mainland. When Dexter spoke, the crowd paid close attention. He told them of conversations he overheard in 1910 as he served several guests who met to discuss the creation of a banking system they chose to call "The Federal Reserve." According to Dexter, the meeting wasn't about banking at all. Rather it was about establishing a single government and monetary system that would eventually rule the world. At the time, there was no way that Mason Edmonds could have known about the role he would be asked to play on the world stage.

On one occasion, Dexter shared with his friends a story that he overheard during one of the Jekyll meetings. It had to do with frogs. One of the bankers said to the others in attendance, "We have to move slowly and methodically. It's like boiling frogs," he added. "If you throw a frog in boiling water, the frog will jump out. However, if you put a frog in a pot of cool water and slowly turn up the heat, the frog will just sit there and be consumed. That's how we will take over the world."

Though most of those present at "peanut boilings" in Copter Country didn't understand banking and financial systems, they clearly understood nature and creatures of all kinds. They also knew about schemes designed to control men's lives. And, Mason was taken by the fact that an island off the coast of Georgia had the same name as one of the personalities in a story that his grandmother had told him. The main character in the story was known both as Dr. Jekyll *and* Mr. Hyde. What Mason didn't know *at the time* was that the men who met on Jekyll Island in the early nineteen hundreds for the purpose of establishing the Federal Reserve System also had two personalities—the one they presented to Congress and the American people, and a more sinister one.

. . . .

    Before dementia set in Laney Lambert was a master storyteller, and for good reason. Rural homes of the early nineteen hundreds had no radios, televisions or electricity. Except in winter months, after the sun went down, Laney and her children gathered on the front porch in the moonlight or by a kerosene lantern, where she entertained them, telling her children about their deceased father and the immigrant families from which they sprang. When the weather turned cold, they moved inside and sat by the fire.

    Angela particularly liked the stories of how the father she never knew laughed and played with her brothers and sisters—how he built tree houses and toy wagons from limbs and logs he gathered from the woods behind the house and cut with an axe and handsaw.

    The only visual image that Angela had of her father, Wilson Lambert, was displayed on a single ragged-edge black and white photograph. In her mind, however, he would forever be bigger than life. The image had been shaped by the stories Laney told about this extraordinary man and loving father.

    Like the girl he married, Wilson Lambert hailed from a poor—but respected—family. He and Laney decided to marry at an early age. Both were only eighteen years old. Wilson's father, Mark Lambert, and uncle, Matthew Lambert, both decorated heroes, died in the Civil War. Though they had fought gallantly, following General Lee's surrender at Appomattox, all Confederate soldiers were told to return home. Before Robert E. Lee dismissed his army, the General said, "If you men will be as good a citizens as you are soldiers, America will be alright." Without another word, General Lee turned and disappeared into his tent. He had done his best to lead a hopeless cause. Now, it was time to send his embattled warriors on their way to rebuild a nation.

    In a letter written and handed off to a fellow soldier on the way home from the war, Wilson's father wrote of many of the things that he and his brother had witnessed. Though the letter arrived safely, its writer didn't.

Wilson's mother, Samantha, opened the envelope and read, "When we came through Tuscaloosa, grown men wept. Under orders of General Sherman, the Union Army had burned everything in sight. They pillaged homes, schools, libraries, and museums, taking from our fellow southerners anything of value. Bruised and battered women told us of how they were gang raped and beaten by Grant's army. Surely, the orders to commit such atrocities didn't come from an American. What the Yankees did to the land and the people who lived on it, was a sin and I told one of them that I was going to tell the world what they had done."

"Oh no, you won't," Mark attributed to a defiant Union soldier. "We've been ordered to see that your kind won't live to tell."

Finding a safe place out of the sight of the Sherman's soldiers, Mark finished the letter he had been writing and handed it off to a fellow Confederate warrior traveling home with him and his brother. "Please see that this gets to my family. I might not make it home. Evil men cannot allow the truth—or those who speak it—to survive." he said to Ronny Smith, a seventeen-year-old fellow Confederate soldier. Mark had met Ronny when the two of them found themselves sharing a barn for the night on a plantation just outside of Atlanta, known as Twelve Oaks.

Mark Lambert and his Confederate colleagues found what appeared to be a safe place to camp for the night. While the campers slept, a platoon of Union soldiers with guns firing and bayonets fixed attacked the camp. Everyone but Ronny Smith was slaughtered. As fate would have it, Ronny had heard the call of Nature and slipped to the outskirts of the camp. When he realized that the raid was underway, it was too late to warn his fellow soldiers. Within minutes, the sleeping journeymen were dead. It was not the first time that murder had been committed to hide the truth. It wouldn't be the last.

CHAPTER 4

No matter how many times he heard Laney's stories, Mason appreciated the fact that his grandmother loved him enough to share a part of America's history that he would not have otherwise known.

On a hot August afternoon back in 1950, Laney's instructional session began like most others. Nine-year-old Mason took his favorite position on the floor at his grandmother's feet. There, the precocious lad learned some of life's most important lessons.

Once he was settled, Laney looked down at him with her loving blue eyes and said, "Some of the things that I am going to tell you may be more than a boy of your age can understand. However, I won't be around forever and I want you to have heard the truth about what people do and why they do it, at least as I know the truth to be. I don't expect you to remember everything, but I want you to write down the lessons that I will share with you in your notebook and keep it with you always. In the same notebook, write down the lessons learned from other people. Read what you have written at different ages and stages of your life. Each lesson is part of a greater puzzle that, in time, will become clear. Even if you don't understand everything now, one day you will. Share the things you learn with your children and your children's children," Laney said. "For, wisdom must never die. It has to be passed from generation to generation, adding new truths along the way. That's the only way to keep evil-minded people from making slaves of the rest of us."

"Tell me everything," young Mason Edmonds begged. "I've got a good mind in my head. I can remember things better than you might think.

"I'm sure you can," Laney said.

As always, she repeated the same preamble. "When I was a girl, times were hard. It was a time of struggle and rebuilding. When The Great Depression hit the nation, the people living in the rural South had not yet recovered from the devastating effects of the Civil War. Both events were created by a small group of people who were out to make slaves of the rest of us," Laney began.

"According to one of the carpetbaggers that the Lamberts had befriended, the War Between the States was conceived and financed by power-hungry outsiders based in Europe. Both the Union soldiers and Confederate soldiers were used as puppets to a great conspiracy.

When the war ended, both sides had suffered more than the loss of lives. Citizens of the Confederacy had emptied their bank accounts as well as money-packed socks hidden under their mattresses to support the reason they were fighting—to keep the federal government out of the lives and businesses of the common man. When the shooting stopped, what little money any Southerner had was not worth the paper upon which it was printed. The South was both broken ... and broke."

Laney sensed that her mental faculties were beginning to slip and she didn't know for how long she would be able to teach her beloved grandson. So, she decided to push the envelope and to move into a previously unchartered territory. She felt compelled to tell her grandson about one of the darkest times in the history of America and disclose to his young mind the real reasons for The War Between the States.

"This was a war like no other this country has fought," she said. "What many believed then—and still do—is that the Civil War was about slavery. However, the vast majority of people who lived in The Confederacy owned no slaves. Only wealthy people in both the North and South did. Slavery was not brought up as reason to fight a war until the North was unable to sell the first reason to its citizens. Like most wars, the War Between the States was launched over *money* and what it could buy—land and what the land produced.

Outsiders from Europe were pressing for a divided America. They knew that the war would cost a lot of money—on both sides—and that both sides would have to borrow from them. Afterwards, both sides of the war would owe the bankers in Europe a lot of money. That meant that they would have to do what the bankers wanted them to do in order to repay their debt. The European banker's ploy was to have the Northern states join with Canada and the Southern states join with Mexico and South America. The result would be just two countries on this side of the Atlantic Ocean for them to deal with. "You mean like when the bully at school picks on one person at a time rather than a group?" Mason interjected. "Exactly", Laney replied, "in their plan to create a single government that would tell the people of the world what to do, they didn't want to have to deal with a united *United* States of America. They wanted to bully it by dividing it and then combining the weaker parts with Canada on the northern part of the continent and with Mexico and Central America on the south. When that didn't work, they inserted an issue they had previously created—slavery."

Though Mason didn't totally understand the division and mergers of countries, he did grasp the fact that a few people wanted to bully all others.

"I have read a book about President Abraham Lincoln," Mason said. "It said that President Lincoln didn't want our country to divide into two parts. It also said that he freed the slaves and that he was killed because of it. Is that true, Granny? I'm not sure I understand exactly how keeping the states together and freeing slaves would cause someone to kill the President," the boy added.

"Well, it might be a bit hard for a nine-year-old to understand," Laney said. "There were several reasons why President Lincoln was killed. In a letter that President Lincoln wrote in 1862 …"

She interrupted her sentence to make sure that she was telling her grandson precisely what the President said. "Would you hand me that book over there on the shelf," Laney asked, "the book of quotations?"

She took the book of Lincoln's speeches from her grandson and turned to the glossary to find the reference that she needed. Turning to page fifty-one, she read from a letter that President Lincoln had written to Horace Greely, on August 22, 1962:

> 'My paramount objective in this struggle is to save the Union, and it is not either to save or destroy slavery. If I could save the Union without freeing *any* slave, I would do it; and if I could save it by freeing *all* the slaves, I would do it; and if I could do it by freeing some and leaving others alone, I would also do that.'

"Those words are profound, meaning that they say a lot about what President Lincoln was facing at the time. He had already written the order that would free the slaves – the one called the Emancipation Proclamation, but had not yet released it."

"What is the Emancipa ...?" Mason asked.

"I'm sorry, son," Laney said, "I'm still using a lot of big words. It was the piece of paper on which the President's official announcement—or proclamation—for all slaves to be released was written."

"You mean that the President can give orders like that?" Mason asked.

"Yes, the President is the Commander-in-Chief of the Army and has certain other powers that are granted to him by the Constitution. The problem is that the South no longer looked upon itself as part of the Union. Southern states had their own President and didn't feel that President Lincoln's orders applied to them. But, The Emancipation was just one of President Lincoln's decisions that upset a lot of people ... on both sides of the line that divided North from South and on both sides of the Atlantic Ocean," she said to her grandson "but I'll try to explain it ... at least as I see it. A slave is a person who has no choice but to do what someone else tells him or her to do, even if he or she doesn't want to do it."

"Kinda like when my Mother and Daddy tell me what to do when I don't want to do it?" Mason asked.

"No, that's not what I mean," Laney responded. "You will always be your Mother and Father's child, but a slave can be bought and sold to other people for money."

"You mean like horses," Mason replied.

"Something like that," Laney answered. "And, the people who owned slaves had paid the people who sold them a lot of money. Just letting them go, meant that the people who had spent money to buy them would lose everything. And, outlawing slavery would mean that the people who were in business of *selling slaves* would be out of business - a very profitable business, operated and supported by the money people of Europe."

"The *money people,*" interrupted Mason.

"Yes, the wealthy bankers of Europe," Laney answered.

"How did people in Europe get into selling slaves?" Mason asked.

"The bankers didn't invent slavery, but they saw an opportunity to make a lot of money. Slavery dates back to the biblical times," Laney answered. "Throughout history the same groups of people have *been* slaves and *owned* slaves. In olden days, it was common practice for the winner of a war to make the losers become their slaves or servants."

"You mean like if my team wins a baseball game, the other team has to come and do all our chores and homework, or if my team loses, we have to do the homework and chores for the other team?" Mason asked.

"I've never thought of it in that manner," Laney replied, "But, it was something like that. The slaves that were brought to America were first captured by other black tribes in Africa. When one tribe defeated another in war, the losers became slaves to the winners. After a while, the chiefs realized that they could sell their slaves to people who would take them to other countries and re-sell them for more money than they paid the chiefs—a lot more money.

During those days, a small group of powerful families in Europe controlled the selling of African slaves to Americans. The same powerful men that brought slaves to America were responsible for the War Between the

States. Some of the African slaves were brought to America and sold to wealthy people and plantation owners. It was all about making money and gaining power."

"Is having a lot of money that important?" Mason asked.

"To some people it is. There are people in the world that would do virtually anything for money, even if it meant selling their souls to the Devil," Laney answered.

"Could you actually sell your soul to the Devil for riches here on Earth?" Mason asked, surprisingly.

"You sure could." Laney replied. "And throughout history, many people have. You just watch. During your lifetime, you will see a lot of people do so."

"How will I know who those people are—the ones whose souls are owned by The Devil?" Mason asked.

"Just watch what people do. The Devil's disciples are easy to identify. They will do evil things and support others who do evil things, as well. They have no conscience. For them 'right' is whatever they need to do to gain power and control over other people ... and make money while doing so," Laney added.

"Like making slaves out of people like us," Mason asked.

"Absolutely," Laney replied. "At the time of the Civil War, slave trading was a business that was carried on throughout the world. But some of the people who write history overlooked the European's and North's role in slavery or the bankers who put up the money to bring slaves here on boats. The over-lookers didn't include those facts in the history books. They still refuse to admit and report on how human beings all over the world are being manipulated into giving up what freedoms we still have left."

"What is an *'over-looker'?*" Mason interjected.

"An *over-looker* is a person who allows his or her personal thoughts to influence what they write or report *as fact.* An over-looker is quick to point out the faults of those with whom he or she doesn't agree, but overlooks their own faults ... or those with whom they agree. The truth is slave owners and traders existed on both sides of the Mason-Dixon Line."

"What is the Mason-Dixon line?" the lad asked. Is that where my name came from?"

"No," Laney smiled, "You were named after a well-meaning organization that your father—like his before him—belongs to. Many of the men who helped shape America in the nineteen seventies were members of an organization of craftsmen—stone and brick layers, carpenters, plumbers ... you know construction workers. I know that your Daddy is a member of the local Masonic Lodge ... and proud of it. You know the ring that he wears on his finger, the one with the letter 'G" on it," Laney said, looking down at her grandson's innocent face?

"Yes, Ma'am," Mason replied. "I never thought to ask Daddy about his ring. He also has a tie tack with the same letter and some tiny tools on it."

"That's the Masonic logo, you know, the symbol that says to the world, 'I am a Mason," Laney explained. "All the men who belong to his lodge are fine men and do good things for the community. You just look for the Masonic logo. If you see a man wearing it, you can know that he believes in God and God's teachings."

Laney continued, "The Mason-Dixon Line was a line on the map that divided northern states from southern states. There were good and bad people on both sides of the line. There were good and kind plantation owners and some who mistreated their slaves," she added, "There have always been good and bad leaders. A long, long time ago in ancient Greece, an evil politician by the name of Draco imposed a set of unreasonable rules on his people. He used human blood instead of ink just to impress upon the people the consequences of breaking the laws he set out. But, we'll come back to this," Laney added. "Just write the name, Draco, in your notebook."

Mason did as instructed, not knowing that when he grew up, he would come to know Draco far better than he wanted.

Laney could see that she had opened a kind of Pandora's Box and wanted to make sure that the lad came away from the lesson with the right impressions. So, she decided to spend a bit more time on the matter than she had originally intended.

Before she could decide where to go next with her lesson, Mason asked, "Did your family own any slaves?"

"No, we were poor, very poor. Like most of the families whose men and boys fought in the War Between the States, our ancestors were not plantation owners," she added, "We had a fifty acre farm and worked it ourselves. The vast majority of the men who were dying on the battlefields were like us. For us, the war was about states' rights, you know the right for a state to decide what is in its best interest, rather than politicians who live more than a thousand miles away deciding for it. Our family," Laney told her grandson, "could more closely identify with the slaves than with the slave owners. The difference, however, was that poor white families at least could move from place to place to pursue opportunities. Slaves couldn't—all except for one family that we knew. They lived on our farm."

"Tell me about them." Mason pled.

"Mason," Angela said, entering the room. "I need you to run down the block to the store to get some sugar. I'm making an egg custard pie for supper and don't have enough sugar. What are you and Mamma doing?"

"She's telling me about when she was a little girl and the things she thinks I need to know about America back then," Mason answered his Mother.

"Well, as soon as you run this errand, you two can continue your conversation," Angela said. "I really need you to go to the store right away. Your father will be home for supper soon. And, he won't have long before he has to go out again. He's trying to finish a job for Doctor Grimsley."

"OK, Mamma," Mason said, "I'll be back as quickly as I can, Granny. Don't forget where you left off. I want to hear everything about the family of slaves that you knew."

As he was running out the door, Angela gave Mason two one dollar bills, which he stuffed in the left front pocket of his jeans.

It was a hot summer afternoon in August. As Mason ran out of his driveway, he could see the setting sun cresting over the oak trees across the street in the Martin's back yard. The sun's rays were beaming through the small openings of the deep green leaves of summer, glimmering as the gentle breeze blew them to and fro. Unlike many children his age, Mason noticed things.

Although the small neighborhood store was only two blocks away, he had worked up a sweat by the time he entered the store. It was almost as hot inside the store as it was outside. Only a ceiling fan stirred the muggy air within.

"Hello Mason," Mr. Asbury said. "It's a hot one today, isn't it?"

"Yes sir," the lad replied, "I ran all the way. I've got to get back right away. My Grandmother is telling me all about the War Between the States."

"You're mighty young to know all that," Mr. Asbury said. "Have you studied about that in school?"

"No sir," Mason replied. "I'm only in the fourth grade. But, I'll be starting the fifth grade in the fall. We aren't supposed to get into American History until next year, when school starts back."

"You are mighty young for a fourth-grader," Mr. Asbury said. "Aren't you just nine years old?"

"Yes sir," Mason answered, "I started first grade when I was five."

"I wonder *whose version of history* you kids are being taught these days," Mr. Asbury said. "What do you need, today?"

"A bag of sugar, please sir," Mason answered. "My Mamma is making an egg custard for supper and she needs it right away."

Mr. Asbury stepped away from the fan at the end of the counter and walked across the floor to the rack where he removed a one pound bag of sugar. "That'll be a dollar twenty-five."

"Mason handed Mr. Asbury the two, one dollar bills that his mother had given him. Mr. Asbury pressed the magic key on the cash register, ringing the bell that signified the cash drawer was about to open.

"Has anyone taught you about the words and symbols on the dollar bill yet?" Mr. Asbury asked, holding the bill up so that the boy could see its two faces.

"No sir, not yet," Mason answered.

"That's a lesson that you need to learn one day," Mr. Asbury added. "Your father is a member of the same Masonic Lodge that I belong to. Get him to tell you about the symbols and words on the dollar bill. They had a special meaning to the men who created this country."

"I will. Why does a bell ring when you open the cash register?" Mason asked.

"You are an inquisitive one," Mr. Asbury said. "It's a built-in safety measure, in case someone other than the store's owner is taking money and making change. They can't open the cash register without someone else knowing that they are doing so."

"So, that helps keep people from stealing money that isn't theirs?" Mason said, more asking than stating the answer.

"Yep," Mr. Asbury said. "Pretty smart on the inventor's part I would say. I'd like for the government to have to ring a bell that could be heard across America every time they open the national cash register and spend our taxes. Somebody needs to keep a check on where our money is going."

"Is there one of those machines big enough to hold all the money in America?" Mason asked.

"No, son, I'm afraid not. But, there should be," Mr. Asbury answered. "The politicians in Washington are printing money and spending it faster than we Americans can earn it. I wish I knew where it was going. And, what's worse, they are selling off our gold reserves. I can't figure that one out, either."

Mason wanted to interrupt Mr. Asbury and ask him about the gold, but didn't want to be impolite. "Those politicians think money grows on trees. I don't trust politicians and bankers. They created the Great Depression and start most wars. As the poor get poorer, they get richer. For them, it's about profits and power ... at the expense of us working people," Mr. Asbury added.

"That's what my grandmother says, too," Mason said.

As Mr. Asbury was making change, he suddenly stopped and turned around, reaching up toward the radio sitting on a shelf behind him. He turned the volume control knob to the right so that he could better hear the voice coming through the speaker.

"We interrupt our regularly scheduled programming to announce that the Supreme Court of the United States had just ruled in favor of Oliver Brown, a Negro who sued the Topeka, Kansas Board of Education. The decision strikes down the *separate, but equal* policy of public schools in America. The case—argued by Attorney Thurgood Marshall—effectively abolishes segregation throughout America. More on the decision on the six o'clock news," the reporter said. "Now we return to our regular program, in progress."

"Son," Mr. Asbury said, "Remember this moment. You've just heard one of the most important announcements of your lifetime. Education in America will be changed forever. Some people are going to be very happy about this decision. Others are going to be fighting mad. Somebody's going to get killed over this. I just know it. That's how it works. Whenever some movement that changes a country comes about, assassins come out of hiding. This court decision will initiate such a movement. It will change the way that you children—and your children—will be educated. For some, it will be better; for others, worse. When averaged out, you kids will learn less about the things you need to know and more about the things you don't need to know. I fear for the America that you kids are going to inherit."

"Like when President Lincoln was shot?" Mason asked.

"Precisely," Mr. Asbury replied. He made some decisions that changed the course of history in America ... in a way that the 'big boys' hadn't planned. And, it got him shot."

"The 'big boys'", Mason answered, "who are they?"

"Men you better hope that you never meet," Mr. Asbury answered.

"I have a notebook that I'm writing lessons my grandmother is teaching me. Should I include what the man on the radio said in my notebook? Is he one of the 'big boys'? Mason asked"

"Ask your grandmother about that, but I think that would be a good idea," Mr. Asbury replied.

As Mason entered the words, "Brown - Education," in his little notebook, he asked Mr. Asbury, "Does this mean that there is going to be another War Between the States?" Mason asked.

"Let's hope that wisdom prevails, but this isn't going to set well with a lot of people. There will be conflict. I hope that I'm wrong, but I'm afraid that some people will use this court decision to create more division among Americans. On that you can rely," Mr. Asbury said. "Here is your change. You'd better get going. Your mother will be waiting."

Mason took the seventy-five cents from Mr. Asbury, placed the silver coins safely in the left front pocket of his jeans and sprinted out the door.

When he came through the back door of his home, Angela asked, "What is wrong? You're all sweaty. Is something the matter?"

"Mr. Asbury just told me that there might be another war and that the President might get shot—like what happened in the War Between the States," the lad said, obviously concerned about what he had just been told.

"Come in here," Laney said. "Sit down and tell me what you are talking about." Angela followed her son into the den, where Laney had been waiting for Mason's return. She had overheard the conversation that took place in the adjacent room.

"When I was at the store, Mr. Asbury and I heard an announcement coming over the radio about courts and schools. Mr. Asbury said that a lot of people were going to be upset about it and that it could cause another war - like the one you were telling me about earlier, the one between the states," Mason said.

"Call the radio station Angela," Laney said. "Ask them about the announcement."

Before she could dial the number, Owen Edmonds walked through the back door. "Did you hear the news?" he asked.

"We heard that there was news, but don't know what it is." Angela replied.

"The United States Supreme Court just made segregation in public schools illegal. From this day forward black children and white children will be going to the same school," he said.

"Is that bad, Daddy," Mason asked Owen.

"No son, the fact that the children will be going to the same school is not bad. But, a lot of powerful people are going to use this decision to create trouble for blacks and whites, alike," Owen answered. "Unfortunately, some people tend to lump the people who live on this planet into groups—like religions or races—and look upon all members of that group the same. This is not a good thing, for in every group, every religion, race, or profession, there are good people and bad people. Just because a few people within a group do bad things, one should not label all the others as bad. Conversely, if a few people within a group of evil people might do a good thing from time to time—for the wrong reasons—one shouldn't immediately forgive a group comprised of mostly evil people for their wrongdoings. But, unfortunately people who sway the opinions of others with propaganda are masters at turning public opinion against individuals or groups that they don't like or don't agree with."

"Daddy," Mason interrupted, "I understand most of what you said, but there is a word you used that I've heard before, but don't really understand: propa ..."

"I'm sorry, son," Owen said. "It's a big word for twisting the truth—you know, lying. Some people are very good at it."

"Now, I understand," Mason said, "How do you spell it?" he asked, writing as his father spelled the word.

"Let me finish what I was saying about how education will be changed forever in America," Owen said. "I want you to understand this. As a result of what the court decided today, the government can now dictate *where* a child goes to pursue an education. However, it can't legislate *whether* a child *gets an education*. The Court did what it had to do, but the result of their decision will be a lowering of standards in the public school systems of

America ... and less discipline for blacks and whites alike. That's how big government works. The things over which politicians exercise control rarely get better. In fact, they usually get worse ... and cost more to operate. Sometimes, I think that is what the 'big boys' want, to make things worse. When things get bad for the people, they get better for the people who control the people."

"How can the powerful people you mentioned—the people in government—tell us what to do?" Mason asked his father.

"They simply see that new laws are passed, telling people what they can—and can't—do and put people in jail or impose fines on us if we don't do what they tell us to do," Owen replied.

"I think I understand," Mason responded. "Before I went to the store, Granny was telling me about slaves and how they were forced to do what the people who owned them told them to do. She said that a family that had been slaves lived on their farm."

"Slavery comes in many forms, my son," Owen said. "I remember reading somewhere that a government powerful enough to give us everything is also powerful enough to take everything away from us. That's why Americans have always been fearful of big government, especially those of us in the South. When we tried to free ourselves from a government that wanted to control us, we lost everything; and, we've had a difficult time overcoming the War Between the States and the perception that all Southerners supported slavery. People all around the world still hold those of us who had nothing to do with slavery—but live in communities located below the Mason-Dixon Line—accountable for the fact that a few wealthy plantation owners in the 1800s had slaves. Those who look down on us tend to forget—or were never told—that there were people in the North who owned slaves, too."

Intent on trying to understand what he was hearing, Mason asked his father, "Is government bad?"

"It was not meant to be," Owen answered. "But selfish people have worked their way into government positions ... for the wrong reasons. Some have been put there by powerful people who use them as ... well, as slaves, to do what they tell them to do. I think that it is a good idea for Granny to tell you the rest of her story now. Perhaps, hearing it may help you understand how people can get along, providing they want to, and trouble-makers let them be.

"Go ahead with your lesson, Laney. I've got to wash up and get ready for supper. I don't have long. I've got to go back to Dr. Grimsley's house. You know, he's adding on a room for his mother-in-law. Rather than helping me tonight, son, I want you to stay here and listen to your grandmother's story. From what I gather, you might be getting the education of your life ... from a wise woman who has lived through some of the most trying times in our country's history."

"Thanks Daddy," Mason said. "I'll miss being with you, but I really do want to hear the rest of the story Granny has been telling me."

As his father went to the bathroom to wash up, Mason resumed his usual position on the floor at his grandmother's feet. "Tell me the story about the slaves you knew," he said.

"I will, but you should remember what your father just told you. There's wisdom in his words. I feel that we are throwing a lot at you ... at a young age. Are you able to take it all in?" Laney asked.

"I think so," Mason replied. "I've read about George Washington, Thomas Jefferson, Benjamin Franklin, and President Lincoln. And, I've seen *Gone With the Wind*. A lot of what you and Daddy are telling me is similar to what's in the movie and the books I've read."

"I'm sure that much of what you've read is true. Keep in mind that although the movie was fiction, it was based on actual events and places," Laney said, and continued. "On his way back from the war—before he was killed—he and his army buddies actually slept in a barn on the Twelve Oaks Plantation—the name of the plantation in the book and movie—right outside of Atlanta. But, that's another story ... for another day."

Laney continued, "At the western corner of our little farm, lived a Negro family—the Henderson's. They had been freed following the death of a cotton farmer in a county just north of our farm. Prior to his death, the farmer drafted his *last will and testament*. In it, he stipulated that upon his death the farm was to be given to his church and the Negro family that had worked his farm with him was to be set free. As their owner, he could do that, "Laney said. "Feeling the need to leave the immediate area, Harold Henderson moved his family farther south, looking for a place to start a new life."

Laney was enjoying telling the story that she had experienced as a young girl. What made it more enjoyable to tell was that her inquisitive grandson was hanging on every word.

"It was a warm Sunday afternoon in April. My Mother, Samantha,—your great grandmother—was sitting in a rocking chair under the huge oak tree in our front yard, cooling off after we had walked home from the tiny church about five miles down the road in the Victory community. She had sent us children into the house to set the table and get ready for dinner. While sipping on a cool glass of well water, my mother saw a Negro family walking down the dirt road in front of her house, heading in the direction of Crestoria. It was an unusual sight. People in our county had never seen folks with black skin, though we had heard about them. This family of Negroes was carrying what appeared to be very few possessions in cloth sacks on their back. My mother called out to them and invited them to come over to the shade. The Henderson's reluctantly responded to her requests.

"Afternoon," my Mother said, "Where are you heading?"

Repeating the words as she originally heard them, Laney continued.

"We don't rightly know, Ma'am," Mr. Henderson replied. "We'ze been freed by our former massa and we is lookin' for a place to live," he added, reaching in his pocket to retrieve a sheet of paper. "Dis piece of paper is supposed to say that my fam'ly and I is free. Does you want to see it? I kant read so I don't rightly know if that is what it really says."

"I'm sure the paper says what you say it says," my mother replied. "What are your names?"

"I'm Harold Henderson. This is my wife, Hattie, and deeze is my chil'en, Moses, John, Mary, and Sally."

"Glad to make your acquaintance," my mother responded.

"Do only white folk live in deeze parts?" Harold asked. Hattie and the four children remained quiet.

"Right now, that's all that live here. What are you looking for?" Samantha asked.

"Anythin,'" Harold replied. "We'll make do with anythin."

"How long have you been traveling?" Samantha asked.

"Two days," Harold answered.

"Have you had anything to eat?" Samantha inquired.

"Just some wild blackberries we pick on the side of the road and a busted watermelon that we found in a ditch," Harold replied.

"Where have you slept?" your great grandmother asked.

"Beside creeks and rivers and under trees," Harold responded. "Where we could get water and wash up."

"*Laney*," my Mother cried out, loud enough so that I could hear her from where I was - in the kitchen.

"I heard her call my name and came to the screen door," Laney said. "Yes Ma'am," I answered.

"Bring me some of those new canning jars from the cupboard in the kitchen and have one of your brothers bring a bucket of cool well water. And ... Laney, bring a plate full of those tea cakes that I made this morning."

"We'll be right there," I said.

. . . .

"How 'bout those tea cakes," Samantha asked. "It's my mother's recipe. She brought it over from Ireland when they came to this country. My family and I could eat a plate full of them a day—that is if we could afford the flour and sugar needed to make them."

Laney continued with her story. "Yas, Ma'am," Harold said. Deeze cakes is the best I evah ate. Ain't dat right?" he asked looking at his wife, Hattie, and their two sons and two daughters.

"All smiled and nodded, agreeing with their father and husband."

"Ma'am," Harold said, "You ought let Hattie cook up somp'um good fo' you and yo' chil'in. Dat's what she done fo' da famiy we work fo.'"

"I'll bet she is a good cook," Samantha said. "We'll see what we can do about that. Now, let me make you a proposition."

"Yas Ma'am," Harold replied, anxiously.

"My husband was killed during a raid on his camp coming home from the war," Samantha said. Taking care of this place without a man is hard. My boys are only 12 and 13 years old. I already had to sell off some of our land. Down the road at the western corner of the twenty acres I have left is an area that I've needed to reclaim from the trees and weeds that have taken it over. I need to plant a bigger garden to feed my children."

"Ma'am, gardens is my specialty. I'd like to show you what I can do," Harold said.

Samantha replied, "The soil in that part of our little farm is rich and fertile, but since my husband died, I haven't been able to cultivate a garden as big as the one we once had. That region has become overgrown with young pine trees and weeds. You know, my children and I live off the land. It's our only source of income. We sell what we don't need in order to buy the things we can't grow," she explained.

Then, Samantha said, "Now, there is an old barn back off the road. It was there when my husband inherited this place from his parents. They homesteaded it. I think that the original log cabin was located just in front of the barn. If you look closely, you can see some of the stones for the foundation and a bit of the old fireplace and chimney. The barn hasn't been used in a long time and it isn't in very good condition, but it has a fairly good roof. If you and your family would like to live there and fix it up in return for helping me clear the new ground to make room for a bigger garden, and help me tend to it until harvest time, I'll split everything we grow with you. And, any wild game that wanders into the area is yours to hunt. There's a small artesian spring next to the barn. The water is fresh and clean. Hattie can help around the house when we and the children are in the fields. What do you think?" Samantha asked.

"I think dat God has answered my prayers," Harold answered. "I won't let you down, Ma'am, I promise. I'll make you proud."

"You make yourself and your family proud," Samantha told Harold. "If you do that, everything will be alright."

Laney continued with telling the story to her grandson. "Harold and Hattie Henderson fixed up the old barn, making it a respectable home for themselves and their children. Within a month, working all day and into the night, Harold and his two teenage sons had sawed down every tree in the five acre tract and burned all the stumps and underbrush. They used our old horse to plow the land, just in time for the spring planting. Harold had done everything he said he would do—and in record time."

"What did ya'll grow in the new garden?" Mason asked his grandmother.

"Peas, corn, butterbeans, squash, watermelons, and potatoes," Laney answered. The revived garden flourished under the tender love and care of the combined families. It took a lot of hard work—on everybody's part—but the new ground bore a bigger harvest than any plot in the entire county, feeding the two families that tended to it and providing enough food to store for at least two winters to come. Even then, there was enough left over to sell to the market in Crestoria. We put aside the best seeds from the harvest to use for the following year. From experience, both families had learned that the crop can be no better than the seeds used to grow it. That's the way with any project that involves people, too. We also knew that we had to keep the weeds from taking over the field and that we would have to fertilize and nurture the field. Left alone, fertile ground will soon be taken over by weeds and briars, destroying the work previously done by the cultivators. That's another metaphor—a good life lesson for you to remember," Laney said to her grandson.

"I'm not sure that I understand it all, but I'll write it down in my notebook," Mason answered, as he wrote, "weeds and briars take over fertile ground."

"Mamma, you're going to have to finish the story after supper, "Angela said. "You and Mason come to the table, so that Owen can get on his way."

"We're coming," Laney replied. "Let's go, before we get in trouble," she playfully whispered to her grandson.

Supper consisted of Mason's favorite: fried chicken, fresh peas, okra from the garden at the Edmonds' farm, cornbread, and freshly-made egg custard.

"Say the blessing, Mason," Owen said to his son.

Everyone bowed their heads and Mason repeated the prayer that children all over the world have repeated for centuries: "*God is great. God is good. Let us thank Him for our food. Amen.*"

"*Amen,*" was echoed by all seated at the table.

With eyes still closed, Mason prayed a silent prayer. "Please God, talk to those people who want to make slaves of other people."

CHAPTER 5

Dinner was delicious," Owen said. As usual, I ate too much."

"Mamma, can I have another piece of pie?" Mason asked.

"Since you were so helpful in going for sugar this afternoon, I'm going to let you have a second piece," Angela answered.

"Ya'll are going to have to excuse me," Owen said. "I'll be back before ten o'clock," he said, kissing everyone—including Laney—on the forehead as he left the table.

Mason said to his father, "Are you sure that you don't need me to help you tonight?"

"No son, not tonight. You stay here and pay close attention to your grandmother. She is a wise woman," Owen said as he went out the back door.

"I'll clean up all by myself," Angela said to her son and mother. "You two can resume your storytelling session. But, Mason, you'll have to be in bed by nine o'clock. Understand?"

"Yes ma'am," Mason replied. "Let's go Granny."

Taking his place once more on the floor at his grandmother's feet, Mason said, "You were telling me about how working together allowed you and the Henderson's to grow more things in your garden and make more money."

"You do have a good memory," Laney said. "O.K., as promised, my mother split all the money and food we made with Harold and Hattie. They got half and we got half. That's why they call the agreement 'share-cropping.'"

"If ya'll grew food on the farm, what did you use money for?" Mason asked his grandmother.

"We used the money for cloth, thread, tools, flour, and sugar. Both Hattie and my Mother made the clothes that our families wore from the cloth sacks used to package fifty pounds of flour. The store-bought cloth was used only to make Sunday dresses for the girls. Mother tried to buy a pair of shoes each year for each child," she added. "None of us had more than one pair of shoes. We wore them to work, to church, and to school - when we could go. Much of our schooling was done at home, by my Mother.

"The Lambert and Henderson families worked together and played together in a color-blind world," Laney told Mason.

"A color-blind world...?" Mason interrupted.

"It's one in which the color of a person's skin doesn't matter. Do you remember what your father told you at supper—that you shouldn't judge people by the color of their skin, religion, or any visible sign that connects them to other people. You have to look into a person's heart and soul before you know that person. In our situation, both families were bound by a co-dependent need to scratch out a living on a twenty acre tract of land. The Henderson's helped us. And, we helped them. My Mother taught us: that's the way God intended for it to be here on Earth." We paid no attention to the differences in the colors of our skin."

"Granny, I prayed tonight that God would help people who want to make slaves of other people," Mason interrupted. He had learned from his grandmother about the kind of relationships that *could* exist between people of different races and backgrounds, but emphasized that there would always be power-hungry individuals who would try to create divisions and cause trouble. That's how they become powerful. That's how they remain so.

Laney told her grandson, "Even in the Confederacy, a few people ruled the rest of us—Negro and white alike. And, they didn't care who or how many had to die as long as they got their way. They were connected to powerful bankers in Europe who intended to profit from The War Between the States. But, we and the Henderson's had a good and healthy relationship, because no one else interfered in our dealings ... at least not directly. And, since there was no one in our way, we could see beyond the colors of our skin and into each other's hearts and souls. Because we worked together—side by side—respected each other, and shared the good and the bad, both families prospered. We were sad to see them leave our farm."

"They left!" Mason exclaimed. "Why did they leave? Where did they go?"

"When he went to the market one day, Harold learned of an opportunity to share-crop with a man who owned a several hundred acres in the county to the west of us," Laney answered. "When he came to talk to my Mother about the opportunity, she told him that it was a chance that he could not let pass. We all hugged and cried when they left. They were like family. Their daughter, Mary, was like a little sister to me. She was the best friend I had as a child. My mother wrote a letter of recommendation on the back of the piece of paper that Harold carried confirming that he and his family had been freed, as slaves. My mother's note read:

> *'To Whom It May Concern*
>
> *Please accept this as the highest recommendation one human being can give on behalf of another.*
>
> *Harold and Hattie Henderson and their four children have share-cropped with me and my family for the past four years. They are proud, honest, and hard working. If you give them a chance, they will make you proud.*
>
> *Please feel free to contact me for any additional information,*
>
> *Samantha Lambert'*

"After reviewing the letter for errors, Samantha handed it back to Harold and told him to go to the barn and harness the horse. 'Hitch the horse to the wagon that is parked behind the barn. The horse and wagon are yours. I don't want you and your children to walk to your next home. I want you to arrive in style', Samantha added.

"Harold didn't want to take the only horse and wagon we had, but my Mother insisted. She told him, that she had been negotiating to swap some of next year's corn crop for a young horse that a neighbor wanted to sell and was sure that they could come to terms. Reluctantly, Harold and Hattie agreed to accept my Mother's gift."

"How can I eva' thank you ma'am?" Harold asked my Mother.

"You already have," she said. "And, who knows our paths might cross again someday ... or perhaps the paths of our children and grandchildren. You know, God works in mysterious ways."

"He do, indeed," Harold replied. "I hopes we does meet and dat our chil'en can stay friends."

"Urge your children to continue to read and learn new things. The world is changing. Who knows what opportunities may lie in their path," Samantha said. "Teach your children—and have them pass on to each generation—a password, just in case our offspring should meet in the future. The phrase is: "God has blessed our work.""

My mother asked for the piece of paper on which she had written the recommendation and wrote "*God has blessed our work.*"

Taking the paper back from her, Harold said, "Does deeze words say, 'God has blessed our work?"

"They do," My Mother replied.

"Ma'am, you knows I kant read, but I'll study deeze words and learn what they say. I will make sure dat day are passed on."

Then Laney said to Mason, "You know, we never got another horse. We used the cow that we milked everyday to pull the plow. Surprisingly, the cow did a good job for us. I always wondered how the Henderson's fared in their new life. I pray that they prospered," Laney told her grandson. "All they needed was a chance to prove themselves. I'm confident that their children turned out just fine. As my mother said to Harold, someday, you might meet up with one of their grandchildren."

"I would like that," Mason relied. "What happened to your farm?"

"My oldest son—your Uncle Lester—still lives in what was once the barn that Harold and Hattie renovated.

When our house burned down, we moved into it. With the help of the neighbors, we spruced it up a bit. After the Henderson's left, times got hard again. We suffered two years of draught. Everything we planted dried up and died. To make ends meet, I sold all but the five acres we used for the garden and the renovated barn where we lived. Selling the other fifteen acres to a neighbor allowed me to raise enough money to live on for the next three years. Though I hated to give up the land, sometimes you just have to do whatever it takes to survive the difficult times. When the draught ended—and due to the efforts of all my children, we raised another banner crop on the five acre garden tract."

"Weren't you sad to leave your home?" Mason asked his grandmother.

"Sure, I was," Laney answered. "But life changes and you have to change with it. As each of the children grew up, got married, and moved away, I was left alone. And, I didn't want to live by myself. As you can see, I love to tell stories. I couldn't tell them to myself. My grandfather used to say, 'A person who talks too much to himself, eventually finds himself talking to a fool.' I certainly couldn't take care of the place—even though it was only five acres. There are times when you need to recognize that what you are doing may not be the best choice ... and do something else. That's another lesson to write down in your notebook."

Transcribing his grandmother's latest lesson, Mason asked, "So, what did you do?"

"Your mother and I talked with Cloe and Danley. We all decided that I would split my time and live a week with each family. All the boys except Lester had moved away. He was the only one living in the county. And, he was renting a small house on the other side of Crestoria. I gave the house and what was left of the farm to Lester so that we could keep at least part of the place where I raised my children in the family."

"What is Uncle Lester doing with the farm?" Mason asked.

"He's working the five acres that I kept and tells me that it still grows the biggest tomatoes, sweetest peas, biggest watermelons, and tallest corn for miles around. Harold and Hattie made their mark. The Henderson's left the land better than they found it," Laney said, in a manner to suggest that her grandson write this one, too, in his book of lessons.

"Tell me more about the Henderson children," Mason pled to his Grandmother, "just in case I meet one of their grandchildren, sometime."

"When the work was done, they were our playmates, Laney said. "They were good children and good friends to my brothers, sisters, and me. As I said earlier, their oldest daughter, Mary, and I had a great relationship. I taught her how to read and shared some of my books with her. She was especially interested in history and past wars. We talked about forming a secret club that would expose bad people and punish them for how they treat those who try to do the right thing. Because of her interest in the war that had just passed—the Civil War—my mother allowed me to share my grandfather's letter with her—the one we reconstructed from memory after the original burned," Laney replied. "Harold and Hattie were outstanding parents and taught their children good manners and respect for people and things. The children worked hard, too—in the fields and at home. Harold and Hattie taught them responsibility and my Mother taught them reading and arithmetic," Laney added.

"She was a teacher?" Mason asked.

"Well, not officially," Laney replied, "But as she had done with us, she knew enough to teach them the alphabet and how to read some of the simple books that my brothers, sisters, and I used when we could attend the little one room schoolhouse in nearby Crestoria. She also taught them addition and subtraction. Like us, the Henderson children were eager to learn ... and quick to do so. They liked hearing my Mother's stories and bits of wisdom as much as we did. Part of learning to listen and be observant was having us repeat portions of her stories as we had heard them recited by my Mother. She also taught Harold and Hattie to read and to add and subtract. Neither of them had attended school."

"Tell me more about the war—the one between the states," Mason asked his grandmother. "Why were they fighting?"

"Well, I'll tell you what I learned from my Mother," Laney answered. "The war originally broke out because Congress'—one of the branches of government—wanted to take from each state the right to rule itself and its people ... the way that the people who created the United States intended."

"Did each state have something like a king or a president?" Mason asked.

"No, in the United States we call them *governors.* And, they don't have near the powers that a king or president would have. In addition, each state has a group of people who make local laws. Congress makes laws for the entire United States of America."

Laney paused and looked into the eyes of her grandson. There she saw a look of bewilderment.

"I'm sorry," she said, "I got a bit carried away. Let's just say that sometimes the history we read is not the way things actually happened. After a war is over, the winner is the one whose side of the story is written down for people to read, forever. To find the truth—the whole truth—you sometimes have to look at the past through the eyes of the defeated. People in power often blame *their own* failures and wrongdoing on others," she said to her attentive grandson. "In the letter that my grandfather wrote on his way home from the war, he said:

> 'Like life itself, this war is a mystery that one day will be solved. The answers to the mystery—though not today apparent—are all around us. Though not in our lifetime, one day the pieces of the puzzle will be pieced together and the world will know the truth, who started this war ... and why.
>
> 'In talking to my fellow Confederate brothers, I have learned that on the slavery issue most of us agreed with the Yankees. Most everyone I talked to

about why we were fighting the Yankees was *against* slavery. Those of us on the battle fields were fighting over keeping the federal government out of our business – to keep people who had no understanding about how we lived our lives from trying to run it and taxing us for things they had no understanding of. The federal government should not impose the wishes of those in power to those who aren't. In that regard, I suspect that we agree with those shooting at us and those we are shooting at. I suspect, if we could have just sat down with the Yankees and talked about our differences, we would have put down our guns and gone home.

'It seems that the little man—those of us with white skin and those with black or brown skin—are the ones that are used by the greedy and powerful to promote *their* causes. Surely, what we have seen from General Sherman makes no sense to us. His actions reminded me of the stories we had read about the barbarian Genghis Khan. Sherman made no attempt to ask who had owned slaves and who had not. His was a wholesale destruction of *a people* ... a way of life. On whose orders was he creating such atrocities? When Sherman was done, it was as though a part of America had evaporated—blown away like dust in the wind, only to live in the hearts and minds of the people who lived it or could tell about it. There has to be another agenda in play. I hope—before I die—that I will learn what it is. We simply have to know and keep the truth alive.'

"That's what we are doing now—keeping the truth alive, you and I," Laney said.

"How do I do that after you are gone," Mason asked his grandmother.

"Remember the things that I have told you. Read books. Observe Nature. Watch people's eyes and body language when they talk to you. Don't judge people by labels and the groups with which they are affiliated—good or bad. Ask questions and don't accept an answer that doesn't make sense or that you don't believe represents the truth. Practice telling stories—as I have. Become good at story-telling. Go to school. Learn how to write so that others can learn what you have learned. Hang out with people who see the world as you do, stick together, and be prepared for every opportunity that comes your way, even if it seems too big to handle."

"You mean like being a general in the Army or Governor, or president of the United States?" Mason asked.

"Precisely," Laney answered. "As you have learned in Cub Scouts, *'be prepared.'* You never know what you might be called to do. Learn about government. Learn about war. Learn what it takes to ensure peace. Learn how people think and how groups of people think. Read the Bible and learn how to recognize Evil."

"Where would I learn this much about people?" the nine-year-old boy asked.

"In school," Laney answered. "Study the human being. Learn what makes us tick and the societies that our kind creates. Learn what makes civilizations fail and what causes them to endure."

"Is this a lesson that I need to write down?" Mason asked.

"It's a piece of the big puzzle that you will put together one day. And, if you save all the pieces as you find them in your notebook, they will be easier to find when you need them ... and you will need them. As strange as it may seem, people today are very much like people were hundreds—or thousands—of years ago. In every generation, people have a tendency to make some of the same good—and bad—decisions that our ancient ancestors made. One of the most perplexing things about the animal who is supposed to be the most intelligent on Earth is that we don't seem to learn the lessons that history teaches," Laney added.

"In the set of encyclopedias that Mamma and Daddy gave me for Christmas last year, I've read about the Romans and Greeks. They were smart people. I don't understand what happened to them," Mason said.

"It's rather complicated," Laney replied. "For now just know that they lost their way. They were misled by leaders that didn't stay focused on the roadmap toward self-preservation and longevity."

"Are self-preservation and longevity places ... like Oz in *The Wizard of Oz*?" Mason asked.

"No, Laney replied, laughingly. "Longevity is not a place. It is a journey. It means *how long* something lasts. "

"You mean like how long the people of Rome and Greece lived—how old they were when they died?"Mason inquired.

"Well, I never thought of it that way," Laney replied, "Longevity can also apply to people and the things people build—like houses, neighborhoods, cities, states, and countries. That's quite perceptive on your part. How l*ong* things live depends on many factors—like how well we take care of whatever it is we want to preserve. When it comes to people, how well we take care of ourselves and whether we do what our doctors tell us to do is important."

"Preserve," Mason repeated, "I know that Cloe and Danley make fig preserves and pear preserves from the trees in their back yard. They store them in the garage for the winter, when the trees don't grow figs and pears."

The process of preserving fruit makes it last a long time ... for later use," Laney replied.

Before Mason could ask another question, his mother entered the room. "It's time to take a break. Go take your bath, put on your pajamas and then you can come back for more of Granny's stories," Angela said to her son. Mamma, you probably need a break too,"

"I'll pour myself a glass of milk and have a piece of your custard pie while you are getting ready for bed,"

Laney said to her anxious grandson. "Hurry, I want to finish this before you have to go to sleep."

"I'll hurry. I promise," Mason said, running down the hall, shucking his shirt along the way.

Sure enough, in record time, the lad returned to the den and planted himself in his favorite spot—before Laney's rocking chair. It had been brought to the Edmonds' house when she moved in. The family heirloom once sat on her front porch. It has been used by her mother when she conducted family schooling sessions. Because the cherished chair was not inside the house, it was the only object retrieved from the fire that had destroyed the Lambert home, so many years before.

Laney placed the half-full glass of milk on the small table to the left of the rocking chair and sat down. "Where were we," she asked her grandson.

Taking a sip of his own glass of milk, Mason said, "You were telling me about preserving things and how to stay healthy and strong. Did you always do what your doctor told you to do?" the boy asked his grandmother. "Is that why you have lived to be eighty-two years old?"

"Truth is, my son, when I was growing up we didn't see the doctor very often. Doctors were few and far between. Hospitals were even fewer ... and they didn't have a lot of sophisticated equipment. Babies were delivered at home. No one had any money for doctors and hospitals. We took care of our aches and pains using folk medicine handed down by our parents and grandparents."

"You doctored yourself?" Mason asked. "Didn't it hurt when you gave yourself a shot?"

"We didn't give ourselves shots. My mother usually treated us with liniments and herbs. Cuts were treated by packing spider webs to stop bleeding and coal tar was rubbed into the wound to keep infection down. In those days, antibiotics hadn't been developed. People were tougher then. We had to be. Life was hard."

"I'm still not sure I know why countries get sick and die," Mason asked his grandmother. "Do the people get sick and die first or do countries die first and the people die later?"

"In the case of Greece and Rome, what died first was *the will of the people*. They stopped caring about the things that had made them strong in the first place. They wanted the easy way out and forgot how to work. They became a victim of their own prosperity," Laney replied.

"Prosper ....?" Mason asked.

"I'm sorry, it means *success*. They forgot what made them successful in the first place?"

"You mean like eating his spinach makes Popeye strong – they forgot to eat their spinach and vegetables?" Mason asked.

"No, like protecting how they lived from people who wanted to make slaves of them." Laney answered.

"Who wanted to make the Greeks and Romans slaves?" Mason queried.

"They had enemies who lived in other countries. These people wanted the land and things that the Greeks and Romans had—like robbers who break into houses and stores to steal what doesn't belong to them. They also had enemies that lived among them—people who lied about being Romans and Greeks, and waved the flags of Greece and Rome, while holding the flags of their mother lands in their hearts. These people twisted everything so as to make it look as though they were committed to Greece's and Rome's success, when—in fact—they were out to see it fail. These were the worst kind of liars," Laney said.

"What other kinds of liars are there?" Mason asked.

"Well, there are white lies, grey lies, and black lies," she replied.

"You mean that lies have different colors?" Mason asked. "How can you tell the difference?"

"White lies contain some truth, but the teller twists the truth to change your opinion about whatever may have occurred. Grey lies are 'they said,' kind of lies. Who 'they' are is usually never revealed, but the rumor or propaganda is out there and inflicts varying degrees of harm to innocent people. Finally, there are black lies. They are the worst kind of lies, because there is usually not a bit of truth to what is told, yet the liar goes out of his or her way to cause others to dislike or distrust someone who is not guilty of any wrongdoing," Laney explained.

"Why would people do that?" Mason asked.

"That's a question for the ages," Laney responded. "That's one that no one has ever been able to answer. Sometimes they feel as though they have to lie to defend themselves and the people they love against those who want to hurt them. Sometimes, people are put up to lying by people on their side or outsiders. During your lifetime, you will encounter people like this, people who will do anything to get their way, including telling black, grey, and white lies without blinking an eye. To these people, 'truth' is whatever it needs to be to help them over a crisis or to get their way. You might not see what they are up to in the beginning, but keep watching. Bad people can put up a front for a while, but their true character will eventually show through."

"Why would a person want to get people on the same side mad at each other by telling lies?" Mason asked.

"Boy, you are asking some tough questions," his grandmother replied. "Let's see if I can help you understand it. Let's say that John and Jack are sitting beside each other in a seat on the front row of in school and you want to sit in one of their seats, but they won't give it to you. If you could tell Jack that John doesn't like him and tell John that Jack doesn't like him in order to start a fight between the two boys, chances are that the teacher would make one of them move away, leaving the seat that you wanted open for you. By creating a fight between two of your classmates, you would get what you want."

"But, that wouldn't be right," Mason responded in a concerned tone of voice.

"No, it wouldn't, "Laney answered. "It's not right, but unfortunately, that's the way that a lot of people in the world get what they want—by creating hatred and fights among people who, if left alone would get along just fine."

"You seem to know everything, Granny," Mason said. "I'm learning a lot and writing down the things you are telling me in my notebook. I thought that you told me that you didn't get a chance to go to school very much."

"I don't know everything. There's a lot I haven't yet learned. I've been learning all my life. I learned what is called 'wisdom' from my parents, grandparents, and people I've read about. I've made it a point to learn history and study how people think and react to similar situations. I'm simply passing along to you the things I've learned," Laney responded.

"What is *wisdom?*" Mason asked.

"Well ... that's another difficult word to put in words. Go get the dictionary and let's see what Mr. Webster has do say about it."

Mason did as asked. He went over to the shelf in the den and retrieved *Webster's Collegiate Dictionary, Second Edition.* Opening the pages to the "W's" he found the word. "Here it is," the boy said, proudly.

"Read Mr. Webster's definition to me," Laney said.

"*Wisdom* ..." he paused. "Granny, there are a lot of big words here. ... *accumulated philosophic or scientific learning,*" Mason struggled to say.

"Go on," Laney said.

"Knowledge; insight; good sense; judgment..." the lad read aloud. "I know what 'good sense' means, Granny."

"Well, that's good enough for now. 'Good sense' it is," she said as she observed her grandson writing the words in his little notebook.

"Even though I am more than eighty years old, I am still learning," Laney added. "Furthering my education has been easier because my mother and father taught me how to see with my mind's eye and hear the unspoken word. Some people call it 'reading between the lines'."

"How can you do that?" Mason asked. "Is 'reading between the lines' the same as 'wisdom'?"

"You bet it is," Laney replied. "With wisdom a person seems to have another eye in our brains?"

"You mean that a person grows another eye inside his or her head?" the boy asked, perplexingly.

"No, the 'mind's eye' is what is called a metaphor. I know that I used that term earlier. Before you ask me what a metaphor is, let me explain. A metaphor means that you use a common example to explain what you are trying to say," Laney said.

"Why not just say what you mean," Mason responded, writing "m...e...t...a...p...h...o...r" in his notebook.

"You are too smart for me, my son," Laney replied. "Sometimes, it is easier for people to understand you if you use an example that they are more familiar with. What I meant by 'seeing with your mind's eye' is: You not only see with your eyes, you let your mind see things before they actually happen. You imagine things that haven't yet happened."

"Can you give me an example, Mason asked.

"Yeah, I think I can," his grandmother replied. "Imagine that you are riding your bicycle down a dirt road. Imagine that your eyes are only looking right in front of your bicycle's front tire. If you only look right in front of you, you might not see a tree that had fallen across the road. Imagine that you suddenly see a tree that had fallen across the road and that you ran into the tree and hurt yourself. If, on the other hand, you heard a crash in the road ahead and that you recognized the sound as that of a falling tree and you said to yourself, 'I bet a tree fell across the road ahead.' As you continued around the curve you not only look in front of you to avoid rocks, you didn't look ahead to see the tree that had blocked the road. By using a familiar sound to visualize or see in your mind something similar, you can prepare to stop or take a path around the obstacle in front of you. Imagining what might happen is what some people call 'the mind's eye.' Does that make sense?"

The boy said, affirmatively, "It's kind of like dreaming, isn't it? What about reading between the lines—seeing words that aren't really there?"

"That's another metaphor. It means that you listen not only to what people say or read the words they write, but you try to understand *why* they are saying or writing those things. You look for the message behind the message."

"Like looking for the golden egg in an Easter egg hunt, lying under a leaf that the green egg was placed on top of," Mason asked.

"Precisely," Laney replied. "If you are going to get at the truth, you may have to look under rocks, behind trees, and in the weeds to find the Golden Egg of truth."

"That's another one of those meta ..." Mason said, pausing to think about the rest of the word. "*Metaphors*, isn't it Granny?"

"It is," she responded. "In this case it is another way to talk about finding *the truth*."

"I understand why someone would want to hide the Golden Egg in a hard to find place, but, why would people want to hide the truth?" Mason asked.

"Sometimes, my son, people do the unexplainable. They do foolish things to themselves and the people and things they claim to love ... selfish things," Laney said. "And, that's what makes the human being a mystery. Sometimes, I think animals make better decisions about their own survival than people do."

"But, I've always thought that people are smarter than animals. Aren't we?" Mason asked.

"Sometimes, I wonder," Laney said. "Let's just say that if you are going to be smarter than the animals and other people, you have to learn everything you can. You have to be prepared *to use* what you know when you have to. It's one thing to know things and another to know how to use what you know." Laney added, watching as her grandson was writing down the last statement. She paused until he was finished; then continued, "In a world that seems caught up in making people of all races and religions slaves, *truth* is the best defense—the best army you'll ever have against evil and those who use it to get what they want."

"Is evil the same as The Devil?" the lad asked, scribbling the words *"truth is the best defense against evil"* on a new page in his notebook.

"The best way I can answer your question, my son, is to say that evil is the opposite of good; darkness is the absence of light; cold is the absence of warmth; death is the absence of life; and *good* is the absence of *evil.*"

"I'm still a child," Mason said, "How will I be able to know what is good and what is evil as I grow up?"

"It's really not that hard," his grandmother answered. "Just listen to that small voice inside your mind—called your *conscience*. If the voice tells you that you shouldn't do something, follow its advice. That voice is God or one of his angels talking to you."

"Yeah, I've heard that voice with my mind's *ears*. I will listen to it always. I promise—Scouts Honor," Mason said, rising to his feet and placing the first two fingers of his right hand on his forehead. "*I will do my best to do my duty to God and my country.* That's the first line of the Scout Oath," the lad added.

"I helped you memorize it when you were eight," Laney asked.

"Yes ma'am, I remember," the boy replied.

"Mason, by hearing the small voice in your mind, you have been in touch with God and His angels. Now, become even more aware of how this world is part of a greater universe. Pay attention to the moon and the stars. Your Scout Oath recognizes who is in charge. Learn not only what God wants you to do, but what you must do *for other people*. In your journey toward understanding why God put us here on earth, you will learn lessons from everyone you meet. Sometimes, you will meet someone that you think is a stranger, but that being is really an angel who has come to protect you or show you the way. Look for them and you will find them."

"You mean that everyone in the world is a teacher ... even angels," Mason asked, taking his pencil and writing "*everyone is a teacher.*"

"Technically, everyone teaches. From some, you will learn what you should do. From others, you will learn what you should not do," Laney replied.

"Is that why God put bad people on the Earth—to teach us what we should *not* do," Mason asked. "Is God always on the side of good people?"

"I wish I could answer those questions, my son. I've never been able to figure out why bad people exist. Just, keep an open mind, and remain focused on the good and the positive. And, when the day comes for you to assume a leadership role, you will be ready. A minute ago you repeated the Scout Oath. It is a good one, but prepare yourself for other oaths—pledges that bind you to good and noble causes. At some point in your life, you will be called upon to solve a major problem—something that will affect the lives of a lot of people. Prepare for that day."

"Will that small voice inside tell me what to do?" the lad asked as he wrote, *"Always be prepared."*

"I am proud of you, Mason. Though you are young in years, you truly understand the lessons that I am trying to teach you and I am impressed that you are writing them down today. Refer to these lessons often and remember: leaders aren't born. Leaders emerge from difficult circumstances that cause them to step to the front of the line," Laney said.

Before anything else could be said or Mason could write down Laney's last statement, Angela stood up from the seat she had taken on the sofa located on the opposite side of the room. Proudly, she had been listening to her mother prepare her grandson for the world that lay ahead.

"I'm sorry to break this up," Angela said, "But, it is past your bedtime, son."

"Do I have to, Momma?" Mason asked, pleading to stay up a bit longer. "I want to hear more."

"You will," his mother replied. "Granny will teach you a lot more. I'm just glad that you are eager to learn what she knows. But, it's late. Give her a kiss and off to bed with you."

"Good night," Mason said, kissing his grandmother on the cheek.

"Good night my little man," Laney said. "Tomorrow, I'll tell you about a book that I want you to read before you graduate from high school. It is a thick novel, but worth the time. It was written by an American who grew up in Russia under a different kind of government than we have here in America. There are a lot of great lessons in it, too."

"What is the name of the book," Mason asked.

"*Fountainhead*," Laney responded.

"I know what a fountain is and I know what a head is," Mason said, "but what is a fountainhead?"

"It means the source of something, you know like where a natural stream comes out of a hillside," Laney replied.

"I've seen lots of them at Uncle Danley and Aunt Cleo's farm," the boy said.

"Well Ms. Rand's *Fountainhead* is a book about young architect who refused to settle for less than the best, simply because influential people, who did, wanted him to do as they did. In the end, he won out, but he had to struggle against insurmountable odds first," Laney said, hoping that her grandson was getting the message."

"Mason," Angela said, "Bed time."

"Sorry, Angela, it's my fault," Laney interjected. "There's so much to teach. And, so little time."

Mason turned to his mother and gave her a kiss. As he turned to go toward his room, he said, "Thank you, Granny. I learned a lot today. And, thank you, Mamma, for letting me stay up later than usual. I love ya'll," the lad said as he walked toward his room, clutching his little black notebook in his right hand.

Just before Mason arrived at the door to his room, he looked back at his mother and grandmother and said, yawning, "How do you spell fountainhead. Is it one word or two?"

"One word," Laney answered.

Mason nodded, waved good night, and disappeared into his room. Angela could only imagine how her son's head must be spinning with questions—as hers had when she and her sisters listened to Laney's wisdom sessions. Still, there were unanswered questions ... lots of them.

"He is a bright young man," Laney said. "I am convinced that he was able to grasp much of what I talked about today."

"I assure you that he did," Angela answered her mother. "He is also a lucky young man, to have you as a teacher ... as were I and my brothers and sisters."

Upon entering his room—as he had done every night he could remember—Mason knelt beside of his bed and prayed: *"Now I lay me down to sleep, I pray Thee Lord, my soul to keep. If I should die before I wake, I pray, my soul you'll choose to take. Amen."*

Having completed his nightly prayer, the boy crawled into bed. He reached for the black notebook and the pencil that he had laid beside it. He added yet another piece of the puzzle to his mounting collection. He entered the word "*Fountainhead*" on the list and turned to the first page in the book. There, he wrote in bold letters the title he had selected: **Laney's Little Book of Wisdom**. He returned his treasured notebook back to its spot on the nightstand, next to the copy of *The Old Man and the Sea*. It was one of the gifts he had received on his last birthday. Laney told him it was the story about man fighting to survive the forces of Nature. A projecting bookmark indicated that the lad was half way through the book.

Exhausted from a memorable day of instruction, Mason fell asleep the minute his head came in contact with the pillow. He took a deep breath, savoring the fragrance emerging from his pillow. The fresh smell was there because his mother had placed the pillow in the August sun, where it had soaked up the life-giving rays for much of the day. The aroma was yet another reminder that his mother cared and that *light* had many affects on both people and things, even when it was not visible to the eye. Angela knew how much her son liked to be reminded of such pearls of wisdom while dozing off to sleep. She was not only Laney's daughter; Angela was her mother's student, too.

Watching from the doorway as Mason drifted off into the world of dreams, Angela whispered. "Good night, my little man. May the good angels look over you 'til the morning's light." When she was certain that he was asleep, she gently closed the door behind her and added, "With all you are learning, I just hope that you don't feel that the weight of the world is on your shoulders though one day, it may well be."

CHAPTER 6

Mason was the consummate student. He looked upon school as an opportunity to learn about things that his parents and grandmother were unable to teach. Because of the instruction he received as a child and the encouragement from his family, Mason sailed through high school and college, earning both academic and athletic honors. Classmates recognized Mason as a natural born leader. They elected him to represent them as their class President and serve as a representative to the school's Student Government Association.

While attending college Mason participated in varsity sports and in student government, even though he was enrolled in a demanding pre-medical curriculum. He made an academic All-American team in baseball and was inducted into numerous honorary societies and fraternities. In athletic arenas, Mason learned lessons the old-fashioned way, by experiencing them.

In his final year of college, the New York Yankee organization drafted Mason as a pitcher and urged him to play professional baseball; however, he turned down the opportunity, go straight to Medical School and marry the girl of his dreams, Norene Bronkston, a beauty queen, artist, and horse enthusiast.

Medical school meant a move from Druidville to Steelton. Norene worked as an art teacher at a Steelton neighborhood school during the first two years that Mason attended Medical School in order to allow her husband to concentrate on his studies. Then, Norene stayed home to care for their first born child, a boy that the couple named Steve.

Medical school required drawing upon the skills and lessons learned from each of the arenas in which Mason had participated, including the one at his grandmother's feet. There was a lot to learn about the human body, the mind, and the inter-relationship between them.

....

At long last, the coveted degree, Doctor of Medicine, was within reach. The dream had come true, not only for Mason, but for his parents.

So as to get a seat as close as possible to the front of the auditorium, Owen and Angela arrived an hour earlier than necessary. This was not unusual. They had been taught to be prompt as children.

Norene was waiting for Owen and Angela in the outer lobby. Down the hall with the remainder of his class, Mason was receiving last minute instructions from the organizers of the event. He and his fellow doctors made last minute adjustments to the traditional mortar board caps and long black robes worn by graduating seniors.

"My Mom and Dad are saving seats for us," Norene said. "Let's go on in and sit down, just to make sure that someone else doesn't take them."

Mitch and Molly Bronkston were dutifully guarding five seats located on the first row behind the section reserved for the graduating class. It was a good thing that they had come early," Norene said to herself, looking around the quickly filling auditorium. Twenty minutes before the ceremony was to begin there was not an empty seat in the auditorium.

The stage exhibited only a simple lectern and five straight backed chairs. This was intended to be a serious occasion, without all the pomp and ceremony often factored into graduation events.

At precisely seven o'clock p.m. the rear doors of the hall opened and a procession of men and women marched down each of the two aisles leading to the reserved seating area at the center of the auditorium. In single file—and in dead silence—the class of seventy-five reverently approached their assigned seats. Dean Parker's predictions four years previously *had not* come to fruition. Only five members of the entering class had dropped by the wayside, not the predicted one-third of the class.

"There he is," Norene said to Angela and Owen, "coming down the right aisle. The parents turned quickly to savor the scene of their son marching toward his destiny. Mason cut his eyes toward the place where he knew his family would be sitting and winked. Tears of joy streamed down Angela's face, while Owen's prideful nod simply spoke volumes.

When the entry procession was complete, three members of the medical faculty and university officials entered stage right.

Dean Clanton Medlock was the first to assume a position behind the lectern. He nodded to the audience, indicating that all present should be seated.

Looking into the sea of black caps and gowns seated before him and the packed house of families and friends flanking the graduates from three directions, Dean Medlock began to speak.

"This is both a joyous and solemn occasion. Tonight, seventy-five new physicians will be initiated into the family of medicine. When we are finished here, each of the young men and women seated in these front rows will leave this hall with the most respected piece of parchment awarded to members of the human race. On it will be printed three words that represent honor and responsibility, *"Doctor of Medicine."* The title is one that has been earned with hard and smart work. It is not an end to anything. It is merely a beginning—an opportunity to further enhance your understanding of the human condition so that you can make life better for your fellowman. You are not expected to know all the answers; however, you are expected to engage in the relentless pursuit of answers to questions known and unknown."

The Dean continued, "You will use the knowledge and experiences gained through the years preparing you for medical school and those gained in these institutions during the past four years as stepping stones toward new horizons. Think great thoughts. Do great deeds. Be compassionate. Extend a helping hand for the hurt and dying. Unless you remain strong in body and mind, you will not be able to lift others up. Live exemplary lives. It is not enough to tell your patients how to live. Show them how to live. Leave a lasting impression on everyone you meet. Your life will never again be the same, for you now shoulder the achievements of all who have gone before you and the dreams of all who will come after. You are my young colleagues, a conduit to both the past and the future."

With those words, Dean Medlock turned and took his seat. As he did, the gentleman to his immediate left arose and walked to the lectern. Although none of the audience had seen him dressed in graduation attire, most recognized the stately gentleman as Dr. Roswell Franks, the university's President.

In a soft, but commanding voice, Dr. Franks said, "To the graduating class and to all who have dreamed of this day through them, please let me add my heartfelt congratulations. The honors to be distributed here, tonight, represent not only the achievements of the young men and women seated before us, but the efforts and support of everyone in these halls. All of you should leave this building with heads held high. For the world will have seventy-five new physicians, whose duty it will become to look out for the health, safety, and welfare of its inhabitants ... everywhere. And, because each of you shared in their education, you too, will share in their future achievements.

"To those of you receiving your degree, on behalf of this great university, its board of trustees, alumni, administrative and teaching staff, let me say to all of you: we are proud to have played a role in the milestone you have reached," the University's President said.

Dr. Franks returned to his seat, indicating that the next speaker was to take center stage. At least to the students, it was another familiar face, one belonging to Virginia Bradley, the school's registrar and admissions officer. Ms. Bradley had overseen the application and acceptance process for each of the men and women seated before her. Mason remembered her as a tough and committed gatekeeper.

From his seat below the stage, Mason's mind wandered back to the day he first met Ms. Bradley. The visit to the medical school's campus was scheduled for face to face interviews with members of the admissions' committee and the person who screened all candidates It was she, who decided who would—and would not—be invited to meet with the admissions committee. Truly Virginia Bradley wielded a lot of power. And, she knew it.

Glancing over his file, Ms. Bradley sneered, "I see from your transcript and letters of recommendation that you earned both athletic and academic honors in college," the grouchy registrar began, "but what makes you think you can make the grade in *this* medical school?" she asked, emphasizing the word *this*.

Shocked by her unprovoked aggressive preamble and believing that Mrs. Bradley was insinuating that as an athlete, he had been given special academic favors, Mason paused for a moment, collected his thoughts and carefully chose the words he would use in response. "Ms. Bradley," he said softly, yet firmly, "I earned every grade on that transcript you hold in your hand. Not only *can* I handle your curriculum, if you and the committee will give me a chance, I will pass *anything* you throw at me." It was a statement that Mason would have to repeat to a nation in the years to come.

Ms. Bradley seemed taken aback by Mason's confident reaction to her probing insinuation. However, she had apparently gotten the response for which she hoped. Within seconds, her stone-faced demeanor broke into a faint smile and she responded, "Perhaps, you will, young man. Perhaps, you will."

On this memorable night—and in front of her superiors—Ms. Bradley was putting her best face forward. She actually smiled when she took her position behind the podium—the first one that any of the graduating class other than Mason had seen.

She went straight to the point. "Will the nineteen sixty-nine graduating class, please stand, turn to your right and approach the stage in single file," the long time registrar said.

Happily, the class followed her commands. Mason couldn't help but wonder how the encounter between Ms. Bradley and him might play out on this momentous occasion.

As a part of the graduation ceremony, Ms. Bradley's job was to call the names of each student and pass the coveted diploma to President Franks, who handed it off to the graduate while exchanging a handshake of congratulations. When Mason's name was called, he walked up the four steps leading to the stage and glanced over at Ms. Bradley. He winked at her. In an uncharacteristic manner, she returned the wink.

"That's good," Mason thought to himself. We both understood the message being sent. I'm glad that she challenged me to prove myself. She probably knew exactly what she was doing. "

Dr. Franks extended his right hand and took that of Mason's. With his left hand he took a rolled up piece of sheepskin wrapped in a crimson-colored ribbon from Ms. Bradley and handed it to Mason.

"Congratulations, Dr. Edmonds," the university's President said. "Display this document with pride."

"Thank you, sir," Mason responded and walked off the stage with his prized diploma. "Doctor Edmonds," he repeated to himself. "I like the sound of it."

Mason walked back to his seat where he remained standing until the remainder of the class had received their diplomas.

When all graduates had received their sheepskin, Ms. Bradley returned to the microphone and said, "Please be seated."

Dean Medlock took his place at the lectern and said to the audience before him, "Will you repeat—with me— the noble-intended oath written thousands of years ago by Hippocrates?" Without notes Dr. Medlock began to recite a modernized version of words attributed to the giant who was most acknowledged to be the "Father of Medicine."

> *"I swear that according to my ability and judgment, I will keep this Oath and this stipulation; to reckon him who taught me this Art equally dear to me as my parents, to share my substance with him ... to look upon his offspring in the same footing as my own brothers, and to teach them this art, if they shall wish to learn it. I will impart*

knowledge of the Art to my own sons and daughters, and those of my teachers ... according to the law of medicine ....

I will follow that method of treatment which, according to my ability and judgment, I consider for the benefit of my patients, and abstain from whatever is deleterious and mischievous. I will give no deadly medicine to any one if asked, nor suggest any such counsel.

With purity and with holiness I will pass my life and practice my Art. Into whatever houses I enter, I will go into them for the benefit of the sick, and will abstain from every voluntary act of mischief and corruption. Whatever, in connection with my professional practice or not, in connection with it, I see or hear, in the life of men, which ought not to be spoken ... I will not divulge that which should be kept secret.

While I continue to keep this Oath ... may it be granted to me to enjoy life and the practice of the art - respected by all men, in all times; but should I trespass and violate this Oath, may the reverse be my lot!"

The Dean paused for a moment, looked deeply into the eyes of his young colleagues and simply said, "Though this oath is intended to be a pact between physicians, it applies to your brothers and sisters in the Family of Man, for the time will come when you will be called upon to serve as a link between the Creator and the created.

"Let me be the first to offer my congratulations to you, my fellow physicians. With this Oath, you enter a brotherhood of service, the honorable Family of Medicine." Then, the Dr. Medlock added, "In my capacity as dean of this distinguished medical school, I hereby certify that—as you leave this place—you are entitled to pursue a valid license to practice the art and science of medicine. Please file out as you entered."

Each student changed the tassel of his or her cap from the right to the left side, signifying that graduation was official. Half of the class turned to their right. The other half turned to their left. Beginning with the two back rows—the opposing columns moved in single files up the aisles toward the rear of the auditorium. Unlike the deafening silence that filled the auditorium when they entered, applause and cheers permeated the air, continuing until the last graduate exited the auditorium.

In the outer lobby, the graduating class exchanged congratulations, handshakes and hugs. It would be the last time that they would be together ... as a single body. From this day forward, each of the doctors would go their separate ways and pursue their own paths toward fulfillment ... ostensibly with the oath they had just taken guiding their thoughts and actions.

CHAPTER 7

The Veterans Hospital in Steelton was under the management of a longtime government man, Lt. Commander Michael Kirby, known to his friends as "Happy" Kirby. The former Naval Commander had worked his way into the chief administrator's position by adhering to the "make no waves" policy. He was, as they say, "*a company man*" through and through.

Happy Kirby was a survivor of the Japanese attack on Pearl Harbor, the dastardly event that brought the U.S. into World War II. The Purple Heart that he proudly displayed on his sport coat was received following a fateful day in 1941. The medal and what it signified gave Commander Kirby an edge over other men with equivalent administrative qualifications. Though he was a war hero, as an administrator in the VA healthcare system, Happy had acquired a reputation for telling everyone what they wanted to hear—with a grin—but doing little to follow through on any suggestion that rocked the status quo.

Mason met Commander Kirby the year before during a ribbon-cutting ceremony that christened the new administrative offices on the top floor of the VA hospital. At the time of their meeting Mason was serving on an Internal Medicine rotation. When the Commander learned that Mason had played football for a legendary football coach, the two men discovered that they had at least one common bond. As a midshipman, Happy Kirby had played the same sport at the Naval Academy.

The Commander's willingness to talk sports at the drop of a hat gave Mason an opening to discuss a recurring problem he surmised was experienced by the surgeons charged with caring for ill and hurting veterans. The surgical staff had met to discuss a far-too-frequent practice. The operating room supervisory staff was quick to cancel surgeries that might extend into the afternoon hours. One case, in particular, was disturbing, and Mason felt compelled to bring it to the Commander's attention. He called the administrative offices and asked to speak to Commander Kirby's assistant.

"Administrator's office, this is Maxine," the pleasant voice on the other end of the phone answered. "How may I assist you?"

"Maxine, this is Dr. Edmonds," Mason responded. "Would it be possible for me to speak to Commander Kirby? I promise I won't take but a minute of his time.'

"He has someone in his office, but let me see when he might be free," Maxine offered. "Hold the line."

Commander Kirby came right on the line. "Mason, how the hell are you," he asked, laughing.

"I'm fine, Commander," Mason answered. "However, one of my patients isn't. And, I'd like to speak with you, when you have a moment, about a recurring problem in the operating room."

"How about right now? I'll be free until two o'clock. Then I have a staff meeting to discuss a new system that we are installing for medical record-keeping. It's state of the art, a computer. Ever heard of them?"

"Just that they are a new way to store data and that they are quite costly."

"Well, we want to stay ahead of the curve at this hospital."

"I'll be right there," Mason replied, and headed to the penthouse level of the hospital.

"Walking into the Commander's office, Mason thought to himself, "It's not the oval office, but it is the center of power in this little kingdom."

. . . .

"Come in and have a seat," the Commander said to Mason, puffing on a pipe. "Do you like my pipe," he asked. "It's a collector's dream. I got it in Cape Town from a vender on the street when we went ashore for an overnight pass during World War II. I've burned up a lot of bags of my favorite tobacco mix in this little bowl." He pointed to the ornamental head of the pipe. "You smoke?"

"No, sir."
"Then how about a cup of coffee?"
"That sounds good."
"How do you take it?"
"Black."
"That's the only way to drink coffee. I've never understood people who make milk shakes out of coffee."

Pressing the intercom button on the telephone, the Commander said, "Maxine, please bring in two cups of black coffee. Thank you.

"Now, my good doctor, what did you want to talk with me about?"

"It's about not being able to do the best job we can to take care of the men and women who come to this hospital for the care they need and deserve."

"How so?" asked the Commander. "We've got a great-looking facility. And this new computer—"

Mason interrupted, "Take today, for example. I had a former Marine scheduled to have a biopsy for a suspected cancer of his tongue this morning. His name is Brady White. We found what appeared to be a cancer during a visit to our clinic six months ago. It took a month to get him admitted so that we could biopsy the area to confirm that it was cancer and to know the kind of cancer we were dealing with. After he was admitted, it took a week to get him on the surgery schedule. And, on the day we were scheduled to perform the biopsy, the chief nurse in the operating room canceled the surgery, stating that there was a policy that no surgery could begin after one o'clock in the afternoon.

"The reason we were late getting to him is that an emergency occurred with another patient. His name was Horace Jacoby, one of the few who made ashore during the invasion at Normandy and lived to tell about it.

"Early this morning, Mr. Jacoby had a massive bleed from a ruptured carotid artery, as a result of an overdose of pre-operative irradiation that was delivered because of a technician's error in reading the radiologist's orders. The tissues over the main artery that supplied blood to the patient's brain died, exposing the artery. Despite all our efforts, we couldn't get a graft or flap to live in the irradiated area.

"We were waiting on a cardiovascular consult to see about inserting a long shunt around the exposed part of the artery. That consult was ordered two days ago. I learned during yesterday's afternoon rounds that the cardiovascular service hadn't received the request. The nurse on the floor didn't follow through with the first order. So I ordered another one. This time, I called the chief resident on the cardiovascular service myself and asked him to stop by. He said that he would see Mr. Jacoby first thing this morning.

"At 5:30 a.m. I received a call from the head nurse on the floor, stating that a patient in the bed next to Mr. Jacoby had frantically come to the nurse's station, screaming, "He's bleeding to death. Jacoby is bleeding to death."

"According to the nurse on duty, she ran to see what was happening, finding Mr. Jacoby lying in a pool of blood. Wisely, the nurse grabbed a towel lying on the night stand and asked the patient who had brought the emergency to her attention to hold pressure on the bleeding artery while she summoned help.

"I called the operating room to schedule an emergency procedure. However, no one answered. So I called the hospital operator and asked her to locate the administrator on duty for me. Ten minutes later, he called me. I apprised him of the situation and he told me that he would have to call a crew in from home, that the hospital was not set up for such procedures 'after normal working hours.' I told him that a man's life was at stake and to do whatever he could to get a crew in here as quickly as possible.

"I took Mr. Jacoby to the operating room where I found two sterile clamps in a drawer and placed them above and below the rupture to keep him from bleeding to death. I looked at the clock on the wall, recording in my head when the first member of the surgical team arrived. It was 5:46 a.m. By the time the instruments and room were set up for surgery, it was 6:45 in the morning.

"When Dr. Johns, asked for a synthetic carotid bypass graft, he was told by the circulating nurse that she had no idea where those devises were kept. Dr. Johns sent a medical student who was rotating on the cardiovascular service back across the street to the university's main hospital to get one of the devises from the CV operating room. A quarter of an hour later, he returned with the graft.

"When Dr. Johns released the clamps I had placed in the ward, Mr. Jacoby lost a half of pint of blood. Mr. Jacoby's heart stopped beating and he stopped breathing. We had to stop surgery and initiate CPR, cardio-pulmonary resuscitation. We were successful in restarting Mr. Jacoby's heart and getting a satisfactory blood pressure so that Dr. Johns could sew in the bypass graft, allowing blood from the heart to pass around the rupture in the artery and provide circulation to Mr. Jacoby's brain.

"We finished the surgery at 8:30 a.m. Mr. Jacoby was taken to the recovery room, where the day shift was preparing for the daily surgery schedule. Everything seemed to be doing fine: blood pressure, EKG, oxygen concentration, etc.

"For reasons that we can't yet explain, Mr. Jacoby suffered a stroke in the recovery room. The staff was unable to resuscitate him this time. He died at 9:35 this morning."

"Commander," Mason said, "If we had been able perform the carotid bypass operation when it had been scheduled last week, we would not have lost this former soldier. *The system* kept us from doing it. As a physician, it is heartbreaking to see a patient die when we have the technology to save him. His cancer appeared to have been cured.

"The reason I went into so much detail about this case was to share with you some of the frustrations that we doctors face in taking care of our patients in this hospital. I realize that I have raised a lot of questions here this afternoon, but I needed to get them off my chest and share them with someone in a position to do something about them."

"Have you ever been in the service?" the Commander asked.

"Yes, sir. Reserve Officers Training Corp and the National Guard."

"Boot camp, but no combat duty," the Commander commented with a cynical grin.

"I tried," Mason answered, "but at summer camp before I received my commission, an orthopedic surgeon examined me and found a compression fracture in my neck and two damaged shoulders from football. My commanding officer and I exhausted all appeals, trying to overturn the orthopedic surgeon's decision, but were unsuccessful. The doctor gave me a draft classification of 1-Y, meaning that I could only be admitted to the service in case of an attack on the U.S. or if I graduated from medical school."

"Were you admitted after graduating from medical school?"

"Once again, I tried, but was told that I was not needed. I exercised the only option left. I joined the National Guard. Last month, I was promoted to Major and Chief of Medical Services for a field hospital unit. You know, like the one on M.A.S.H?"

The Commander nodded.

Mason continued. "As Chief of Medical Services, I know a bit about red tape and the administrative side of medicine as practiced in the military. Each year, when my unit goes to summer camp I butt heads with some of the active-duty Army hospital personnel, trying to get them to provide training for our paramedical and hospital support staff. They seem to look upon the National Guard enlisted personnel as replacements rather than soldiers in training. I want my staff to be ready if and when we are ever called up to active duty or to handle a domestic disaster."

"Then you understand what I am up against, Mason," the Commander added. "Congress has cut way back on VA appropriations for the past two years. I don't know what this year holds. Since we are tied to the whims of politicians, we have to work within whatever budget they negotiate among themselves."

Mason looked around the office in which he was sitting. The plush carpet, the down-stuffed chairs, mahogany paneling on the walls, the hand-carved desk behind which the Commander was sitting, and the three-foot bronze sculpture of an American Civil War icon, the infamous Admiral David G. Farragut, the naval officer to whom is attributed the phrase, "Damn the torpedoes, full speed ahead." The impressive bust was sitting on a six-foot-long ormolu chest standing against the wall to his left. Then Mason then looked at the *Vista computer system* (an acronym for Veterans Health Information Systems and Technology Architecture) sitting on a credenza behind Commander Kirby's desk.

The Commander picked up on what the doctor was doing. "Expenses for administrative services come out of a different part of the budget," he offered, with the first sheepish grin Mason had ever seen on the Commander's face.

Mason simply nodded, but thought to himself, "I'll bet it comes from a different part of the budget, right off the top, just like in Washington, D.C. One day, I'd like to go there and change the way that the people's money is spent."

"Anyway," Commander Kirby said, "it's hard to get people who are entrenched in a way of doing things to change. The operating room supervisor in this hospital has been here longer than I have, and she has friends in high places, lots of them. I've tried to get her to instill some more efficient policies in her area on several occasions. Each time I do, she reminds me that she is a tenured government employee and that if I want to remain administrator of this hospital, I'd better not force her hand. I'll talk to her about why it took so long to get things set up for Mr. Jacoby's surgery, but I can't make any promises. Thank you for caring, Dr. Edmonds, and for making me aware of some of the problems in my hospital. I'll look into the issues you've raised. You can count on it. Have a good rest of the day."

The Commander ushered Mason to the door and patted him on the back. "What kind of team is the university going to have this year? You know, I'd like for you to introduce me to the coach one day. He's my kind of man."

Mason left the administrative offices, saying to himself, "The coach I know is anything *but* the Commander's kind of man. The coach I know, who rightly is known nationally by just that title alone—*The Coach*—makes things happen and tolerates no excuses from anybody. When he learned of what happened here last night, my former coach would have made heads roll and dared the politicians to challenge him on the decision."

Based on the lack of interest in what he had just heard from Commander Kirby, all Mason expected was more of the same, more tolerance of more government intervention in the delivery of healthcare, more bureaucracy, more red tape, more defiance from staff members who resisted the right kinds of change, even when it meant providing better care for more veterans like Mr. Jacoby. The future into which Mason could see would mean that too many of America's former heroes were destined to die before their time while waiting for hope and promises that would not come.

Before he could finish his thoughts on the subject, Mason's beeper went off. He went to the closest phone and called the PBX operator.

"This is Dr. Edmonds," he said to the operator. "You paged me?"

"Yes, doctor. Mrs. Jacoby is in the chapel area and would like to talk to you. I still have her holding on the phone."

"Tell her I'll be right there," Mason answered.

Walking down the stairway to the main floor of the hospital, he thought to himself, "How can I possibly explain to the wife of a man who survived Normandy that her husband died because of a broken system encumbered by the inactions of career-minded politicians, tenured government employees, and paper pushers?"

The fact was he couldn't. Only those who experienced government-run healthcare first hand could possibly understand why veterans often received less than the best of everything, especially the brave men and women who had risked everything for their country. "They and their families deserved better than the government they had protected chose to provide," Mason thought.

Turning the corner of the hallway leading to the chapel at the end of a first floor corridor, Mason could see Mrs. Jacoby and a man who appeared to be in his early fifties, wearing his VFW cap, who he recognized was her son. He had met him during one of the family's routine Sunday afternoon visits. Next to Mr. and Mrs. Jacoby's son stood two younger men, one dressed in Navy whites and the other in Marine fatigues. Mason's heart dropped into his stomach.

"How can I face these people?" he thought. "What will I say to the family of a man whose system he fought to protect and preserve, betrayed him?"

Mrs. Jacoby took charge of the situation. "Dr. Edmonds, I'm Grace Jacoby. Don't you feel bad. I know that you did everything you could to help Horace. He told me about you every time I talked with him. He was so appreciative of the fact that you always stopped by on your way home from a two-day shift to make sure that he was okay and that you came by the first thing in the morning before you started your morning rounds.

"Dr. Edmonds, my husband knew that he was going to die. He told me so and that I should not worry. He was ready to go. He had made peace with God and forgiven everybody who ever wronged him. I had fifty years of marriage with the finest man I ever knew. Although my son and these two fine grandsons standing here in their uniforms are going to miss him, we know that he is in a better place and that he is going to be okay, and so are we.

"Doctor, if you ever come through our little town of Ashton, please give me a call. Here is my telephone number. I'll cook you the best fried chicken and fresh vegetable dinner you've ever had," she said, and hugged him.

With tears in his eyes, Mason took the small piece of paper, folded it and tucked it away in a special part of *Laney's Little Book of Wisdom*.

. . . .

The following year, as part of his moonlighting job with the Pathology Department of the Baptist Hospital, Mason was called to perform an autopsy on a newborn child who had died shortly after birth. The call came late Saturday evening while covering the Emergency Room and ICU units at the hospital in Steelton.

"I can't get up to Ashton until tomorrow morning. Tonight I'm on duty here at the hospital. Will that be okay?" he asked the pathologist covering weekend calls for the hospital group. "I can be in Ashton by 10:00 tomorrow morning."

"Tomorrow morning will be just fine," Dr. Causey answered. "I'll call Dr. Smith back and tell him that you will see him tomorrow."

It was fortuitous that the call came on one of the few weekends that Mason had no in-hospital or residency responsibilities. He had never been called out of town to perform an autopsy. All others had come from local hospitals.

Drew and Joan Williams, neighbors of Mason and his wife, Norene, agreed to take care of their two young children so that Norene could accompany Mason on the trip.

. . . .

After Mason had completed the postmortem examination and revealed his preliminary findings to Dr. Smith, the attending physician invited Mason and Norene to come to his home for lunch.

"I'd love to have lunch with you," Mason said, "but, I need to make a house call on a friend who had already invited me to have lunch when I was in town. I can come by, though, for a glass of tea and a short visit beforehand."

"Great," Dr. Smith replied. "I'll call my wife and let her know that we are on our way."

When Mason and Norene arrived at the Smith home, Mason asked to use the telephone.

"Sure," Dr. Smith said. "Use the one in my study. You'll have some privacy in there."

Settling into Dr. Smith's desk chair, Mason called the number given to him by Grace Jacoby months before.

"Hello," was the melodic answer he heard on the other end of the line. "This is Grace Jacoby."

"Mrs. Jacoby, this is Dr. Edmonds. Does that invitation for a chicken dinner still stand?"

"You bet it does!"

"Will your son be there?" Mason inquired.

"I'm afraid not, he's on a hunting trip this weekend, somewhere up around Lookout Mountain."

"What about your grandsons? I know that the last time I saw them they were in training. Are either of them in town?"

"No, they're both on active duty now, somewhere in Asia, but we don't know exactly where. You know, top secret stuff. I'm here by myself this weekend. I'd like to have some company."

"Well then, company's coming," Mason replied. "I'm at Dr. Smith's house. I came into town to assist him in finding out what happened to a newborn baby on Saturday."

"Do you mean George Smith?" Mrs. Jacoby asked.

"Yes, Ma'am."

"George is my doctor. He's a fine man and a great doctor. You know that he was a pharmacist before he became a doctor, don't you?"

"No, Ma'am, I didn't know that."

"You tell him I said hello and that he and Wanda are welcome to come with you. If they can, that is."

"I will. And, Mrs. Jacoby, I actually know about top secret stuff. Your grandsons must be special to be involved in it. Can you tell me how to find your place?"

"It's easy. First, you go to the center of town—where the red light is—and turn east on Riley Avenue. Go two miles and—"

CHAPTER 8

Some things are impossible to change. One of them is the influence of genetics on the human mind and body. Following her mother's health line, Angela developed dementia and eventually required skilled nursing home care. The only one in the area that barely met the minimum standards required for continued licensure. The staff seemed more interested in putting in their hours than in going the extra mile for residents. Mason and Norene were constantly frustrated by the lack of attention the staff paid to Angela's hygiene. She was often left alone while other residents participated in planned social activities.

The nurses and aides hated to see Mason and Norene come through the front door of the facility. They knew that they were about to be called on the carpet for signs of neglect. Mason had served as Medical Director and physician of a first class nursing home operation during the early years, after he received his medical degree. He knew how a nursing home should be operated and the kind of care that was possible.

On his way out of the nursing home one Saturday afternoon, Mason glanced into the dining room at the empty chair where his mother formerly took her meals. Angela's current condition required that she remain in her room. On either side of the empty chair sat two other residents of the senior care facility. One was a gentleman in his early sixties. He had been confined to a wheel chair for the past decade.

"Hi Jeremy," Mason said, sitting down in a chair beside him. "Everything looks clean around here today."

"Yeah," Jeremy replied, "They got word yesterday that the state inspectors were going to make an unannounced inspection because of a complaint by one of the resident's family, so they cleaned the place up," Jeremy said. "Just one time, I'd like to see the inspectors show up without warning. They might shut this place down."

The other man seated at the table was a World War II veteran, Charles Shivers, a Marine Sergeant who'd been a combat correspondent. He was only seventy-two years old and still sharp mentally.

"Hello, Charles," Mason said to the retired Marine. Charles had been injured while Japanese machine guns rained bullets down on the soldiers of Easy Company during the Battle of Iwo Jima. Sergeant Shivers documented the battle from the base of Mt. Surbachi, though he didn't participate in the historic flag-raising incident that was captured by a photographer's camera. Because of those injuries, Charles' legs had given way at an earlier age than expected, causing him to rely on a wheelchair to move around the facility.

On the days that Angela refused to be awakened from her nap, Mason often sought out Sergeant Shivers and wheeled him into Angela's room. While Angela slept, the two men exchanged stories. After the war, Charles had become a sportswriter for an Atlanta newspaper. He knew sports.

"How's the team going to do on Saturday?" Charles asked.

"Hard to tell," Mason replied. "One thing I learned from my coach is that one can never tell what a group of nineteen-to-twenty-two-year-old men are going to do in the heat of battle. You should know that."

"Well, what are we going to talk about today?" Charles asked.

"What if I tell *you* a war story—of sorts?" Mason replied.

"I'd like that," Charles said. "You know that when I was in the Marines one of my jobs was to report on our activities to the press."

"I know," Mason said. "That's why I thought that you might enjoy hearing about some of the things I've learned about today's military."

"I would. Tell me everything you know."

Mason began, "One day in the early nineteen nineties, I received an invitation from the Department of

Defense to participate in the National Defense University's civilian outreach program at Fort McNair, located on a small island in the Potomac River."

Mason was a good storyteller. It was a craft that he had learned from his grandmother. "My participation in the outreach program was suggested by a former Naval Commander whom I had befriended through community service work. With the invitation came a directive to visit the local FBI headquarters for a security clearance.

"I adjusted my schedule to attend the once-in-a-lifetime event and flew to Washington, D.C., for what would prove to be an incredible three days. I was met at Reagan National Airport by a young Air Force Lieutenant Colonel, who escorted me to the loading and drop-off area, where a military busload of other civilians was waiting.

"Upon boarding the bus, I realized that I was the last of the group to arrive. The first face I saw after scaling the vehicle's steps was none other than that of my friend, Jack Williamson, the former Navy Commander who had been responsible for the invitation.

"'Welcome to Washington,' Jack said as I sat down in the seat next to him. 'I saved this seat just for you. I've been here since yesterday.'"

"'That doesn't surprise me,' I replied. 'Once a Commander, always a Commander, right?'

"Jack just smiled and turned to the other guests who had previously boarded the bus, saying, 'Gentlemen, say hello to Dr. Mason Edmonds.'"

"The group waved as I waved back.

"'You'll have a chance to get to know each of these guys over the next couple of days,' Jack said to me. 'Like you, they have been selected from a pool of millions throughout the country. Each has made a significant contribution to our country and/or his profession.'

"Briefly interrupting himself, Jack barked in a commanding voice. 'We are ready, driver. Anchors aweigh!'

"'Aye, aye, sir,'" came the reply from the young Navy ensign driving the bus."

"I miss those days," Charles said, interrupting the storyteller before him. "Those were some of the happiest days in my life, times when I was part of a proud and honorable team of sailors. We loved each other and the country for which we were fighting."

. . . .

Mason acknowledged the old Marine's comment, and continued. "At the security gate on the mainland side of the bridge that connected Fort McNair with the island, the credentials of the bus's passengers were pored over by the guards. After being satisfied that we were who we purported to be, the gates were opened and our bus entered the fort.

"Impressed by the high level of security exhibited, the civilians were immediately ushered into a classroom where the traditional coffee and donuts were served, in buffet style of course. I introduced myself to a man in his early sixties whose name tag read: 'James Pickett, Oklahoma City, OK.'

"'I see that you are from Oklahoma City,' I said. 'Do you happen to know my friend, Dale Robertson, the cowboy actor?'

"'Sure, I do. Everyone in Oklahoma knows Dale. Not only is he recognized as a great actor, Dale was an all-sports athlete. Did you know that only Jim Thorpe earned more athletic letters in Oklahoma than Dale Robertson?' Pickett asked.

"'I did know that,' I replied. 'And Dale was recently inducted into the Cowboy Hall of Fame. The honor is well-deserved. Dale is a great American and devoted patriot.'

"'These days,' Pickett noted, 'Dale spends a lot of his time making public appearances to help raise money for charities, and plays in a charity golf tournament every week somewhere.'

"'That's how I met him,' I replied. 'We played in a tournament to raise money for Special Olympics together. The two of us hit it off and stay in touch with each other. In fact, my wife and I flew out to Oklahoma last spring to play at a tournament he helped organize at the Oak Tree Club, just outside Oklahoma City.'

"'I know it well. I'm a member there. Sorry I didn't meet you while you were in town.'

"'Yeah, me too,' I said. 'I enjoy golf. It is a game of strategy and adjustment. You have to deal with the golf course and the obstacles that the designer put there to trip you up. Changing conditions of the weather and the mindset and skills of your opponent add to the challenge. But most of all, golf is a game that you play against yourself. It keeps you trying harder to achieve a near-impossible dream, to better the best score you ever shot.'

"'You know,' Pickett said, 'we seem to have a lot in common.'

"'Seems that way. I'll bet as we get to know each of the others here at this event, we'll find that all of us have things in common. How do you know Jack Williamson?'

"'I'm in the oil business. Jack has invested with me in some wells. Fortunately, one or two of them hit—hit BIG!'

"'The oil business, huh? I want to know more about that. Maybe you can help me understand why America imports most of our oil rather than buying it from guys like you.'

"Before we could say anything else, the door to the classroom opened and two men dressed in military uniforms entered the room."

"'Good morning, gentleman. Would you take your seats? I am Commander Self, U.S. Navy. I hope that each of you had a pleasant trip and that you are ready for a day of intensive work.'"

"None of the guests had been apprised of the content of the program upon which we were about to embark.

"I thought to myself: Work? I wonder what the Commander means by work? I glanced around the room at the strangers who were there with me. Each had the same look of surprise on their faces that I was certain could be seen on my own.

"'Today, you are going to learn about things that very few people know, things that no civilians know. Only those of us with top-secret clearances have been privy to the intelligence that we are going to share with you. After

Lt. Colonel Kearney makes her first presentation, there will be time for questions.'"

"I was both surprised and intrigued that I and a group of strangers were about to enter the inner sanctum of military secrets. It was both exciting and a bit scary that this much trust was to be placed into the hands of a group of civilians.

"Lt. Colonel Kearney went directly to the world map hanging on the wall behind her and began to talk about political unrest, military conflicts and secret operations taking place around the world. Not only did she explain *who* was involved in the conflict, but the role that the United States played, including which side our military supported, and why.

"For more than half an hour, the Colonel revealed top-secret information to the group seated before him. Then, she said, 'Any questions?'

"My hand was the first in the air. I said, 'Yes, Colonel. I have one.'"

"'Go ahead, doctor,' the Colonel said.

"I was somewhat surprised to hear the Colonel address me as doctor. My name tag only read 'Mason Edmonds.' Nevertheless, I asked: 'Why in the world would you bring a group of civilians here and tell us all these things?'

"The Colonel smiled and replied, 'Doctor Edmonds, you forget that we had you checked out before you arrived here. I know that you recall going through an FBI clearance. I hope that you recall the oath you signed not to divulge the details of what you will learn here today. We expect you to live by that oath and intend to see that you do."

"Naturally, I nodded, indicating that I understood both the answer and the order that was skillfully woven into it.

"'I am happy to answer your question, doctor,' the Colonel said. 'You are a focus group. We want to know what you think you know about world affairs. Let me ask you, doctor, were you familiar with any of the events and operations I just addressed?'

"I replied, 'No, Colonel. None of them.'

"'I would have been shocked if you did, doctor,' the Colonel replied. 'We can't trust the media. We leak to them only what we want them to report. Sometimes we intentionally provide them with press releases containing information that is one hundred and eighty degrees from the facts. We know that our enemies around the world also read newspapers and watch television. We don't want our enemies, foreign and domestic, to know that we know *what* we know, how we obtained the intelligence, or what we intend to do with it.'"

"As the Colonel was completing her answer, I reflected on a lesson learned from my grandmother, who told me about white lies, grey lies and black lies," Mason told Charles. "I must admit that I was a bit surprised to learn that the U.S. Military engaged in all three colors of propaganda—in the name of 'national security'."

Once again, Charles interrupted Mason's story. "When I was a combat correspondent, I always wondered how my stories got changed after I submitted them. There were times I hardly recognized what I had written after it was printed."

"Well, I gathered from the Colonel's remarks that this happens quite often," Mason said, and continued with telling the story of a trip into the inner sanctum of military intelligence. 'Some of our enemies call themselves Americans. Are there other questions?' she asked.

"A gentleman on the opposite side of the room from me raised his hand.

"'Yes sir, Mr. Butler,' Colonel Kearney said. "You have a question?'

"'I'd like to know what percent of what we read and hear in papers each day is true.'

"I was impressed that the Colonel knew each of the participants by name," Mason told Charles. "Surely, she and her colleagues had done their homework."

"'Mr. Butler,' the Colonel answered, 'I'd say about a third of what the networks and wire services report is the truth, the whole truth and nothing but the truth. Much of what is printed or aired falls under the 'white propaganda' spectrum; however, there are some progressive socialist in the media who engage in propaganda of the black kind.

Over the years, we've learned that we can't trust the media, at least not the mainstream media. I don't know whose side they are on. It would not always be in America's and our allies' best interest to publicize everything our military does. We keep America safe by keeping some things secret.'

"Next, a thin, athletic-appearing guest in his early forties, who sat to my far left, raised his hand.

"'Yes, Mr. Cooley, what is your question?' the Colonel asked.

"'How closely do you work with the CIA?' Mr. Cooley inquired.

"'As closely as the law allows,' the Colonel replied. 'The men and women in the Central Intelligence Agency do a great job. They rarely get credit for their efforts, nor do they expect it. Without the CIA, America would not be a safe place to live. There are a lot of people out there that would like to see us—*The U.S.*—out of the way. Some of them have set up shop here in our backyard. In short, the enemy is among us, and we know it. We just can't get the orders from our Commander-in-Chief and his Vice President to take them out, but that is not to be repeated outside these walls. Understand?' the Colonel stressed.

"All in attendance nodded, indicating their pledge to honor her instructions.

"For the next two hours," Mason told Charles, "a parade of military officers representing the three major branches of the U.S. Armed Forces came into the classroom and briefed the group of civilians on world affairs. At the end of the morning, my newly sworn colleagues and I had learned about more than a dozen wars being fought around the world, why the U.S. considered them important to its interests and security, and who was supporting the enemy.

"'Now, let's have some chow,' said Commander Self, who had reentered the room during the last two minutes of the morning's final presentation. 'This afternoon, we will travel to the Naval Operation at Norfolk, Virginia. Tomorrow, you will get a chance to see some of the finest maritime war machines and technology in the world. Then tomorrow afternoon, we will board a converted C-

130 and fly out to one of our nuclear-powered aircraft carriers in the Atlantic. You will land on the carrier, employing 'tail-hook' technology. This promises to be a memorable experience. *I guarantee it!*'

"'After evening chow, you will be briefed by the carrier's Captain and spend the night in the officers' quarter's bay aboard the vessel. You will see, up close and personal, a floating military city, staffed by a crew whose age averages nineteen and one-half years. I think that you will be both amazed and impressed at what kind of men and women this country is still capable of producing.'

"All of this was much more than I had envisioned," Mason told Charles. "I had no idea that my fellow focus group members and I were going to be taken on board of a nuclear submarine, a destroyer, an amphibious craft, and a nuclear aircraft carrier. I could only imagine what other surprises awaited."

"I would like to have been involved in that focus group," Charles interjected. "I could have told them a thing or two about the press."

"Since you were so close to the press, they wouldn't have trusted you," Mason responded.

"You're probably right," Charles said. "I've learned that nobody seems to trust my profession."

"Can you blame them?" Mason asked.

"No, I really can't," Charles responded.

"My time is growing short, so I'm going to move forward in the story a bit now," Mason said, "I want to get to some of the other parts before I have to leave."

"'Cross your arms and tuck your chin tightly across your chest,' Commander Self ordered, as the C-130 prepared to touch down on the deck of the carrier. 'On my command, take three deep breaths and hold the last one until the craft has safely landed,' he added.

"I looked out of the small window in the side of the airplane to catch a glimpse of the massive floating fortress upon which my colleagues and I were about to land. *Impressive* would be an understatement. I had seen photographs and documentaries depicting U.S. Navy carriers, but seeing one this close was a totally different story.

"'Prepare to touch down.' Commander Self ordered. 'Take three deep breaths and hold the last one, *NOW!*'

Within six seconds, Mason and his colleagues felt as though they had hit a brick wall, Mason told Charles. The C-130 tail hook had been engaged with the cable coursing across the carriers' landing surface, bringing the plane to an abrupt halt.

"'This has to be where seat belts came into existence,' I said to myself.

"I'm glad mine held. Otherwise I would have gone flying through the cockpit of the plane," he told his audience of one.

Within seconds of landing, the plane was taxied off the landing area and onto the right side of the carrier's top deck. Happy—Mason was sure—to have two feet on a solid surface, all passengers embarked.

"'Keep your vests and helmets on until we are inside,' Commander Self ordered our group and ushered us toward the vertical tower to the right side of the massive vessel. There, we entered a steel door and found ourselves in a well-lighted, roomy, air-conditioned environment.

"'Take your helmets and vests off and follow me,' Commander Self said, leading the group of visitors through a series of hallways into a conference room. 'Hand your gear to the sailors who approach you, grab a cup of coffee over there on the counter and take a seat.'

"Within a minute, a tall, distinguished man, sporting a crew cut, entered the room. All military personnel jumped to attention.

"'As you were,' the newly arrived individual ordered. 'Gentlemen, I am Captain Morris Currier. It is my honor to serve as Captain of this wonder of the world upon which you have just landed and to welcome you to it.'

"'Wonder of the world,' I thought to myself." He commented to Charles that, though it was quite different from the Taj Mahal, the giant craft was awe-inspiring in its own unique way.

"You've seen the Taj Mahal?" Charles interrupted, raising his eyebrows.

"I have—but that's another story. Let me finish this one today," Mason replied.

"'Over the next several hours,' Captain Currier continued, 'you men will have an opportunity to experience what only a handful of civilians have ever experienced. You will be taken into the guts of this floating steel fortress and see its weapons systems and intelligence centers. You will see one of the best trained and most dedicated groups of men and women in the world carry out their daily activities with enthusiasm and efficiency. This carrier, like all of the Nimitz-class carriers, has three hospitals on board that can treat several hundred people. Our hospitals are nuclear powered and can supply emergency electrical power to shore facilities.

"'This carrier also has three cafeterias with the capacity to feed 3,000 people three meals a day. It can produce several thousand gallons of fresh water from sea water each day and it carries a half a dozen helicopters that can be used in transporting victims and injured warriors to and from their place of injury. Not only are we prepared for war activities. We are a floating humanitarian flotilla ready to spring into action should disaster occur anywhere in the world.'

"Turning to Jack Williamson, I whispered, 'I had no idea.'

"'It is amazing, isn't it?' he replied. 'Our entire defense system is based upon preserving the peace and promoting human rights around the world, but you won't read that in the papers or see it on the mainstream media's news.'

"'I'd like to see the hospitals on board,' I said to Jack.

"'That can be arranged. I'll see to it,' Jack said to me.

"Captain Currier continued, 'While you are here, we want you to be as comfortable as possible. Colonel Self will be with you at all times, except of course when you retire for the evening. He has assembled a team of sailors who will provide whatever you need. Now, let's go to the chow hall and eat some of the best food you'll ever taste.'

"We did as ordered. Captain Currier had not understated the quality and amount of food that was served. It would have put some so-called five-star restaurants to shame.

"After dinner—or I should say 'evening chow'—my group of civilians gathered back in the conference room where Captain Currier told how the nuclear carrier fit into the overall defense system of the United States and what some of the other carriers in the fleet were doing at the time. The session only lasted about twenty minutes, at the conclusion of which he said, 'Now, you will be shown to your quarters to prepare for an evening of rest. We will get started bright and early tomorrow morning—at 5:30 a.m. I'll see you then.'

Mason paused and stood up from his chair in the nursing home's dining room. "I need to stretch a bit. I'm going to go into the kitchen and get a cup of coffee. Would you like one, too?" He asked Charles.

"That would be great." Charles replied.

"How do you take it?"

"Black. Is there any other way to drink coffee?"

"Not in my book," Mason answered, and went on his errand.

. . . .

Handing Charles the cup of steaming coffee, Mason said, "Now, let's get back to the story. I'm going to have to leave soon. Norene will be worried.

"Laying my head on the pillow of my bunk," he continued, "I thought, being here, somewhere in the Atlantic Ocean on a military marvel, is a far cry from Prideville. America has truly come a long way. No wonder our enemies want to do away with us. No wonder they won't take us on out in the open. They'd get clobbered in a New York second."

"Don't you mean minute?" Charles interrupted.

"No, I mean *second*. Those weasels, and the people behind them, are threatened by our might. I can see why they would resort to political and domestic terrorism.

"Though I was caught up at the moment and in the incredible things I had seen and heard over the previous twenty-four hours, I also knew that tomorrow was another day and that I needed to go to sleep. To assist in my winding down, I used the meditation techniques I had learned from my daughter when she was training for Olympic sports. Within two minutes, I was dreaming."

"Didn't your feet hang off the end of the bunk?" Charles asked. "Those bunks on ships are usually not made for men of your height."

"The bunk was a bit short, but I was so tired that a little inconvenience didn't matter. And when I thought of how some of our troops have to sleep while in combat, I felt as though I was basking in the lap of luxury," Mason answered.

"At 5:00 a.m. the promised knock came on the door of my cabin. 'Rise and shine. We'll be leaving for the conference in twenty minutes. We can't be late.' The voice had a distinctive Southern drawl. It sounded like that of one of the young sailors from my home state, the one that I had met the previous evening at dinner, or I should say 'chow.' Colonel Self had assigned to each guest a seaman from an area of the country from which he hailed.

"I hurriedly shaved, showered, and dressed. I was ready when the next rap on the door came at precisely 5:20 a.m.

"Morning chow (not breakfast) took place in a dining hall that efficiently served what appeared to be a thousand sailors as much food as they desired. More eggs, bacon, ham and biscuits than I had ever seen in one place were available for the taking. Surprisingly, there was no waste. The mess-hall crew had their job down to a science, as well. From observing the habits of the ship's crew, and the daily schedule of activities they were able to accurately predict how much, and what kinds of food needed to be prepared for each meal.

"After morning chow and a short debriefing session, our group of civilians was escorted back to the deck of the carrier to observe how jets were launched from the vessel at incredible speeds. The force of the catapult pulling the plane down the deck, combined with the engine power, was enough to accelerate a jet to 165 miles per hour in just two seconds and allow the aircraft to takeoff in a distance of only 300 feet, the length of a football field. In between takeoffs, other jets landed, using the tail hook system at the opposite end of the runway. Though it occurred with the sound of thunder, it was poetry in motion.

"Our group watched as young men and women on the deck carried out their duties with surgical precision and efficiency," Mason added.

"It's been a long time since I was one of those baby-faced Marines," Charles said, "a very long time. In those days, I had good legs. Now I am mostly confined to this wheelchair. Getting old is hell. Sorry to interrupt, but the excitement of reminiscing got the best of me. I want to hear more about how those jets landed and took off from the carrier."

"For a half an hour, our group observed takeoff and landing exercises. Such power, such precision, such technology," Mason said. "It was awesome. Then Commander Self said, 'Let's go aloft, to the bridge.'

"I was most taken by the opportunity to enter the seat of command and sit in the Captain's chair. The rather massive chair seemed to have been tailored for the oversized frame of the carrier's Captain. It was strategically stationed behind a panel of controls that were capable of turning the floating fortress on a dime, or so it seemed. In fact, the Captain told the group that Jack Williamson had devised a series of maneuvers that could return a ship to the exact spot in which a man—or in today's Navy, woman—fell overboard. The maneuver was appropriately called 'the Williamson Turn.'

"'In honor of the man that the Navy, in its appreciation of the creative skill involved, still considers an inguenological hero, it will be my honor to demonstrate the maneuver that Commander Williamson devised,' Currier said, and called down to the ship's deck, instructing a seaman to cast a rubber raft overboard.

"Captain Currier took over the carrier's controls and explained his actions. 'First,' he said, 'I will put the rudder over full, toward the port side—sorry, the left side of the vessel, for you non-sailors, since that's the side to which the raft was tossed overboard. Then, I will set our course to sixty degrees from our original course and shift the rudder full to the opposite side, to the ship's starboard, or right, side.'

"We were amazed at how the massive vessel responded to the Captain's maneuvers.

"'We will now head twenty degrees short of the reciprocal course and position the rudder amidships—sorry, parallel to the center of the vessel,' the Captain continued, pressing the appropriate buttons on the control panel to make the carrier carry out its pirouette-like dance, while our audience of civilians watched in utter amazement.

"Amazingly, the carrier returned to the original course, in the opposite direction, back toward the exact spot at which the raft had been thrown overboard. Within minutes, the visitors in the control tower could see the orange rubber raft floating on the waves to the left of the carrier.

"'Well done, Captain,' Jack Williamson said when the maneuver had been completed. 'Although the turn was originally created by using a destroyer, I'm glad to see that it works with a carrier," Jack said, as the group respectfully applauded the ingenuity and precision with which the Williamson Turn was carried out.

"'Many lives have been saved as a result of Colonel Williamson's ingenuity,' Captain Currier said to our group. 'He has played a major role in the National Defense University's civilian outreach program, the one created to recognize other Americans who have made contributions within their respected fields of endeavor. That's why each of you has been invited here today.'"

Mason leaned back in his chair and said to Charles, "Afterwards, each of us civilians took the opportunity to sit in the chair of the man who called all the shots and viewed the events taking place on the flight deck with the eyes of an eagle, those of Captain Currier, a decorated sailor with more than twenty years of service.

"Captain Currier was both a field general—or should I say a sea general—and a politician. He knew how to handle his fighting force and the visitors who were observing their tax dollars in action. The Captain was happy to have his photograph taken with each civilian who sat, even for a brief moment, in the chair that wielded such power that a single command could wipe out a small country if necessary.

"'It's time for noon chow. You see, keeping our crew fed is an important part of how we take care of them,' the Captain said. 'It's not only to nourish their bodies. It feeds their souls, or spirits. They not only need a break from the intensity of their work, eating the kinds—and amounts—of food with their fellow sailors. It is part of the bonding process. It is also an expression that the American taxpayer, who provides all this, is behind them. Seeing each of you here today affirms that message. Now, Colonel Self will escort you to the mess hall.'

Sitting in Angela's nursing home room, Mason looked at Charles and said, "I must admit, the thought had never entered my mind. I didn't realize how important the little things are to our fighting forces. It made me realize that we need to remind them of how much we appreciate their every effort every time one of them is in our presence."

He continued, "We began to head to the small door leading from the bridge. Captain Currier reached out and touched me on the shoulder, indicating that he wanted to have a private word with me. 'I understand that you would like to tour the hospitals we have on board,' he said.

"'If it isn't too much trouble, I would really like to see them,' I replied.

"'We'll swing by the medical facilities, while the rest of the group is making its way to the mess hall,' Currier said.

Charles interrupted here. "Though I spent a lot of time in a military hospital after the injury to my legs, I was never in one on a ship. Tell me what you saw."

Well, in keeping with the carrier's other facilities and technology, the hospitals were state of the art," Mason replied. "Nothing was spared. The latest CT scanners and MRI's were aboard. The operating rooms can accommodate any life-saving procedure and the laboratory was capable of running the kinds of test necessary to determine the cause of most illnesses. In addition, the craft's pharmacy had all the medications necessary to keep sailors healthy and fit.

"The word, cleanliness, could have originated from an American aircraft carrier. The facilities were spotless. Floors had been shined like a brass belt buckle, deserving of a merit of accommodation. And the air didn't have the typical rubbing alcohol smell of some medical facilities. It was fresh and clean. Sheets on empty beds were stretched so tightly that a dime would bounce into the air if dropped on them. Medical personnel were focused on the task at hand. When spoken to, they responded in a professional, but courteous, manner."

Again Charles had a comment. "I wish some of the people who operate and work in this nursing home and the hospital across the street could visit such a facility and see just how it is possible to care for people," was his observation.

"I know," Mason agreed. "My mother has been here for three years and Jeremy has told me a lot of what goes on behind the scenes. It's just a matter of time. One day, the inspectors will show up without someone leaking the fact that they are coming."

"When I toured the carrier's medical facilities, I said to the carrier's Captain, 'Now this is the best government-run hospital I've ever seen. I wish those ashore were operated in such a manner. Perhaps, one day, I might be able to tell people in Washington about the way that hospitals and nursing homes should be operated."

"Amen," Charles interjected. "I've been in a few VA hospitals during my time, too. I wanted to clean house, literally—but get back to your story."

Mason nodded, and continued. 'Doctor,' the Captain said to me. 'Out here, we have a zero-tolerance policy. We have to. Not only are the lives of our sailors at stake, the security of our country could ride on how well these men and women feel and how well they are able to carry out their responsibilities.'

"'Clearly, this is the model for healthcare, Captain,'" I said. 'I just wish there was a way that we could instill what I have seen here throughout America's healthcare system.'

"'Send all the people who are involved in caring for Americans to us for a month and we will show them how it should be done,' Currier said.

"'I'm sure you would,' I answered. 'Today, we would have to send you Congress, the Commanders-in-Chief and the White House staff. They are the ones out to run—or should I say ruin—healthcare. Do you think we could get them out here?' I asked.

"'I see what you are getting at,' Captain Currier said. 'But we'd better join the rest of the group in the mess hall.'

"After noon chow, Captain Currier invited all of us visitors into the ship's conference room once more," Mason said to Charles. 'It was his way to prepare us for sending us on our way."

"'Gentlemen,' the Captain said, 'on behalf of the United States Navy and America's fighting forces around the globe, we hope that you have enjoyed your brief odyssey into our world and that you liked what you saw. When you go back into *your* world, just know that there are a lot of people on vessels much like this one riding the waves every day and night, trying to keep America safe from those who would destroy our way of life. It is the hope of all of us who are sworn to keep America safe from its domestic and foreign enemies that, in years to come, you will always remember your time on the high seas with fond memories. Tell others of what you have witnessed. Encourage them to support these brave young men and women who put their lives on the line for the country they love each day and night.

"'Now, as you return to your world, all of us aboard the U.S.S. John Stennis pray that God will bless each of you and that He will continue to bless the country that we all love. I know that each of you have sworn at some point in your life to defend and protect it and its Constitution. When you return home, each of you can put your head on your pillow and know that these young men and women whom you have seen in action on this carrier will be doing their job to the best of their abilities, night and day. And, thousands of their fellow servicemen and women will be doing the same somewhere in the world.'

"With that," Mason told Charles, "Captain Currier departed the room and returned to the carrier's deck to resume his duties. Commander Self took charge, saying, 'Now, my staff will usher you to your quarters to gather your belongings and prepare you for the trip home. Seaman Cortez will prepare you for launch. You will be jettisoned off the carrier as are the jet fighters you have observed. If you've never experienced the force of 2-G's, you are in for a thrill.'

"The officer was correct in his explanation of the effects of two times the force of gravity on the human body. As the converted C-130 carrying a group of duly impressed civilians was catapulted off the carrier's surface, I felt as though my chest was being compressed against my spine. Surely, the walls of my heart were being compressed as well," Mason told Charles. "For more than ten seconds, it was impossible to breathe. Expanding the chest against the extreme forces of gravity created by the carrier's catapult would have been an impossible task. I could understand why my colleagues and I had been told to take several breaths and hold the last one prior to takeoff. It was not until the craft was airborne and assumed a speed of 130 mile per hour that things normalized in the cabin."

"That must have been an awesome experience," Charles said.

"Beyond description," Mason answered. "I glanced at the men to my right and to my left. Everyone seemed relieved to have endured the experience of a lifetime, without undue consequences.

"When the C-130 landed back at Norfolk, my colleagues and I deplaned and boarded the bus that had been waiting to take us back to Fort McNair. The trip took less than two hours. Along the way, I reflected on all that I had seen and experienced. Though I had never visited Disney Land as a child, it must have been what any child would feel on his or her first visit. And being far beyond the Disney Land or Disney World stage, I felt as though I had been invited into an inner sanctum, a world that only a select few truly know, a world of order, efficiency, and unparalleled discipline, one in which its participants were *totally* committed to the oath each took upon entering the military – to 'defend and protect.' And, the amazing part of it all was that those upon whom the nation depends to protect us against our enemies are so young, yet so capable."

"If every American could see what I had seen over those two action-packed days," Mason said, "they would better appreciate what it takes to keep America safe. Every member of the President's Cabinet and Congress should be required to spend a night on a carrier. Perhaps they would see how the *Ship of State* could be run more effectively."

Mason rose from his chair and said, "I've enjoyed sharing my story with you, Charles. You are a good listener. Now, it is time for me to go."

"These days, about all I have to do and can offer is to listen," Charles replied. "My time has come and gone. The future is in the hands of you and your generation. Make sure the young people in America know the truth about why we enjoy the freedoms we have."

"I will, Charles, I will," Mason replied. "And thank you and your generation for the sacrifices you made."

CHAPTER 9

Being one with nature came natural to Mason Edmonds. As a lad, and while visiting the Littlejohns' farm, he often stole away and sat, like a rock, under a big oak tree near the small creek that traversed the woods behind his Uncle Danley and Aunt Cleo's wood-frame house. In the wild, truth is a constant. There, the mind can connect with the soul and an Intelligence far greater than that of any human and become one with Nature.

With .22 rifle in hand, Mason would sit quietly waiting for the squirrels to come home to their den for the evening, Time in the woods provided opportunity to examine the presence of God all around—the insects, worms, and ants—all living life to its fullest in their own tiny universes. On most days, though the furry little squirrels were clearly in range, Mason simply watched them frolic, never raising his rifle to take a bead.

In the wild, he studied the trees, marveling at how their root systems spread out in the ground below to anchor them to the earth, and seeing the community of tree and plants all around. Though anchored in the earth, each reached toward the heavens with all its might. Day by day he watched the leaves change colors, announcing that one season was ending and another was about to be born—once again. He also noticed that some trees never lost their leaves or nettles. Appropriately so, this genus of the plant kingdom was called evergreens. Even though some of Nature's secrets remained undisclosed, everything seemed to have a place and purpose in the grander scheme.

To those who paid attention, the Creator seemed to be saying: "Constancy and change are each parts of our universe." What Mason learned as a young man out-of-doors was that with the change of seasons comes a promise of renewed birth, new leaves, grass, and flowers, each being created from the apparent lifeless seed or root beneath the surface. And, those parts of nature seemingly unaffected by the changing of seasons seemed to be reminding the new growth that it was not the first to make its presence known.

By studying the world around him, Mason became more aware of his own mortality and the interrelationships that must certainly exist between human beings and human beings, as well as between human beings and our Maker. He noted how the stars, sun, and moon dance in the skies to a symphonic tune generated in some faraway place by some omnipotent entity who so masterfully engineered a plan that it is beyond human comprehension. Laney had told him: "To those who seek answers to the mysteries of life, revelations are as plain as day itself." Though he had written his grandmother's statement in his *Little Book of Wisdom*, it wasn't until he visited Africa that Mason Edmonds truly understood its meaning.

During his medical training, Mason had looked for more than the physical relationships of body organs and branched systems. He searched for the meaning of life itself; how the brain and the body are related to the physical and metaphysical universe in which they exist. He was haunted by recurring questions: What are the secrets embodied in life and death? What causes cells to grow in numbers and size? What causes them to shut down and die? What mysteries are hidden in the human genome? Is it possible that the genome of man was created for the sole purpose of evolving into something greater? Is the destiny of man sealed at birth or is our fate written by our own choices and decisions?

These were questions that plagued Mason Edmonds. He had been taught that nations behaved in much the same way as the people who gave them birth and nurtured them. As he learned about the human body and mind, he went again and again to his Bible, trying to identify the links between theology and science. It would be years before he found the answers he sought. Many of the questions he had were answered in the corner of the earth where many believe that Homo sapiens first walked upright, answers that he would one day share with the world.

....

During a photographic safari in Africa in the early nineteen-nineties, Mason, Norene, and their daughter, Roma, observed the cycle of life and food chain, up close and personal, as God had created it. With an armed guide from the camp known as Londolozi accompanying them in an open Land Rover, the expedition parked within a few yards of wild lions, elephants, hippopotamuses, and less threatening species such as water buffalo, rhinoceros, giraffes, and cheetahs. The Edmonds felt very close to the so-called untamed part of the planet. And, yet, never had any member of the family felt so attached to the enigmatic Being responsible for it all.

They saw the ascending nature of the "food chain" and how one species seemed to be created for the sole purpose of supporting another. More amazingly, no animal contributed to the destruction of the environment they shared. The Edmonds family saw the hand of God in everything great and small.

Upon returning from Africa, Mason took his Bible off the shelf and began to read the *Book of Genesis.* He read Genesis 1:26 for probably the fiftieth time in his life and was suddenly stricken by two words that had gone unnoticed in all the previous readings: "us" and "our." He read the verse again, "And, God said, let *us* make man in *our* own image after *our* own likeness." The words seemed to jump of the page, calling out for contemplation.

Mason reread all the verses leading up to verse 26, and noted that *prior to the making of man,* God uttered eight commands beginning with "Let there be light ..." Then, God issued decrees relating to the firmament, waters, dry land, grass, fruit trees, lights in the heavens separating day from night, moving creatures emerging from the waters, and foul that fly in the skies. The Creator went on to order the existence of cattle, creeping things, and beasts of the earth. Only after all these things were made by God commanding them to be, he decided to make something else, something unique: *a human being.* However, when it came to creating humankind, an all-powerful Creator asked for assistance and participation, saying to someone in His presence, "Let *us* make man in *our* own image, after our own likeness."

"Who are *us* and *our* revealed in this single verse of the Bible?" Mason asked as he read the words given to Moses on Mount Sinai. The answer would not be immediately forthcoming. He searched other scriptures looking for additional clues, including scientific links to the biblical rendition of creation, wondering what Moses meant by the term "dust" from which the Bible declares the human form was shaped. "Was the scriptural writer referring to 'genetic dust,' he asked himself, and how did the human race change after the "sons of God" fathered children with the "daughters of man?" Were all the hybrids destroyed by the Great Flood? Could the hybrids that survived the flood—the Annunaki—be the ancient ancestors of the modern-day global cabal of conspirators known as the Illuminati?

Mason tried to square the plethora of clues with those he had learned in Sunday school and during the time he spent in obstetrics and gynecology. It was in the scientific fields of genetics and reproduction that Mason discovered some possible answers. He learned that it was possible to create a human fetus—using microscopic genetic materials—*outside* the womb, a process called *in vitro fertilization,* and to implant the fertilized egg in the uterus of a woman. He also learned that genes could be manipulated in a scientific laboratory, making the new creature different from its parents. Then he learned of emerging research that could allow geneticists to create an exact replica of the donor from which the genetic material used for the experiment was obtained.

Mason's mind began to spin. Was Charles Darwin only half right? Could it be that God was skilled in using genetic technology millions of years ago and used it to create all life on earth, including human beings in His own image? And, exactly what did God and His helpers look like? What did the hybrids, the "sons of God" who mated with the "daughters of man," look like? What did their offspring look like? And, where are they now. Are they us?

Young Dr. Edmonds continued to ask questions and look for answers. Did God assign the task of using such technology to create a new species, like their own, to a team of beings who existed, with Him, in some far-off realm or universe? Did they defy His orders?

He wondered if the human genome was created with the capacity to evolve, as evidenced by archeological findings and confirmed by the written and photographic history of the species. Was *this* 21st century revelation of genetic engineering the long-awaited link between theology and science, *Creative-Evolution*, divinely engineered by the entity, or entities, that created all things, living and not?

"Perhaps," Mason reasoned, "the answers to these questions will be forthcoming within my lifetime. It would be good to know how it all came about and what the future of the species might hold."

Mason continued to search for answers to the questions of life, keeping in mind Laney's statement: "To those who seek answers to the mysteries of life, revelations are as plain as day itself."

It was entirely possible, he surmised, that he hadn't been looking in all the right places. Africa opened a whole new avenue of questions.

CHAPTER 10

"Dr. Edmonds," one of his office nurses said, opening the door to an examination room. "I know that you have instructed us not to interrupt you when you are with patients, but the Governor is on the phone and asked if he could speak to you."

"Will you excuse me for a minute?" Mason asked his patient. "I'll be right back. I have a few things I want to discuss with you before you leave."

"Certainly," she replied, "And, while you have him on the phone inform the Governor that a lot of us have some bones to pick with him. We'd like to know what he's going to do about the rising cost of insurance on the Gulf Coast and the mess left by the oil rig disaster of 2010. I have a condo there. The prices of real estate have hit rock bottom and I can barely afford to pay the flood and wind insurance on my unit, let along the taxes. This oil thing smells like the work of environmental terrorists, you know, the ones who set fire to forests and upper-scale neighborhoods in California."

"If I get a chance, I'll ask him," Mason replied. "I'll take the call in the staff room," the doctor said to his nurse.

"How's the family?" Governor Roberts asked.

"Everyone's fine. And yours?"

Mason and Roswell Roberts had known each other for years. Their daughters were members of the same sorority during their college years and their sons, Steve and Rod, had been best friends while the two of them were in college. Mason had supported his friend's run for the Governor's office when he decided to seek the state's highest office.

"We're all good," the Governor responded. "Mason, I read your op-ed in the newspaper and I like some of the things you said in it, especially about how to get a handle on the rising cost of healthcare. I'd like for you to come up to the capitol and meet with a small committee I'm putting together to discuss what role this state can play in curtailing this spiraling problem. Will you do it?"

"When is the meeting going to take place?"

"Well, I'd like to do it as soon as possible. How about the middle of next week? You have your secretary talk to mine and see which day and time is best."

"Who else are you planning to invite?" Mason asked his friend.

"I want to get representatives from the main players—you know, the stakeholders—in this healthcare issue."

"Some of them might not like what I will have to say," Mason said. "My experience with stakeholder*s* is that their main concern is to protect their own interests not to solve problems."

"I know," the Governor replied, "but we have to put all the cards on the table and see what can be done. This state, like many others, cannot afford the status quo, especially when it comes to the cost of healthcare premiums for its employees and teachers."

"If you want me there," Mason said to the Governor, "I'll make arrangements to attend. There is one person that I would like for you to invite to the meeting. His name is Baker Arrowsmith. Baker is an attorney who knows more about the healthcare industry than almost anyone I know. Will you invite him?"

"You let Ellen know how to contact him and I'll extend the invitation," the Governor promised. "Tell Norene and the kid's hello for me."

"I will," Mason replied. "And you give Betsy and yours my regards. By the way, how is your stallion doing—the one who had the bad foot?"

"How did you know about that?"

"One of my mares had a similar problem. When I took her there for treatment, the Vet School told me about your stud."

"He is fine," the Governor replied. "We can't let him compete any more, but he is a great stud, throwing off beautiful colts and fillies. He won the Grand National Championship in Shelbyville a few years back, you know."

"I know. Our stallions are half brothers," Mason reminded him.

"See you next week." The Governor hung up the phone.

At the meeting the following week, Governor Roberts thanked the assembled group. "I am deeply concerned about the rising cost of healthcare for the individuals insured by our state. The cost of caring for teachers and state employees has gone from a quarter of a million dollars to over a billion dollars in just five short years. And, no one seems to be able to tell me why. Those dollars come out of the general fund of the state's budget, money that we could put to better use, providing better education for our students, paving roads, rebuilding bridges, and building facilities that would attract more tourism to this beautiful state."

"I wish I could take Ross on board the aircraft carrier that I visited a few years back," Mason thought to himself. "He'd see the efficiencies exercised by the medical staff on board and how fit the crew is. Then, he'd know why it costs the state so much to pay medical bills for its employees."

The Governor continued laying the foundation for the meeting. "The reason that I've brought each of you here today is simple. I want to get to the heart of the problem and see if we can find a way to slow the growth or reverse the trend. We have here today representatives from the insurer that manages our state's health benefits program, the head of the state Department of Public Health, a physician who has long been involved in the private delivery of healthcare, the executive director of the state Health Planning Agency, and the attorney who wrote much of the legislation that deals with the delivery of healthcare in our state."

Mason had his doubts. "These people won't be interested in making the kinds of changes that would be required," he whispered to Sean McDonough, the state representative from his district, whom the Governor had invited. "Stakeholders will try to defend the way they are doing things."

The Governor glanced Mason's way, guessing that something about the makeup of the group was a concern, then added, "I think it would be appropriate to have the representative of the insurer of the state's health benefit package tell us why our medical insurance costs are so high."

"Governor, our company has never been involved with cost savings. As you know, this state is self-insured. You do not have a contract with our company to provide benefits. You simply hire us to process the claims submitted by those you insure. We charge you a fee for each claim we handle."

"And what is that fee?" the Governor asked.

"Well, it generally amounts to 10 to 12 percent of the amount of the claim," the insurance representative answered.

"So you're telling me that if a state employee is admitted to the hospital and his or her hospital bill runs $10,000, the state of Alabama pays your company a thousand dollars just to process the claim," the Governor figured.

"Yes, sir, that's the contract we negotiated with the state many years ago," the insurance representative replied.

"Who determines where patients can go for treatment?" Governor Roberts asked.

The representative said, "As per our agreement, state employees and teachers have to go to one of the preferred doctors and hospitals we have under contract."

"You mean that doctors and hospitals are required to negotiate contracts with you, and you make the decisions as to which doctor or medical facility a teacher or state employee can go to for treatment, and how much you are going to pay the doctor for the care that he or she renders?" the Governor queried.

"Yes, sir. That's the way it works."

"Who determines which hospitals and clinics qualify for state-funded reimbursement?"

"That would be my agency," the executive director of the state Health Planning Agency answered. "In the 1970s the federal government mandated that each state develop a long-term health plan to determine how many hospital and nursing home beds it needed. We have been bound to that plan, and unless it can be demonstrated that the needs of a given region of our state change, we are locked into a forty-year-old document. As much as I'd like to change it and open up the healthcare industry to competition, the law prevents me from doing so."

"Can we change the plan?" the Governor asked.

"It's not that easy. The state Health Planning Board hears the requests and makes the decision to leave the plan as is or to change it," the executive answered.

"Who sits on the board?" the Governor wanted to know.

The planning authority executive named the individuals who held positions on the board.

"It sounds to me that the board is stacked with people and institutions that could have a vested interest in keeping newcomers out. Is that right?" the Governor asked. "I am a proponent of free enterprise, you know. And, it seems that a relatively small group of people have a monopoly on the delivery of healthcare in our state."

"Well, sir, the board serves at the pleasure of the Governor," the executive answered. "You have the authority to change the board's makeup, if you see fit. My job is to enforce the statute that created the board. I'd be honored to work with anyone you appoint to make the necessary changes."

"Let's hear from the state Department of Public Health. What programs do you have that are designed to cut the cost of healthcare in our state?" the Governor asked.

"We have initiated a wellness program to nip disease in the bud. That's how we think that we can keep the more expensive costs under control," Dr. Phillip King, the director of public health answered.

"Tell me about your wellness program."

"Well, sir, we have six nurses who cover the state and hand our literature to some of the schools. We give flu shots during the flu season to those who want them."

"What else?"

"That's about it, right now, Governor," Dr. King said. "We're looking at adding a commercial weight-loss program on a voluntary basis for state employees and teachers."

"That's it? That's your wellness program?"

"Yes, sir."

"I want to hear from the attorney next. I'm saving the doctor for last," the Governor said. "Mr. Arrowsmith, how do you see the current problem?"

"Governor," Mr. Arrowsmith said, "I have spent most of my career working with healthcare providers and the legislature, trying to ensure that the health, safety, and welfare of the people of our state are looked after. We live in a changing world. The ways of solving the health needs of the citizens of this state, today, are different than they were forty years ago, when the state health plan was written and adopted. It is my opinion that we are still bound to policies and procedures whose times have passed. And that is why we are paying more and getting less. I am shocked to learn how much of the healthcare dollar is taken by people who shuffle paper. We need to stop debating how we are going to pay for healthcare and come up with answers as to why the healthcare we now have costs as much as it does.

"I know that Dr. Edmonds will probably speak to some of these issues in more detail. I am somewhat familiar with his opinions and I think that he is right on target with both his assessment and some of the solutions to a problem literally growing out of control.

"If you truly want to know my opinion, it will take a few minutes for me to develop it," Mr. Arrowsmith said to the governor.

"Go ahead, that's why I asked you here," Governor Roberts replied.

"We are looking at a new set of rules. Under the old system of 'cost-plus' reimbursement hospitals were rewarded for driving up costs. As the insurance representative explained earlier, how his company was paid 10 to 12 percent for simply processing a claim, hospitals were reimbursed for all costs and guaranteed a profit of 10 to 12 percent profit on those costs, regardless of how they spent money—building new buildings, advertising, salaries, new equipment, etc."

"Under cost-plus reimbursement," Arrowsmith added, "it was impossible for a hospital to fail. All hospitals and the insurance companies that were paid on a percentage basis for processing claims were incentivized by the system to drive costs upward. By doing so, they were guaranteed a higher profit. Then, along came a new way to reimburse hospitals. It was called 'Diagnosis Related Grouping' (DRG). Medicare and Medicaid decided that it would only pay a hospital a set fee for a certain type of admissions and procedures. For example, for a woman admitted for the purpose of having a baby, the global fee paid to the hospital would be preset. No matter whether the mother and baby stayed for an hour or a week, the hospital was paid the same amount of money. Suddenly, the incentive for hospitals changed. Admission and discharge policies changed accordingly. Instead of encouraging doctors to keep patients for prolonged admissions, hospitals were putting pressure on doctors to discharge the patient as quickly as possible. But shortening hospital stays didn't save patients money. The costs to the carrier were the same for a one-hour stay as for a one-week stay. What we now have is essentially a 'drive-through' delivery of babies system, and the same applies for many other diagnosis-related conditions."

"Yeah," the Governor said. "When my daughter delivered my grandchild last year, the doctor sent her home the next day. I thought that was the doctor's choice. When my wife delivered our daughter twenty-five years ago, both my wife and the baby stayed in the hospital for five days."

"Sorry to interrupt," Mason said. "In the case of your granddaughter's delivery, the hospital more than likely put pressure on her doctor to discharge her."

"A lot has changed," Arrowsmith inserted. "The way doctors are compensated changed, too. Medicare and Medicaid payments to physicians have gone down every year for the past two decades. Although the cost of living and running a business goes up at the rate of 4 to 6 percent per year, the payments to doctors have gone down an average of 4 to 6 percent over the past twenty years. And the national healthcare plan proposed by the current administration is expected to cut physicians' reimbursement even more, by 20 percent. Based on inflation, doctors are paid less than half of what they were paid for the same treatment ten years ago, and with dollars that are worth only about half what they were a decade ago. This is in part due to what is called 'managed care' or 'preferred physician organizations,' Medicare and Medicaid being the largest of such organizations."

"I hadn't thought of Medicare and Medicaid as being HMO's," the Governor observed, but we aren't here to address doctors' problems. I am concerned about the financial health of this state.

"Medicare and Medicaid are the biggest HMO's in America and growing exponentially, especially if universal healthcare and the so-called 'public option' become law," Arrowsmith pointed out. "In the wars of control propaganda runs rampant. Some insurance companies advertise to the public that they are looking out for their clients' interest, when in fact they are only looking out for their bottom line and a greater share of the market—government-run health insurance plans included. They put pressure on doctors to sign onto their plan or be excluded from seeing the large pool of patients, companies, and organizations they insure. By signing on, the doctor agrees to accept whatever payment the insurance company decides to pay him or her for services. The only recourse for the doctor is to resign from the plan and reduce his or her access to the patient pool insured by the company or demanded by the Federal Government. And, in this state one company insures more than ninety percent of our citizens. That same company administers Medicare and Medicaid for citizens who qualify for those programs. If a doctor orders more tests than the insurance company—or the government—thinks is appropriate, or refers the patient to a specialist without prior approval, the physician could be penalized at the end of the year and runs the risk of being dismissed from the plan. And, the more that government becomes involved in the healthcare industry, the more convoluted the system will become."

"Now, what does this have to do with the reason you called us here, Governor?" Mr. Arrowsmith said, but added quickly, "Let me answer my own question."

Mr. Grey, the representative from the insurance company interrupted. "Hold on for a minute. I take offense to your blaming this whole mess on our company and our industry. We are a *not-for-profit* company."

"Well, I know that is what your charter states," Mr. Arrowsmith said, "but what do you do with all the millions of dollars you collect each year by processing the claims of state-run programs alone? If you processed one billion dollars of state-reimbursed claims last year, you would have earned one hundred million dollars on the state-handled claims alone. And, that doesn't even count the thousands of small and large business accounts you serve."

"Hold on, gentlemen," the Governor interrupted. "We don't want this to turn into a finger-pointing session. I'm not looking for blame. I'm searching for solutions."

"Governor," Mr. Arrowsmith replied, "you said that you wanted us to identify the problems and try to come up with solutions. If we can't be forthright in what each of the professions and industries each of us here today represent, we will leave from this place with nothing but more of the same."

"You are right, Mr. Arrowsmith," Governor Roberts replied. "I served in Congress. I can attest to the bureaucratic red tape that stifles government. Continue."

"Dr. Edmonds will speak to the physician side of things, but I want to continue with the *regulatory* aspect of healthcare costs and services, if you want me to," Mr. Arrowsmith said to the Governor.

The Governor nodded.

"With the Federal Government embracing a nationalized healthcare system, we can expect more regulation, leading to more bureaucracy and inefficiencies. More dollars will go to shuffling paper, handling telephone inquiries, and scanning electronic data entries than will be spent to take care of patients," Arrowsmith continued.

Governor Roberts said, "I recall hearing someone explain it in this way, 'if you like the compassion of the

Internal Revenue Service and the efficiency of the Postal System, you'll love nationalized healthcare.' And, some of the recent data coming out of Washington suggests that the Postal System is billions of dollars in debt."

"It is," Arrowsmith substantiated. "To keep costs under control, Americans can expect less care and longer waits for the care they need. Hospitals will have the incentive—if not the mandate—to monitor access and restrict medical treatments from the medical staff. Doctors will also be challenged if they order more tests or procedures than some federal mandate stipulates."

"I know that I am scheduled to speak last, Governor," Mason interrupted. "But I need to stress what Mr. Arrowsmith just said."

"Go ahead."

"Thank you," Mason responded. "With more restrictions placed on physicians, the doctor-patient relationship will be no more. There will be a third partner, the government or the government represented by a local insurance company that manages the nationalized health program. Healthcare will be rationed, regardless of what the politicians say. Everywhere in the world that government runs the healthcare system, the people are taxed as much as 60 percent of their income to pay for a plan that offers delays and disappointment. I have traveled to countries whose healthcare is nationalized. I've performed surgery in their facilities. I've seen what their patients go through to have their concerns and needs addressed. 'Health care' is a 'big lie,' shaded by propaganda of the blackest kind. You see, under government-run systems, death is considered more economically feasible than extended care. Physicians are pressured to make decisions or choices for their patients based upon economic parameters set by bureaucrats."

Dr. King, the director of the state Public Health Agency chimed in. "We won't allow that to happen. We will see to it that the doctors and facilities that take care of old people continue to take care of them."

"How will you do that?" Mr. Arrowsmith asked. "If your funds are cut off, how will your agency provide even the ineffective programs it now offers?"

"Sir, I take offense to your comments," Dr. King said. "We do a very good job in taking care of those who need our services."

"Look at the facts," Mr. Arrowsmith said. "In every county of this state where the Public Health Department provides a large part of the care—rural areas—people are more obese, suffer from a higher rate of diabetes, high blood pressure, arthritis, and heart disease than in counties where you have a lesser presence."

"That's because there is a shortage of doctors in those counties," Dr. King replied.

"Partly true, sir," Arrowsmith answered. "And, if the trend of the past four decades continues, there will be even fewer doctors in the future. Already many of the best and brightest American students are selecting other fields of endeavor. Bright minds will not work under a system which simply makes them robots or technicians. Doctors will not subjugate themselves to bureaucrats who know less about managing a problem than he or she knows. More and more of America's doctors are graduates of foreign medical schools. Our state, our nation, is at a crossroads. With all due respect, Governor, this state can either be a follower or a leader. We can resolve to make the kinds of changes that curtail costs and sustain quality. I know that these words are near and dear to Dr. Edmonds' heart. So I will stop for now and let him speak for himself and his profession."

"I must admit, Mr. Arrowsmith," Governor Roberts said, "You have raised some issues that I hadn't considered. I doubt that very many of the people of this state and the owners of the companies and businesses that pay the premiums for healthcare are aware of them either."

"Mason," the Governor said to Dr. Edmonds, "Let's hear what other thoughts you have to add to all of this. I have read some of your thoughts on the subject, but bring them into the context of what has already been said here today."

"I hardly know where to begin," Mason said, looking around the table. "The problem facing our state and nation is at least in part due to decisions made by all the stakeholders around this table. There are others who are not here: the pharmaceutical industry, the nursing home industry, medical supply companies, the trial lawyers, and the public in general. Because I have had dealings with each of these segments of healthcare, I think I can at least address some of their contributions to the problem and suggest changes that each could make in becoming part of the solution."

"I heard that you were once the medical director of a nursing home conglomerate and that you initiated an innovative health prevention program for the state's Educational Association," the Governor interjected.

"That is correct, Governor," Mason replied. "Perhaps, the best way for me to demonstrate how difficult it has been, and will be, to solve the rising cost of healthcare and preserve quality is to summarize a program that I was instrumental in introducing to the state teachers' organization a couple of years back.

"At the request of Dr. Herbert Paulson, the health board of the teachers' association, I conducted a pilot program in my county to determine the current state of health of teachers and school employees. The mission was to identify risk factors and see if, through early intervention, we could reduce those risk factors, keeping teachers out of doctor's offices and hospitals and in the classroom, teaching the state's children. The program that we created cost the teachers nothing.

"At our direction, a team of health screeners went into the schools, gathered pertinent health data, took blood samples, weights, body/mass indices, blood pressure, etc., and plugged the data into a computerized program that collated the data and gave a health profile for each participant. Those teachers who were found to have the highest risk factors were counseled on ways to lose weight, eat more healthy diets, engage in prudent exercise activities, and learn about the conditions they were found to have. After six months, the same measurements were taken, demonstrating that if—and here's the clincher—the teacher complied with the recommendations, all parameters that measure health improved."

"Did it work?" Governor Roberts asked.

"The biggest obstacle we faced was participation," Mason explained. "Even though the program was offered at no charge to the teachers, only about one-third of them participated. We were never able to get the state's teachers' association to place either positive or negative incentives on the members they insured. And, Dr. King, I know that you will take offense at what I am about to say, but though your representatives participated in the discussions leading up to the pilot program, the state Department of Public Health offered no assistance or support in taking the program statewide. The result was that the pilot program ended and the cost to the people of this state to provide healthcare for its teachers and school workers continued to rise, going from five hundred thousand dollars to one billion dollars in the next four years."

"Don't blame the increased cost on me," Dr. King responded offensively.

"I'm sorry that you are offended by the truth," Mason replied. "However, if your agency had been willing to work with us, Dr. King, I am convinced that, together, we could have slowed the growth of the state's financial responsibility to teachers' healthcare. There are other factors. From my forty years of being a physician, surgeon, medical director of a senior care facility, original member of the state's medical licensure commission, and businessman, I have learned that unless the recipient of health benefits takes some responsibility for his or her own health and does the things that he or she can do to control weight, limit high sugar and fat diets, engage in physical activity, neither this state nor this nation, will ever be able to afford or provide the kind of healthcare that politicians are promising."

"We haven't set next year's budget yet, so I don't know what we will request—and the legislature will appropriate—for healthcare," the Governor noted.

"I can almost guarantee you that whatever is both requested and appropriated will exceed last year's amount, Governor," Mason assured him. "You are dealing with a powerful lobby that satisfies its constituency by getting them what they want, regardless of whether it is good for our state. Only though prevention and early intervention of disease processes can we get control of costs and sustain the kind of quality that Americans have come to expect. And, that's going to be painful for some. It's like taking candy away from a baby. The baby will pitch a temper tantrum when you take away what you previously gave to keep it quiet."

"Okay, you've presented your version of the problem. What solutions do you suggest?" the Governor asked Mason.

"We must let the free enterprise system work in healthcare and do away with monopolies that pose as not-for-profit entities. Encourage entrepreneurs to build new hospitals, nursing homes, and clinics. Allow private enterprise to compete with less efficient and service-oriented facilities."

As he spoke, Mason paid close attention to the body language of those sitting at the table as he spoke.

"This state's and this nation's healthcare woes are but a symptom of our loss of focus on the things that made us a great state, a great nation, a proud and caring people. In the name of compassion, we have lowered standards; and we are paying for it. We must encourage private health initiatives and cease from rewarding mediocrity and demand that providers and recipients alike take ownership of the challenge of keeping America healthy and strong. We must put government, elected officials, and government employees on the same kind of budget that we have to exercise in our own households—not to spend money we don't have and to hold those who abuse the family budget accountable—or replace them with lawmakers and administrators who will do these things."

Everyone present could feel the tension in the room. Out of the corner of his eyes, Mason could see Mr. Grey, the representative of the state's most powerful insurance company, whispering to Dr. Paulson, the director of the state employee's insurance fund. Although he couldn't hear the words they were speaking, he assumed that they were discussing how they could counter his proposals.

Dr. Edmonds continued, "We must pass and sustain tort reform. Malpractice abuse is a costly process in time and money. You would be surprised to learn how many days away from treating patients that doctors spend in depositions and in court defending frivolous lawsuits."

Arrowsmith interjected, "Dr. Edmonds interrupted me a time or two. I feel compelled to insert a comment on this topic. I know that this might sound strange coming from a lawyer, but he is right. I defend doctors. We should petition the Supreme Court for this state to redefine the meaning of 'malpractice' and provide disincentives for attorneys who file frivolous lawsuits that drive the cost of healthcare up. With the current tort system, doctors are forced to order unnecessary tests and often make unnecessary referrals to specialists, not in the name of practicing 'good medicine,' but to protect themselves from hindsight analysts who prey on doctors and hospitals."

"Thank you, Mr. Arrowsmith. You lawyers do have a way with words. We may have the cart before the horse," Mason added. "If we had nationalized legal care, or 'no fault' liability insurance, America's healthcare system might not be in the predicament it is in. Doesn't every American deserve access to quality legal care? How many Americans are mistreated by a system inundated with delays and incompetency? Now, don't get me wrong, just like there are great doctors, there are great lawyers, but the legal system in America can't even come close to comparing with our healthcare system. Why aren't we as concerned about it as we are about healthcare? Aren't people's lives and livelihood at risk when they enter the courthouse? You know the reason, because lawyers are running our government, some of them among the most incompetent of the profession. I know. I have a law degree as well as a medical degree. I have seen the legal system from both sides. If lawyers were held to the same standards as physicians, the courts would be overrun with lawsuits against attorneys. With all due respect, Governor, if politicians were held to the same standards of accountability as physicians, many of them would have been run out of office long ago."

The Governor said, "I'm afraid that we can't solve the problems with the legal system. Right now, we have to focus on getting a handle on healthcare."

"I'm sorry, Governor, that's part of the problem. No one is willing to address the disease of corruption and waste that this state and this country are facing. It's like a patient with cancer and blood poisoning who is being treated with an aspirin tablet and a Band-Aid. If we doctors only addressed part of the problem, and did it with the attitude with which politicians seem to address the ills of our nation, the patient would die every time. Government—including the one that runs this state—is refusing to deal with all the maladies facing a country on life support."

"Because I know that your remarks are well-intended and not personal attacks, I take them in the spirit in which they are offered, but you're asking a lot of me," the Governor said to his friend.

Mason said, "Ross, I'd like to see this state take a leading role in demonstrating to others that the American spirit is still alive and well. As it has done on so many other occasions, America is ready to rally, ready to tell politicians to 'butt out.' Americans are ready to take control of their destiny.

"Governor, you could be the Governor who solved one of the greatest dilemmas this state has ever faced. It would be your legacy. No, it won't be easy. However, this is how I see us taking a step forward to solve the problem you brought us here to address. Unless we take action on the problems identified, we will continue to feed the monster. And it will, one day, consume us, no matter how much money we throw at it."

"Well," the Governor replied, "does anyone else have anything else to offer?" No one uttered a word. "Then I will take these matters under advisement and get back to each of you within the next few weeks. Thank you all for coming."

"Mason," the Governor said, as the group prepared to leave. "Can you stay for a minute? I'd like to ask you another question."

"Absolutely," the doctor answered.

When just the two of them were alone around the Governor's conference table, Roswell said to Mason, "It looks like I've got a tiger by the tail. This problem seems to be bigger than I thought. I'm not sure how to attack it. The people—and the companies and/or departments they represent—are in a position to affect the kind of change needed to correct the problem seem *to be* the problem."

"Precisely," Mason said. "It's time for the truth to come out in the open. I've long been concerned about what is happening to my profession and the entire healthcare system in America. National healthcare will be a disaster. It will drive America into bankruptcy. I wonder if that's not its intent. I've been active in both local and national medical movements that are trying to affect the kind of change that America needs. Several years ago, I was the chairman of a legislative affairs committee representing the largest country medical society in this state. Every year, we went to Washington to meet with our Congressional delegation to provide input into matters affecting healthcare in America. I think it helped. But, for whatever reason, the fix was in. Doctors could do nothing."

Ross Roberts nodded. "As you know, I was a member of Congress. I am quite familiar with how Washington works—or should I say, doesn't work. But how do we maintain quality and get a handle on cost?"

"It's a matter of getting the people who use the system to take some responsibility for their health, to provide both incentives for those who take better care of themselves and disincentives for those who don't. The insurance industry does this for other types of insurance. Safe drivers pay less. And people who live in areas not subject to hurricanes or floods pay less. It is about creating a free marketplace, removing the constraints on entrepreneurs who could offer competition to the monopolies now in place. People who reduce healthcare risks and costs should be rewarded for their efforts and—"

"Governor," Ellen said, cracking the door to his office, "please forgive me for interrupting, but Senator Braxton is on the phone and said he needs to speak to you. There is a bill before the Senate that he has to cast a vote on and wants to ask your opinion."

"Put him through," the Governor said to his assistant.

On the phone, he asked, "What's up, Jeremy? He listened a bit. ... Yeah, I know a little bit about it. As a matter of fact, I was just discussing this matter with a mutual friend of ours, Mason Edmonds."

Turning to Mason, the Governor said, "Jeremy said to give you his regards." Mason nodded in acknowledgment.

"Jeremy, this bill would have a positive impact on our state. Already we are going broke paying for healthcare costs, and Mason has just explained to me that tort reform is one of the ways we can reduce those costs. The government already imposes limits on what doctors are able to earn. Limiting the amount that lawyers could earn on so-called malpractice lawsuits would be fair. If you want my opinion, capping the awards for medical malpractice suits would go a long way to turning this heath cost crisis around. If nationalized healthcare becomes a reality, the lawyers are going to be out in the cold anyway. Have you thought about introducing a bill to nationalize legal services? Doesn't every American—legal or illegal—have the right to quality legal services?" the Governor followed up, with a bit of sarcasm, realizing that the Senator was an attorney.

Following a moment of listening to Senator Braxton's reply to his comments, the Governor said, "You are welcome. Do you think you have enough votes to push this nationalized tort reform through? Most of the people voting on it are lawyers, you know. Well, good luck, and keep me posted. I will. Take care."

"Jeremy said that it would be a stretch, but that someone was trying to tie a tort reform amendment to the Medicare reform bill. And the law lobby had determined that a bit of reform would be better than removing their ability to sue for anything. Part of the administration's revised plan removes the ability to sue any individual or institution that signs onto its plan."

"That's a double-edged sword." Mason replied. "I wonder who inserted this amendment into the bill?"

"I understand," the Governor said, "that one of the senators heading up this part of the bill is a physician from some western state. I think he has been spearheading our party's attempt to make sure that our children and grandchildren won't be left with a bigger debt than they already have hung around their necks.

"You know, Mason, you seem to have a handle on this whole healthcare dilemma. I think I'll make you the health czar of this state and have you bring all the stakeholders in healthcare to the table again to try and work something out. I'd like to see our state take the lead in addressing these matters on a national level."

"What the hell is a health czar? The term seems a bit daunting."

"It just means that you would have the ability to call meetings and ask tough questions of the businesses and professions that impact healthcare in the state. I can appoint you through what is called executive order. Will you do it?"

"Ross, I'm not looking for another job. I have a full time practice and a lot of other interests, but I have long felt that if we doctors don't become involved in helping preserve the best care available at a reasonable price, we would lose employees of the Federal Government. I worked in the VA system several years ago and I have seen government-run healthcare at work. It is a huge step backward from what Americans enjoy today. If I am going to do this, I want you to let me assemble a blue-ribbon committee representing knowledgeable and experienced people who will work toward making the kinds of change that we need, not just trying to protect the interest of the current stakeholders."

"You got it," the Governor assured him.

"Then, I'll go to work today. I'll let you know whom I recommend so that you can make the appointments to the committee."

"Thank you for taking this on," the Governor said, shaking his friend's hand and ushering him to the door. "How many horses do you have, now?"

"Too many," Mason replied. "Norene and I have twenty-three. How about you?"

"Only fourteen, but I am looking for a registered Tennessee Walker black mare that I could add to my herd," Ross said.

"I've got her. She's a three-year-old and gentle as a lamb, fifteen-and-a-half hands tall," Mason responded.

"Send me some photographs. I might be interested."

"I'll email them to you tomorrow," Mason promised.

"I'll be on the lookout for them. And say hello to the family," the Governor added.

. . . .

As promised, within a week Mason had put together a distinguished panel of physicians, pharmacists, administrators, attorneys, financiers, and businessmen and businesswomen. He told each of them to expect a call from the Governor's office issuing a formal invitation for them to serve on the Healthcare Analysis Committee.

Mason waited for the Governor to follow through with his promise. Weeks turned into months and months turned into years. All the time, the cost of healthcare for the state continued to rise. Politicians met and passed bills designed to pay for the rising costs. The tort reform amendment, sponsored by Senator Braxton and his Republican allies, failed to pass the Senate.

In like manner, no new legislation or bills were introduced nor passed to instill the corrective measures for the state. The recommendations suggested by Mr. Arrowsmith or Dr. Edmonds were looked upon as a serious threat to "stakeholders." Their powerful lobbyist went to work, killing the Governor's Healthcare Analysis plan—and the state's hopes of controlling the rising cost of insuring teachers and state employees.

To its credit, the teachers' association offered a voluntary commercial weight-loss program. As predicted by Dr. Edmonds, without proper incentives, or disincentives, the program failed to achieve its intended goals. And, after a year of trial, the "window dressing" was taken down. The monster got fatter. And expanding nationalized healthcare remained at the top of Washington's "progressive" agenda.

Disappointed that the opportunity to save the system—at least at the state level—had been missed, Dr. Edmonds did not abandon his oath to care for humanity. It was not his nature to give up or give in. He had sworn, years before to not only take care of individual patients, but to look after the human race, to "... prescribe regimens ... according to his ability and judgment ..." And, according to his judgment, America's healthcare system was approaching a near-death experience and in need of a physician's attention.

In reflecting on his failed attempt to help solve his state's healthcare crisis, Mason was reminded of the words of another physician, Dr. Orison Swett Marden. In his book, *Pushing to the Front,* published almost one hundred years ago, Dr. Marden wrote:

> "Every experience in life, everything with which we have come in contact in life is a chisel which has been cutting away at our life stature, molding, modifying, and sharpening it. We are part of all we have met. Everything we have seen, heard, felt or thought has its hand in molding us, shaping us ... Your whole career will be molded by your surroundings, and the character of the people with whom you come in contact with every day . . . A strong successful man or woman is not the victim of his or her environment. He or she creates favorable conditions. His or her own inherent force and energy compel things to turn out as he or she desires."

Mason had made it a point to enter a portion of Dr. Marden's statement in *Laney's Little Book of Wisdom:* "Create favorable conditions," underscoring the word "create." Dr. Marden must have experienced similar circumstances in the 1900s as America was working its way through the Great Depression, he surmised.

Like the mythical Phoenix that rose from its own ashes, Mason had visions of a miraculous cure for America's current healthcare and financial crisis. While he had been instrumental in constructing facilities that delivered the level of care that he felt his aging mother and other senior citizens deserved, he envisioned a day when the American people would rise up and let their voices be heard, a day when they would tell government to butt out of their lives and once again take control of their destiny, a day when politicians would worry less about being elected and more about doing the right thing.

Though he had failed in his attempt to make the kinds of positive changes that his state needed, Dr. Mason Edmonds was not a quitter. Giving up was not part of his genetic makeup. He had been knocked down before, only to pick himself up and get back into the game.

As he had often done when answers were needed, Mason looked to the heavens. As euphoric sensations of resolve began to flow through his veins, he raised his right hand and pledged to his Maker: "If you will give me strength and wisdom, I will carry the fight to those who want to enslave your creations rather than help us become self-sufficient."

In answer to the doctor's prayer, doors opened.

CHAPTER 11

"I'm no politician. I have a full-time surgical practice, a medical institute to run, an eldercare center to oversee and a horse ranch to manage," Mason said to the three people sitting around his conference table. "I can't put all those things on hold and run for political office, especially one that would require my spending much of the year in Washington, D.C. I don't think that I'm your man."

"It's because you are not a politician that we are here to urge you to run for Congress. America is at a crossroads. And the politicians have led us to the brink of collapse," Cecil Raferty, Mayor of Gulf Town said. "The country needs people like you. Unless we have people who understand what is at risk and do what the founding fathers did—put their country first—we are in danger of losing whatever is left of the free enterprise system in America. Already the government controls a lot of our lives and taxes us to support social programs. We represent a group of one hundred business and professional men and women who have concluded that you are the person to be our next congressman."

Cecil added, "The group is willing to fund your campaign and work to get you elected. What about it?"

"Let me add to what Cecil has already said," Shirley Hodnett, a local real estate broker, said. "We have looked all around the district and we are convinced that you will be elected in a landslide."

"Yeah," Dr. Warrington Minor offered. "As president of the county medical society, I can assure that all of us will be with you. My medical school roommate, Michael Batson, is the president of the medical society in the adjoining county, the second largest in the state. He has promised to throw his support your way."

"I don't know," Mason responded. "This is a big decision. I love my life. I am where I want to be, doing what I want to be doing, with whom I want to be doing it.

I'm not sure that I am cut out for the political scene. And I am responsible for my ninety-three year old mother, who is not well."

"Mason, I know that you have been president of virtually every society and association in your specialty. You know how to be a leader. And, at this time in our history, we need someone to go to Washington and stand up for the people. You understand what it takes to run a business, to make decisions based on sound financial principles and how to look *wrong* in the eye and call it what it is," Cecil said. "I saw you in action when we served on the health foundation together. Please consider what we have proposed."

"I don't know. I'll have to go home and think about this. My decision will affect all those who look to me to take care of them. This would turn my world upside down," Mason said hesitantly.

"It would," Shirley replied, "and it would alter in a positive way the lives of millions of people throughout America; plus, we would have someone in Washington that truly understands the two largest issues to impact the lives of the American people—healthcare and the 2010 oil disaster in the Gulf."

"I'll call you in a few days," Cecil said, "Think of all the good you could do for this district and for the country I know you love. You see, I've read your books and op-eds. I know how much you care about America."

. . . .

When Mason told Norene of the meeting that had taken place earlier in the day, she said, "They must be out of their minds. They want you to drop everything and become a politician!"

"No," Mason replied. "They absolutely do not want me to become a politician. They want me to go to Washington and be myself, to say to the people making laws the kinds of things that you and I have talked about as we watch the news and see how shortsighted some of America's leaders can be. They want me to be 'the peoples' voice on healthcare, national defense, for supporting our allies around the world, and the free enterprise system. They want me to remind Americans of the country that our Founding Fathers created, one established with God as its cornerstone. They want me to speak up for what's *right* with America and speak against what's *wrong* with some people and policies currently bleeding it to death."

"This is not how I envisioned us living out our lives," Norene said. "I saw us spending more time traveling for pleasure, walking on the beach, playing golf, riding horses, and reading books together. If you win, we may never share any of those things."

Realizing what she had just said, Norene paused and walked to the window, staring across Fountainhead Ranch and the herd of black Tennessee Walking Horses grazing on the plush green grass. Mason sat quietly while Norene collected her thoughts. After a minute or so, she turned and looked at her husband. "I always knew that God had a plan for you. I thought it was to be a doctor—a surgeon—and take care of people who needed your help," she said. "I now realize that a lot of people need your help. Your country needs your help. The world needs your help. So, my love, if this is what you feel you must do, I will be by your side, all the way—as I have always been."

"If you are with me, the world can be against me and I'll be all right," Mason said.

"You can be sure that a large part of the world will be against you. If you become 'the people's voice,' the people who don't agree with you will do everything in their power to discredit and destroy you. You are a student of history. You know this to be true. Your adversaries will go to no ends to smear you and our family. That's the system that you are about to enter. That's the nature of mankind and the adversarial system. Are you ready to arouse the dragons?" Norene asked.

"I'm very much aware of the consequences," Mason replied. "At this stage in my life, I have so many knife wounds from backstabbing that the scars have merged, creating a kind of shield between my shoulder blades."

"Just as long as you know that," Norene responded, "don't let them and the system they represent get to you. If you are going to do this, stay focused on your goal."

"Honey, you are an incredible woman, the best partner that any man could ever hope to have."

"Before you make a final decision, let's drive down to the beach and take a long walk. You know how you've always said that you can think more clearly there—in God's sanctuary," Norene suggested.

"I think that's a great idea," Mason replied. "My mind is so much clearer there. The roar of waves rushing ashore seems to speak to me. At times, I've thought I heard the voices of God and his angels speaking to me between the calls of the gulls flying overhead. With my toes planted in the sugar-white sand on the beach, questions don't seem to be so insurmountable and answers seem to be more forthcoming."

"Then, let's go," Norene said, "I'll grab a bag of kettle-cooked potato chips and a small bottle of cabernet. When we are tired of walking, we'll just sit quietly and admire one of those magnificent sunsets."

. . . .

"I've given your offer a lot of thought," Mason told Cecil, Shirley and Warrington. "If you still think that I should run for Congress, I'll do it."

"*All right!*" the mayor said, raising both arms in the air. Then he jumped up from his chair and grabbed Mason's hand, shaking it in a moment of celebration. Warrington and Shirley followed suit, grabbing Mason's hand to shake on the deal, before he could change his mind.

"Let's not celebrate just yet," Mason said. "We have not even begun to fight. All we have done is to identify the objective and the enemy. There is a lot of ground to capture and a lot of mine fields we have to maneuver before we can even think about celebrating. This will be a tough fight. My platform will ruffle a lot of feathers. The Administration and all its minions will be against me. The trial lawyers, the hospital association lobby, the state's largest medical insurance carrier, and the teachers' union bosses will be against me. They know that I have information on how they have worked together to drive up the cost of healthcare in this state.

"The ACLU and Lambda will be against me, as will the global warming and environmentalist radicals. So, we're up against some powerful lobbying groups who don't mind making their opposition known, and they have the mainstream press in their pockets. They will use all the dirty tactics they can muster to try and discredit me as a human being and as a candidate. Do you still think that I am your candidate?"

"Absolutely," Shirley replied. "Let me tell you who will be for you: everyone who has ever served in the Armed Forces or has a family member who has or is serving; everyone who has ever been treated unfairly by insurance companies, hospitals, nursing homes; everyone who has paid more than their fair share of taxes and been harassed by the IRS; everyone who believes in traditional family values; everyone who runs a business or values their job; everyone who loves the America of Teddy Roosevelt, Harry Truman, and Ronald Reagan; everyone who has seen God removed from the American way of life and wants to see Him return to His rightful place in America; everyone who values life, liberty, and the pursuit of happiness without government interference; every parent and grandparent who is concerned about the debt that has been hung around the neck of their children and grandchildren. These are just a few of the people who will be for you—and that's a majority of the American people. I know it is a majority of the people in this congressional district."

"I hope that you are right," Mason responded to Shirley's encouraging words. "If we are going to do this, there are a few caveats that I want to set out from the start. So, let's come back down to earth and talk about the obligations I now have to satisfy.

"First, I have to get the doctors on my staff to agree to take up the slack. I want my administrative and support staff to agree to help keep the practice alive during the times that I am away. I will not stop being a doctor or surgeon. If I am elected—and during the months that Congress is not in session—I will return home and continue to perform surgery, take care of my clinic and the patients to whom I've given my word to care for as long as I can. I also have to see that the eldercare facility named after my mother and grandmother continues to be the model for the manner in which senior citizens suffering from dementia should be cared for. If we are going to talk the talk, we have to walk the walk.

"I would not be going to Washington as a politician. I would be a doctor following the tenets of the Hippocratic Oath, taking care of those who put their trust in me, both in Congress and in my clinic. In order to do all these things, I will need your help and the help of those who want me to run for this office, not only in getting elected, but in helping me affect the kind of change that makes America what Ronald Reagan envisioned: the '*shining city on the hill.*' Are these terms acceptable?" Mason asked.

The three people sitting before him raised their right hands and said, "We swear."

. . . .

Mason decided to announce his candidacy on a day of the year that meant a lot to him and his family, the Fourth of July, a day of celebration set aside to commemorate America's birth.

A crowd of five thousand filled the bleachers on the south side of the football stadium. American flags could be seen in every hand. Marching bands from the county's six high schools surrounded a platform decorated in the traditional red, white, and blue, which straddled the goal line at the east end of the stadium.

The ensemble of bands played familiar John Philip Sousa marches and theme songs of each of the branches of the nation's Armed Forces. Mason could not keep his right foot still. Involuntarily, it was tapping to the rhythm of the marches that he had played on his trumpet when he was a member of his high school's marching band.

Sharing the stage with candidate Edmonds were three familiar faces to the people who had gathered for the event: the retiring congressman, George Blanton, Mayor Cecil Raferty, and Neal Logan (Chairman of the party's National Election Committee).

Cecil Raferty was first to speak, "Ladies and gentlemen, would you please stand for the playing of the national anthem, and remain standing for the pledge of allegiance."

All present turned their attention to the fifty-yard line, where an honor guard composed of two Eagle Scouts and two Gold Award recipients representing the Girl Scouts of America, proudly displayed Old Glory, the state flag, and the flags of Boy Scouts and Girl Scouts. Combined bands of over 300 musicians played the *Star-Spangled Banner*, sending chills up and down the spine of the people in the stands and on the platform.

The honor guard peeled off, revealing a gentleman who had been sitting behind them in a wheelchair. Bringing a hand-held microphone to his mouth and mustering all the strength he could, Charles Shivers said to the crowd in a somewhat raspy voice, "Please join me in repeating the Pledge of Allegiance." Five thousand proud voices followed the lead of the World War II hero, reciting the familiar pledge, emphasizing the phrase, "under God."

As the words, "with liberty and justice for all" echoed from the end zone stands, Charles looked to the stage where Mason was sitting, raised his right hand to his VFW hat and saluted. Mason knew that it was Charles' way of telling him to climb the congressional hill and put the flag and all it stood for back in its rightful place.

Holding back the tears, Mason winked at his storytelling companion, nodding that he understood the message.

After the emotionally charged beginning, Mayor Raferty moved to the lectern and introduced Blanton. The congressman stepped briskly to the microphone and thanked those in attendance for the support that they had given him over the past two decades.

"I am here to endorse the candidacy of Dr. Mason Edmonds as your next congressman," Blanton said. "What about you?"

The crowd cheered, "Mason ... Mason ... Mason ..."

When Congressman Blanton had finished his remarks, Neal Logan took center stage and explained to the people present why the country needed Edmonds in Washington. He asked for each person present to take it as a personal responsibility to see that Dr. Edmonds was elected.

The crowd cheered and chanted, "Mason ... Mason ... Mason ..." The sound was deafening, indicating that the people were enthusiastic about the opportunity to send their man to Washington to instill reason back into government.

After the national committee chairman had completed his remarks and introduced Mason to the crowd, the candidate stepped up to the microphone. "I stand before you today to announce my candidacy to represent you in the Congress of the United States of America in the seat vacated by the retirement of the Honorable George Blanton."

The crowd cheered, chanting "Mason ... Mason ... Mason ..."

"This will be a hard-fought race. There are those who will be threatened by the message that you want me to bring to Washington and the agenda I will put before the Congress on your behalf. I will need the support of every one of you here today and all the people you know in this district. I am not a politician. I never have been. I never will be. I am first and foremost a physician.

"There is one promise that I will never break; I will never lie to you. No matter how ugly the truth might be, I will give it to you—straight up ..."

The crowed interrupted his statement once more, chanting, "Mason ... Mason ... Mason..."

He raised his hands asking for quiet; and when the noise lessened, he continued, "And I plan to approach the problems facing our country in the same manner that I have always approached any disorder. America is ailing; and it needs a doctor. In fact a lot of doctors, doctors who are ready to go to Washington and help stop the spread of infection that is eating away at this great nation. That's what I intend to do."

Once again the crowd rose to its feet, chanting, "Mason ... Mason ... Mason ..."

Regaining order, Mason continued once more. America is suffering from a disease of corruption, a life-threatening condition imposed upon it by politicians who have been willing to sell their souls for political favors, politicians who have mortgaged your children's future for social programs that are destined to weaken the very foundation upon which this nation was built, just so that they could remain in power and pad their own bank accounts."

Then Mason said to the crowd before him, "I once read a statement attributed to a man born during the Great Depression. He forewarned Americans about socialism and those who would prosper by giving other people's resources away."

The doctor reached in his back pocket and pulled from the *Book of Wisdom* in his right hip pocket a 3x5-inch index card, on the back of which was written the words he read aloud.

> "You cannot legislate the poor into freedom (or prosperity) by legislating the wealthy out of freedom (or prosperity.) What one person receives without working for, another person must work for without receiving. The government cannot give to anybody anything that the government does not first take from somebody else. When half of the people get the idea that they do not have to work because the other half is going to take care of them, and when the other half gets the idea that it does no good to work because somebody else is going to get what they work for, that my dear friend, is about the end of any nation. You cannot multiply wealth by dividing it."

"These prophetic words were written by Dr. Adrian Rogers, the esteemed minister from Memphis, Tennessee. A similar message was offered by former British Prime Minister Margaret Thatcher, who advised against socialism, reminding such reformers "that sooner or later, you will run out of other people's money."

The crowd roared with cheers and applause.

Mason continued, "Why is it that we Americans have allowed ourselves to be led down the self-destructive path that our nation is on, by those who would lose a nation to gain and maintain power? As your congressman, I will do everything in my power to bring this message to all Americans and to try and convince my fellow lawmakers in Washington to end the mad march toward socialism."

The crowd rose to its feet and cheered. Mason realized that though his words had resonated with the people in attendance, he had a major hurdle ahead of him beyond the confines of the athletic stadium in which his candidacy was being announced. "Can one man, one voice, make a difference?" he wondered to himself, waiting for the crowd to quiet down.

"When I get to Washington, I will refer to this little book of wisdom," Mason pledged, holding up the notebook he carried in the pocket of every pair of pants he had worn since he was nine years old.

"This small notebook is filled with lessons I learned from my grandmother and other wise teachers and instructors, pearls of wisdom that have stood the test of time. I will also use the skills I learned in becoming and being a physician and in earning my law degree. I will assess the problem, make a diagnosis, and offer the best remedies possible to correct the conditions draining life from the greatest nation the world has ever known. When I use every available resource to discover the cancers eating away at the American way of life, I will take drastic measures to either cut it out or cut off the source of its existence."

Again the crowd rose to its feet, chanting, "Mason ... Mason ... Mason ...."

Raising his hands for silence, Mason continued, "I pledge to you that I will go to Washington with the compassion of a physician, but with the mentality of a surgeon. I will cut out everything that I find to be detrimental to America's vitality and longevity and be an advocate for free enterprise and freedom of thought and action. I will do everything in my power to justify the confidence that you place in me. As I swore an oath to uphold the traditions of my professions upon graduating from medical school and law school, this one I now swear to you. If you see fit to elect me as your representative to Congress, I will look out for the health, welfare, and safety of this great nation and use every ounce of energy in my body to make America well again. So help me God."

The crowd jumped to its feet and applauded for the better part of three minutes. Eventually, Mason was able to conclude his remarks.

"My fellow Americans, it is not yet time for celebration. We have work to do. As a great coach once told me, 'When the work is done and you have won the contest, there will be time enough for celebrating.' That night will be on the second Tuesday in November, assuming we all pull our share of the load. Let us not tell people what we are going to do. Let's *do it* and let them report on what we *have* done."

With those words, Mason stepped back from the lectern. The bands struck up Lee Greenwood's ballad, "Proud to Be an American," and Mason stepped down from the stage, making his way into the crowd, shaking the hand of every person who offered it. He felt the connection. The doctor realized just how hungry average Americans were for the kind of leadership they deserved, and the Founding Fathers had envisioned.

That evening, after all election committee members and guests invited to Fountainhead Ranch, including Charles Shivers, had left, Mason and Norene sat in their den, reflecting on the events of the day.

"What do you think, Honey?" Mason asked Norene.

"I think that you made the right decision and that a lot of people are very happy with your willingness to be their advocate in Washington."

"Maybe some of the things I learned in law school will pay off yet—you know, the advocacy system. If I win, I'll be operating in a den of lawyers."

"No doubt," Norene responded. "I've heard you say many times: it's not the enemy that you can see that is to be feared, but the one hiding in the shadows." I particularly like the fact that you promised to get the truth to the people, no matter what the consequences."

"I hope that I am wrong, but I fear that the one's in the shadows—the global Shadow Government—are pulling the strings of a lot of America's politicians and the mainstream media that protects them."

"I, too, hope that you are wrong. However, when it comes to zeroing in on the cause of a problem, your track record is pretty good," Norene said. "Now, it's time for you to get some rest. During the next four months, it will be important to look after yourself so that you can look after all those who will put their trust in you."

"Thank you for being by my side," Mason said to his wife as the two of them walked toward the master suite of their home. "We do make a good team, don't we?"

"We always have," Norene replied. "I'm sure you remember the oath that you and I took on the day we were married, don't you?"

Mason thought for a moment and repeated, "to have and to hold from this day forward, for better or for worse, for richer, for poorer, in sickness and in health, to love and to cherish; from this day forward until death do us part."

"You did remember!" Norene said. "I'm impressed. Though the vows didn't say anything about running for political office, I'm sure that 'for better or worse' might apply to such undertakings."

"You are incredible," Mason said, giving his wife a great big hug. "Let's go find a good movie. We've had enough excitement for one day. Or have we?" he added, with a mischievous smile

CHAPTER 12

The campaign lived up to its expectations. Mason's opponents pulled out every political antic in the *Devil's Guidebook of Dirty Tricks*—and then some—using all colors of lies and propaganda in order to try and destroy his credibility and wreck his candidacy. Through it all, the doctor took the high road, repeating his pledge to look out for the people's interest, to identify the problems tearing the country apart, and to use the precision of surgeon's knife to cut out all waste and abuse he could find.

The doctor's approach to the political process paid off. On election night in the year 2012, Mason Edmonds became a United States congressman. With him were elected enough conservatives to change the power structure of the legislative branch of government.

Appropriately, Mason Edmonds was appointed to represent his party on the congressional committee that dealt with healthcare issues. Though he was a "freshman" congressman, he was not intimidated by the Washington, D.C., machine and quickly earned the respect of his colleagues.

On November 11, 2012, the House Subcommittee on Healthcare Reform was scheduled to meet with the Secretary of the Department of Health and Human Services. Entering the room, Mason recalled the time when he sat at the witness table and testified before the same congressional committee. At the time he served as president of an international facial surgery association and was there to tell his association's side of the intergroup conflict between warring plastic surgery organizations. Following a lengthy investigation, the Federal Trade Commission had concluded that a group of doctors engaged in total body plastic surgery were guilty of restraint of trade violations to the Sherman Anti-Trust Bill. Mason and his facial surgery colleagues were invited to provide testimony to the committee confirming the

FTC's findings. Presenting a number of documented examples in which the plastic surgeons under investigation he said had used "guerilla warfare tactics" to prevent qualified surgeons from being admitted to hospital staffs to perform the surgeries for which they had been duly trained and were qualified to perform, Dr. Edmonds convinced the House subcommittee that antitrust violations existed within the medical profession and should be dealt with swiftly and authoritatively.

The accused plastic surgeons were also present, trying to defend their actions before the congressional committee.

Today, however, Mason's role was quite different. He would be part of the group asking questions. He and his fellow congressmen and women were there to investigate concerns as to how some of the healthcare stimulus money had been spent.

Reading from the talking-points document that had been prepared for her by the White House, the Health and Human Services Secretary was trying to make her case for expanding government-run healthcare. For more than an hour, Mason listened as the HHS Secretary attempted to make the Administration's case before the congressional committee.

When his time came, Mason asked the Secretary a question that, to the amazement of all, she was unable to answer. He respectfully asked her to name one aspect of the Health Reformation Act of 2009 that had cut cost while at the same time had improved efficiency and quality of services.

The Secretary said, "I don't know that I can answer that question."

Mason responded to her reply by saying, "Madame Secretary, since you have no answer to the question, allow me to suggest that there is one branch of government that goes about its business without fanfare. It is the active duty healthcare providers of the United States Armed Forces. I have seen them in action. I have also seen what government-run Veterans Administration provides to these brave young men and women after they have served their country. And all I can say is that if you had seen some of the ways in which these heroes are treated after they return home and try to get assimilated into society, you would be ashamed. And may I remind you and all who are present in this chamber what this country owes to its veterans.

"It is the veterans of this country, not religious leaders, who have given us the freedom to worship Almighty God. It is the veterans, not reporters or media moguls, who have given us the freedom of speech and freedom of the press. It is the veterans, not the campus or community organizers, who have given us freedom to assemble or dissent. It is the veterans, not lawyers or judges, who have given us the right to a fair trial. It is the veterans, not politicians or their political party affiliations, who have given us the right to vote without fear in free and open elections. It is the veterans who not only salute the flag while serving, but for the rest of their lives. And, it is the veterans, not political activists, who swear an oath to defend this nation and its' Constitution against all enemies, foreign and domestic," Mason said solemnly. "And, as a grateful nation, it is our responsibility to take care of those who have taken care of us: our veterans."

You could hear a pin drop in the room as Congressman Edmonds continued.

"I know these things, Madame Secretary, because I have seen them with my own eyes. This nation's veterans deserve more than we can ever repay them, including the same kind of care that they received when they were on active duty. I've seen *the best* of government-run health care—on board one of our modern nuclear aircraft carriers. It is the standard that we should demand of every government-run or -supported healthcare facility on land or at sea. Madame Secretary, have you ever visited an aircraft carrier?" Mason asked.

"No, congressman," the Secretary answered.

"Perhaps you should. And, you should take the entire Cabinet of which you are a member with you. That's the model you, the Administration, and my fellow members of Congress should be emulating, if positive healthcare reform is to come about," Mason added.

"Madame Secretary, you come before this committee asking us to support legislation that would expand—to everyone in America—the same inefficient system that exists today in too many of America's VA hospitals. With all due respect, Madame Secretary, how dare you! When you and the bureaucrats who run the existing government-run healthcare facilities and programs can come before this committee and demonstrate how you intend to provide quality care in a caring and efficient manner to Americans who have little choice but to accept what you now offer, please come back to these chambers.

"Oh, and one more thing, before you go, I have one final question," Mason added. "Can you tell this committee precisely how the one hundred and fifty billion dollars allocated by Congress two years ago for improvement in healthcare for rural communities, who have no doctors or hospitals, have been spent?"

The HHS Secretary couldn't answer that question, either.

"Then, Madame Secretary, before asking the Congress of the United States to consider funding and supporting more of the same kind of injustice, waste, and inefficiencies, I beseech you to demonstrate that the current plan that you and your Administration have rammed down the throats of the American people is working and affordable."

Leaning into the microphone, Mason said, Madame Secretary, are you familiar with a political concept known as '*Problem-Reaction-Solution Propaganda?*' "

"Yes, Congressman," the Secretary replied.

"Then, if you were sitting in my chair, could you see why I might be concerned that this whole stimulus ordeal and the rush to pass healthcare legislation might be looked upon as an example of 'Problem-Reaction-Solution Propaganda?"

Before she replied, the Secretary was silent for several seconds; then answered, "I could see why you might think that possible."

"Thank you, Madame Secretary. Mister Chairman, I yield the remainder of my time to the gentlewoman representing the great state of Arizona."

"Mister Chairman," the congresswoman from Arizona said, "I have one question for the Secretary." Looking over the top of her glasses, she asked, "Madame Secretary, can you account for the ninety million dollars that were promised to the State of Arizona to secure our southern border and build public health clinics for illegal aliens? To date, we haven't seen one dollar of the aid promised."

She continued, "On another note—and although securing the nation's borders does not fall under the jurisdiction of your department—you do sit in on Cabinet meetings with the Secretary of the Interior, do you not?"

"Yes, congresswoman, I do," the Secretary answered.

"Then, you must know what your administration intends to do about the flow of illegals into our state or cleaning up the so-called Mexico-U.S. Superhighway in the Sonoran Desert just outside of Tucson. If you haven't seen what the people coming across our borders have done to the desert, let me just say that the areas they have trashed would make any garbage dump look good. It is a not only an eyesore, it is a public health disaster, a breeding ground for filth and disease. And, I know that public health matters fall under the jurisdiction of the department under your supervision."

"I'm sorry, congresswoman, I was unaware of the problem, but I will look into it."

"Thank you, Madame Secretary," the congresswoman said, reaching forward to turn her microphone off. "Mr. Chairman I don't have any further questions. However, as previously stated by Congressman Edmonds, I look forward to a time when the Secretary returns to demonstrate how she and her cohorts in this Administration have taken the measures that should have been long ago taken."

"Madame Secretary," the Chairman said, "do you have anything further to add?"

Stunned by Congressman Edmonds' remarks and the Arizona congresswoman's comments, the Secretary answered, "No, Mr. Chairman."

"Then my colleagues and I thank you for coming. We look forward to having you back here soon."

The chairman sounded the gavel, and announced, "This committee is adjourned until further notice."

. . . .

Outside the congressional chambers, the only network that approached Congressman Edmonds was VOX News.

"Congressman," the reporter asked, "You were pretty tough on the Secretary in there. You put her on the spot about the VA system and how some of the so-called stimulus money of 2009 was spent. She seemed to be unprepared to answer your question."

"I only asked the Secretary the same question that my constituents back home are asking me," Mason responded.

The reporter followed up, "Where did you learn about the treatment of our veterans and the possibility that some of the stimulus money appropriated by the previous Congress may not have found its way to the intended sources?"

"I once worked within the VA system," Mason replied. "And, before I took the oath of office as a congressman, I visited the VA hospitals in my district and surrounding areas. Then I came to Washington and visited the one here. If the American people could spend one day in the typical VA hospital, nursing home, or one of their outpatient clinics, there would be an uprising against anyone who suggested that we turn over the responsibility of keeping America healthy to a bunch of keyboard jockeys or governmental bureaucrats. I was sent to Washington by some of the people who have experienced the inefficiencies and failures of government programs."

"Can you elaborate on some of the 'efficiencies and failures' to which you have referred?" the reporter asked.

"I want all your viewers to remember one thing: government may be the worst managed monopoly in existence. It is in violation of its own antitrust laws. Government can print more money when it needs it, or raise our taxes. It can pass laws that place restrictions on hiring and firing practices of private companies, ensuring mediocrity. The businesses run by Americans have no choice but to dumb down their businesses. I'd say that's an unfair advantage."

"And what about the efficiencies and failures you mentioned?" the reporter asked.

"Anyone who is impressed by the compassion of the Internal Revenue Service; the efficiencies of the Postal System, and how Medicare, Medicaid, Fannie Mae, and Freddie Mac have been handled should step forward and lead the march to expanding the nationalized health care system from what was created in 2009."

"What about the congresswoman from Arizona's questions? Do you have any comment on them," the reporter asked.

"Only that I am familiar with how illegal immigrants are destroying the landscape in her state. I've seen the photos taken of the immigrant trafficking superhighway to which she referred. It is an environmental and public health atrocity. I have to wonder where the environmentalists are on this one."

"Well," the VOX reporter said, looking into the camera. "You have heard it from a doctor who has come to Washington to—in his words—look after America. Although he is a freshman congressman, he doesn't seem to mince words or be afraid to take the establishment on. Now back to our studios in New York."

. . . .

"Mason, I saw the congressional hearing with the Secretary of HHS on C-Span. You were pretty tough with her. She wasn't prepared to answer your questions about the VA system," Norene said on the phone. "I bet the Administration and all its vultures will descend on you with the wrath of God tomorrow."

"If they bring God into it, I won't worry," Mason said to his wife. "I worry more about the demons that I am finding here in Washington, those who are out in the open and those working from the shadows. God seems to be an uninvited guest in many of the offices and chambers up here."

"Are your own party's leaders in the House and the Senate supportive of your efforts?" Norene asked.

"For the most part, they are. They seem to be comfortable in letting me play the role of 'sacrificial lamb,' letting me speak my peace and take the heat, but that's okay. I've been in this position before. I know that I am speaking for the people who sent me here to be their voice. As long as I have *their* support—and yours—I can fight off the demons. I've never looked upon myself as a career politician. My job is to do what I came to do, and get back to being a physician."

. . . .

On VOX News the following Sunday morning, the host said, "This is Curt Waters. Today, on "Tell It Like It Is," we have Congressman Mason Edmonds in the studios with us. Welcome, congressman.

"This week you were involved in the committee before which the Secretary of Health and Human Services appeared to make her case for expanding the nationalization of healthcare in America that the current Administration has been pushing since 2009. You raised an issue that the Secretary didn't seem prepared to address: the government-run healthcare system offered to the veterans of this nation. You insinuated that the care being provided to the men and women who have bravely served this country is second rate. Is that your opinion, sir?"

"Mister Waters, I'm sorry to say that in some cases second rate would be an overstatement. When I worked in the VA system a number of years ago, I witnessed unnecessary delays that caused men and women who had endured the perils of war to lose their lives from curable conditions, simply because the system failed them. When I decided to run for Congress, I interviewed scores of veterans and their families who more recently depended on the VA system for their healthcare needs and visited a number of VA hospitals."

"And, what did you find out?" the host asked.

"I learned that over the past forty years not much has changed. The current VA system and many nursing homes are examples of government-run healthcare *in action*. We don't need to look ten or twenty years into the future, when the federal government totally controls health matters for all Americans, to see what kind of system my colleagues in Congress and this Administration are advocating. We only need to look at the model already in place, and change it first. Change it now. This is the kind of change that we were promised by this Administration, but haven't yet seen.

"Congressman, you mentioned nursing homes in your comment about government-run healthcare, aren't most nursing homes owned by private corporations or individuals?"

"When the government dictates what a corporation or proprietor can do, it doesn't matter whose name is on the door," the congressman replied. Our senior citizens and war heroes deserve the best that this country has to offer. Examples of long delays in treatment and where disease has spread to patients receiving care for nonrelated matters are a matter of record. Reckless dissemination of erroneous notices, sent out by incompetent administrative personnel, has caused unnecessary upset to veterans and their families."

"I am familiar with the examples to which you refer and understand your analogies, congressman," the host interrupted, "How does the expansion program now before Congress differ from the VA system in place today?"

"As different as a six is to half a dozen," Mason replied. "It may be wrapped in a different package and have a pretty bow tied around it, but inside it is the same old inefficient and costly socialized policy of the 'government knows better than the people what is good for them.' Look how deeply we are in debt because the administration sold the American people on expanding the so-called stimulus package. Only a fraction of the money allocated by Congress can be accounted for. And when I asked the HHS Secretary where some of the money appropriated for expanded VA services and community health programs is, she could not answer the question. That she couldn't answer these questions should raise the brows of every American citizen. That's sloppy business and accounting practice; but what would you expect from an Administration, the members of which, never ran as much as a lemonade stand? If the IRS can trace every dollar we average Americans make and spend, it certainly should be able to account for the money the government who controls it spends—assuming it wants to do so."

"Are you suggesting that there is a government cover-up at play?" Waters asked.

"I'm only saying that a lot of money—hundreds of billions of tax dollars—are unaccounted for. And the fact that the money is missing should be an invitation for every investigative reporter in America to dig as deeply as necessary for answers. Yet, not one member of the so-called 'mainstream media' has raised the question. And the American people are joining me in wanting to know *why.*"

"So, you believe that members of the media are not digging as deeply as they should?" Mr. Waters asked.

"This may be the biggest story of the new century and no one is following up on it. Where are the 21st century versions of Woodward and Bernstein? I think that we might be witnessing the greatest example of what is known as 'The Problem-Reaction-Solution Paradigm' in recent history—a 'Big Lie.'"

"Could you elaborate on what that is—the paradigm you mentioned," Mr. Waters asked.

"Sure," Dr. Edmonds replied. "It an old tactic of political warfare in which a problem is either created or exploited by conspirators who shift blame for the crisis they created to someone else, in this case the U.S. President who preceded the Padgett Administration. A concerned populace reacts to the contrived crisis by turning to government for protection and help. "Help" comes—at a price—in the form of a solution that was planned long before the crisis was created. The result is that rights and liberties are exchanged for the illusion of protection and help."

"And, according to your comments to the HHS Secretary last week, you believe that the Padgett Administration created the need for a stimulus package and for universal healthcare," Mr. Waters asked.

"I do. It is as plain as day," the congressman said. "The kind of cover-up going on in Washington today—the grey and black propaganda kinds—make the Watergate cover-up of the 1970s look like a nursery rhyme. Yet, the mainstream media are silent on the issue."

"That's why we are here. This network wants to know what you know so that we can investigate any misconduct and give the American people a fair and balanced report.

"Now, congressman, what alternatives do you see for a healthcare system that comprises more than fifteen percent of the total budget for this country?" the host continued.

"As has been demonstrated in every war that America has faced—and won—or in any illness ever diagnosed, once the problem has been identified and the outcome envisioned, the bureaucrats need to get out of the way and allow the forces of human nature to do what they were created to do, to right wrongs. If there's a business that government should be involved in, it would be the business of empowering people, giving citizens the tools to rebuild, and rebuilding it takes place."

"We only have about thirty seconds left, congressman. Is there anything else that you would like to say to our viewers?" Mr. Waters asked.

"Just this: from everything I can determine, protecting our borders and empowering the citizenry is what the founding fathers intended. That's why those of us who have taken up their mantle should be trying to preserve their intentions with all our might. My hope is that all the people listening to us this Sunday morning will say a prayer for the leaders who are deciding the future of this great nation and that my colleagues and I will do what is best for each and every citizen in this great nation."

"Thank you, Congressman Edmonds, "Will you come back and keep us apprised of your efforts?"

"I'd be honored, Mr. Waters. Thank you for having me."

. . . .

"I knew he was the right person for the job," Cecil Raferty said to his wife, Bobbie, turning off the television set. "I think I'll call him and tell him how proud we are that he is unafraid to speak his mind. He not only speaks for those of us along the Gulf Coast, he speaks for the vast majority of Americans. But I'm concerned about his safety. "You know he is stepping on a lot of toes—powerful toes, at that."

"Everyone present could feel the tension in the room. One way or the other, they will try to silence him," Bobbie said.

"That's what concerns me. The powers that be have a lot of tricks and emissaries at their disposal."

"When you speak to Mason, tell him to very careful," Bobbie urged.

. . . .

"Congressman Edmonds," the President said, as Mason entered the door to the Oval Office. "Thank you for coming. Have a seat over here on the sofa and let's talk about the new health reparation—I mean *reformation*—amendment before Congress. You've been pretty outspoken about your feelings relative to how the Healthcare Reformation Act of 2009 is being managed and you've created quite a bit of confusion about what we are trying to accomplish with the expansion program now before Congress."

"With all due respect, Mr. President," Mason said. "I'm not confused. I don't know who you are referring to. I think I know precisely what the effects of this legislation will have on the delivery of healthcare to the average citizen in this country for generations to come. It's like giving a dying patient another dose of the same poison that created his or her illness in the first place. More of the same will not correct the ills of this nation either."

"I saw the video of your interview on VOX. I think you've been watching too much of their propaganda over the years. They are against everything my Administration proposes," the President said.

"No sir, Mr. President. "I haven't had much time to watch television. My comments come from my own personal experiences as a physician. I have seen the ugly side of healthcare. I have also seen the best. And, the best comes when doctors and their patients are allowed to solve problems without outside interference, when doctors are empowered to exercise their training and judgment to take care of patients without having to get permission from some bureaucrat, who often *denies* a doctor's request to do what is in the patient's best interest; and when the free enterprise system allows fair and balanced competition in the health-delivery marketplace."

"Well, now that you are one of us, here in Washington, you'll see things a bit different—from the top down."

"Once again, sir, and with all due respect, I hope that day never comes. For if it does, I will have violated the oath I took the night I was awarded my Doctor of Medicine degree, the pledge I made to the people who sent me here to be their voice in this wilderness that they know as Washington, D.C., and the oath I took when I was sworn in as a congressmen to defend and protect the Constitution against all enemies, foreign and domestic."

"Mason," the President said, changing his demeanor to one of a more threatening nature, "If you know what is best for you and your family, you'll remain a bit quieter until you learn the ropes of this town."

Mason stood up from the sofa. ""Mr. President, if that's all, I have work to do. I am writing my own accountability amendment to your healthcare legislation that will require you and your Administration to explain to the American people how the Act of 2009 improved the quality of healthcare in America and how you intend to pay for all the promises you have made."

"You'll be back here, asking me to forgive you for the insubordinate manner in which you've talked to me today, congressman. Next time you come through that door, it will be on your hands and knees."

"I'll die first, sir."

"You might, congressman, you just might. You're ruffling the feathers of people who yield more influence and power that you can imagine."

"Mr. President, not only am I aware of the power wielded by the people about whom you speak, I know their names. What you don't know is that I am not afraid of them. For too long, they have worked behind the scenes, making free men slaves to their selfish ways, some of which might have been your ancestors. I know it is this same shadow government that put you here in this office to do their bidding."

The President seemed shocked at Mason's comment. It was as though a secret had been discovered.

"When you sent for me," Mason added, "I suspected that it would be to strong-arm me into backing off. I knew that if I refused to do so, that I would be considered a threat to a greater plan to bring America into a global world order. I know about that plan, and how you are being used to by the powerful overlords to whom you answer."

"You are skating on very thin ice, here, congressman," the President warned.

"I have bought an insurance policy against your threats," Mason added. "In three safety deposit boxes in different locations around this country are envelopes that contain the names of these power brokers and why you and they would want to see me out of the way. I have also created a DVD that is contained in each envelope, explaining everything I have learned about how some of the 'stimulus' money intended for Americans has left these shores and found its way into secret bank accounts. On the DVD is a twenty-minute monologue about this secret society and your ties to them, including where the money to finance your campaign came from, how the fifty—and one hundred—dollar gift cards found their way into the hands of ACORN, community organizers, and spiritual leaders who supported you throughout the nation. I know what your Administration's agenda means to America and the world the Illuminati intend to create by instilling Orwellian and draconian laws."

"Be very careful, congressman. You can't prove any of these charges."

"Are you willing to take that chance, Mr. President? The television network that you mentioned earlier, the one that you say doesn't report anything positive about you, has specific instructions that if something should happen to me, they are to open the boxes with the keys I have given to three of their executives and reporters and read the contents of the letters on the air, then broadcast the DVD to the world," Mason said, restraining his anger.

"No one will believe anything broadcast on VOX. We have seen to that. Our people are implanted throughout the mainstream media. That's who the vast majority of Americans believe."

"If you think that VOX's first expose of ACORN was revealing, sir, you haven't seen anything. The biggest political blockbuster in history is waiting to be aired. Let's just say that the questions of your place of birth have been answered and the people who were involved in forging your birth certificates are caught on tape and on camera, revealing who told them what to do, how to do it, and how much money they were paid to do as they were told. We have friends in Hawaii, too."

"There's no way that you could have tapes of these alleged events!"

"Again, sir, you underestimate the U.S. and Israeli intelligence communities. You see, some of the individuals your people and the Shadow Government paid off were undercover CIA agents—you know, the agency that your Attorney General has been out to discredit. Others were Israeli intelligence agents—you know, the country that you have refused to support on the international stage."

"So this is blackmail," the President cautioned.

"Wrong again, sir. It is a matter of gathering and documenting the facts. The monies that changed hands to allow you to run for this office have been traced back to their sources. That's how good the intelligence agencies that you and members of your Cabinet have been out to castrate are. Mr. President, you and the overlords you serve have a lot riding on keeping me alive—and those letters and the DVD that accompanies them locked up in a safe place for a very long time."

"I don't think you have the guts to put your life and that of your family on the line for this far-fetched political agenda," the President said. "Are you after my job?"

"Not in the least, Mr. President. It is not an office to which I have aspired. However, if you are willing to take the chance of having me eliminated, you go right ahead. If you are willing to test my guts, you go right ahead. But first, you should tell those who pull your strings of the consequences. In the meantime, I suggest that you and I find some common ground. Doing so will allow you to appear as though you are living up to some of your promises until the next election comes around. I'm sure that you can find some reason to improve upon the VA healthcare system and improve healthcare in rural communities while doing away with as much red tape and waste as possible. Unleash the free enterprise system on the healthcare dilemma and preserve the best of what remains of the best system in the world.

"Abandon, or at least slow down, your agenda of socializing America. Stop spending money this country doesn't have or assuming the debts of other countries whose paths we are following into the graveyards of history. Now, if you will excuse me, I have work to do. Good day, Mr. President."

"You'd best be very careful driving home and crossing the street," the President said as Mason saw himself out.

Leaving the Oval Office, Mason felt as though he might have just signed his death warrant. Were the President's admonitions genuine, wishing for him to remain safe from harm, or were they a veiled threat? That was a question that Mason could not answer. However, one thing was clear. He was a marked man. The powers that be would be putting their heads together to figure out how to deal with him.

....

Due to President Padgett's failed stimulus policies, the largest national debt ever recorded, rising unemployment, and his failure to earn the respect of America's enemies on the global front, the polls showed that less than half of the Americans surveyed approved of the President's job performance.

To make matters worse, the enormous price tag placed on his initial nationalized healthcare program by the Central Budget Office, and the added cost of his expansion package, the newly seated Congress decided to conduct further investigations as to how to pay for some of the President's programs.

The HHS Secretary never appeared back before the congressional Committee on Health Reform to discuss the deficiencies posed to her by Congressman Edmonds regarding the VA system, claiming that she was still "gathering information." However, in the budget presented to Congress by the White House, Mason noted a twenty percent increase in Veterans Affairs appropriations for the upcoming fiscal year.

"That's how government thinks they can solve everything—throw more of the people's money at it. And if the money to throw isn't there, just print more," Mason thought, as he read the appropriations request. "More money is not the answer. It never has been. There has always been enough money in the VA system; it is how the money is spent, the lack of initiative on the part of many of the people who administer the system, and a failure to hold bureaucrats accountable that is the problem," he muttered, tossing the fourteen-inch thick budget binder onto his desk.

Mason reflected on the nineteen seventies' conversation he had with Commander "Happy" Kirby, the administrator of the VA hospital in which the doctor had worked during portions of his medical training. He recalled how the treatment of Horace Jacoby, one of the Marines who made it to the beach at Normandy during the D-Day invasion of World War II, had been delayed, leading to his untimely and unnecessary death. The incident and the unwillingness to correct the problems encountered by Mr. Jacoby on the part of the hospital's administrator had remained in Mason's mind through the years. Though he had been unsuccessful in affecting positive change in VA policies and procedures during his surgical residency, perhaps now he could help make a difference in how healthcare, or sometimes the lack thereof, was administered to Americans, especially those who had offered to pay the ultimate sacrifice.

"Martha," Mason said, pressing the intercom button on his phone, "Would you please get the HHS Secretary on the phone for me?"

"Right away," the administrative assistant answered.

. . . .

"Madam Secretary," Mason said, "I haven't heard back from you. You were going to get investigate where some of the money appropriated for projects under your jurisdiction is."

"Yes, Congressman," the Secretary answered. "I'm working on that. You know how the wheels of government turn, not always as quickly as one would hope."

"Precisely," Mason responded. "That's why I have concerns about government taking control of America's health needs."

"I was truly embarrassed that I was unable to answer your questions as to where some of the stimulus money appropriated for the Department of Veterans Affairs had gone. I knew nothing about the public health issue along the Arizona border," the Secretary said. "Sometimes, I feel as though I am just a figurehead. I was handed the talking points that I was expected to present to your committee just thirty minutes before I was to testify."

"I understand, Madam Secretary," Mason replied. "However, I plan to have the Chairman call you back to testify before our Committee on Health Reform in two weeks. I do hope that you'll have the information by then."

"I'll sure do my best, congressman. But I can see that some of the information I have already requested seems to be making a lot of people around here very nervous. And that it makes them nervous makes me nervous."

"Madam Secretary, we are dealing with people who are masters at hiding the truth. Be very careful in whom you place your trust."

. . . .

Three days later, Martha buzzed her boss and said, "Congressman, may I step into your office for a moment?"

In the office, she asked, "Have you seen the news flashes on television?"

"Nope, I haven't had a chance to turn the TV on. I've been working on this information that our staff has compiled in preparation for the HHS Secretary's appearance before our health committee. I think that she's going to be quite helpful."

"That's what I wanted to talk to you about," Martha said. "The Secretary was killed in an automobile accident on her way to work this morning."

Mason laid his pen down and took off his glasses. Recalling his conversation with the President just a few short weeks ago, he thought, "As a result of the pressure that I had put on her, the HHS Secretary must have begun to dig and ask questions that someone, or a group of individuals, didn't want answered."

"Martha," Mason said, "This is scary stuff. How did the accident happen?"

"All that the reporter said was that her brakes failed. She ran through a stop sign and under an eighteen wheeler, decapitating her," Martha replied.

"Thank you, Martha. Will you leave me alone for a minute? I need to think."

. . . .

Shortly thereafter he called her. "Martha, would you please see if Dale Jackson at the FBI is available. I need to speak with him."

"Mason, how the hell are you?" Dale asked. "I haven't seen you since I beat your pants off on the golf course last summer. Are you up to a repeat performance? I need some spending money."

Mason said, "Dale, I am calling you about a matter of grave concern. I need to speak with you in a place where we will not be seen nor overheard."

"Man, this must be serious."

"It is."

Dale knew they were both familiars with the Capital City Golf Course, so he said, "Meet me in the rain shed on the 13th hole at six o'clock tomorrow morning. No one will be on the course that early. That's the middle of the night for most of the people who live here."

"I'll be there. And don't tell anyone that you are meeting me."

"You got it."

. . . .

At the rain shed, Dale said to his long-time friend, "This must be something of great importance for us to be meeting like this." Dale had once served as director of his state's Bureau of Investigation when he and Mason worked on a sting operation to catch a nurse who was in cahoots with a pharmacist in her neighborhood, forging prescriptions and selling prescription drugs to teenagers.

"Before you jump to conclusions and think that I am a paranoid conspiracy theorist, hear me out," Mason began. "I'm sure you've heard that the HHS Secretary was killed yesterday morning."

"Yeah, she ran through a stop sign on her way to work and hit an eighteen wheeler. She was driving a convertible and when she went under the trailer she was decapitated."

"The early reports said that there was a problem with her brakes," Mason replied.

"Yeah, that was the initial report, but they retracted that and said that she was talking on her cell phone and didn't see the stop sign," Dale said.

"I have conducted a bit of my own research. It is my understanding that the Secretary came to and from work using the same route every day since she has been in Washington. She has passed that four-way stop intersection twice a day for months. What are the chances that she ignored the stop sign?"

"That's a good point," Dale answered. "What are you getting at?"

"I have been pressing the Secretary to disclose sensitive information regarding the stimulus money that was appropriated for her department. I spoke with her four days ago and told her that she was going to be called back before our congressional oversight sub-committee. She indicated that her inquiries were making a lot of people nervous and that they were getting concerned, giving her reason to be concerned about her own safety. Yesterday, she died in a mysterious accident," Mason said.

"These kinds of accidents happen every day, all over the country. What makes you think that her death had anything to do with anything?"

"A few weeks ago, I was called to the Oval Office. The President asked me to back off on tracking the HHS stimulus money. When I told him that I couldn't do that, he threatened me with my life," Mason replied.

"The *President!*" Dale exclaimed in amazement.

"He did," Mason responded. "Dale, I think the Secretary's death is connected to my investigation of the department she oversees and her apparent willingness to come forward with answers."

"When did you become a detective?"

"When I became a doctor," was the reply. "Doctors do detective work every day. You see, in our medical training we are taught to look at the obvious and not-so-obvious signs and symptoms that could be responsible for a disorder. Then, we are taught to gather additional information to either confirm or refute our suspicions. The best doctors are those who consider all possibilities and narrow them down to a common thread that runs through the case, you know, go to the source. Dale, the common thread in the Secretary's death is my delving into this healthcare legislation and asking hard questions. While leaving the Oval Office, the President in a threatening tone told me to be careful crossing streets and driving. A few weeks later someone who may have been thought to be helping me in my investigation died driving her automobile on a familiar route. Does that not raise questions?"

"It does," Dale replied. "But, that's still a stretch for a charge of murder against the President of the United States."

"There's more. I have learned that hundreds of millions of dollars appropriated within the stimulus package were earmarked for veteran's activities. The problem is that no one can account for where the money is or has been spent," Mason added. "Whatever is going on at the highest levels of government today could make Watergate pale in comparison."

"We need a 'deep throat,'" Dale replied. "You know, like in the Watergate scandal, and reporters with the zeal of Woodward or Bernstein to go after and report the truth."

"Good luck," Mason responded, "in getting any member of the mainstream media to be that aggressive against this Administration."

"What about VOX?" Dale asked.

"I have some contacts over there," Mason replied. "But to get to the root of this, your agency—the FBI—will need to become involved, and perhaps the CIA."

"I know that a lot of people in our agency and over at CIA are not that happy with this Administration," Dale said. "We have been tracking the campaign money that came in from out of the country during the last election. And, it looks as though much of it was funneled through students and church organizations in fifty—and one hundred—dollar prepaid credit cards. As you know, it is hard to trace who originally bought the cards, but it appears that it was orchestrated from Belgium, from the office of a group that often refers to itself as 'Moriah,' or the 'Conquering Wind.' They are also known by other names, such as 'the Illuminati' or 'the Shadow Government.'"

"I am familiar with these terms," Mason replied. "Isn't this the group that met at the Hotel Bilderberg in the nineteen fifties? Its Inner Circle is composed of a dozen or so powerful families who believe that they are direct descendants of the Annunaki, the giant 'sons of God' that Genesis tells us intermarried with the 'daughters of men.' Their offspring—the self-designated 'illuminated ones'—are out to establish a New World Order that will assume control of world affairs in the name of Lucifer, their leader?"

"That's them," Dale replied. "Electing this President, orchestrating America's implosion, and creating an Orwellian-like state in America seems to be part of their plan."

"George Orwell was trying to warn the world about them in his book, *1984*," Mason said.

"Precisely," Dale replied. "Like Orwell predicted, Big Brother has eyes and ears everywhere. And, to this group, people are no more than chattel. Everyone is dispensable, especially if they get in the way. We'll have to be careful."

"Yeah, I know of at least one person who may have been killed because she was becoming a liability," Mason drove home.

"Let me nose around and see who I can trust," Dale answered. "I'll be back to you in a few days. This is a good place to meet, but we'd better go now. The groundskeepers will be arriving soon. And, in Washington, everyone is a sleuth."

"Oh my God," Mason said, recalling his meeting with President Padgett, "I just remembered. Right before the President threatened me I mentioned that I knew about how his campaign funds came into this country and who supplied much of them."

"Be careful," Dale advised. "They know that you are on to them."

The two men left the rain shed, heading in opposite directions. When Mason arrived at his car, he thought to himself, "This could be the last time I crank this car."

When the engine turned over, nothing happened. Mason breathed a sigh of relief. However, before he left the out-of-the-way lot behind the maintenance building, he checked his brakes and power steering, just in case.

CHAPTER 13

"Congressman, President Padgett is on the phone," Martha announced over the intercom that connected her office with her boss's.

"Mason," the President said, "we need to talk. Can you come over to the Oval Office right away?"

"Will I be asked to come through the door on my hands and knees?" Mason asked.

"Don't be foolish," the President replied. "You know that I was just joking about all that."

"I didn't take it as a joke, Mr. President, and the look in your eyes wasn't that of a joker."

. . . .

In the Oval Office, President Padgett said, "Have a seat on the sofa."

"If it's okay with you, Mr. President, I think I'll just stand."

"Stand if you wish," the President replied, leaning back in his chair behind the desk that had been used by commanders-in-chief for many decades. "I think we need to bury the hatchet. It's not good for the country if we are on opposite sides of the issues. I have a way that we can solve this impasse between us. How about if I appoint you as Secretary of Health and Human Services, to fill the seat vacated by the untimely death of the last Secretary? That way, you could play a major role in helping restructure the way Americans receive healthcare from this time forth. It would be win/win. How about it?"

Mason felt that he was being set up. Quickly, he thought to himself, "If I accept this position and am prevented from making the kinds of change that are needed—and the healthcare system continues to deteriorate—I will be blamed for it."

"The polls show that the American people are very unhappy with nationalized healthcare and that the estimates of what it is going to cost were grossly understated," Mr. President."

"That's why we need to put a new face on it, and yours is the face that I want."

Mason saw through the President's plan, but remembered the advice once given to him by one of his mentors, Dr. Jay Andrews, who said, "You can't fight city hall from the outside." Although he didn't hear it from his grandmother, he had, nevertheless, written the lesson down in *Laney's Little Book of Wisdom*.

Hoping to test the President's sincerity, Mason said, "It's going to take more than a new face to make your healthcare plan work, Mr. President."

"Whatever it takes, you'll have my support. I have to make this work," President Padgett replied.

"Perhaps, if I can get some guarantees, it would be worth the risk," Mason said to himself. Then he said aloud, "Mr. President, you should know by now that I am a man of principles. I can't be bought off. I took an oath to serve humanity as a doctor. Then I took an oath to serve the people of my district in Congress, looking out for their health, welfare, and safety. I am not one to break promises."

"Precisely, and, that is what I'm now asking you to do, be true to your oaths."

"Mr. President, if I accept your offer, you must know that I will dig into a lot of things that could turn out to be embarrassing to you and members of your administration. Even more, it could cause trouble for you in even higher places," Mason added.

"Higher places?" President Padgett replied, staring into Mason's eyes.

"Yes sir, from your biggest supporters, if you get my drift."

"What I have learned about politics," the President answered, "is that sometimes you have to give a little to get a lot. And, that there are people in the world who neither you nor I want to get at odds with—powerful and unforgiving people. These people only measure results, and my seeing that America's new healthcare system doesn't get derailed is essential—if you get *my* drift. My staff tells me that the amendments I have submitted to the healthcare stimulus package in their current forms are unlikely to pass the newly elected House of Representatives. I need them to pass. Will you help me do that, Mason? I am willing to compromise on some of the points that are important to you."

"If providing quality healthcare is your mission, if you are serious about getting government off the backs of doctors and add tort reform to the new amendment, I'll consider it," Mason answered.

With at least that promise, the President said, "Good, then we have a deal." He extended his hand to the doctor.

"There's one more thing," Mason said, leaving his right hand at his side. "You must call off those men driving the black SUV who tail me everywhere I go."

"They've been providing protection for you, congressman."

"You mean the kind of protection that the former Secretary of HHS received?" Mason responded.

"That was an accident, Mason, an unfortunate accident."

Realizing that he was about to enter the biggest crapshoot of his life, Mason said, "I'm sorry, there is another caveat if I am to take the job. Mr. President, before I leave the White House, I want you to promise me that you will let me select my own team of Secret Service agents and my own personal bodyguard. I know that there are a lot of people in high places who won't be happy with the fact that you may have even offered the HHS position to me. Who, other than you, knows that this meeting is taking place?"

"The lady who let you in, that's all," the President replied.

"Can she be trusted?"

"With *my* life," the President replied.

"With *your* life?"

"With *our* lives, then."

"Do I have your word about my choice of bodyguards and Secret Service team while I'm considering your offer?"

"You have my word," the President answered.

"May I use a secure telephone to make a call?" Mason asked, extending his hand for the ceremonial handshake to seal a deal. But Mason, still mulling acceptance of the offer, was thinking, "Have I lost my mind? Have I just taken the first step toward making an unholy pact with the enemy?"

"Use the phone in my study. It's the first door to the left, right out that door. It's a secure line." The President pointed to the door opposite the one through which Mason had entered the Oval Office.

. . . .

On the phone, Mason said, "Dale, you won't believe what just happened."

"Are you all right? Where are you?" Dale asked in a concerned tone of voice.

"I'm at the White House, in the President's private study adjacent to the Oval Office."

"You are joking. Right?" Dale responded. "Is the door locked from the outside? Check around you and see if the smell of gas is in the air."

"I'm not joking. I'm as serious as a heart attack. Dale, I need you and two of your most trusted agents to come here right away. And make sure that you are armed. You and I are about to be given the assignments of our lives."

"How do I get through White House security and to you?"

"It will all be arranged," Mason replied.

. . . .

The trio of FBI agents soon arrived.

"Mr. President, this is a long-time friend, agent Dale Jackson of the FBI, the gentleman that I spoke with you about. As you agreed, he has brought two of his agents with him. This is the team that I want to be in charge of my security. Is that agreeable?"

"Pleased to meet you, gentlemen," President Padgett said, stepping forward to shake the hand of each.

"Congressman Edmonds drives a hard bargain. I've decided that I want him on my team. I have learned the hard way, if you can't beat them, you may have them join you," the President said, smiling.

Turning to Mason, President Padgett asked, "When will I have your answer?"

Mason answered, "Soon, very soon."

"You guys take good care of him," the President said, gazing at the Edmonds security detail. "I understand that he has some secret safety deposit boxes that we want to remain secret forever."

Dale looked at his friend with a confused expression on his face. "Don't worry," Mason said, "it's a deal between the President and me."

As the men left the White House, Dale whispered to Mason, "You didn't take a payoff, did you? That's not what your safety deposit boxes are for, are they?"

"Dale, you know me better than that. I have some things that could be very embarrassing to Padgett stored away in safe places. In fact, they could cost him the presidency. Just in case anything should happen to me, there are two high-profile reporters at VOX News who have keys and are instructed to open the boxes and reveal their contents to the world. They won't find any money in *those* boxes."

"You'd better give me a key, too," Dale replied. "Things can happen to reporters, you know."

"I do, indeed. This Administration is not very happy with the ones over at VOX."

. . . .

That same evening after dinner, Mason told Norene that he had a matter of importance to discuss with her.

"I know this is going to take you by surprise, because it shocked me. President Padgett has offered to appoint me as the new Secretary of Health and Human Services."

"You can't be serious! The President who threatened your life now wants you to join his Administration?"

"That's the gist of it. I remember reading somewhere: 'Keep your friends close and your enemy's closer.' If I become HHS Secretary, I may be able to do more for the medical profession and for the people of America—from the inside looking out, rather than from the outside looking in. What do you think?"

"I think you are venturing into very dangerous territory," Norene replied. "You know these people. We've long talked about who runs the world, and that they will do anything to promote their agenda.

"You will need an army to protect you," Norene added. "You have been openly critical of the President's policies and people with whom he's surrounded himself. I know that you have heard that some groups believe that the President is their Messiah. Some people believe that even his name represents the phrase, 'He is with us.'"

"One of those who openly proclaimed as much is the man who calls himself "the leader of the Nation of Islam" here in the U.S.," Mason replied. "Others are convinced that the President, himself, believes his destiny is to be the savior of the world and that the position he now holds is merely a stepping stone to the office of Secretary General of the United Nations."

"You've said that to me before," Norene replied. "He was pandering to the UN even before he was elected. With his latest appearance before that Assembly, it looked as if he was still on the campaign trail. Do you believe that he thinks he has been anointed to change the world?"

"If he does, the world that he is out to create is quite different from the world that you and I would create. We've had many conversations about prophesies in the Book of Revelation," Mason responded. "I read a book last year entitled *Let Us Make Man*. The author discussed how mankind can choose its destiny. Before the Messiah comes, there is to be an antichrist or false prophet, who will survive a mortal head wound, and the people will believe that he is a god. From what I can gather from the Scriptures, humankind can choose to follow the antichrist or to reject him. And, based on what I have seen and know, it is more likely that the man who now sits behind the desk in the Oval Office is more apt to fit the role of antichrist than Messiah."

"You know," Norene said, "I watched a program last month on the History Channel about this subject. A professor was discussing the similarities between Napoleon and Hitler. He explained their rise to power and the conditions that existed in their countries that allowed them to do so."

"I've studied about the rise of these two butchers," her husband noted. "That's the term that Nostradamus used to describe them hundreds of years before they were born. I can guess what the history professor said. In both France and Germany, there was an economic recession. Times were hard. And the people were restless. Both Napoleon and Hitler came along and told the people what they wanted to hear. Each of them was an accomplished orator and identified a scapegoat whom he could blame for their country's woes. The people chose to give Napoleon and Hitler absolute power. Then, like the children in the Pied Piper story, the people followed each man to their own destruction. Does that sound familiar?"

"Too much so," Norene replied. "It sounds as though history may be repeating. But, who is today's scapegoat?"

"Well, Israel is one." Mason replied. "Sound familiar?"

"Oh my God," Norene said. "Who else?"

"The other scapegoat is not necessarily a person or country, but a way of life—capitalism, and individual freedoms, the freedom to live life without Big Brother monitoring or controlling every move," Mason answered. "With what we now know about the Illuminati, you have to wonder if the economic downturn of 2008 wasn't caused by this group of overlords so that *this* President— the perfect figurehead for the times—would win. I'm truly concerned about America's future. A lot of people seem to want America, the modern-day paragon of human rights, to bleed, including some of my colleagues in Congress and the people now occupying the White House."

"You know how scary it is to talk about this, even between the two of us, and in our own home. Sometimes, I think that the walls have ears."

"You may be right," Mason replied. "Information is power. And, information about one's adversary leads to absolute power, the kind of power that a Shadow Government has to have."

"If you decide to accept President Padgett's offer, what are you going to do to ensure your safety?"

"I don't know that there is any way to ensure one's safety, but Padgett has allowed me to select my own security force headed up by my long-time friend, Dale Jackson."

"How big is Dale's army?" Norene asked derisively.

"He'll have four men with me at all times."

"That's not a big enough army to go up against all the President's forces, especially if he is who we fear that he might be," Norene said.

"Dale is not only an FBI agent. He was a special ops guy in the Army in Viet Nam. I feel safe with him and his men watching my back. And he's going to see that the same kind of security system used in the White House is installed here in our home."

"I want you to know that I don't like it, "Norene said. "It scares me to think that you are going to be any part of this Administration. I've heard you say that 'if you play with dirty playmates, you get dirty.'"

"Yeah, that's what my grandmother used to tell me."

"I don't trust them," Norene counseled. "I certainly don't trust the people who put them in office, you know, that group that you and I talked about during your campaign for Congress, the Illuminati. But if this is what you must do, then I'm with you."

"You always have been," Mason replied, giving his wife a hug. "It may be our best chance to learn if a global shadow government, the Illuminati, really does exist and what they intend to do with America."

"I'm concerned about what they might do with *you*," Norene said, taking her husband's hand in hers.

"It wouldn't be the first time I've jousted with a dragon. It seems that I've been doing it all my life."

"Yeah, but this dragon is the granddaddy of them all. And, it lives in the shadows, out of plain sight."

. . . .

President Padgett began his Cabinet meeting by introducing its newest member.

"Ladies and gentlemen, let us all welcome, Dr. Mason Edmonds to his first Cabinet meeting. As the new Secretary of Health and Human Services, Dr. Edmonds will be helping save the Health Reform Act that I signed into law last March from the new Congress' attempts to repeal it, but he will be doing more. I have asked him to tell those of us around this table how we can make the one now in place even better. Although he comes to us from the opposite side of the congressional aisle, I have been convinced that he is the man of the hour.

His knowledge of the medical profession and how care is delivered at every level of this society gives him a unique perspective on how to best achieve the revolutionary goals this Administration has set and to preserve the best of the current system. I want to ask each of you and your staffs to give Dr. Edmonds your fullest cooperation. Dr. Edmonds, would you like to say a few words?"

"Thank you, Mr. President," Mason said. "I know that many of you are wondering how I came to be a part of your cabinet. The answer is simple. The President asked me to do it and promised his full support to me. I have taken him at his word."

Mason looked around the table at a group of people whose motives and judgment he had often questioned—and who knew it. Nevertheless, the Commander-in-Chief had asked him to help solve a problem facing the nation.

Looking deeply at his fellow Cabinet member, Mason said, "As you know, I have been quite outspoken about my feelings with the healthcare bill passed a few years back and the current amendment to repeal much of it that Congress is being asked to consider. In its current form, the amendment being offered by your party does not address the solution to making America a healthier nation. In fact, unless portions of the repeal amendment pass, healthcare and the U.S. economy are heading for a train wreck. The President has told me that he doesn't want to see such a disaster and I must assume that none of you do either."

The doctor waited for a reaction from those seated around the table. That he only met silence caused him to wonder if disaster was precisely what some of the Cabinet had been instructed, or paid off, to ensure.

Mason continued, "While many of your advisers have blamed doctors for the high cost of healthcare, what has not been taken into account in the revamping of healthcare in America is that doctors' salaries only account for about ten to twelve percent of the entire healthcare budget. Many doctors are already leaving the profession, entering other professions. Some are becoming lawyers. Others are running for political office. Further reductions in compensation will lead to a mass exodus by doctors from nationalized healthcare, leaving the President and you, his Cabinet, with the blame for the physician shortage.

"By including illegal aliens and the intentionally uninsured onto the rolls, the healthcare legislation already passed has placed a tremendous burden on the nation's budget. Already, costs have exceeded projections. And, we are still in the infancy stage of the life span of a growing monster.

"If universal healthcare fails, your legacies will be tarnished. I can't believe that is what you want. A failed healthcare system is certainly not what the American people want. You don't want history to hang the yoke of a bankrupt America around your neck, do you?"

For a brief moment Mason paused. Still no response, nothing but long faces and stern eyes. He could see that he was getting under the skin of some of his fellow Cabinet members. Strangely, he was beginning to believe that a failed America is what some of them had in mind. Nevertheless, he continued with his remarks. He noted that the Presidential historian was recording every word he spoke.

"So, if you will work with me and encourage your party's members in Congress to work with me, I am sure that we can come up with a plan that will help cover the uninsured in America, without destroying the entire system—if that is what you truly want.

"To make the program work, we will have to inject both incentives and disincentives into the system. Doctors, hospitals, and administrators that produce a better product need to be rewarded. Those who do poor jobs need to be penalized or closed down. Governmental departments that fail the people they serve should live by the same rules. It's the proven policy: 'reward achievement; punish failure," he said, placing his hand over his right hip pocket, acknowledging to himself the source of the time-honored words of wisdom that he spoke.

"America's government and healthcare system need to be run like a business, because government has now become a business, running businesses. This Administration has taken on the responsibility of overseeing many of the businesses and industries in America. If you think that the banking system and making automobiles are challenges, you haven't seen anything yet. What if people could walk into a bank or automobile dealership, sign a piece of paper and leave with a pocket full of money or a new car without paying for it? Though this example may seem ridiculous, providing all the health that all the people want, when they want it, at no cost to them, is unreasonable and unsustainable.

"Healthcare consumes a major part of our budget every year because 'health' has been politicized. Health is now designated a *right* rather than an *objective* or *privilege*. It is unreasonable to ask one American to ensure the health of another. A government can't give health to its people. It can only fund the system that attempts to provide an indefinable entity: health. The fact is, like money, health has to be earned. People have to do the things that tend to keep them healthy and some people are better at it than others. Some people inherit the ability to remain healthy; some people squander their inheritance; and some people never had it from the start.

Health is not a commodity that can be traded to the highest or lowest bidder. Like love, health cannot be bought, sold, guaranteed, or regulated. And, like love, we know that health exists, but it is difficult to define."

From the body language of many of his fellow Cabinet members, Mason could sense that the former lawyers and academicians around the table were very uncomfortable with what he was saying. Most of them embraced liberal or progressive views. They had been indoctrinated by their own teachers and role models to believe that government could solve all problems. However, Mason concluded that he might have only one chance to speak the truth to people who didn't seem to want to hear it. More importantly, at least to the doctor, his comments would be a matter of record.

Mason continued, "I know that this Administration is heavily invested in the matter of human rights and protecting the planet. Well, the planet includes the people in America who live on this planet. And, I look upon human rights as those rights that enhance life for humans. However, with all due respect to each of you, imposing a system upon the people that is destined to provide a lesser quality of healthcare does not enhance life in America. Regardless of what your advisers may be telling you, a government cannot assume the role of caring for humans who won't care for themselves. There will never be enough money in the public coffers to do so, regardless of how high you raise taxes.

"We have to stop politicizing healthcare and look upon some illnesses as addictions, because many illnesses are self-imposed, made worse by feeding the cravings of those who are already abusing the system. Before we can address the things that illnesses do *to* people, we have to address the things that people do to themselves. Then we can find a way to address the conditions that happen to people, regardless of the personal commitment they make to being healthy."

Once again, Mason paused for a moment and tried to read the expressions of the President and the other members of his Cabinet. The atmosphere in the room was so cold that a chain saw might have difficulty cutting it.

He could tell that his message was falling on deaf ears of the social reformist in the group. Nevertheless, he didn't back off on speaking the truth.

"I know that this is not what many of you want to hear, but, the facts are: in order to save your healthcare initiative and bring quality healthcare to America, we have to depoliticize healthcare.

"In every country that has nationalized healthcare, care—and life—end up being rationed. Lives are shortened because of delays and denials of the kinds of care that have been proven to extend life. People suffering from pain have to live with it while they stand in line for corrective treatment and surgery that may never come.

"I am one of the few people in America who have read the 2,000-page Health Reform Act of 2010. Portions of it give government-paid insurance clerks and bureaucrats the ability to exclude senior citizens from procedures that will be available to younger Americans or illegal aliens. I ask you: If healthcare is a right, is there an age at which that right is forfeited or denied? Is it 'right' to impose a system on Americans that punishes excellence and ensures mediocrity? I would submit that the answer to this question is 'No.' If these things are known beforehand, and we still go forward with a plan that is destined to fail to enhance the lives of Americans, we will have committed one of the greatest human rights atrocities in American history. We will be guilty of political malpractice. And, the people of America should hold us accountable, individually and collectively. I for one cannot be a part of such a plan."

Mason was on a roll. His juices were flowing. He had waited for years to say some of the things he was saying to the people who were responsible for many of the problems facing America. He continued, "Now, if you truly want to do what is in the best interest of all Americans, this is what I and my staff will attempt to accomplish. We will:

1. Review the current state of health in America, including availability, utilization, delivery, administration, and costs of services and products;

2. Research and identify the factors that impact health and well-being in the private and public sectors, including prevention and early detection of disease;
3. Recommend pro-active measures designed to remedy deficiencies and/or inefficiencies throughout America's health-related network;
4. Recommend measures to provide all the healthcare that America can afford –no more, no less;
5. Organize the citizenry in a nationwide initiative designed to promote healthy lifestyles. Care for those who are truly unable to care for themselves. Reward those who are compliant. Penalize those who are not;
6. Instruct the congressional members of our respective parties to include meaningful tort reform and provide relief to physicians and help eliminate costly and duplicitous defensive medicine.

"With the bipartisan measures, we can cut cost without sacrificing quality and efficiency. But, as your HHS Secretary, I cannot accomplish this mission without the support of everyone in this room. I need each of you and your friends in Congress to take the role of leadership. Announce to the American people that we are going to repeal portions of the healthcare plan and that we politicians and our staffs have joined the same system that we are asking them to accept, that we are going to govern by example."

With that, Mason could see spines bristling. He had truly hit a nerve. Now the issue was becoming personal. He paused and looked at President Padgett, searching for his reaction. He was not alone. Everyone in the room tried to read the President's body language.

"Go on," President Padgett said to Mason. "We want to hear everything you have to say on the matter."

The doctor continued, "Now, I know that I have proposed some things that may not be very popular with many of you. I am an outsider who has just come into your inner sanctum. However, unless I can be assured that

I have the full support of everyone in this room, I will give the President this letter of resignation that I have already prepared, right now," Mason said, reaching his pocket and pulling an envelope from the inside pocket of his suit pocket. "I will simply request from the presidential historian a full and unedited transcript of the remarks that I have made here today and end my participation in trying to help save America's healthcare system as quickly as I came into it."

The President, realizing that Mason had dropped the proverbial bomb on his Cabinet, said, "Dr. Edmonds, you have done precisely what I asked you to do. You have given us your views on the tasks at hand."

Looking around the table at each member of his Cabinet, the President asked, "Is everybody in?"

Though without any visible degree of enthusiasm, all present nodded affirmatively.

"Then, Dr. Edmonds, we will look forward to having you present the details of your changes in the upcoming amendment that we intend to submit to a bipartisan group of Congressmen and women and Senators to add further reform to the Health Reform Act of 2010. We look forward to hearing the details of your recommendations at the next Cabinet meeting on Monday morning? Now, let us turn to fiscal matters. Secretary Rommel, what can you report from the Department of Treasury?"

. . . .

Early in his career, Mason had learned that when important decisions need to be made, one should seek the advice of people who have lived the experiences you may be facing. To do this, he called to mind the team of experts he had assembled when the governor of his state had asked him to establish a health commission to address some of the same issues now facing the nation. He decided to contact the individuals he had assembled for that task. He knew these people. He could trust them.

Mason contacted each person on the list and asked for their help. All agreed to do so. "Time is of the essence," he told them. "I need you to come to Washington right away, two days from now."

Without exception, the group gladly complied with Mason's request.

CHAPTER 14

Gathered in the conference room of the Health and Human Services Building were some of the sharpest minds Mason had known. The group included:
- Dr. Marion Washburn, a dean of the college of community health at a major medical school, who was also a physician who had trained at Walter Reed Medical Center,
- Dr. Sherry Jolly, a PhD pharmacist with both clinical and research experience, who currently ran the pharmacy department at a large Veterans Affairs hospital,
- Dr. Bonita La Batre, a family physician who had served as president of her state medical association and on the board of trustees for the American Medical Association. She also had experience in public health and children's health,
- Dr. Lora Blackburn, a dean of a college of health and human services, with a PhD in physical education, sports medicine and exercise physiology,
- Mrs. Frances Delano, a financier and former banker with a masters' degree in business administration who had served on a state health planning agency. She also had created a veteran's memorial organization and served on numerous health-related boards,
- and Jackson Hunter, a former president of a large insurance company and resident of the human resources division of one of the nation's largest communications network.

Mason felt as though the brain power and experience gathered around the table could clearly define some of the issues facing America's healthcare delivery system. Each of them had seen both the good and bad, from the personal side and from that of the companies and organizations they represented.

"When I contacted each of you three years ago," Mason began the meeting, "little did I know that we would one day be discussing the nation's healthcare issues, but as I thought about it, those facing the nation are the same as those facing virtually every state in the Union. It's just a matter of adding more zeros to the numbers. Over the next two days, my objective is for us to boil the national issue down to a proposal that I can put before the President and the rest of his Cabinet. Does anyone have a question?"

Mrs. Delano, the former banker and financier, spoke up first and said, "It looks like we have a huge task before us. Let's get to work."

. . . .

By the following afternoon the select committee of advisers had hashed out the problems facing America's healthcare dilemma and come to a consensus on a half a dozen ways to eliminate waste and maintain quality. Dr. Edmonds gathered the notes that had been taken during the meeting and, with his administrative assistant's help, began to draft a document that could be presented to the President's Cabinet on Monday morning.

. . . .

Reviewing the document that had been circulated by the new HHS Secretary's assistant, the President looked at Mason as they and the Vice President met, and said, "This is impressive. How did you come up with these ideas so quickly?"

"I've been thinking about these matters for years. Solving them is really not that difficult, assuming that solving problems is the objective," Mason said, pausing and peering over his glasses at his fellow Cabinet members in a subtle, yet vilifying manner. "The handwriting has long been on the wall. I knew that someday America would have a nationalized healthcare policy. So I just pulled together a group of experts who I felt would see the problems from the outside in, and asked them to tell me what they would do if they were asked to advise the President of the United States or his advisors."

The President said, "What makes you think that we aren't interested in solving problems or that any of your friends are qualified to advise us?"

"That's the question I need answered," Mason responded. "My question to them was what would you do *if* you were put in charge of correcting the ills of the new healthcare plan? Isn't that what you asked me to do?"

"That's precisely what I asked you to do. I just wanted to make sure that neither you nor any of them wanted my job. Just keep in mind who you answer to."

"That's a question to which I already know the answer," Mason replied, sensing the President's hair bristling on the back of his neck. "What you have in front of you comprises the thoughts of a good cross section of healthcare providers, recipients, business people, financiers, and administrators. And if you would allow me to be so bold, I believe that what came out of this three-day meeting is a better alternative than what Congress offered in its two-thousand page bill. It's a business plan, one that is not loaded down with pork or pet projects—one that America can afford and will get the people involved in becoming part of the solution to the healthcare problem."

"That's a fairly bold indictment of Congress."

"I'm sorry for being so blunt. But, the facts are the facts," Mason said forcefully. "Mr. President, clearly there are some smart and caring people in Congress, but as I have reviewed the collective decisions of the legislative branch of government during the past few years, the collective IQ of the group when deciding this nation's fate would be well below the national average of the people they were elected to represent."

"As the presiding officer in the Senate, I take offense to your remarks," the Vice President retorted.

"Once, again, Mr. Vice President, I apologize only for my boldness. But the facts speak volumes," Mason said, and continued. "The solutions before you are offered by caring Americans who only want what is best for the nation and every citizen of this nation. They are not concerned about satisfying special interest groups, illegals, political correctness, or getting reelected. Mr. President, you gave me a job to do, and if you truly want to solve America's healthcare problems, the proposals that my committee and I have recommended represent the bones of the platform that I would like to see you and this Cabinet throw its full support behind."

"Thank you, Dr. Edmonds," the President said. "We will all study this proposal and give you some feedback at next Monday's meeting."

....

On the following Monday, the Cabinet was prepared to react to Dr. Edmonds' task force recommendations. The Chief of Staff led off the comment session regarding Mason's changes in the current healthcare legislation. He outlined a number of reasons why the plan would be hard to maneuver through Congress. So many lawmakers had promised favors to the people who had helped them get elected.

The Secretary of State spoke second. She pointed out several areas of concern, including how other nations that have nationalized healthcare would react to the U.S. repealing the one it just passed. And although the matter didn't concern state matters, she expressed concerns over restrictions on government-funded abortion benefits for unwed mothers and full coverage for the children of "undocumented" aliens. "The National Organization of Women would raise holy hell," the Secretary of State predicted, "if these benefits were repealed."

Next, the Secretary of Defense expressed his concerns that some of the military leaders and enlisted men and women would be upset if they learned that the VA system was about to be reorganized.

Then the Secretary of Education said, "Teachers throughout America will walk out of their classrooms. Asking them for a co-payment for obesity-induced conditions and yearly health screening will be offensive."

The Secretary of Commerce added, "Labor unions will take to the streets. There is no way that they are going to work without the health and retirement benefits guaranteed in the negotiations of 2010."

"We simply have to look at the data," the Secretary of the Treasury said, "A large part of the healthcare budget is spent on people over the age of seventy. We simply can't pay for procedures and medications for old people who sit around in nursing homes and sleep all day. We can't allow them to become even a greater drain on society than they already are."

Mason bit his tongue as his fellow Cabinet members defended a healthcare plan that the experts had already said would bankrupt America.

Finally, the President himself spoke. "Dr. Edmonds, while I asked you to bring solutions to the cabinet, you have gone too far. The changes that you have proposed will not be popular with a large segment of this Administration's political base. After you spoke yesterday, I took a poll of the other members of the Cabinet and congressional leaders. The vast majority are unwilling to give up the healthcare plan that our positions provide and support the kinds of reform that you suggest. Because of the special pressures imposed on us and the responsibilities we bear, we are entitled to a different healthcare plan than is the average citizen. I'm afraid that you will have to go back to the drawing board."

Mason's first reaction was to pull the resignation letter that he carried from his jacket pocket and throw it on the table. However, he gathered his emotions and instead said, "I think that you are right, Mr. President. I need some time to think and plan. I do need to *go back*— back to my roots, back to my family where I can consider all that I have heard here today. I want your blessings to take a leave of absence to clear my head and see if I can look at things the way you and the members of the Cabinet do. With your blessings, the Assistant Secretary of HHS can oversee things for a few weeks."

At first, President Padgett was speechless. He did not want to appear to overreact to one of his Cabinet members who had asked for time to consider doing what he and the other members of the Cabinet wanted him to do.

He said to Mason, "You know that time is of the essence. I want to put your party's efforts to repeal my healthcare program to rest before the summer recess. We can't allow the other members of your party and friends to shoot holes in it for a month like they did in 2009 and 2010 during so-called 'town hall meetings.' I want to cut the legs out of the Tea Party movement. However, I have asked you for your advice. So, I agree with your taking time off so that you can come back with a plan that both major political parties can live with. I'm sure that after you have considered all you have heard here today, you will see things our way. Now, you are one of us, aren't you?" the President asked, putting Mason in an awkward position.

Trying not to choke on his own tongue, Mason replied, "Yes, sir, Mr. President. We are all Americans. We all want what is best for America, don't we?"

Everyone present looked at the President for his response.

After a short pause, realizing that the session was being recorded, the President responded. "Absolutely, we are all in this together. What will we tell the press?"

"My suggestion is that we tell them the truth, that healthcare is an important matter and that I wanted to personally research the possibilities for making the changes that you are supporting as thoroughly as possible." Mason replied.

"You're the man for the job at hand," President Padgett replied. "That's a good answer. That's what we will tell them, that since you are also a doctor, you are conducting your own personal research. I like it. That's what you will be doing, right?"

"Yes, sir," Mason answered. "When I come back, I will have some answers and roll up my sleeves to make healthcare better than ever for the American people at an affordable cost."

Mason asked to be excused and rose from his seat. He went to his office and gathered a few things, but did not want it to appear as though he was leaving his post, only taking a sabbatical for further study on a complex issue. Before he left the room, he called his wife.

....

"Norene," he said, "We're going home."
"You mean you are *coming* home?" she asked.
"No, honey, I, or rather *we,* are going home, back to the *real* world, to Fountainhead Ranch. I'll see you in about half an hour. Pack a few things for the trip."

....

As Mason exited the HHS Building, a mob of television and newspaper reporters met him.

"Mr. Secretary," the AAC reporter asked, "is it true that the President asked for your resignation because you failed to provide him with an analysis he had asked for on a timely basis?"

Mason looked into the camera being held by an assistant next to the reporter and said, "Absolutely not, with the President's blessings, I am taking a leave of absence to conduct research on how he can reform healthcare so that it works for the American people and America's budget."

"Where will you go?" the CSS reporter asked.

"Wherever I need to go to gather the facts. First, I will go back to my ranch and create a plan of action. Then I will look at every angle of the healthcare challenges facing this country and the people who have been charged to oversee the task of taking care of Americans."

"Where will you begin such a search?" a reporter from the UBS asked.

"I plan to personally visit private and government-operated hospitals, nursing homes, and clinics to get a good feel for the current state of healthcare in America. My mother is in a nursing home. I can attest to the fact that late-life senior care is one phase of the healthcare industry that has made little, if any, progress over the past forty years. I intend to spend a lot of time trying to find ways to improve the care that senior citizens and veterans are receiving. It is a sad state of affairs. And with what the Health Reform Act of 2010 calls for, the kind of care offered to America's aging population won't get any better."

The CLN reporter asked, "Who will be overseeing the Department of HHS during your absence?"

"The Assistant Secretary," Mason answered. "She is a capable administrator."

The CLN reporter followed up, "How do you explain your appointment at HHS, anyway? You don't seem to have much in common with this Administration."

"You know," Mason replied. "I think that's why the President asked me to accept the position. He told me he wanted to hear from people who don't always agree with him."

The VOX reporter asked, "Mr. Secretary, do you not agree with the President?"

"Not on all issues," Mason answered. "I think each of us is hoping to convince the other to take a new look at an old problem. The challenge is to do so with an open mind. President Padgett is an intelligent man and savvy politician. You don't become President without winning a few debates and the hearts of a lot of people. My role is to gather the best information possible and to present it to President Padgett so that he can offer the best recommendation possible to Congress. That's how I think each of us sees our roles."

"Do you think that healthcare is a *right* of every American?" the ABS reporter asked.

"I don't think that the Constitution says that it is," Mason responded. "Nowhere in the Constitution can I find the word 'health.' Only the Declaration of Independence even remotely refers to it. And it states that it is the '*pursuit of* life, liberty, and happiness' that the Founding Fathers thought were inalienable rights."

"Doesn't the fourteenth amendment of the Constitution address the health issue?" asked the reporter from CCN.

"It only talks about 'public health' like sanitation, drinking water, epidemics, and the like. Any reasonable person would find it hard to believe that the framers of our Constitution intended for the federal government to foot the responsibility of delivering babies, lowering blood pressure, regulating blood sugars, treating depression, or performing abortions. It is hard to believe that the Founding Fathers envisioned a government 'of the people, by the people, and for the people' to provide everything that the people desire, including keeping every American healthy, cradle to grave. And, like love or happiness, health is not an easy condition to define. One person's health may be another's incapacitation. It's a matter of degrees and attitude."

"What do you mean by degrees?" the CCN reporter followed up.

"Take something as simple as a headache. Some headaches are more severe than others and some people deal with pain more easily than others. Some people would take an aspirin and go to work with a headache. Others would require a narcotic and go to bed. So how can the federal government ensure against headaches, and who will decide on behalf of the patient how severe his or her headache is, and what treatment is required? The answer is that a bureaucrat can't. And, that's what some politicians think that they or bureaucrats they oversee can do. There are more lawyers than doctors involved in making these rules. It would be inappropriate to have a doctor representing a client accused of wrongdoing in a courtroom. Neither should the American people allow lawyers to administer healthcare or make the rules for those who are trained to do so."

"Then who will decide these things?" the UBS reporter asked.

"As is the case in all health matters, the decision for treatment should be left between the patient and his or her doctor. If government wants to be involved, it has the right to decide what it can afford *to pay for*—no more, no less. Government's role in healthcare may eventually be an issue for the Supreme Court to decide."

"Thank you, Mr. Secretary," the reporter said, turning to the camera. "You've heard it live. The Secretary has not resigned, but is on a fact-gathering mission with the President's blessings. Clearly, health is a major issue facing America, one that may be left for the Supreme Court to decide. Now, back to our studios."

....

"Honey, I saw a replay of your interview on VOX. None of the other networks showed any of your remarks," Norene said.

"That doesn't surprise me," Mason responded. "My remarks didn't fit their agenda."

"So, what will you do now? Are you going to come back to Washington?"

"I'm not yet sure that being Secretary of HHS is where I need to be. I am being played for a fool. For one brief moment, I thought that the President truly wanted my help. Not only did he make a fool of me, he made a fool of the committee of caring people I brought to Washington who thought that they were going to make a difference. I'll never make that mistake again. If I stay in this arena again, it will be in a position that will allow me to call the shots. Maybe I need to put my legal hat on and think like they do—like lawyers do. You know that most of the politicians here are lawyers. That's part of the problem. I think that what the American people need is leaders who understand the Constitution and the Golden Rule. They also need someone who knows how to diagnose and correct the ills of the nation in duress. And I'm going to do all I can to help find those people."

"You don't mean what I think you mean?" Norene replied. "You aren't considering running for President, are you?"

"No, I don't intend to run for President. In the first place, I don't think I could get nominated or elected. I'm not sure that either party likes me now. I'm an Independent. The Republicans think I'm a traitor and the Democrats don't trust me. I've said what I came here to say to the people who needed to hear it. Maybe I just need to go back home—back to being a full-time doctor, where I can help change people's lives, one-by-one. I thought that I could make a difference here in Washington, but I have seen that the only difference that I could ever make here was if I was part of an Administration and Congress that thought the way most Americans think. I was willing to do the people's work because—well, because it is the people's work, like the Founding Fathers did. Right now, I just need some time to clear my head."

"Yes, you do. I think you are right. We need to go home for a few weeks, away from this atmosphere of—how did you say it—intentional ill-doing and seduction?"

"Those were not my words. They were written by Hippocrates in his oath."

"You'd think that Hippocrates may have spent some time in politics," Norene said.

"He spent time in a similar situation in ancient Greece. And this country is on the same tract as that once-great civilization, toward being torn apart at the seams. You'd think that we could learn from history, but the human race just seems to keep on losing its way and making the same old foolish mistakes. I don't know if America can be revived. It would take a miracle."

"Well, you know miracles *do* happen," Norene said. "Let's pray that God is not done with America, not yet. Somewhere in the Constitution, I bet you could find that Thomas Jefferson and the other framers anticipated what is happening today. I'll bet that Jefferson crafted the document with the Illuminati in mind. He had seen them at work in Europe and expected them to come after America. All you need to do is to uncover the part of the Constitution that he and his colleagues put there for this dilemma and set the wheels of justice in motion, in the right direction. For a very long time, America's enemies have been slowly—but surely—having the Constitution re-interpreted to their way of thinking by appointing Left Wing judges to the Supreme Court. Put on both your legal and medical hats and put together a prescription for reason. Washington, D.C., could use a big dose of it."

CHAPTER 15

It was Tuesday morning in the early part of July 2012. The top half of the morning sun could be seen peeking over the huge water oak trees at Fountainhead Ranch. On the veranda outside his study, Mason was having his first cup of coffee, while admiring his heard of black Tennessee Walking horses. The events of the past few weeks had taken their toll on the doctor. Not only was he thinking about his future, but that of his beloved country. Through the closed door, he heard the ringing of the phone on the desk in the study.

"Who could be calling this early in the day," Mason said to himself as he rose from his chair and opened the study door. Norene was still asleep, so he hurried to pick up the receiver.

"Mason, this is Dale," the caller said. "Did I wake you?"

"No," was the reply. "I've been up."

"Do you have a minute to talk? Sorry to call so early, but I thought that you'd want to hear what I've learned."

"Right now, I've got a lot of time on my hands. In fact, when you called, I was trying to decide what to do next. I am so frustrated with the events that took place in Washington that I am seeing red, no matter in which direction I look. The President made a fool out of me in the Cabinet meeting," Mason said. "He let me go way out on a limb and left me hanging there, alone. I've come to the conclusion that he only wanted to learn the details of what I and some other members of Congress would offer up as an alternative to his healthcare plan so that he and his cronies could shoot holes in it. He never intended to go along with my plan. I trusted him. I took a chance and got burned. I was betrayed, and wasted the time of those who trusted me, for a second time."

"Well, that's what I want to talk to you about, but I can't discuss matters of this nature over the phone. I can come down to your ranch to see you. How about Thursday?" the FBI agent asked. "I could come in late Wednesday evening and we can talk the following morning."

"Thursday will be fine. Just come over to our house when you get up," Mason said. "Ring the bell at the gate and I'll let you in."

"I'll be there about eight o'clock if that's all right."

"Great," Mason replied, "Can't wait to see you. We have some catching up to do."

"You said it," Dale responded.

. . . .

As promised, Dale made the trip to Fountainhead. On Thursday morning he and Mason poured cups of coffee went outside to Mason's favorite spot, on the veranda looking out over the lush green pastures of his ranch.

"What is so important that you had to come all the way down here to talk with me about it?" Mason asked his long-time friend on Thursday.

"Well, our investigation into the HHS Secretary's death is now complete and it looks as if you were right. It was no accident. Several eyewitnesses reported that before the Secretary arrived at the stop sign, a black SUV with tinted windows was chasing her, bumping her vehicle from the rear repeatedly. Dents on the rear bumper and trunk area confirmed that a number of lesser impacts had occurred on the same day. And her cell phone found in the floor of the car indicated that she had dialed *the first two* digits of the emergency 911 number, apparently trying to call for help. And to top it off, the brake fluid in her car had been drained. Someone set her up to die so that it would look like an accident," Dale said. "Didn't you tell me that the President threatened you if you didn't back off on your inquiry into the way that some of the healthcare money appropriated by Congress had been dealt out?"

"Yeah, he told me that I should be very careful driving home or crossing the street," Mason replied. "I took it as a direct threat."

"Our investigation also revealed that the HHS Secretary had compiled a lot of the information you had asked her for and that she was going to present it at the next hearing before the congressional subcommittee on which you sat," Dale said. "According to her personal secretary, the Secretary was about to blow the lid on the greatest heist and cover-up in American history. Like you suspected, it appears that some high-ranking government officials were on the take. They were funneling large sums of money into sham corporations or to overseas corporations for political favors. We found corporate documents that were ostensibly going to create jobs by building new medical clinics and hospitals in rural areas, but nothing happened. Some companies were set up to purchase new medical equipment for the VA system and to refurbish older facilities. The problem is that although the contracts were let and money was paid, nothing—absolutely nothing—happened."

"That confirms my suspicions," Mason replied. "What else did you learn?"

"A lot," Dale answered. "We are talking about hundreds of millions of dollars. Maybe billions. Many of the companies to which the money was given no longer exist and no one has a clue as to where the money is. More than a trillion dollars of Federal Reserve monies is unaccounted for. One of our agents is following a lead that a lot of it may have been transferred into the International Monetary Fund or World Bank. It appears that the former HHS secretary was on the trail of the people who were involved in these scams."

"So they eliminated her."

"Precisely," Dale answered. "Someone implemented the 'Rothschild Formula.' Mason, this could be *big—really big*. It appears to involve people at the highest levels of government. And, we have to be very careful how we go about gathering information, or we might be next on the list."

"I'm afraid that I am already on the list," Mason replied. "I suspect the only reason that they haven't come after me is because of the letters and DVD's I have stowed away in several safety deposit boxes around the country. I think they decided rather than killing me, physically, they would try to set me up and destroy my credibility, you know, like they probably did to Ted Kennedy at Chappaquiddick and Sarah Palin when she ran with McCain."

"You may be right," Dale said. "I'm not yet sure who else we can trust."

"We need to explore our options. Maybe somewhere in between my legal and medical training and your criminal justice training we can come up with an answer. The American people have been taken for a costly ride and we can't just let this thing drop," Mason said.

"We have to be very careful. We don't know who else is involved in this massive transfer of wealth and resources," Dale replied. "Clearly, we can't trust the President. I feel that very soon he may have a new name attached to his many titles: 'Liar-in-Chief.'"

"Unfortunately, I have that same feeling," Mason said, "I think I know someone we can trust," Mason said. "Like you, he is also a former special ops agent. At one time, he was involved in national intelligence. That's where I first became aware of his connections and skills. He still knows how to get at classified information and into virtually any computer. Other than you, Dale, he would be the first person I would turn to."

"Then, let's contact him," Dale said, "the sooner the better."

. . . .

The following day, another member had been added to the early morning meeting on the veranda of Mason and Norene's home.

"Dale Jackson, meet Gabriel Shade," Mason said, introducing the two men in whom he was about to bank his future—and perhaps a whole lot more.

"Pleased to meet you, Gabriel," Dale said. "Mason has told me a lot about you. However, he said that as well as the two of you know each other, there are still things about you that he doesn't know."

"That's true," Gabriel answered. "If I told him everything I know, I'd have to kill him.

"Just kidding," Gabriel added. "However, the doctor is pretty good at reading between the lines. There are a few things the oath I took when I signed on to the intelligence community prevent me from telling anyone, even my wife—you know, classified stuff."

"Yeah, classified stuff," Dale replied. "I just hope that all that classified stuff is true. These days, you never know. The world seems to run on propaganda," Dale added.

"Mason tells me that the two of you have worked together in the past," Gabriel said to Dale.

"We have," Dale replied. "We first met when our state's Bureau of Investigation was conducting a prescription drug ring in Steelton. Mason suspected that one of his former nurses might have been connected to the ring and called us. For months, the bureau and country sheriff's office used an empty office on the second floor of his clinic as our base to conduct our sting operation. During that time, we got to know each other pretty well. I told Doc that he had a knack for undercover work."

"Yeah," Mason interrupted. "What he really told me was that I'd better stick to my day job and let the criminal justice system handle the rough stuff. Things got pretty testy there at the end, didn't they, Dale?"

"But you seemed to love every minute of it," Dale said to his friend.

"I did," Mason replied. "You know that I actually worked in the criminal justice system between college and medical school. I was an assistant probation officer. I learned a lot about the criminal mind and its seeming insatiable appetite for breaking the rules. It was eye opening to see the extent to which some people will go to defy the law and the risks they are willing to take."

"How did you and Mason meet?" Dale asked Gabriel.

"We were both involved with a medically related company that was trying to help doctors and dentists prepare for the coming nationalization of the healthcare system," Gabriel explained.

"How long ago was that?" Dale asked.

"It was in the late nineteen nineties. Many of us have seen the writing on the wall for years. We knew it was just a matter of time before social constructionists would shove their version of healthcare through. Mason was a huge help. He had long ago seen what was on the horizon and began to get independent of hospitals and health insurance companies before many of his colleagues even considered the move."

"I didn't know that about you," Dale said to Mason. "We never talked about such things."

"We were too wrapped up in trying to catch the bad guys. And gals," Mason answered.

"What happened with your project?" Dale asked, looking at both Mason and Gabriel. "The one to help doctors prepare for socialized medicine?"

"We were ahead of our time," Gabriel spoke up. "We couldn't convince the medical profession that nationalized healthcare was eminent. The big healthcare insurance companies kept telling doctors and hospitals that nationalized healthcare would never come; that they had a powerful lobby in Washington and could forestall any effort. They were successful in blocking universal healthcare when the Clinton Administration tried it, and became complacent and apathetic when the Clinton plan failed."

"Apathy, that's one of the phases in the 'Cycles of Democracy' that Alexander Tyler described," Dale interjected. "Unfortunately, it is one of the end phases of the cycle."

"Yeah," Mason added. "But one thing that trusting Americans can't seem to learn about social constructionists is that they are both patient and persistent. They may appear to back off for a while, but they retreat only to regroup and come back again, constantly chipping away at the foundation of whatever it is they have their sights set on."

"In this case, they have their sights set on the United States," Dale put in. "The ring leaders, or at least their lieutenants, may be regrouping right in our own back yards. They feel that this is the best chance they've had, or will ever have, to invoke their system upon Americans."

"Very perceptive," Gabriel added. "You might recall the time that the former Russian leader, Nikita Khrushchev, looked into the eyes of the U.S. ambassador and said, 'We will bury you.' At the time, the American people didn't understand what he meant. They thought he meant that the Soviet Union intended to defeat us on the battlefield, on the seas, and in the air. What he meant was that the atheistic communists intend to *outlast* us.

"You have to give the communists credit for being persistent," Mason said.

"And cunning," Gabriel added. "They have learned from history and from the draconian group that gave birth to communism. They clearly understand the natural history of democracies, that once the masses realize that they can vote themselves into a state of relative prosperity they kill the goose that lays golden eggs."

"Why is it that this simple lesson we all learned as a child seems so hard to get across to adults, especially politicians?" Dale asked.

"There are many fables that America seems to have forgotten: the Pied Piper, the Boy Who Cried Wolf, Pinocchio, Snow White, and the Uncle Remus stories," Gabriel replied. "Each of them contained a moral or lesson that warned against the consequences of evil. Communists expect to be around when capitalistic America is laid to rest, choked on its own Constitution or led into the sea by elected officials who tell the masses what they want to hear and then distribute the wealth while raking a goodly portion off the top for themselves."

Although Dale and Mason already were aware of much of what Gabriel was telling them, they were enjoying the manner in which he repeated the lessons learned from children's books and history. The relaxed setting of Fountainhead Ranch allowed one to reflect on simple solutions to complex problems. In Washington, it was the other way around. Simple things were made more complex, by design.

"America's adversaries have studied the U.S. Constitution and probably know what it says better than most of our politicians," Gabriel continued. "They figured out a way that they could use our Constitution for the purpose of eroding American values and expanding government, contrary to the intent of this country's founders."

"I've long believed that the enemy is among us," Mason said. "The signs and symptoms are everywhere."

"They are," Gabriel replied. "They have infiltrated every aspect of our society. Anti-capitalistic professors have been planted on every college campus in America, disguised as 'progressive' academicians. Since the nineteen sixties, socialist liberals have been indoctrinating our young people to their way of thinking. They supported politicians whose liberal views ran contrary to the current of the Founding Fathers. They changed the face of the entertainment industry, challenging morals and seeing that high-profile people who agreed with socialistic views became involved in the political arena."

"I assume that you guys are solving the world's problems," Norene said coming through the veranda door with a steaming pot of coffee in her hand. "I thought that you'd need a warm up."

"We may not have solved them all," Dale said, "But the morning is not yet over."

"I'll be back in a while with a fresh pot. It looks like y'all will be here for a while," Norene said, returning to the inside of the house.

"Where were we?" Mason asked.

"Talking about the Hippies," Gabriel answered.

"Yeah, the hippie generation didn't go away," Dale said, wanting his two colleagues to know that he, too, had been following the political trends taking place in America. "They just cut their hair, shaved off their beards, took a bath, changed clothes and took their agenda into the political arena. In the last two Democratic Administrations, the White House has been occupied by the Woodstock generation. Their new aphrodisiac is power. And, they have been served a big dose of it by the invisible empire that first instigated the demonstrations at the corner of Haight and Asbury in San Francisco in the 1960s.

" Mason said, "What so many people have either forgotten or didn't know is that to avoid immediate opposition from the Right, the hippie movement started out being called the 'Jesus Movement,' but their behavior and agendas were far from anything that Jesus preached or did."

"Did you ever see a photograph of Bill and Hillary Clinton when they were hippies?" Gabriel asked.

"I didn't," Dale answered.

Mason said he had seen it.

"Scary, isn't it. Bill had shoulder-length hair and a full beard the same length. Hillary had dirty stringy brown hair and wore John Lennon glasses. The photos were taken when Bill was organizing the anti-American, anti-Vietnam demonstrations in Moscow. It is amazing how the media can cover up the past of those who promote their agendas and with whom they agree," Gabriel observed.

"Like the current President's past and the fact that he went to college on a foreign student scholarship," Dale added. "This whole thing about his eligibility to hold office has been swept under the rug."

"The hippie movement, anti-Vietnam War movement, and Global Warming thing have been fabricated and financed by the powers that be, to change the way Americans view themselves and the world," Gabriel said. "And there are still unanswered questions about the oil disaster in the Gulf of Mexico in 2010. What happened and when it happened seems too coincidental."

"One day, I want you two guys to meet another friend of mine, a retired general in the U.S. Army. If I've heard him say it once, I've heard it a thousand times: 'there are no coincidences,'" Mason said.

"The environmentalists are operatives of the powerful group that calls themselves the Illuminati. Evidence is mounting that they may have sabotaged the British Petroleum rig in the gulf, creating a disaster that would help them stop oil drilling in and around America, making us more dependent on the people who they already control—OPEC," Gabriel said.

"Do you know these things to be true?" Mason asked.

"I do," Gabriel replied. "The Clintons' activities have been clearly documented. When they were young, Bill and Hillary were all wrapped up in the Hippie movement and influenced by the same people who now control the environmentalists and PETA. They are the same powerful families who are promoting Global Warming, using all colors of propaganda. A lot of questions about the past two Democrat Administrations, as well as the candidate who ran against George W. Bush in 2004 remain to be answered."

"Speaking of questions," Dale interrupted. "What about the eligibility of the current President to serve? His original birth certificate has not been produced. The one that he and his supporters have produced is not authentic. To the 'invisible empire,' truth is whatever it needs to be."

Gabriel nodded and continued. "Hundreds of private e-mails and documents obtained from a computer server at a British university caused a stir among global warming skeptics in 2009. The cyberspace conversations show that climate scientists conspired to overstate the case for a human influence on climate change. Some e-mails exposed their plans to discredit scientists who questioned the global warming conspiracy by challenging the veracity of the skeptics' credentials and research. That tactic is known in Illuminati circles as The Rothschild Formula: 'eliminate any obstruction by all means necessary.' It is how the Shadow Government works. They bend rules and ruthlessly go after the reputations of anyone who stands in their way. I can't say much more about it right now. I'm still gathering data. But, clearly, there is a greater agenda afloat that meets the eye. Dale knows what I'm talking about, I bet," Gabriel added.

Dale nodded in agreement and said, "This much I can tell you, Mason. "Long before Al-Qaeda, America's enemies had worked their way into every phase of American life—government and the court system, effectively opening its borders to anyone who wanted in, anyone, that is, who could be used for their cause. They have flooded the U.S. military with people who they think will side with them when the next 'civil war' occurs. It has been a well-thought-out and ingenuously executed plan, a plan that has worked. Divide and conquer.

"It's a proven strategy of war," Gabriel pointed out. "Those who are out to destroy our way of life have used every conceivable opportunity to create division among Americans, setting the stage for civil unrest within our borders and painting the U.S. as the 'problem' to other nations, even though we have emptied our treasury to provide aid to those who hate us."

"Amen to that," Dale said. "The Marshall Plan rebuilt Europe and Japan with American taxpayer dollars. And billions of aid has gone to African nations and other third world countries, now controlled by warlords who despise us."

"Many of the same people who have drained our treasury over the years are behind the current state of the American economy and the nationalization of industry and healthcare, aren't they?" Mason asked.

"They are. And that's where it gets a bit complicated," Gabriel answered. "It will take a lot longer than I have today to answer that question. And, I'm only going to give you two guys the big picture. Some of these things I learned when I was involved in military intelligence."

"All of us have seen the world change during our lifetimes. When I was a child, our greatest fear was that the Soviet Union would rain intercontinental ballistic missiles down on us and wipe us off the face of the earth," Mason added.

"In those days, the Illuminati or Invisible Empire created an enemy that would serve their purpose," Gabriel answered. "Keep in mind that chaos is the Illuminati's greatest weapon. The Soviet Union collapsed not because of a military campaign, but the Illuminati realized that the USSR had served its purpose. The economy was in shambles throughout the Soviet bloc. And Moscow couldn't keep up with the arms race going on between it and the North Atlantic Treaty Organization. The Illuminati stopped funding the Soviets and the U.S.S.R. collapsed. Then the Illuminati found another ally that wouldn't require nearly as much capital: Radical Islam. In the process, the Russian 'Bear' was not destroyed. It was simply placed into a state of hibernation. Remember what I said earlier. Fabian-styled socialism is very patient. Its architects plan farther ahead than most Americans think."

Mason interrupted, "When NASA announced that it would no longer access the International Space Station with its own shuttles and that all future trips to the station would be aboard Russian shuttles, I could see the handwriting on the wall. Ronald Reagan must have turned over in his grave. The space station is an important strategic outpost. If this has been a part of the Illuminati's long-range plan, no wonder they chose not to compete with the U.S. Without firing a single shot, this Administration gave them control of the most important outer space offensive and defensive weapon in the history of the world. It pains me to think that, while Americans have worked to build a way of life for ourselves and children, our politicians have been outmaneuvered in the global and universal arenas."

"That's the way the Illuminati work," Gabriel responded. "They are masters at figuring out how they are going to take what belongs to others and use it for their own good and they don't care who gets hurt in the process. A moment ago, Mason, you referred to how the Soviet Union suddenly decided to change its policies on the world stage. That didn't just happen. It was carefully orchestrated. At the Shadow Government's instructions, the communists stepped aside and let West Berliners tear down the Wall, as President Reagan suggested in the most emphatic manner he could. It was a clever tactical move. In appearing weak, they were taking a step away from the front line and letting others do their bidding. Tearing down the wall was a symbol of lifting the Iron Curtain and inviting people on both sides of the Curtain to come and go as they wished. By doing so, the Illuminati could encourage 'investors,' meaning U.S. taxpayers, to come into Russia to help them rebuild, buying the loyalty of communist leaders. What has never been revealed is that the Russian Mafia is the real winner. And, that's okay with the Illuminati. They use the Mafia throughout the world."

"Now, that you explain it that way, the plan promoted by the Illuminati's Soviet puppet, Mikhail Gorbachev, in the late eighties—the one called Perestroika—takes on a different meaning," Mason interjected.

"It was a masterfully created charade," Gabriel replied. "By telling the world that *they*—the Soviets—had decided to 'restructure' their government and economy, world attention could be shifted elsewhere, to the newly created chaos generator, radical Islam.

"It certainly appeared that billions of dollars were injected into the Russian economy and that Russia and Iran have developed a cozy relationship," Dale chimed in.

"Perestroika was a clever 'stimulus' campaign, financed by outsiders, many of whom were former enemies of the Soviet Union. It's an old tactic: use other people's money to do one's bidding. Make it appear profitable for people and corporations to invest money and resources that the Shadow Government intended to confiscate at a later date," Gabriel said. "Trillions of dollars of aid from the U.S. and our allies were poured into the Russian economy and emissary military. Much of it found its way into Iran—the newly created enemy of capitalism on the world stage. The "powers that be" concluded that radical Islam was a much more effective way to infiltrate and destroy capitalism than communism ever was. The Soviet warriors were not anxious to die. Islamic radicals look upon such a death as a ticket to heaven. Human beings have always been more loyal to religion than politics, sometimes blindly so."

"So you think that a lot of the 2009 stimulus package ended up in Russia," Mason interjected.

"Hard to tell yet, but I suspect much of it did," Gabriel replied. "Russia seems to be involved in a 'money laundering' scam. They are creating an army for hire, ready to participate in any revolution that needs them and is willing to pay a price. Much of the foreign aid given by the U.S. and its allies has found its way into Iran, Iraq, and Palestine, including a lot of what was meant for Haiti following the massive earthquake that wiped out a lot of their infrastructure. The rest of it found its way into Switzerland and the Cayman Islands, in secret accounts and to buy off politicians and warlords in the U.S. and third world countries, ensuring their vote in the United Nations. And, the current Administration in Washington appears to be part of the conspiracy."

"I am convinced that Gabriel is right," Mason said. "It would be interesting to track the money that British Petroleum was forced to put into a so-called escrow account for the Gulf disaster and see how much of it was actually used for the intended purpose. The U.N. has not always had America's best interest at heart. Slowly, but surely, the UN is becoming the framework for a 'one-world government, financed by U.S. tax-payer dollars.'"

"They are close to having everything in place," Gabriel replied. "The financial crisis in the United States and the spending spree that is fueling the fires of economic collapse is intended to bring this country to its knees. This whole economic crisis is being orchestrated. Who has bought much of our debt?" Gabriel asked, looking at both Mason and Dale.

"China," Mason answered.

"Precisely. China." Gabriel answered. "I once heard it said that whoever controls debt controls everything. And, what form of government does China have? Communism, the same as Russia. And who controls the communists? The Illuminati. By creating the massive debt that the U.S. has mounted under the current Administration, and the fact that China controls much of the U.S. debt, it could mean that whoever is pulling China's strings controls the destiny of the United States. And the puppet masters are the thirteen families who rule the world, the Annunaki descendants who call themselves the Illuminati."

"And we are so distracted with Iraq, Iran, Afghanistan, and the oil crisis in the Gulf of Mexico that we lose sight of the Chinese agenda," Mason inserted.

"Precisely," Gabriel replied. "That's how they work. From my sources, it appears that China is about to make a move on acquiring controlling interest in British Petroleum."

"It's no wonder there wasn't any rush to plug the well by this Administration or to accept help from the seventeen nations who offered it. If BP stock and public opinion plummet, a Chinese takeover would be better accepted by the world," Mason interjected."

"Absolutely," Gabriel replied. "While the Russians and Chinese don't like each other very much they like wealth and power. Long ago the Shadow Government convinced the communists that they have a common enemy, capitalism," Gabriel said. "And how do you destroy capitalism? You create massive debt, interject distractions, nationalize as much of the free market as possible, and bring down capitalism. Who in today's world is the paradigm of free enterprise? Who is the remaining bastion of democracy and capitalism?" he asked.

"The United States of America," Dale answered. The look on his face said that he was adding things up. "That explains a lot of things."

"And, there's another part to the global puzzle that the average American doesn't know. Do you know who controls the Panama Canal, the only intra-continental waterway connecting the flow of goods between the Atlantic and Pacific Ocean?" Gabriel asked.

"Panama does, doesn't it? The Carter Administration gave it to them as its first act of business in the nineteen seventies," Dale answered.

"That's just part of the deal. We also gave Panama tens of millions of dollars a year to maintain it," Gabriel answered. "However, the Panamanians turned around and leased the canal to China. That's how 'One World Order' politicians work. They take money from taxpayers and distribute it among themselves and the people and governments they purchase. This group of so-called 'intellectually elite' has intentionally screwed up the United States' ability to control its own destiny in the world. Though Jimmy Carter was not one of the Inner Circle, he was a Trilateralist, a third-tier Illuminati organization. Carter was simply carrying out the orders he received from Belgium," Gabriel explained. "He received his marching orders from the American member of the Inner Circle at the time, David Rockefeller. Through China, the Illuminati control the world-wonder waterway that the U.S. built to protect its trade routes. Once again, the Shadow Government outsmarted the American people, and we were oblivious to their actions, because the mainstream media was and is in bed with them.

"My own experience in such matters tells me that the other part of the puzzle that so many Americans haven't yet figured out, including some of our well-meaning politicians, is that our enemies live by the rule: the enemy of my enemy is my friend,'" Dale said.

"I thought that phrase was attributed to the Mafia," Mason declared.

"Remember what I said earlier, that the Illuminati use the Mafia. The statement to which you referred is an old axiom, going back to Machiavellian politics," Gabriel declared. "Machiavelli's principles arose from Annunaki documents that were the precursors to the *Protocols of the Learned Elders of Zion*."

"And, to social deconstructionists, distraction is a part of warfare. When attention is diverted away from a cancer or an uncontrolled infection it grows until it consumes the person. The same applies to a society," Dale added.

"I am duly impressed," Mason said admiringly. "You two guys are an incredible tandem, playing off each other's lead. It was better than a Bill O'Reilly and Glenn Beck show. Though I was familiar with some of what y'all have bandied back and forth, I didn't know a lot of the details."

Once again, the veranda door opened and Norene stuck her head out, asking, "Do you guys need anything. You've been out here for more than an hour. Would you like to have anything to eat? I have some great tasting breakfast protein bars."

"That sounds great," Mason answered. "And could you bring us another round of coffee?"

"This may be the coffee-drinkingest trio I've ever seen," Norene said.

"When you've spent as much time in the military and in the intelligence community as some of us have, you learn to drink a lot of coffee," Dale answered.

"No problem," Norene said. "I'll be right back with coffee and protein bars. Is chocolate and peanut butter okay with everyone?"

"Each of the men nodded.

"Making every effort to constrain himself, Gabriel immediately jumped back into the conversation. "The Shadow Government knows that history is on their side. There is a natural progression in the life of a capitalistic society." He reached for the wallet he carried in his left hip pocket and pulled out a laminated card. "I have carried this card with me for years. It contains what some have called *The Law of Alexander Tyler*, a Scottish history professor at the University of Edinburgh in the seventeen hundreds. He said, "A democracy is always temporary in nature: it simply cannot exist as a permanent form of government."

Mason interrupted, "Now, I do know about that. And with respect to the United States as it exists today, Tyler's Law is not very encouraging. Do you think that Nostradamus was prophesying or revealing the written plans of the precursors of The Illuminati?" Mason asked, waiting for either of his two friends to answer.

"It is clear that Nostradamus had unusual insight," Gabriel answered. "Though he was born a Jew, his family was forced to convert to Christianity during the Spanish Inquisition. As a child, he was taught the canons of Judaism and Kabbalah by his grandfather, who would have been familiar with the advice received from the Grand Sanhedrin (elders of Zion) to the Jewish people's plea for advice on how to deal with the Spanish Inquisition. One would have to assume that Nostradamus' grandfather would have shared the Elders' advice with his grandson. It is highly possible that Nostradamus was sharing what he had learned of the plan received by the chief rabbi of Spain about the time that Columbus set sail for America. It appears that a plan conceived strictly to assist Jews in Spain was confiscated by Adam Weishaupt and a group of power-hungry mercenaries who saw it as a way to take over the world, and that hidden in the lines of his quatrains Nostradamus was trying to warn future generations about the sinister plans of a self-anointed elite and the consequences of their intentions."

"I have read that many dictators, including Napoleon and Hitler, were familiar with Nostradamus' works and felt as though it was their destiny to act out the course of history that had been described, and that Adam Weishaupt, founder of the Order of the Illuminati, was a student of Nostradamus," Mason contributed.

"Man, the History Channel should have been here. This would make a great television series. You have done your homework," Gabriel commented. "The connections are quite obvious to the student of history willing to look not only at the lines, but between them, and connect the dots."

"I'm curious. Who were Alexander Tyler's mentors?" Dale asked, "If you know."

"I do," Gabriel answered. "But, at this time, I can't recall their names. However, Tyler was a Scottish history professor in the seventeen hundreds. He was considered an expert on the Greek and Roman Empires and is famous for the following statement." Gabriel read from the card he had retrieved from his wallet: "A democracy will continue to exist up until the time that voters discover that they can vote themselves generous gifts from the public treasury. From that moment on, the majority always votes for the candidates who promise the most benefits from the public treasury, with the result that every democracy will finally collapse over loose fiscal policy, (which is) always followed by a dictatorship."

"I thought we had put the Tyler connection to rest," Dale injected.

"We touched a bit on it," Mason said. "However, I want to make sure that we are all on the same page. Let's review it again. Collapse is what the Illuminati are encouraging and are counting on. Isn't it, Gabriel?" Mason asked.

"It is. "But how long *this* democracy lasts is really up to the American people. We have a chance to prove *Tyler's Law* wrong. We have a chance to replace socialistic-leaning public officials with conservative ones who understand that taking from Peter to pay Paul is a sure formula for disaster."

"That seems to accurately describe what is happening to the United States," Dale remarked. "I think it was former British Prime Minister, Margaret Thatcher, who said, 'Sooner or later, you run out of other people's money.'"

"Yeah, and with what is happening in the European Union with its economy and growth of radical Islam, these days, you hear or read Mrs. Thatcher's advice a lot," Mason told the other two. "I carry the statement to which you just eluded right here in this little notebook in my right hip pocket," he added, patting that region of his trousers. "Like Gabriel, I carry words of wisdom with me that I have learned from others for quick reference when needed."

"Well, let me read the rest of the card that I carry with me," Gabriel added, "Listen to the rest of Tyler's Law." He read: 'the average age of the world's greatest civilizations from the beginning of history, has been about two hundred years. During those two hundred years, those nations always progressed through a predictable sequence: from bondage to spiritual faith; to great courage; to liberty; to abundance; to complacency; to apathy; to dependence; and, back to bondage."

"It seems like the three of us are preaching to the choir," Dale interrupted. "We are all saying the same thing. America is in trouble. The question that we need to address is: what do we do, what can we do?"

Gabriel answered, "I think that this was a healthy conversation, like reviewing one final time the game plan before a football game or before meeting the enemy on the battlefield. We needed to vent and make sure that we are all in agreement with what has brought us to this point."

Mason responded by using a medical metaphor, "Saving America is no different than saving a patient with an infection. The right diagnosis has to be made. The right treatment has to be offered. The sick patient must accept the side effects of the treatment. The treatment has to be carried through aggressively until every infecting organism or pathogen is destroyed. And, finally, a close check needs to be kept to see that if any signs of infection recur they must be treated immediately and aggressively. That's how one cures any potentially lethal malady. And, that's how we Americans can defy Tyler's Cycle of Democracies."

"But doctors aren't in control of the White House and Congress," Dale said.

"Exactly!" Mason replied. "One of America's problems is that too many lawyers are running the show in Washington. After I was sued for malpractice when none was committed, I decided to attend night school and get a law degree. When I was in Law School, we were taught the adversarial system, to argue both sides of the issue. We were taught that it is not up to the lawyers to determine 'right' or 'wrong.' That responsibility is left up to the judge or jury, as the case may be."

"Well, as I see it, Washington has it wrong again. The politicians should be debating the issues and let the people be the judge and jury." Dale interjected.

"That's the way it works, only the people only get to vote every two years. Congress could vote every two hours on something that would take years to undo," Gabriel added.

"In Medical School, we were taught a different system: that there is only one 'right' diagnosis and that all other diagnoses are 'wrong.' As a physician, one's role is to be both the judge and the jury, to address the disease and make the patient well again."

Dale responded to Mason's explanation by saying, "I wonder what would happen if we had more doctors in Washington?"

Mason replied, "In some respects, things might be a lot better. I've heard many of my medical colleagues say that they are considering running for political office. And the benefits and workload are a whole lot better than practicing medicine under the new healthcare bill. A congressman's pay is higher than the average income of doctors. There are more perks and benefits, shorter work days, more vacation days, better health benefits for them and their families, and an incredible retirement plan."

"You mean members of Congress don't have to use the same plans they imposed on the rest of Americans?" Dale asked.

"If they had been forced to use nationalized healthcare or live on social security following retirement, they wouldn't have been so eager to impose them on us," Mason replied. "These are the kinds of things that the American people deserve to know and be reminded of often. Keep in mind that so-called 'healthcare reform' is not at all about care; it is about control. It's the biggest step in Orwellian politics, a form of governance in which 'Big Brother' calls all the shots. And, that's the message we have to have the American people understand."

"Can I get a copy of that card you were reading from earlier, Gabriel?" Dale asked.

"Yeah, sure," Gabriel added, "And remember that America's enemies are as familiar with *Tyler's Law* as we are. Global slave masters have systematically supported people and programs committed to ensuring that the United States, Israel and other Capitalist countries follow the Greek and Roman Empires to the graveyards of history. They are out to pave America and Israel's way back to bondage."

"Dale, "Mason said, "It is sad that Americans can't see what is happening. They are blinded by empty promises and hopeful rhetoric. However, I think Prime Minister Netanyahu and many Israeli leaders have long seen the Illuminati's plan to destroy capitalism and governments committed to self-determination. Gabriel and I have discussed this on many occasions and are convinced that there's a clandestine agenda behind the things happening today in America, as well as in Israel. As a child, I remember hearing the phrase, 'As General Motors goes, so goes the nation.'

"Yeah, Dale interrupted. "And we know how GM went. General Motors has now become Government Motors. Do you know who owns much of the wealth that once was America's?"

"OPEC, the Illuminati's worldwide collection service," Gabriel answered, before Mason could answer.

"Right! The shift of debt, money, prosperity, and poverty is also being orchestrated by America's enemies, 'foreign and domestic.' Many of the people who are running the U.S. government are on the take, bought like prostitutes by those who have pledged to destroy us and our way of life," Dale said. "A closer look at what was couched as an oil shortage during the Carter administration was no shortage. It was an intentional embargo orchestrated by powerful members of the Shadow Government intended to drive out the smaller independent oil companies so that the big five could control the gasoline and oil industry in America. That's what is happening to banking today."

"So the Doc has made the right diagnosis," Gabriel said. "The question is: can the patient—the United States of America—be saved? What remedies are available? Which ones would you recommend?"

"That's what the three of us have to explore," Mason replied. "We've done a lot of airing for the last hour or so. Now it's time to put on the gear and get to work. We're up against some very powerful individuals and organizations, gentlemen. And many of the American people are clueless. The uninformed are being led like sheep to the slaughter. Is there anybody powerful enough and strong-willed enough to save this country and the free world?"

"Here we are," Norene said, "coming through the door with a tray loaded with chocolate and peanut butter protein bars and a thermos of coffee.

"Thanks, Hun," Mason said.

"You're the perfect hostess, Ma'am," Gabriel added.

"If you keep spoiling me like this, I'll be back every week," Dale said.

"You guys don't scare me with your threats. But, I wouldn't want to get on your bad side. I pity those who do," Norene said, setting the tray on the table and returning to her inside duties.

"Where were we?" Mason asked.

"You were talking about the need to inform the American people about some of the things that we know and who would be powerful enough to withstand the wrath of the Rothschild Formula," Dale replied.

"I don't know about the powerful enough part of it, but I can speak for the strong-willed part," Gabriel replied, peeling the wrapper off a chocolate protein bar and taking a bite. "I have been trained as a soldier, how to survive when survival seems uncertain. I've been involved in many situations where drastic measures were called for. When I entered the military, I took an oath to defend this country against its enemies. The way I see it, some of its enemies are some of its so-called leaders, pretending to fly the flag of the United States—while within their hearts—plotting to topple it by whatever means necessary. The Trojan horse is rolling into every major city in the U.S. Only today it's called by different names and abbreviations: stimulus package, ACORN, SEUI, PETA, GREEN PEACE, to name a few. If you two guys are with me, I'm willing to see if I can get a shot at Achilles' heel. You know what you told me about your investigation into the billions of dollars that had gone missing, when it was supposed to be used to build healthcare facilities for veterans," Gabriel said, looking at Mason. "As a vet, I take that personally. Gentlemen, there is one thing that you must never forget about the human race. Greed and power are inseparable traits. There is one thing that you must understand about the thing that underlies greed and power: *money.* Wealth does not vanish. It simply changes shape and hoarders. If the money was there it can be traced. There is another possibility. Perhaps, the money was never there."

"*Never there?*" Dale blurted out.

"Never there," Gabriel replied. "It is highly possible that this whole stimulus thing is a sham. Like the oil embargo in the nineteen seventies and the swine flu scare of 2009, It is possible that both the crisis and the solution were created to make it *appear* as though America was in trouble in order to destabilize the economy, push social construction programs through, and allow a very powerful group of men and women around the world to gain control of people's lives and the free enterprise system. At some future date—when the globalist have taken charge—the money might be suddenly dumped back into circulation, making it look as though they solved the crisis. These kinds of artificial 'recoveries' generally occur around the times that their people are in office. I may know how we can get to the root of this and expose the perpetrators."

"This is all about trust and betrayal," Mason said. "We have all taken oaths to uphold the Constitution and the codes of our professions. Each of us has a military background. You guys much more than me, but let's give our operation an appropriate name."

"What is it that you doctors call the emergency when you are called to revive a patient who is dying?" Gabriel asked.

"Code Blue," Mason answered.

"That may be a bit obvious," Gabriel replied. "What about something less obvious, like *'Operation Annuit Coeptis?'*"

"Aren't those words imprinted on the dollar bill?" Dale asked.

"Then that's perfect," Dale responded. "Let's hope that Providence will favor our attempts to bring America back from—what did you call it, Mason—a near-death experience? What do you think?"

"I'm in." Gabriel replied.

"Me, too," Mason added.

"Give me a day or so to sort out my thoughts and I'll be back with you," Gabriel said. "Now, if you will excuse me, I have a war to fight."

Gabriel shook the hands of the other two members of his lean and mean covert army, grabbed a handful of protein bars from the tray on the table before him, took a huge gulp of coffee, and left.

"Do you realize what we just did?" Dale asked his friend, the doctor.

"I think we just made a deal to join a soldier in the biggest battle of his life." Mason answered. "You know, when he said he took an oath to defend America against all enemies, I couldn't help but think of the oaths we both took, too. In many ways they all say the same thing; we swear to do the *right* thing, whatever the cost. In that respect we are all soldiers. We simply use different weapons and tactics. And, although we may come at the enemy from different directions, the mission is the same, to see that *good* prevails and that *might* is used for *right.*"

"You're beginning to sound a bit like a preacher," Dale said to his friend.

"Yeah, at one time, I thought about going into the ministry."

"What haven't you thought about trying," Dale asked.

"Right now, I'm trying to keep things in perspective," Mason answered. "We not only have to be committed, we have to be smart. I often think about the prayer that my grandmother told me was adopted by people trying to kick an addiction. You know the one that says, 'God grant me the serenity to accept the things I cannot change; the courage to change the things I can; and the wisdom to know the difference.'"

"You know that there is a lot more to that prayer than just the sentence you just quoted, don't you?" Dale asked.

"No, I thought that was all of it," Mason replied.

"I'll get the rest of it for you," Dale said, making a note on the legal pad he had in his lap.

Reaching his right hand behind his back to stroke the little notebook in his hip pocket, Mason added, "I think that's where we are here. We have to look at the wisdom contained in the prayer—determine what we *can* change and what we can't. None of us who met here today likes the taste of failure."

"What was it that you called President Padgett when we talked a few days ago?" Mason asked.

"Liar-in-Chief," Dale replied.

"Well, there is a Bible story in which a small boy with a slingshot defeated a giant with a sword," Dale replied. "Perhaps, as God guided the mind and hands of the boy who would be king, he will see fit to favor our undertaking to reveal the truth."

CHAPTER 16

Later that evening Mason went into his study and pulled down from the shelves the Military Code book that had been given to him in his earlier years. He wanted to review the oath that he took upon becoming an officer in the ROTC and later in the National Guard. Gabriel's comment about the oath taken by a soldier had stirred his interest. He wondered how it compared to that of a physician and attorney. He opened the book and began to read:

> "I, _____, do solemnly swear (or affirm) that I will support and defend the Constitution of the United States against all enemies, foreign and domestic; that I will bear true faith and allegiance to the same; and that I will obey the orders of the President of the United States and the orders of the officers appointed over me, according to regulations and the Uniform Code of Military Justice."

He read the oath over and again, dissecting every word: "... to defend the Constitution ... against all enemies, foreign and *domestic* ..." and ... "*obey the orders of the President* of the United States. ..."

"What if it was determined that the President had betrayed his oath to defend the Constitution and the Republic for which it stands?" Mason asked himself. This would present a conflict of interest, a violation of Constitutional law. The President could not serve two masters: the Constitution *and* the enemy of the Constitution. Mason recalled a statement written by the President in one of his books, to "... stand with the Muslims should the political winds shift in an ugly direction." Radical Muslims were self-professed enemies of the United States, planning and conducting mass genocide with acts of terror throughout the land. Clearly, the winds were changing. Was President Padgett siding with the radical Muslims? It was a question that deserved an answer.

Mason began to reflect on the meetings of the Cabinet that he had attended and the people with whom the President was associating. He knew more about many of them than they imagined. Mason had done his homework. He was "prepared." Or so he thought.

From comments made by President Padgett and members of his Cabinet and from what he had previously learned and observed, Mason was becoming increasingly convinced that these people didn't intend to live to the oaths they had taken when assuming their offices. They didn't love America, at least not a free, safe, and prosperous America. In fact, Mark Hyman's article in the November 2009 edition of *The American Spectator* had pointed to a number of statements and actions that would lead one to believe that members of the present Administration despised the United States, blaming it for the world's ills.

Mason opened the bottom right file drawer of his desk and retrieved the copy of Hyman's article that he had filed away for future reference several months before. As he read the words, it was apparent that the author had chronicled a long series of events, comments and writings that affirmed his opinion, that the President carried an animosity for the United States and its policies, consistently pandering to Americas' professed enemies while shunning its allies. He even suggested that the Veterans Affairs administration no longer provide medical care for America's servicemen and women, leaving them to be responsible for the injuries they incurred while fighting to defend their country.

The article mentioned a string of anti-American individuals with whom the President had associated as a young man and whom he had appointed into Cabinet and "czar" positions after he took the oath of office.

In a television interview, President Padgett had asked the American people to judge him by the people with whom he surrounded himself. The article mentioned a string of professed anti-American individuals with whom the President had associated during his life, as well as those he had appointed to Cabinet positions and as czars *after* he took the oath of office.

Hyman's article was stirring; pointing out that the President had a lifetime of comments and actions that revealed his real attitude toward the U.S. and to his native religion, Islam. It was baffling that he could have been elected President of a Judeo-Christian-based nation after promising that he would side with Muslims in a time of conflict and crisis.

Laying the article on his desk, Mason got out of his chair, opened the door to his study, and walked out on the terrace, gazing into the nighttime sky. He could hear the mating calls of Whip-0-Wils in the distance and the symphony being played out by different species of frogs in the lake just beyond the charcoal-colored wooden fence that surround the pasture where he could see his horses grazing in the moonlight.

In this open air sanctuary, he had often found answers to perplexing problems. Knowing that on the opposite side of the moon's face the landscape was always dark provided a clue. People, can be two-faced, too, presenting one to observers, while at the same time concealing a darker side.

Mason could see why he had been treated as an outsider at the most recent Cabinet meeting and how he was being used as window dressing by the President and the overlords who were pulling President Padgett's strings.

Mason's thoughts were interrupted by the ringing of the telephone. Heading inside, he said to himself, "Who in the world would be calling at this time of night? It's 10:30." He lifted the receiver to his ear and uttered, "Hello," as though he had been awakened from sleep.

"Mason, is that you?" the voice on the other end of the call asked. The doctor recognized the voice. It belonged to the man who was already weighing heavily on his mind.

"Yes sir, Mr. President," he replied, clearing his throat as though he had been sleeping.

"I'm sorry to call so late, but I wanted to wait until everyone around here had gone to bed. It's 11:30 in Washington. What time is it there?"

"It's 10:30, sir, we are on central time."

"Were you asleep?"

"I had dozed off."

"Listen, Mason," President Padgett began. "I just wanted to check with you and see how your research is coming. Have you found what you are looking for—you know, the kinds of things that you said might be responsible for why my healthcare plan isn't meeting the expectations that I promised?"

Mason had a sneaking suspicion that the President was trying to find out how much he had learned. Still trying to act as though he was not fully awake, Dr. Edmonds said, again clearing his throat, "I've learned that this might be more complicated than I first thought. I have some credible leads but I'm not yet prepared to point any fingers."

"Can you tell me what you have learned?" the President asked, "We are on a secure line. I'm in my study, adjacent the Oval Office. It's the one you used when you called the man from the FBI that you have chosen as your security detail. All communication devices here in this area are secure. I've had the best minds in my Administration see to it."

"I understand, Mr. President. You might not like what I uncover, sir. Did you ever think of that? You didn't like my suggestions during the Cabinet meeting. Neither did most of your Cabinet."

"Don't let that concern you. I want to know everything you know," the President said. "I *need* to know everything you know."

"Yes sir. You will. I assure you that you will."

"Keep in touch, Mr. Secretary," the President said. "Good night. Oh, and one thing more. When will you be coming back from your leave of absence?"

"When I have the information that I am seeking, Mr. President. Good night, Mr. President," Mason replied, hanging up the receiver. For a while, he had forgotten that he still held the title of Secretary of Health and Human Services.

"Who was that, calling at this time of the night?" Norene asked, opening the door to Mason's study.

"It was Padgett."

"What in the world did he want?" Norene asked.

"I guess he's burning the midnight oil, too. I can tell from his voice that he is not his usually confident self. He's concerned about what I might learn about him and some of his people. I'm dealing with a clever man. He didn't get where he is without the ability to fool a lot of people. Now he is playing games with me, pretending that he wants to know what he already knows. What he wants to know is how much of what *he* knows, do *I know*," Mason said. "Every day, I become more convinced that he is a worried man, trying to cover his tracks. Political winds do sometimes blow in an unpredictable and ugly direction."

"I've heard that last statement of yours somewhere," Norene said. "But it's too late for me to think about that right now. And, you can't untangle this web tonight, my dear. Come to bed. Tomorrow's another day."

"I'll be there soon. Even if I laid my head on a pillow right now, there is no way that I could sleep. I've got to think through this situation. A lot is riding on these next few weeks."

"Have you learned more than you knew when you decided to take a leave of absence?"

"I don't know that I have learned more, but a lot more questions came to light while Dale and Gabriel were here. We got it all out. Each of us was surprised to learn how much we thought alike. You go on to bed. We'll talk in the morning."

"You won't stay up too late, will you?" Norene asked.

"No. I promise. Good night."

"Good night," she said and closed the door.

Mason went to the internet and pulled up the Constitution of the United States. He remembered that when in law school and studying constitutional law, the professor often repeated the words of a former U.S.

President. In his 1985 inaugural address, President Grover Cleveland said:

> *"He who takes the oath today to preserve, protect, and defend the Constitution of the United States only assumes the solemn obligation which every patriotic citizen ... should share with him. The Constitution, which prescribes this oath, my countrymen, is yours; the government you have chosen him (Cleveland) to administer for a time is yours."*

Professor Milton Cohn opened and closed every class on constitutional law with the words: "The Constitution which prescribes the oath you will take on the day that you are admitted to the bar, my fellow attorneys, is yours to protect and defend . . . for as long as you live."

As much as Cohn's admonitions meant to Mason as a law student, they were never as cogent to him as today. Much of what once belonged to the American people had been taken from them. If the money had been stolen, the thieves were guilty of larceny. If the money had never been appropriated and the government had confiscated the banking, automobile, insurance, and healthcare industry as part of a fraud, the statute of frauds also applied. If the former HHS Secretary's death was an assassination, criminal proceedings would need to be explored. With any or all of these felonies, impeachment proceedings should be initiated.

It had been a while since Mason had called upon the insights he had learned during law school. Perhaps, he had finally found a way for his two professional degrees to come together. Recalling the story of Dr. Jekyll and Mr. Hyde and having concluded that *Doctor* Edmonds should consult with *Attorney* Edmonds, he put his best diagnostic skills to work, researching the differential diagnosis of the ills that faced the nation and the alternative methods of treatment that were available to heal America's ills.

Operation Annuit Coeptis was under way. He, Dale, and Gabriel, along with the colleagues they were about to recruit, could only hope that Providence was with them in their undertakings.

. . . .

"Raley, is that you?" Mason said to his old law school classmate when he answered the phone. "This is Mason Edmonds."

"Is this Doctor Edmonds or Attorney Edmonds calling," Raley replied, poking a bit of fun at his old friend, even though not knowing that Mason had been sorting out the same distinction.

"Both," was the answer. "I have a situation that I need to bounce off someone I can trust. I figure if I hire you as my lawyer, the attorney/client privilege statute will prevent you from sharing the nature and content of our conversation with anyone else. Is that right?"

"You did learn something in law school, Doc," Raley Stovall said. "And, by the way, I've followed your advice. About half of my practice involves suing incompetent lawyers and accountants. It's almost as good as if I owned a money-printing factory—you know, like the U.S. Government has."

"That answers one question before I ask it," Mason said. "I have a situation in which there might be a whole slew of lawyers and accountant types that we may want to bring both civil and criminal actions against."

"I can help you with the civil part," Raley answered. "We'll have to get someone else to handle the criminal part."

"I understand," Mason replied. "This thing is too big to discuss over the phone. When and where can we meet?"

"Well, I'm in Capitol City, where are you, now?"

"I'm at my ranch." Mason answered. "I'd really like for you to come here so that I can get you to meet with some of the other people working on this project with me. I can't afford to let anyone see us together. My ranch is a secure setting. You can't see our house from the road. We can meet in absolute privacy."

"This must be something *big*," Raley said.

"It is, really big." Mason replied. "Raley, don't tell anyone that you are coming here to meet with me. Find an excuse to come to the coast for a day or so. How about Saturday morning? Do you work on Saturdays? I know how you lawyers are," Mason said poking some fun back at his former classmate.

"Well, some of us work on Saturdays," Raley answered. "What time do you want me there?"

"It should take about three hours for you to drive here. So, why don't we meet about eleven o'clock? I'll pick up a quart of gumbo and some sandwiches so that we can work through lunch and into the afternoon. You can sleep over on Saturday night, here in the house with us. We have plenty of room."

"I usually command a suite," Raley said, jokingly.

"Then, a suite you'll have," Mason said, playing along with his friend.

"That sounds good. It will be good to see you again, Mason. I heard about your taking some time off as the HHS Secretary. Does this have anything to do with that?"

"Let's wait until we are face to face to ask or answer any more questions."

"You're the client, Doc," Raley answered. "That means you're the boss, too. I'll see you Saturday. And tell Norene that I'm looking forward to seeing her again."

Before he let Raley go, Mason affirmed, "Remember, attorney/client privilege. I've just hired you as my lawyer. So, no discussions with anybody about where you are going or with whom you are meeting. Agreed?"

"Agreed," Raley replied.

"As soon as we get off the phone, I'm dropping a check in the mail to you. Then, we have a contract—you know, offer, acceptance, and consideration. You are hired. Will three hundred dollars cover the cost of this conversation, counselor?"

"It will—today," Raley answered in jest. "We're running a special for doctors with law degrees. Former classmates get an extra ten percent off. I'm impressed that you remembered the tenets of contract law. Just joking, Mason."

"I know you are. But we're about to get into some serious matters. I hope that after we do we will still be able to laugh. The check is in the mail. I'll see you Saturday, counselor."

. . . .

"Come in, Raley," Mason greeted his friend at the front door. "The other two people are already here."

"I brought my briefcase and lots of legal pads and pens. I didn't know how much we had to talk about," Raley, who always tried to inject a bit of levity into a tense situation, answered.

"You didn't bring a tape recorder, did you?" Mason asked.

"No, should I have?"

"No. This will be a meeting that we do not want recorded. It might cost us our lives."

"I'm getting more nervous about all this by the moment," Raley joked.

"Raley, meet Agent Dale Jackson with the FBI and Gabriel Shade, former Army intelligence officer. Gentlemen, this is Raley Stovall, a former law school classmate. Don't let his cavalier persona fool you. Behind that devil-may-care façade lies one of the brightest minds I know. He finished first in our law school class."

Raley broke in. "What the Doc, here, didn't tell you is that I only beat him by one-tenth of a quality point. He came in a very close second. Imagine what he could have done if he wasn't practicing medicine during the day and taking care of a family."

"Enough of that," Mason said. "Let's get to the reason why I have brought you all here. I have long believed that there were some shenanigans going on in Washington."

"Shenanigans? Washington?" Raley said sarcastically. "Man, is that the most understated description of our nation's capital in the twenty-first century that I've heard."

"Be serious for the next few minutes," Mason scolded.

"I'm sorry," Raley replied. "I apologize. Go ahead."

"The bills coming to the floors of Congress and the decisions being made by the White House seemed to run counter to reason. That is, if one is interested in the long-term survival of the United States", Mason said. "Legislation laid before us is so voluminous that no one has a chance to study the bill's content or the amendments before we are asked to vote on it. In the last year alone, Congress has spent more money, defined by more zeroes, than I can write on a piece of paper. And I think I'm about as smart as any of the other people in Congress. I'm not even sure how many zeros are in a trillion—and neither are my colleagues. The signs and symptoms of fiscal suicide are everywhere. And no one seems to be taking notice."

"Why do you say that?" Raley asked.

"You may have been watching the news. But if you have to ask that question, you may not have been reading between the lin*es*. The government of the United States, in concert with a powerful cartel of globalist, has been bleeding the American people to the brink of death. While it is a sure way to create a feudal system, it's an old and failed way to solve the ills of the people. In the dark ages, doctors cut open the veins of sick patients, believing that ridding the body of bad 'humors' that they believed to be contained in the blood would make the patient well again. Washington has taken up an old and dangerous practice. Spending money this government doesn't have has become just as foolish. Everywhere one looks within the current political system, the seven deadly sins are obvious: gluttony, avarice, greed, discouragement, wrath, envy, and pride. Plus arrogance."

Gabriel interrupted, "I like the idea of bringing in sins against God as well as sins against humanity. It will strengthen our case and win a lot of favor with the American people. But we'll need to define 'pride' as 'national pride,' something other than the kind of pride associated with narcissistic behavior."

"As we begin to draft how we are going to explain all this to the American people, keep in mind that the preamble of the Constitution makes a direct reference to God," Raley added.

"That's a good point. Many of the people running the show in Washington remind me of children whose parents have given in to their errant ways," Dale said.

"Yeah," Mason echoed. "I recall how Ronald Reagan compared government to an infant. He said that government is like a **baby, an alimentary canal** with a big appetite at one end and no sense of responsibility at the other."

"What do you expect?" Gabriel asked. "The American people are not holding its elected officials accountable for their actions. Except for those involved in the Tea Party Movement and the three of us, the people believe that they are helpless. I know that I keep harping on children's stories, but Americans are being led by Pied Pipers who are taking us into the seas of destruction. Right now, if I were a betting man, the way things are going I'd have to place a bet on communism outlasting capitalism. Perhaps Khrushchev had attended an Illuminati Inner Circle meeting, or two. He could have been right. Wow! I never thought I'd let such words come out of my mouth."

"Okay, guys," Raley interrupted. "I think that we can all agree that a problem exists. Now, let's look at our options. Tell me what you know."

Gabriel said, "I'll start. Since I last met with Mason and Dale, I've been able to hack into the computer at the Treasury, the VA system, and the Defense Department. I figured if Chinese teenagers could get into those computers, so could I. You can't believe how easy it was to do so."

"You realize that in breaking into the government's computers, you have broken the law, don't you?" Raley said. "But, we can deal with that later. Continue."

Gabriel complied with Raley Stovall's request. "The contract to install those computers and to encrypt the information they store must have been let to the lowest bidder or some powerful government official's son-in-law. So far, I've learned that a huge chunk of the so-called stimulus packages has in fact been distributed. What I haven't yet been able to determine is where the money went. This much I can say. It did not go where it was intended to go, at least not much of it."

"Where did it go?" Mason asked.

"Can't yet say for sure, but I have learned that there have been a whole bunch of new secret accounts opened up in Swiss and Cayman Island banks within the past two years and that the calls to open the accounts originated from the United States, more specifically from the White House. The Federal Reserve is in up to its ears in this thing. I just haven't yet figured out how they are involved. Swiss banking computers are a bit harder to get into than are our government's, but give me a couple more days. I think I can get in."

"This sounds a bit like bank fraud could be at play," Dale chimed in. "Especially if the money went first into U.S. banks and was transferred out of the country. We see this kind of thing at the FBI frequently. You can bet that whoever is behind this tried to cover their trail. I'll try to get into the FBI computer and find some answers."

"If you have trouble getting in, let me know," Gabriel said. "I might be able to help there, too."

"What?" Dale said in amazement. "Is there any computer that you can't hack into?"

"Haven't found one yet."

"Have you been able to get into the Defense Department's and Department of Veterans Affairs computers yet?" Mason asked Gabriel.

"Yeah, I got in, but some of the budgetary stuff is encrypted with a different code and it is going to take me a while to break the codes."

"I wonder if any of the money that was earmarked for defense may have been confiscated by the politicians in high places." Raley added. "If so, the Joint Chiefs could be interested in this operation—what do you call it, Operation Annuit Coeptis? That's a Latin term, isn't it? Doesn't it mean God is on our side?"

"It is and it does. That's why we chose the name," Mason replied. "America's vital signs are not looking good. We need a miracle to bring it back to a healthy state."

"Gabriel, you move forward on getting the information," Raley said in the most serious of tones yet. "Does any one of you know a general or admiral in the military services?"

"I have a long-time friend who is a general. I thought he had retired, but learned last week that he is still on active duty," Mason answered.

"Great! Contact him and ask how well he knows one of the Joint Chiefs of Staff," Raley said. "I have an idea. Perhaps we can bring the cavalry to the rescue. If Defense money found its way into a secret Swiss or Cayman Island bank account, the Joint Chiefs will be livid. Mason, do you know anyone who served in the JAG corps in the military?"

"Yes, I do. My brother-in-law," Mason replied.

"First, use some of your legal training and look at the rules for court martial. I think that's Section 32 of the Uniform Code of Military Justice. Find out if the Commander-in-Chief of the armed forces is subject to the same laws as those he or she commands," Raley said.

"Where are you going with this?" Dale asked.

"If, as Mason has suspected, the wrongdoing goes as high as the Oval Office, even with the outcomes of the 2010 elections the current makeup of Congress will never initiate impeachment proceedings against this President. On the other hand, if the oath of office of the President as Commander-in-Chief makes him subject to Section 32, the Joint Chiefs could initiate punitive action against him."

"I knew that I had called the right man," Mason said. "You learned a lot suing lawyers and accountants, my friend."

"Well, many of the people in Washington are lawyers who use accountants to shuffle the money around so that no one can find it. So, in many respects, this challenge is just a little bigger, and might I say more risky, than some of the other cases I've handled against our brethren of the bar," Raley added.

"I know a bit about court martial proceedings," Gabriel said. "When I was in the Army, one of the colonels in the quartermaster corps that provided supplies for my unit was thought to be selling supplies meant for the troops on the black market, instead. He was subjected to court martial proceedings and I was called as a witness."

"That helps," Raley said. "But we need to do our homework and explore all options. If we find out that the taxpayers' money has ended up in secret accounts of the politicians, we will have to use any and all measures available to us, on behalf of the American people. Is there anything else we need to discuss today?"

"No, I think that we accomplished a lot in a short time. We don't need to sit around and talk. We need to get to work," Gabriel said. "And, I'm already on it," he said, closing down his laptop. While you were talking just now, I was able to break the code into the Department of Veterans Affairs in Washington. By tomorrow evening, I'll have some of the information we need and call each of you to let you know what I found. Because of the way telephones work today and how easy it is intercept conversations, I'll just say, 'I found the key that I was looking for. It was in my back pocket.' If I haven't found what we need, I'll say, 'I'm still looking for the key I lost.'"

"Gabriel, how should we communicate with each other?" Mason asked.

"As little as possible," Gabriel answered. Let's refer to Operation Annuit Coeptis as 'Norene's skin cancer operation.' We'll talk about healing as a measurement of how things are progressing with Annuit Coeptis. Poor healing, wound breakdown, or infection, will mean that we have hit a snag. Future meetings will be referred to as when Norene has to come back into your office for follow-up visits. A reference to the cancer recurring will be a sign that an emergency meeting is needed. And, if it's okay with you, Mason, we should probably meet here in your house. Words to the effect that you have told Norene she didn't need to return to your office for follow-up visits will mean that someone has suspected what we are doing and that we should cut off all telephone or internet communications until further notice."

"I will give each of you a password to get into my super-encrypted email system," Gabriel added. "You won't have to worry about anyone eavesdropping on us, but we will still use the Norene's skin cancer as a way to communicate. Is that clear?"

Everyone nodded in the affirmative.

"Oh, by the way, Mason, has Norene ever had a skin cancer?" Gabriel asked.

"No, not really, she had some keratoses—you know, pre-malignant spots that we've treated with a chemical peeling solution—but never any cancer." Mason answered.

"Well, *now* she does," Gabriel replied. "Start talking to your staff and friends about your ongoing concerns about all her years of sun exposure and the need to keep a close watch on her skin. Talk of future biopsies that may be needed to keep a close check on her. Lay the foundation, just in case anyone begins to snoop around asking questions."

. . . .

The email read:

"Dear Mason,

I'm really pleased to know that Norene's pathology report came back and that the news is good. I was also pleased to know that she is healing well and that you she is scheduled to have the sutures removed tomorrow afternoon. I found some information that might be useful to you. It is a research project on a new topical solution that can be used to attack cancerous cells. It looks promising. Early results are encouraging. I'll let you know more when I learn more. And, give my best to Norene.

Gabriel.

P.S. I enjoyed the fishing on Saturday with you, Dale, and Raley. Although we only got a few bites, I learned a lot about fishing in different waters. I found the key I thought that I'd lost. And thanks for the tip about using the new sun-block preparation. We will all need to be more aware of the dangers of exposure to the elements, especially in the heat of the day."

"By George," Mason muttered under his breath. "He got in. He broke the encryption code of the VA and the Defense Department. The guy is a phenomenon. I've never seen anything like him, not on this earth."

Mason also noted that Gabriel had copied the others with his email. He was anxious to learn what Gabriel had discovered. He went to work, researching the Uniform Code of Military Justice, concentrating on Section 32. He wanted to be prepared when he met with his brother-in-law, Morley Bronkston, to discuss the court martial process, should it be determined that the current Commander-in-Chief was guilty of wrongdoing.

. . . .

"Doc," Morley said, "this kind of a thing has never been done. The way I read Section 32 suggests that any commanding officer can bring charges against anyone who took the oath of service, including the Commander-in-Chief. But in order to initiate such a proceeding, you will need to get an active military officer to file the charges. That, within itself, is a major obstacle."

"Maybe not," Mason replied. "I have learned from General Daren Borden, a friend that I mentioned earlier—and who served with one of the current Joint Chiefs—that America's Armed Forces are very unhappy with this Administration. Promises have not been kept. The Administration is gutting the defense system, refusing to support initiatives that the Joint Chiefs believe to be in the best interest of this country. It is also holding up on needed manpower, armament, and technology that field generals are requesting. General Borden tells me that if we had to fight a war, we would have to do so with one arm tied behind us, and that it is becoming more difficult to keep moral up."

"No wonder the Joint Chiefs are upset," Morley replied. "Something has to give. As part of JAG, I was involved in several court martial proceedings. However, I can tell you that there is no precedent for initiating such proceedings against the President of the United States."

"Are you saying that it can't be done?" Mason asked.

"No, that's not what I am saying. I am saying that there is no precedence. Nevertheless, if your investigations show that he has either ordered or been involved in the misappropriation of military and veteran's funds, converting any of them for personal gain—for him, any of his friends, or America's enemies—it would be an actionable offense. The bigger question is in which venue such proceedings would take place. With the composition of Congress, I'm sure that he and his supporters would try to have it resolved there so that they could bury it. You will recall that although President Clinton was impeached, he was never punished and served out the remainder of his term, receiving full benefits afterwards. Do you want to risk this and end up with a similar outcome, or less?"

"No, if we find that wrongdoing has occurred, I want the perpetrator or perpetrators to have to answer to the American people and pay for their actions," Mason answered.

"Then, it looks like you will need to wait until you hear from Daren. I remember him from college. Wasn't he in ROTC with you and me?"

"That's him," Mason replied.

"He is a good man," Morley added. "I knew that he would go on to do good things."

CHAPTER 17

"Thank you for agreeing to meet with us in this manner, General Purcell," Daren Borden said, entering the other General's office. "Allow me to introduce everyone. I'm sure that you remember former congressman and HHS Secretary, Dr. Mason Edmonds. This is agent Dale Jackson of the FBI; Gabriel Shade, U.S. Army retired, an information specialist extraordinaire; Raley Stovall, an attorney; and former JAG member, now a practicing attorney, Morley Bronkston."

Each of the men shook General Purcell's hand and exchanged pleasantries.

"Have a seat," he said to the group. "I guess that General Borden told you that he and I once worked together."

All nodded, indicating that they knew of the two Generals' prior relationships.

General Borden began the conversation. "General Purcell, we are here to discuss a matter of grave consequences and to ask for your assistance. The actions you will be asked to consider involve your boss and some of the most powerful men and women in the U.S. government and around the world."

"You mean the President of the United States. The Commander-in-Chief?" General Purcell asked.

"Yes, sir," Daren replied.

"This must be serious stuff."

"It is, General Purcell. If what Gabriel has discovered is true, President Padgett and his comrades have come close to pulling off one of the greatest heists in the history of the world, while aiding and abetting America's enemies."

"I'm all ears," General Purcell replied.

Gabriel took charge of the conversation. "With all due respect, General, I have been able to access the computers of the Defense Department, Veterans Affairs,

HHS, and U.S. Treasury. What I discovered is that there is absolutely no evidence that the so-called stimulus money intended for national defense projects and veterans' affairs was disseminated and that most of what was disseminated was not used for its intended purpose."

The General sat even straighter in his chair, asking, "Where did our money go?"

Gabriel replied, "My investigation shows that millions of dollars have gone into a number of private escrow bank accounts assigned to high-ranking officials of this government. In short, General, the American people have been betrayed and defrauded. That's one reason why the stimulus didn't work. The money never found its way to where it was intended. It appears that a colossal scam has taken place.

"So far, I can trace about nine hundred million or so that was removed from the general fund and deposited in forty-nine secret accounts in Switzerland and the Cayman Islands. The transactions took place from the computer system at the White House. "General, from what I can determine the transactions were generated on the computer in the President's private study adjacent to the Oval Office."

"Can you say for sure that President Padgett was involved?" General Purcell asked.

"What I can say is that the President's computer was involved. And from what I know from my years in top-secret intelligence operations, the President's computer is like the red telephone that used to have a direct line to the Kremlin. President Padgett was the only person who is authorized to answer or use the red phone. The same policy exists when it comes to his computer. He is the only one who has the password to get into the computer."

"What if someone else used his computer?" General Purcell asked.

"Even that is a violation, sir," Gabriel replied. "The President is the only one authorized to use it. He, alone, is responsible for its password and sworn not to divulge it to anyone."

"Well, this looks pretty damning," the General replied, rubbing his chin and shaking his head from side to side. "Why would anyone in such a high position risk the consequences of this kind of an action?"

"Money and power, sir," Daren Borden answered. "You and I have spent our lives fighting against those who want to control other men for the power and riches that come with such control."

"But the President of the United States?" General Purcell replied. "He is already the most powerful man in the world. Why does he need more?"

"Because there *is* more. It seems that when some people get a taste of the kind of exhilaration that comes with fame and power, they become addicted to the sound of their own voice or the roars of the crowd. They lose the perspective of what it is they sought in the first place. We're not too sure that President Padgett isn't passing through this presidency on his way to becoming Secretary General of the United Nations," Mason told the General.

"And narcissistic dreamers tend to surround themselves with underlings who always tell them what they want to hear," Dale Jackson said.

"Except when President Padgett appointed Mason Secretary of HHS," Gabriel inserted.

"What do you want me to do?" General Purcell asked.

"General, the usual channels of investigating such a matter or bringing about justice will not apply to this situation," Raley replied. "With much of Congress eating out of the President's hands, investigation is unlikely. And, impeachment is out of the question."

"What are our options?" the General asked.

"Appointing a special prosecutor—even if Congress would do so—will be a waste of time and money. It would be a sure formula for cover-up."

"That's one option that we can dismiss," General Purcell said.

"So far, we are all in agreement," Raley replied. "The best way to bring about justice in this case is to file a Section 32 under the Uniform Code of Military Conduct. We believe that court martial proceedings can be brought against the Commander-in-Chief."

"Who gave you such an opinion?" the General asked.

"I did, sir," Morley Bronkston took the lead. "During the years I served in the Army, I was attached to JAG and was involved in a number of courts martial. All that is needed is for a command-level officer to file charges against one thought to have violated his or her oath as an officer of the military. In reviewing the Constitution, I believe that a strong case can be made that the Commander-in-Chief is the ultimate military officer and is bound by the oath of office, according to the Code, to '... faithfully execute the office of President of the United States ... and to defend and protect it against all enemies, foreign and domestic.' And, the office of 'Presidency' means Commander-in-Chief, as well."

The General sat motionless, listening to what he expected to be the option of choice. It was clear that the wheels in his mind were churning in high gear.

"Clearly, sir, "Daren interrupted, "if what Gabriel has learned is factual, President Padgett has violated his solemn oath and should explain why millions, if not billions, of dollars were converted from the Defense Department of his country into personal accounts. He should have to answer questions why hundreds of millions that were appropriated for veterans' healthcare and benefits ended up in accounts in Switzerland and the Cayman Islands."

"Will you do it, General?" Mason asked. "I've spent the past two years trying to find answers. I feel confident enough about the answers that have come forth to stake my life and that of my friends and family on it."

"That may well be what you are putting at stake and asking the rest of us to do, too," General Purcell answered.

"Earlier, you made reference to oaths," the General said, looking into the eyes of his fellow General, Borden. "From what I know about everyone in this room, at one time or the other we have all taken oaths, lots of them. The one that is common to all of us is the one we took when we became officers in the United States Armed Services and the Reserve branches that support it, to defend this country and its Constitution against all enemies, foreign and domestic. Even though all of you, with the exception of Daren, are no longer in the military, the oath you took then didn't expire when your tours of service ended. Yes, gentlemen, because of what I see in your eyes and the love each of you has for this country, how could I say No? I want to see for myself the information that you have obtained, Gabriel."

"I have it right here," Gabriel replied, reaching into his briefcase and pulling out a three inch binder of documents.

Taking the binder from Gabriel, General Purcell said. "I'll look this over. In the meantime, you lawyers, with the assistance of the former JAG officer, move forward and draft the documents that you want me to sign. Gentlemen, we are at war. And, I've never entered one I didn't intend to win," the General said, standing up from his chair. What did you say you call this operation?"

"We didn't say, General," Mason answered. "We call it Operation Annuit Coeptis."

"Operation Annuit Coeptis," the General replied. "I like it. It's on the dollar bill. It means Providence has favored our undertakings, doesn't it?"

"Precisely," Mason answered. "As previously mentioned, we have all sworn to various oaths that bind us to noble causes. I'd like to propose one that I have especially created for the operation to which we have agreed.

Reaching into the inside pocket of his suit jacket, Mason retrieved a single piece of paper.

"I drafted this last night," he said, unfolding the paper. "It says:

> 'We, the founding members of Operation Annuit Coeptis, do solemnly swear and avow to use all means necessary to protect and defend the Republic that is the United States of America and the freedom-loving peoples of the world against individuals, organizations, or governments that

engage in or support activities intended to undermine or undo the Declarations and Constitution crafted by the Republic's Founding Fathers and the laws of God. Furthermore, we pledge to expose, and bring to justice, all who participate in acts of deceit, treachery, and treason against the Republic and its lawful citizens. And, as we go forth to fulfill the terms and conditions of this oath, we pray that God will look favorably upon our undertakings.'"

"Well, what do you think?" Mason asked, laying the piece of paper from which he had been reading on the coffee table before him while looking into the eyes of his colleagues.

"I think the words clearly state our resolve and mission," General Purcell replied.

"Are you asking us to sign our names to the oath?" Raley Stovall asked.

"You know that it's not necessary that we sign anything," Mason answered. "I just wanted to formalize and affirm what I hoped we would agree to undertake."

"Although it is not essential that we do so, I'd like to sign the document," General Purcell said. "You don't have a problem with that, do you, Mason?"

"Absolutely not," Mason replied, reaching for the document lying on the coffee table before him and into his jacket pocket for a pen. "Who wants to go first?"

"Let me add here, that although I am sure Daren wants to be a part of this, he needs to remain behind the scenes. I would not recommend that you sign the document," General Purcell said to his colleague.

"You know that I would," Daren replied. "I want to be a part of this, too."

"Just in case this document finds its way into the wrong hands, we are going to need an unnamed friend on the inside. And you are the person I would want to be there," the General added.

"I'll go with your wishes, Harold," Daren answered. "But I want it to be known among us, though, that I wholeheartedly swear to this oath."

"Duly noted," General Purcell responded.

"Though it is unlike a former sergeant to step in front of a general, if it's okay with you, General Purcell, I'd like to be the first to sign," Gabriel said, reaching for the pen that Mason was holding up.

"Go right ahead, sergeant," the General said, "On this matter, rank is irrelevant. We are all in this together."

"So, Gabriel gets to be John Hamilton of the Oath of Annuit Coeptis," Raley Stovall said jokingly.

"Since we will look to him to provide the proof we need, I think that is appropriate," Mason interjected.

As the others watched, Gabriel wrote his name in bold letters, immediately under the line that read, "And, we pray that God will look favorably upon our undertakings."

"Who's next?" Gabriel asked, holding up the pen.

"Allow me," General Purcell said, taking the pen from Gabriel's hand and leaning forward to place his name directly underneath that of Gabriel Shade.

"Mason?" the General said, "Would you like to go next?"

"Thank you, General," Mason replied, "but, I think I should go last."

Reaching for the pen, Morley said, "Allow me." When he had finished, he handed the pen to Raley.

"You guys realize that we could be signing our death warrant, don't you?" Raley said, inscribing his name underneath that of Morley's.

"I think that we all realize that, but it's a risk we have to take," Mason responded. "It's either ours or that of the United States of America."

"I know you're right," Raley said, handing the pen to Mason, who after adding his name to the list of signatories, carefully folded the document and placed it inside a small notebook that he had retrieved from his right hip pocket. "

"I will see that this is kept in a safe place," Mason said.

"What if others want to sign on?" General Purcell asked. "I can think of a half a dozen men and women who would do so if they were given the opportunity."

"I'd like to see every American swear to the Oath of Annuit Coeptis," Mason replied, "but this piece of paper—" He patted his right hip pocket— "is special and I'd like to keep it that way if that is okay with you guys."

All nodded in agreement.

"What will you do with the pen we used?" Morley asked. "History may be in the making."

"If it's all right with you guys, I'll keep it with the document, safely stowed away," Mason replied. "Morley may be right. What we have launched here today could change the course of history, and for the better. Perhaps we can urge the judge who signs off on the court martial verdict that puts the perpetrators away to use this pen, as well. Now, that would make it special."

"Let's don't get ahead of ourselves, here, gentlemen," General Purcell interjected. "We've still got work to do before we are ready to take my complaint to a military judge."

Having completed the first part of the mission, Mason said, "General, I know that you are busy. We won't keep you any longer. We'll be back in touch in a few days."

"The hint of a drawl in your manner of speaking suggests that you may have grown up in the South," General Purcell said to Mason.

"I did," Mason replied. "In a little town call Prideville."

"Is it next to Fort Chamberlain, where the Army's helicopter training center is based, isn't it?" General Purcell asked.

"Yes, it is. Are you familiar with the area?"

"Copter Country, they call it. I was stationed there for two years. I was a helicopter pilot in the Viet Nam War," the General said. "My father was one, too, in the Korean War. That's when helicopters were first being introduced in combat. He learned to fly them at Chamberlain, but I grew up in Oklahoma. My father became a helicopter instructor at Fort Stiller."

"Would the rest of you gentlemen excuse Dr. Edmonds and me for just a moment," General Purcell asked. "I'd like a private word with him."

Raley, Gabriel, and Morley said their goodbyes and closed the door behind them.

When the two men were alone, General Purcell said, "Prideville, huh?"

"That's right. It is where I was born and raised," Mason replied. "Are you from a long line of military career people?"

"No, just my father," the General replied. "His people were farmers. In fact, my great grandfather was a share cropper on a farm near Prideville. He had been a slave, but was set free before the war was over," the General added. "We'll talk more about this later. Right now, all of us have work to do."

When Mason joined the others waiting outside the General's office, Raley was the first to ask, "What did the General want to talk with you about?"

"It looks like members of our two families have crossed paths before," Mason answered.

"It is a small world, isn't it?" Daren added.

"Indeed, it is," Gabriel interjected, "But if the Illuminati gets its grip on all of it, the vice will become so tight that no one will be able to breathe without permission."

"If Operation Annuit Coeptis is successful, perhaps we can forestall their efforts," Mason interjected.

"That depends upon how favorably God looks upon our efforts," Gabriel declared.

. . . .

Four days later, Mason, Gabriel, Raley, Daren, and Morley returned to General Purcell's office. The general signed the court martial papers, initiating a precedent-setting action against the highest ranking officer in the Armed Services, its Commander-in-Chief.

. . . .

The following day, General Purcell's aide alerted him to a phone call.

"Is this General Purcell," the voice on the other end asked.

"It is," he answered. "Who's calling?"

"General, this is Barton Wiley, President Padgett's Chief of Staff. I have in my hand a document ostensibly signed by you bringing Section 32 charges against the President. I'm sure that this is some kind of a joke and just wanted to call and get the word from the horse's mouth, so to speak, before I trashed the document."

"Mr. Wiley," General Purcell said, "The document you apparently have before you is no joke. I have already begun to convene the panel of JAG judges and appointed a JAG prosecutor to handle the case. I suggest, sir, that you find one from the JAG corps to represent the President."

"What have you been drinking? Are you out of your mind, General?" Wiley responded in an agitated tone of voice. "With the stroke of a pen, as Commander-in-Chief the President can dismiss the case."

"You need to check the Uniform Code of Military Conduct, Mr. Wiley," the General answered. "Once charges of misconduct are levied against an officer, as its Commander-in-Chief, the President is an officer of the Armed Services, and his command is immediately placed in suspension."

"Then the Vice President becomes President?" Wiley said.

"Until this matter is resolved, he does, Mr. Wiley," General Purcell replied.

"General, you know that as soon as the Vice President takes the Presidential Oath of Office we will have dismissal, pardon, or whatever papers are necessary ready for him to sign, don't you?" Wiley replied.

"I'm already a step ahead of you, Mr. Wiley," the General replied. "You forget that you are dealing with an old soldier who has been in many battles. The first thing we learn in officers' school is to already have Plan B and C and D in place before Plan A is launched, something I'm sorry to say, your Administration hasn't yet learned.

Upon taking the presidential oath of office, the former Vice President as the new Commander-in-Chief will be served with court martial papers. We already have enough data on him to bring him before another court that I have already appointed. The prosecutor for that court is already in place. And, in case you continue to play the game, similar documents and proceedings are already in place for the Speaker of the House and the President Pro-Tem of the Senate, if necessary. No, Mr. Wiley, I'm afraid that you may be playing in a bigger game of chess that you are prepared for. And any king you put into the game is already in checkmate."

"I'll have your head, General!" Wiley shouted over the phone.

"I expected that response from you," General Purcell replied. "Be very careful. We already know about some heads you and your Administration have had."

The next thirty seconds were filled with nothing but absolute silence. Then Mr. Wiley said, "General, I think we need to talk. Where and when can we meet?"

"Has anyone else seen the documents you hold in your hand?" General Purcell asked.

"No sir. No one," Wiley replied.

"Then, put them is a secure place and don't show them or discuss them with anyone. Is that clear?" the General said.

"It is, General," Wiley answered.

"Do you want to meet in a public place, like here in my office or some place more private?" General Purcell asked.

"Private, if you please, sir," Wiley replied.

"I'll meet you at the park bench under the split-trunked oak tree to the south of Lincoln's statue located in the park's center at 7:30 p.m. There will still be enough light for us to recognize each other. I'll be wearing a black jogging suit with a red strip on the sleeves and pants and a ball cap with an insignia of two crossed arrows on its front. I know what you look like, Mr. Wiley. I have a photograph attached to your file, here in front of me. And, Mr. Wiley, come alone, without a bug. I'll have on my person, equipment that can detect such devices and a

M1911 pistol that got me through a lot of situations in combat.'

"Sir, you don't need to be concerned about any of that. I'll see you at seven-thirty."

. . . .

"You remember my instructions, Mr. Wiley?" the General asked as the two men sat down on the bench. Each knew that there would only be about ten minutes more daylight before their meeting would be conducted in the dark. "If you had a bug or a weapon, this little black case here inside my warm-up suit would have already sent me a message."

"I have already told you that you didn't need to worry about such things, General. I know the game of chess well. I know that when a good player voices the term checkmate that he has already considered all moves available to his opponent. Sir, I'm tipping over my king. I know when I'm beaten. What can I do now to save myself?"

"I'm not sure that you can save yourself—from us," General Purcell replied. "We know that you have been involved in the largest scam ever perpetrated on the American people, the people who put their trust to change this country and the world for the better, not for just a few, but for all. You and your friends have betrayed the trust of your fellow Americans and you will have to pay for the wrongs you've done. However, if you are willing to cooperate with us, we may ask the judges to consider your cooperation when they render judgment."

"I'll tell you everything I know, General. I am so sorry. I knew that what we were doing was wrong. I was assured that it was what the President wanted and that there was no way we could get caught, that the systems we were using were secure and that the plan was foolproof."

"You were misinformed, Mr. Wiley," General Purcell replied. "What you should have been told is that the kind of things you and your friends tried to pull off was proof that you are fools. You are dealing with the greatest intelligence and fighting force the world has ever known. Fortunately you and your cohorts don't own them—at least, not yet. Even though you and friends have tried to destroy it, there are good men and women who love this country so much that they have reaffirmed their pledge to protect it from all enemies, foreign or domestic."

"What do you want me to do?"

"I want you go back to work tomorrow as though nothing has changed. You will be my eyes and ears, my 'deep throat,' like during the Watergate investigations of the 1970s. I want to know what they know and how they react to what is about to break. I want to see how they plan to cover up what has taken place. You meet me here every evening at this same time and tell me what I want to know. And next time wear a jogging suit and running shoes," the General ordered. "Look as though you are looking after your health. From the looks of your waistline, it looks as though you could use some exercise."

"Yes, sir," Wiley replied.

"And, Mr. Wiley, no matter how hot the kitchen gets over there," the General said, pointing toward the White House, do not expose me or our plan. You will be put under the jail or worse. And, your jail won't be one of those country club prisons. You are now dealing with the United States Armed Forces. And we are fighting mad. We've been around a lot longer than that team of politicians that occupies that sacred house with the huge white columns on Pennsylvania Avenue. Is there any doubt in your mind as to what you are to do?"

"No sir. I'll see you tomorrow," Wiley said, rising up from the bench.

"And, jog out of the park, Mr. Wiley. Throw your jacket over your shoulder and make it look as though you are on one of those afternoon runs that you will be taking for a while."

"Oh," General Purcell called out, motioning for Wiley to come back to him. "Look shocked tomorrow when the documents appear on the President's desk. Don't blow your cover."

CHAPTER 18

"Barton, get in here," President Padgett screamed through the intercom, calling his Chief of Staff into the Oval Office. "Look at this. Who the hell does General Purcell think he is? I'll show him who is in command of this country's defense. Get him over here."

"What is it, Mr. President? What should I tell him it is about?" Wiley responded, appearing to be confounded by the President's actions and comments.

"This son of a bitch thinks he's going to bring me before a court martial. I'll have his head," the President said.

"A court martial," Wiley asked. "Can he do that?"

"I don't know," the President replied. "You guys advised me to try the terro... uh, enemy combatant who masterminded the 9/11 attacks in the military courts, didn't you? I recall that you said, as Commander-in-Chief I would be able to have more control of whatever punishment came down on them. This whole commander-in-chief thing could backfire. Get me the Attorney General. NOW!"

"Yes sir, Mr. President. Who do you want first, the Chairman of the Joint Chiefs or the Attorney General?"

"Janis Horton, the Attorney General," the President replied. "I'll need to get her take on this before I hand that damned general his hat and marching orders right out onto the streets of this city."

"Yes sir. I'll get right on it. Is there anything else?"

"Yeah, don't breathe a word about this to anyone else, especially not the press. And ask Mary Ann to bring me a bottle of Rolaids."

. . . .

"Can he do this—bring court martial proceedings against me? Can't we get this moved into a civilian court?

The Oath/McCollough

If we pick the right judge, I think we can get all charges dropped," the President said to the Attorney General.

"I don't know, sir," the Attorney General answered. "This sort of thing has never come up before. The document claims that as Commander-in-Chief you are subject to all laws that govern military conduct. This could be a problem. If any part of these charges are true, this could pose big trouble for you and a lot of your friends and advisers. Is there any validity to the claims in this document?"

"Are you my lawyer?"

"Well, sir, I'm not sure about that either. If these proceedings take place in a military-style court martial all lawyers will have to be JAG officers. I wouldn't be able to participate in your defense."

"Then I'm not answering any more of your questions," the President replied. "Get me someone who knows something about this—what did you call it—JAG?"

"The letters stand for Judge Advocate General Corps."

"Find out who runs that operation and have them come to me NOW," the President shouted. "I'm still Commander-in-Chief and they have to follow my orders."

"Yes, Mr. President," the Attorney General said, closing the door behind her.

. . . .

A JAG officer didn't make the President happier. "Mr. President, I'm sorry to inform you that we have determined that as Commander-in-Chief of America's Armed Forces you are subject to Section 32 of the Uniform Code of Military Justice and that the charges against you and some of your Cabinet and friends appear to have teeth," the JAG officer appointed to handle the President's court martial said. "You can fight the charges and the venue. However, you should know that the prosecution is willing to make a deal."

"A deal, what kind of a deal?"

"You, the Vice President, and the Speaker of the House will resign effectively immediately for 'personal' reasons. All moneys currently held in secret bank accounts for everyone involved will be returned to the U.S. Treasury. Checks, representing equal distribution of all such funds will be issued to Social Security recipients, veteran pension funds, and the servicemen and—women currently in uniform around the world, without explanation, except that the Congress voted to give them a stimulus bonus. That's the deal that has been offered. Is that clear?"

"Or what? What if I refuse?"

"Well, sir, the prosecution has already anticipated that question. If you refuse their settlement, they will release to all media tomorrow morning at an internationally televised press conference the charges and details of their findings," the JAG officer replied.

Turning to his press secretary, sitting in on the meeting, the President asked, "What would be the political fallout of such a thing?"

"In a word sir, devastating."

"Will all of you excuse me for a few minutes? I need to have some time to think," the President said, rubbing his forehead with his left hand.

. . . .

"Mary Ann," the President said, pressing the intercom button that connected him with his personal secretary. "Is the First Lady in the house?"

"I believe she is, sir. Can you hold while I check with her secretary? Are you all right, Mr. President? The President had sounded dejected.

"Yeah, I'm all right. Tell her it is not that kind of an emergency, but I would like to meet her in the drawing room of the private quarters in five minutes."

. . . .

While he waited to join the First Lady, President Padgett reached for the red telephone sitting on the credenza behind the desk in the Oval Office. The phone had once been connected to identical handsets located in the Kremlin and in the French chateau that only the Inner Circle of the Illuminati knew existed. Since the Cold War warmed up, the direct line to Moscow had been disconnected. On the other hand, numerous calls back and forth to Europe had taken place using the red phone since this President took the oath of office.

"Yes, Mr. President," a deep authoritative voice weighted with a distinctive French accent said. "What is the purpose of your call?"

The President instantly recognized the voice as the one belonging to a man he had never met. He knew its owner only by a code name: Solomon.

"Grand Master," President Padgett said. "We have a situation here and I wanted to let you know about it as soon possible."

"Go ahead," Solomon responded.

"I have learned that a small group of Americans have hacked into our supercomputers and that they have traced a lot of the funds that were used for my election. They also seem to know where money approved by Congress for the 2009 project ended up. It is my understanding that they have obtained the bank account numbers set up for our friends in the Cabinet and Congress here in Washington as well as our friends in other countries. This group of troublemakers has threatened to expose what they know unless I and my Cabinet resign. I need to know what you would have me do."

After a lengthy pause, the voice on the other end of the line, said, "What else do they know?"

"It is hard to tell, Grand Master, but these people seem to know what they are doing and could pose quite a danger to our greater mission," President Padgett answered. "They have a computer hacker who appears to be able to access anything, including the computers of the major newspapers and television networks around the world. They are threatening to run a story exposing you, the other members of the Inner Circle, and your connection to the American government, banking system and the United Nations."

"Do you have any idea who is behind this?" Solomon asked.

After a short pause, the President responded, "The only person I can think of is the doctor whom we appointed Secretary of Health and Human Services a few months back, Mason Edmonds."

"Where is he now?" Solomon asked.

"He is on leave. I think he's home, on his ranch."

"If it is him, do you think we can bring him and whoever it is he is working with into the fold? " Solomon asked.

"Are you asking if we can buy them off?" the President responded. "I don't think they are after money."

"Everybody has a price. See if you can find what his is."

"I will try," President Padgett said. "In the meantime, what shall I do?"

"Say nothing, to no one. Do you understand?"

"I understand," the President said. "I just can't believe that Dr. Edmonds would put himself and his family at such risk. If he knows what we think he knows, he must know who he is up against."

"You must have a mole on your staff, as well. Someone is cooperating with the troublemakers. You have to find out who it is. Play along. Do as they ask. For now," came the answer. "I will contact our people at the Federal Reserve and have the Chairman inform our friends at the Trilateral Commission and Foreign Relations Committee about the security breach. We will pool our resources and prepare to strike. Our friends at the Times and the Post have always been helpful. I will have Spartacus contact the television networks."

"You are going invoke the Rothschild Formula, aren't you?" President Padgett asked.

"Precisely," Solomon said in a response that sounded as though it originated in the depths of Hell. "This is war. And, we aren't accustomed to losing!" Solomon slammed the phone down on its cradle.

President Padgett sat motionless, still holding the red telephone receiver next to his ear. How could he and his advisers have been so naïve to think that by bringing Mason Edmonds into the Cabinet they could prevent him from striking out against them? A formidable adversary was not only given access to the inner sanctum of his Administration, he had been given a master key that gave him access to the very weapons he needed to bring the Administration down.

"What have I done?" President Padgett muttered to himself, returning the red handset back to its resting place.

. . . .

"Mr. President," Mary Ann said over the intercom, "the First Lady will meet you as directed."

"Thanks," President Padgett replied, seeing his dreams turn to ashes. He stood up from the leather chair positioned behind the desk that he had hoped to use for several more years, gathered his coat and walked to the door. He turned and took one long last look at the Oval Office and all the memorabilia that graced it. He knew that he might be returning to gather a few personal items and prepare for his exodus. However, the office was no longer truly his. What his future held was a mystery.

"Would this turn of events torpedo the promise that the Inner Circle made to him some years back? Is my dream to become Secretary General of the United Nations dead?" he thought. "Perhaps, if I were to lie low for a while, Solomon would get things back on track. After all, I have become a multimillionaire since becoming President. Solomon and the other twelve members of the Inner Circle could do anything they felt promoted their agenda at least that is what I have been led to believe. I am their man, the one chosen to bring the One World Government to fruition. Too much had been invested in the plan—and me—to let the mission be thwarted by a small group of amateurs. Surely, this is merely a bump in the road, a temporary setback."

With the riches that the Illuminati had funneled into secret bank accounts and safety deposit boxes, President Padgett was set for life. Millions of U.S. dollars, gold, and silver had been socked away for him. He and his family could live like kings for the rest of their lives, even if he had to retreat from the limelight. And the chateau on the French Riviera that had been promised would make a wonderful place for him and his family to live out the rest of their lives in luxury, or to disappear for a while until he and those he served could regroup.

"I deserve to live like a king," Padgett assured himself. "I was born to change the world. I have been groomed for a position within the New World Order. I have served the Masters well, doing everything they asked me to do, saying precisely what they had told me to say, when they wanted me to say it. I have brought the Muslims into the global debate and held Israel off from destroying Iran's nuclear power plants. I created a debt from which the U.S. may never recover, shifting power and riches to other world players. They owe me. They all owe me. I am the chosen one, or so that's what they led me to believe. Surely, I am the one foretold in prophesy. Like the Phoenix, I shall rise from the ashes. It is my destiny to do so.

"Or have I served their purpose? I know what they do with people they consider a liability. How could things be turned upside down so quickly?"

There was a lot of questions that remained to be answered, but so little time ... at least for Kennan Ahmad Padgett, the "anointed one."

CHAPTER 19

The East Room of the White House was packed to capacity. Every facet of the media had gathered to hear what they had only been told was an "important announcement" from the President of the United States.

In the back of the room stood six men who were not members of the press corps, other media, or the President's cabinet. Flanking General Purcell were Dr. Mason Edmonds, Gabriel Shade, Raley Stovall, Morley Bronkston, and Dale Jackson. The General, dressed in his military uniform, simply told inquirers that the visitors were five "average citizens" who had been selected at random as token representatives of the American public to hear the President's remarks.

That seemed to be good enough for a stunned group of media types who were concerned that their love affair with the President might be in jeopardy and were eager to hear what he had to say.

From across the room, another soldier in uniform, Daren Borden, winked at Mason and his colleagues. After reviewing Daren's continuing role as an unidentified member of Annuit Coeptis, the group decided that it would be best if he didn't wear the usual insignias of his rank and kept his distance.

President Padgett stepped onto the platform that had been temporarily placed as a stage. The First Lady was at his side. The President approached the microphone. From his body language and the look on his face, it was obvious that this was no ordinary press conference. The room got deathly quiet. What could be so important that the press hadn't been forewarned about the nature of the meeting? It was generally provided with the President's prepared remarks beforehand.

"Ladies and gentlemen, thank you for coming. I have a very short announcement and will not be taking any questions." Reading from Teleprompters that were located to his left and right, the President said, "Today, I have made one of the most difficult decisions of my life. I have decided that in the interest of my family, I am resigning my position as President of the United States of America, effective twelve o'clock noon Eastern Standard Time tomorrow. I can only say that my decision is based upon personal reasons and that I wish for all of you and the person who follows me in this office God's speed. Thank you."

Except for the members of OAC, no one could believe their ears. What had caused the President to take such drastic measures? If he was resigning, where was the Vice President? There were scores of valid questions, but no answers.

When President Padgett exited the room, TV reporters scrambled, stepping over, around, and on each other to get in front of a camera to comment on the story of the new century. What could have happened that would initiate such drastic measure? The evening talk shows had a field day speculating on the events that taken place and those to follow. The morning headlines around the world read, "U.S. President Resigns." People everywhere were in a state of shock.

Another press conference was called for the Rotunda of the Capitol Building for the following morning at 11:55. The White House Press Secretary would say only that "more news would be forthcoming."

This time the Vice President, the Speaker of the House of Representatives, the Senate Majority Leader, and the President Pro-Tem of the Senate took center stage. The Vice President spoke first.

"Ladies and gentlemen, thank you for coming. I have a short announcement and will not take any questions. I have decided that in the interest of my family, I am immediately resigning my position as Vice President of the United States of America ..."

"The Vice President is reading from the same script that the President read to us yesterday," a reporter from the Washington Times said to his Washington Post counterpart.

"Yeah, and I'll bet you a baked chicken dinner that we may hear the same thing from the three other people standing behind him," The Post reporter replied.

He was right. Within five minutes, the four most powerful people in the United States government other than the President had announced their resignations, effective immediately.

A reporter from CLN leaned over to one with a VOX news logo on her shirt and said, "You realize that the government of the United States is effectively shut down, don't you?"

The VOX reporter replied, "For once in my lifetime, the American people can take a deep breath and know that they aren't being shafted. America will be just fine. There are lots of qualified people who can sit in the seats held by the five people who have resigned during these last two days. I just hope that our industry will give whoever takes over the reins half the chance that we gave those who just resigned."

The frowning CLN reporter was speechless.

. . . .

That evening the group composing Operation Annuit Coeptis sat around a conference table in a part of the Pentagon used only for high-level meetings. Because the gathering took place at 9:00 p.m. the building was essentially empty, save for the occasional member of a cleaning crew or security guards, who the group could hear walking down the hall outside the room.

"These have been two historic days," Dale said. "Never in history have the top five political leaders in America resigned within a forty-eight-hour period. Now what?"

Raley Stovall answered Dale's question, "According to the protocol of succession the Secretary of State will assume the office of the Presidency. That would be Secretary of State Helen Crompton."

Morley Bronkston interrupted, saying, "That's always been her ambition, anyway. Do you think she may have set this whole thing up, knowing that's the quickest the way for her to assume the office of her dreams?"

Gabriel replied, "That's a good theory, Morley, but she's not behind this. In fact, she is part of it. Today, I obtained some of the information that I have been after. This whole affair goes much deeper than any of us imagined, very deep into the Cabinet. In fact, so deep that seven members of the cabinet, other than the Secretary of State, are involved. All but one member of the Cabinet is involved."

"All but one," Mason replied in astonishment. "What did these people think they were doing? And, they almost got away with it. Who are the others?"

"The Secretaries of Treasury, Defense, Interior, Agriculture, Commerce, Labor, and the Attorney General," Gabriel replied.

"What!" General Purcell exclaimed. "Who does that leave?"

"Well," Daren Borden replied, "hold onto your seats. I've already looked into the line of succession to the presidency and guess who would be next in line, assuming that all of the people I just mentioned resign?"

"It's been a long time since I studied this kind of stuff," Raley Stovall said. "Tell us, for God's sakes."

Daren looked at Mason, who already knew the answer. The doctor was leaning forward holding his face in his hands, slowly shaking his head from side to side. "The one cabinet member who was not part of the scam, the Secretary of Health and Human Services," Raley revealed.

"You mean that you'd become President?" Morley turned to Mason.

"Think about it," Gabriel interrupted, "Mason comes back from voluntary leave, assumes the position of Secretary of HHS, and when the others resign, he steps into the presidency."

"This is too much for me to digest," Dale replied. "And, how do we know that those in line ahead of him will resign?"

"I have the same information about each of them that I had on the President, Vice President, Speaker of the

House, and the President Pro-Tem of the Senate. When they see the walls caving in around them, they will follow suit," Gabriel said.

"I wouldn't be so sure about the Secretary of State," Raley interjected. "She's not one to give in easily. She's a fighter and she's had her sights on the office for years."

"When she sees what I've got on her, she will resign," Gabriel replied.

"What is our next move," General Purcell asked. "You know, as a military man I need to be thinking two steps ahead."

"General," Daren responded to his fellow soldier, "I think that you should call a meeting of the remaining members of the President's Cabinet for the purpose of catching them up on matters of national security."

"That's not protocol," General Purcell responded. "I would usually go through the Secretary of Defense and the President's National Security Advisor first."

"Tell them that due to the urgency of the situation, you don't have time to follow protocol and that they need to meet you here at 7:00 a.m.," Daren replied.

General Purcell said, "Its nine-thirty now and my aide is waiting down the hall in my office. Hand me that phone. I'll call him and tell him to get on it."

. . . .

Within twenty minutes, there was a knock on the door. "General," the aide said, "I reached everyone. They will be here as you asked."

. . . .

"What was the reaction to the request?" the General asked his aide.

"Sir, everyone seemed very nervous. You know, not their usual confident selves. The Secretary of Defense was ticked that he was asked to be here with everyone else."

"I'll handle that tomorrow morning," the General replied. "When he arrives, put him in my office and I'll tell him the purpose of the meeting before we join the others. That will satisfy protocol. With what they've done to the American people, these people shouldn't worry about protocol or formalities.

. . . .

In his usual fashion, General Purcell arrived at his office at 6:00 a.m. on the following morning. Waiting on a loveseat in the hallway across the door from his suite was the Secretary of State.

"General, I need to speak to you for a moment prior to the meeting," she said.

"Madame Secretary," General Purcell replied, "I am sorry, but I can't do that. You know that any information I have must be first discussed with the Secretary of Defense."

"But General, these are unusual times. And I'm sure that you are familiar with the succession protocol to the Presidency. Within the next twenty-four hours, I will be sworn in as President. Now, you don't want our new relationship to get off on the wrong foot, do you?" the Secretary said in a sarcastic and threatening tone of voice.

"No, Ma'am, I sure don't," the General replied. "However, if you will excuse me, I am expecting the Secretary of Defense in a moment and I've got a lot to do this morning."

"You are making a terrible mistake, sir," the Secretary said.

"Maybe I am, Madame Secretary. Maybe I am. But, right now, I must go inside. I'll see you in the conference room down the hall in a few minutes," the General said, pointing to the double doors and the end of the hall to his right.

The Secretary stormed down the corridor toward the conference room. She was not accustomed to being told NO by anyone.

. . . .

General Purcell opened the door leading to his outer office, where he found his top aide and the Secretary of Defense waiting as requested.

"Come on in, Mr. Secretary," the General said, opening the door to his private office. "Have a seat. This will be short and sweet. I don't want it said that I didn't talk to you first. So I'm talking to you. Now, let's go join the others."

"General," the Defense Secretary said, "aren't you going to tell me what you brought us here for?"

"Yep," he said, "You'll hear it when the others do. Now, let's go," the General said, rising from his chair and inviting the Secretary out of his office.

. . . .

"Thank you for coming on such short notice," General Purcell said, entering the room with the Secretary of Defense following a step behind. "Now, let's get right to it. For the past several weeks, a team of special investigators has been looking into where large sums of so-called stimulus monies that were ostensibly earmarked for defense and veterans affairs have gone. I'm not going to play games with you. The reason that you are here is that we have irrefutable evidence that each of you has been involved in one of the greatest schemes ever uncovered, one that makes Bernie Madoff's Ponzi scheme look like child's play.

"You and those who own you have robbed the American people and its proud defenders of what they deserve—what your Congress appropriated for them. We had similar evidence on the President, Vice President, Speaker of the House, and President Pro-Tem of the Senate. This is why they resigned. Now, as head of Operation Annuit Coeptis, I am giving each of you that same opportunity."

"What the hell is Operation Annuit Coeptis?" the Secretary of State asked. "And who authorized it in the first place?"

"The Founding Fathers, Madame Secretary," the General replied. "In their wisdom—and proceeding with what they believed to be God's blessings—they had the Latin words, 'Annuit Coeptis' placed on the dollar bill. They also created the oath of office sworn to by each of you in this room. They went even further by constructing a way for the citizens of this country to hold their elected officials accountable when that oath was violated. It is now clear that each of you has betrayed your pledge to protect America against all enemies, foreign and domestic, and the country is suffering greatly from your actions. In fact we are on the verge of collapse, collapse that you and those who own you orchestrated."

"Who made you an expert on constitutional law?" the Attorney General asked.

"No one," the General replied. "However, as a soldier, I learned a long time ago, when you have been trained to conduct a special ops mission, you call in the people who have been prepared to get the job done. That's what I did. Trust me when I tell you ladies and gentlemen, if this were a game of chess, each of you is in checkmate. There is no other move you can make but to topple your king and surrender."

"I knew that we should have moved more quickly to get rid of that General," the Secretary of State whispered to the Secretary of Defense. "Never trust a man or woman who wears those two crossed arrows on his or her uniform. Special Forces soldiers don't understand globalist matters. They are gung ho America."

"Now, just in case any of you are already scheming to fight us on this, I have already prepared a story revealing each of your involvements in a clandestine scandal that was intended to result in a regulatory capture of the U.S. government. If you don't do as I say, the American people are going to learn the truth about the people you serve— the Inner Circle of a Shadow Government that has been playing monopoly with the world. The self-anointed sovereignty that owns you believes it their duty to make decisions for the rest of us.

"Do you think that he is bluffing?" the Treasury Secretary whispered to the Commerce Secretary."

"I don't think that we can take that risk. If we allowed this story to come out, it would be a major setback for the greater initiative. We'll go along and let the dust settle for a while. We will be back," the Commerce Secretary replied, cupping his hand over his mouth so that no one could overhear his remarks.

The General continued, "The people will be told how you and your friends on Wall Street, in the Federal Reserve, the United Nations, and the International Monetary Fund converted taxpayer money into secret bank accounts in Switzerland and the Cayman Islands. They will be told how American's money was used to fund programs designed to destroy America. The article outs the names of warlords and dictators whose favor you and your comrades have bought in trying to create your 'one world government' and provides the account numbers of each account and the bank in which the account exists."

"How the hell did he get this information?" the Treasury Secretary said under his breath.

"At my command, the story will be automatically inserted onto the front page of every major newspaper in the world," the General said.

"How can you do that?" objected the Secretary of Commerce, aloud. "The newspapers have secure computer systems to prevent just such a trick."

"Well, sir," the General answered. "Our computer guys are a lot smarter than theirs, or should I say, yours. Are you willing to risk the public humiliation and criminal charges that will be brought to bear by the Administration that follows yours?"

"Just who do you think will assume the presidency and all our positions?" the Secretary of State asked.

"Madam Secretary," the General answered, "surely, you know the answer to that question. The only member of the Cabinet that was considered an outsider by the administration you serve."

She looked around the room and began to count heads, aligning them in the order of succession. Then she said, "It's the Secretary of Health and Human Services, but she is only Acting Secretary in Dr. Edmond's absence."

"Precisely," the General replied. "The next President of the United States will be Dr. Mason Edmonds. He has already been contacted and is in Washington as we speak. He will deliver to the Oval Office this morning a letter announcing his return from administrative leave."

The room was deathly still. No one knew what so say. They just hung their heads in defeat.

"Now, each of you should go to your office and prepare your own letter of resignation. Then gather whatever you can put in a briefcase or purse and make a quiet exit. The letters will be gathered at ten o'clock and delivered to the current Chief of Staff. A press conference will be held at eleven o'clock during which he will announce that your letters of resignation have been submitted," General Purcell ordered. "Are there any questions?"

"Yeah, I have one," the Secretary of State asked. "Who else is part of Operation Annuit Coeptis?"

"Some things, Madame Secretary, are truly 'top secret,'" the General replied. "Just know that all of the participants in this operation have taken an oath to defend this country against its enemies foreign and domestic, and mean it! It is unfortunate that you and your co-conspirators didn't."

"I see what you mean," the Secretary of Defense whispered to the Secretary of State. This Purcell guy is as gung ho as they come. No wonder he moved through the ranks."

"Perhaps our party's affirmative action plan has worked too well," the Secretary of State replied in a voice intended to be overheard by General Purcell and the others at the table.

Though he heard the Secretary's remark, General Purcell ignored her obvious attempt at distracting and upsetting him, and continued, "Now, let each of us do the right thing. Expect one of my aides at each of your offices at ten o'clock sharp to pick up your letter of resignation. And please keep in mind that what transpired here this morning never happened. You haven't seen or heard from me in months. If any of this leaks or the public ever learns about Operation Annuit Coeptis, the newspaper articles waiting on a very secure computer at a very secure place will be released. Even in years to come, it will be a hot story. Is that clear?"

With no objection being voiced or openly indicated, the General left the room, leaving a group of once-powerful people with little choice but to save themselves—at least temporarily—by following the General's orders.

. . . .

"Sir, I have everyone's letter," the General's aide said to his boss.

"Very well. Were there any holdouts?"

"Yes sir," the Secretary of State was the last one to give in."

"That was predictable," the General replied. "Bring the resignations to me, please."

"Yes, sir," the aide replied and proudly walked into General Purcell's office.

"Sir, may I speak freely?" the aide asked.

"Certainly, Colonel," the General replied.

"On behalf of all fighting forces that now wear—or have ever worn—the uniform of the United States of America, I want to thank you for what you have done. It has been a long time since someone went to war for us, the men and women who have worn and are wearing the uniforms of the Armed Forces of the United States of America," the aide said, holding back the tears pooling in the corners of his eyes.

"Colonel," the General replied, "I was just the messenger. It was a group of what some would call average citizens who went to bat for us, patriots who are committed to taking America back from those trying to hijack it."

"Sir, with all due respect, there is nothing average about the men who worked with you on this mission to bring down a corrupt administration," the Colonel insisted.

"You are right, Colonel," the General answered. "But their identities can never be revealed. There are powerful people in the world who had invested a lot in the men and women who are tendering their resignations. They would be very angry if they knew who was involved in bringing them down."

"What about you, sir? Everyone will know about you," the aide answered.

"Only if the other members of Operation Annuit Coeptis, you, and the people who were in the conference at seven o'clock this morning are willing to take that risk," General Purcell replied. "I'm not going to tell anyone about it. You aren't going to tell anyone. And, I don't think that the people whose letters I have in my hands are going to do so either. They have too much to lose."

Later that morning another press conference was held—the third one in as many days.

. . . .

"Ladies and gentlemen, in my capacity as Chief of Staff to the office of the Presidency, I stand before you to announce the resignations of a number of members of the President's Cabinet," Barton Wiley began. "This morning, I received letters of resignation from the Secretaries of Treasury, Defense, Interior, Agriculture, Commerce, Labor, Transportation, Energy, Education, Veterans Affairs, Homeland Security, and the Attorney General. Each of them stated that they are resigning for personal reasons and would not comment any further on the matter."

Hands went up around the room in which the press conference was taking place. Reporters called out the Chief of Staff's name asking to be recognized.

"Who the hell does that leave," the Washington Post reporter asked his Times counterpart?"

"I was listening as closely as I could. If I'm right, the Secretary of Health and Human Services is the only Cabinet position not mentioned."

"What does that mean?" the Post reporter asked.

"I'm not quite sure. But, there is definitely a succession plan and I know that it involves the Cabinet," his Times colleague replied.

"I will not be taking questions or commenting further on this matter at this time. However, as soon as we have further information, we will release it to you," Mr. Wiley added, and left through the same secure door in which he entered.

The clamor to get outside and break the news created frenzy. The past three days had been filled with more "news" than the reporters and the networks and media they represented could handle. The resignation of the chain of command of American government made headlines around the world.

There were more questions than answers. It didn't take the media types long to do the math and conclude that the Secretary of Health and Human Services was next in line for the presidency. And he was on sabbatical.

Attempts to reach the Assistant Secretary of HHS, who was acting as its director, were "unsuccessful," all media outlets reported. Photographs of Dr. Mason Edmonds were displayed on the front page of newspapers and magazines as well as electronic media throughout the world. Headlines read "President by Default." Not since the unexpected death of entertainer Michael Jackson, had one person received as much attention.

"Change has truly come to America, but what kind of change are we now in store for?" one reporter asked, signing off her nightly television program. It was a good question. And no one knew the answer, not even the man who was—by default—about to assume an office to which he had never aspired.

The VOX host said, concluding his popular show that evening, "Not since the Founding Fathers convinced the people to convert plows, axes, and saws into weapons and take up arms against a tyrannical monarch has America had the opportunity to start afresh with new leadership and prove Alexander Tyler wrong.

"A revitalized America's leadership has come once again from the heartland—from the people, by the people, and for the people. It appears that the Oval Office may be occupied by a man with somewhat unique credentials, a man who is the product of 'Middle America', a physician who has taken on the most challenging case of his life. Is he up to the task? Time will tell. Good night.

CHAPTER 20

"How do you feel?" Norene asked her husband as they were about to enter the White House for the ceremony to swear in a new President.

"Overwhelmed," Mason answered. "This has all happened so fast. And I haven't prepared for this job."

"Oh yes, you have," his wife replied. "You've been preparing for this job since you were a child. You just didn't know it. Every experience, every instructor whom you've encountered has prepared you to be President, to identify what's wrong, to seek the advice of wise and competent people and to take the most appropriate course of action. Now you have the opportunity to teach the Americans who never learned such things—who they are, where they came from, and where they can go—to lead them toward health, safety, and well-being. The country that you love is waiting for you to make it well again, Mason."

"You've always had a way to lift me up whenever the load gets heavy. America is lucky to get such an incredible woman for its First Lady. How do you like the title, First Lady?" Mason asked.

"Like it belongs to someone else," Norene answered. "I'm not going to like all the attention. I really like my privacy. If it didn't mean being away from you and supporting what you are doing, I'd be painting the country sides of Florence, Italy, or Provence, France. But right now my place is with you, and yours is with America."

"Then, let's go do it," Mason said, holding his wife's hand as the two of them entered the East Wing of the White House, where a small group had gathered. Mason had insisted that the event be understated. The Edmonds' children and grandchildren were there, as were Gabriel, Dale, Raley, Morley, and General Harold Purcell.

An officer dressed in full uniform was stationed at the door to the East Room. His was an unfamiliar face to reporters and most of the attendees. It was that of General Daren Borden, though on this occasion the General wore the bar of a first lieutenant.

First, the Edmonds and Bronkston families gathered for a memorable family photograph. Norene stood at Mason's right. He insisted that two spaces to his left remain vacant. "These are reserved for my mother and father," he told the photographer.

Following the family photograph, Mason was joined by Gabriel, Dale, Raley, Morley, and the General Purcell. Once again, it was decided that General Daren Borden's association with the group be kept top secret. It was the first and only photograph of the Operation Annuit Coeptis team—minus one. Mason simply told the others present that these were long-time friends who had helped him along the way and he wanted to show his appreciation by having them attend the ceremony.

Following the photographic session, the Chief Justice of the Supreme Court, Mason, and Norene moved to a predetermined area in the room before the television camera. The Chief Justice asked, "Are you ready?"

"I am," Mason replied, with his mind momentarily flashing back to the August afternoon in 1951 when he had stood before Laney, saluting as his scoutmaster had taught, and repeated then the words, "I will do my best to do my duty to God and my country. ..."

"If you are ready, place your left hand on the Bible, raise your right hand and repeat after me," the Chief Justice said,

> *"I, Mason Lambert Edmonds, do solemnly swear and affirm that I will faithfully execute the office of President of the United States, and will to the best of my ability preserve, protect, and defend the Constitution of the United States, so help me God."*

Mason repeated the oath as required.

"Congratulations, Mr. President," the Chief Justice said. "May God be with you."

"Thank you, Your Honor. I will need all the help I can get, including yours," Mason replied, gazing into the eyes of the Chief Justice with a look of both resolve and humility.

"You've got it, Mr. President," the Chief Justice said, leaning in so that bystanders couldn't overhear his remarks, "with everything that the Constitution allows."

"That's all any President should ever ask for," Mason replied.

As the newly sworn President and Chief Justice were exchanging words, Raley bent toward Morley and said, "My friend, you have just witnessed the oath that will be heard around the world."

....

Following the ceremony, Mason turned to the television camera and made a short statement that was broadcast around the world. He spoke from the heart and used no notes or teleprompter.

"My fellow Americans, you have just heard me repeat the words of an oath that every President before me has repeated. I have sworn on God's word and on the Constitution of this great nation to 'faithfully execute the office of President of the United States of America.' Those words mean that I have pledged my allegiance to you, the people of the United States of America, that I will do everything in my power to keep this nation and its citizens strong, healthy, and safe from those who have sworn oaths to destroy her. And, to live up to these promises, I need your help.

"I am not a politician. I am one of you; a citizen who has been called to duty, an 'average' American who believes his time on this earth is to be spent in such a manner as to leave this great nation better than he found it. However, this dream, this responsibility, can be realized only if you join with me, putting all the things that have divided us aside and come together as the pledge we repeat each time we stand before our flag says: 'one nation, under God, indivisible with liberty and justice for all.' If you will pledge allegiance to the flag, which signifies this great republic, and no other, we can, once again, become 'one nation.' If every American will let this time-honored pledge of allegiance be your compass in all aspects of your lives, the United States will rise from the ashes that we see mounting around us as did the mythical Phoenix and rise to newer and greater heights.

"In our quest to keep America safe, we have to realize that the kinds of wars fought by our fathers are no longer. There are no 'front lines.' The whole world is a battlefield. And, like a fog, the enemy is able to cover the entire landscape, engulfing us in every corner of America and in every phase of our lives. Simply stated, the 'War on Terror' is, in truth, a 'War for Sovereignty.' It is a war in which every American is a warrior every minute of every day. In such a war, vigilance is not a sometimes thing. It is an all-time thing.

"To win the battles facing us as a nation, we have to remain both united and committed to a common cause, the preservation of a way of life that once made us the envy of the world, and a united front that our enemies feel the need to divide for the purpose of burying us in a common grave.

"Tomorrow I will ask the newly revised Congress to confirm General Harold Purcell as Vice President of the United States of America. General Purcell is not only an accomplished defender of this country, he is a tested patriot and capable leader, the kind of man that I need at my side, the kind of man that America needs to help regain the respect it has lost around the world in recent years.

"On this occasion—and in accepting the office of President of this great nation—I also wish to announce that I will not seek, nor accept, the candidacy for this office in the next election. I will return to doing what I love, and would like to believe I do best, being a physician and surgeon.

"I have just taken an oath to defend the Constitution and the nation it was constructed to preserve. Now I make this pledge to you. During the time I hold this office, I will give you every ounce of my being, every fiber of my body. Every waking moment will be committed to righting America's 'ship of state,' a vessel that has temporarily ventured off course. I will surround myself with patriots who are smarter than I, patriots who are dedicated only to America's success and longevity and not that of nations who are self-proclaimed enemies of this Union.

"I will delegate tasks to the individuals best qualified to complete them, regardless of race, religious preferences, or any other so-called politically correct identification. I will insist that people who are responsible for doing your work—the people's work—

carry out their responsibilities with honor and integrity.

"I will appoint people to judgeships and offices of authority who I believe know right from wrong and will do what is right for this nation and mankind because they believe it their God-given duty to do so.

"I will never use this office for personal gain. And I will call upon you, my fellow Americans, to take it as a personal challenge and responsibility to once again turn our country away from failed policies and self-serving agendas. In an act of solidarity behind our Constitution, I will ask those of you who identify yourselves as 'hyphenated' Americans to drop all letters and hyphens before the word American. Tear down all barriers that divide us. Hold hands and stick together.

"Join me and the capable people who I will ask to assist me in making America the icon of freedom and opportunity, a nation respected by those who choose to be our allies as well as those who, from this day forward, foolishly choose to be our adversaries; for we will not be overtaken from within or without. We know who the enemy is and we intend to keep that enemy at bay.

"I call upon parents throughout this nation to become masters of your own home, your families, teaching your children right from wrong. Teach them American history—as it actually occurred. Teach your children the meaning of tough love, and what it means to be loyal to the family unit that makes us all Americans. Make your homes and neighborhoods shining examples of

American pride and dignity. Wear symbols of and/or fly 'Old Glory' with pride.

"Get off the sofa, put down electronic games, and move about neighborhood, cities, and states, doing productive work and engaging in activities that enhance not only your own lives, but those of others. Take responsibility for your own well-being. Do the things that lead to longer, healthier, and more fulfilling lives. Pursue life, liberty, and happiness with vigor and enthusiasm. But most of all let us stop apologizing for being the world's advocate for freedom and human rights. Be proud to call yourself an American.

"You will teach these things best by demonstrating them to your children. And, as you lead by example, I ask that you work with me and my new Administration to put government back in its rightful place, as *a servant* to the people, and not what it has become, the people's master.

"Let us begin anew. Let us look to the past and revisit the basis of our being; yet let us also look into the future and create a Republic of our own doing, one that personifies the visions of our Founding Fathers and the yet undefined dreams and aspirations of our children and our children's children.

"My fellow Americans, some will say that these are ambitious undertakings—that the world I have described has outlived its time. I take exception to such fatalistic delusions. The world of which I dream was once a reality and it can be, again; but only if people like you and me do what we are being called to do—stand up to the true enemies of human rights, those who would make man dependent on government.

"America is the world's last hope; and you and I are America. What will the historians write about us? Will it be that we saved our country from the graveyards of history, that we rallied around our flag and raised her from the beastly dragon that was about to consume her? As we ponder this question, let us realize the implications in our collective answer. Then move forward with 'the chance of a lifetime in a lifetime of chance.' Good night. May God bless you, and may God bless America."

Mason was joined by Norene and their family, who wrapped their arms around him and told him how proud they were of him. "I wish your mother and father could have been here today. They would have been so proud of you," Norene said.

"I, too, wish my parents could have been here," Mason replied. "As I was speaking, I felt their presence. At least yours are here in the flesh."

Then the members of Operation Annuit Coeptis approached their partner and exchanged manly hugs. "Can you guys stay for a while? I'd like for you to come to the Oval Office so that we can talk about some of the things I just promised the American people," the newly sworn President asked.

"It would be our honor, Mr. President," Raley replied.

"Listen, guys. When it's just us, can we give that Mr. President stuff a rest?"

"With all due respect, Mr. President," General Purcell protested, "you must allow us to show the office of the presidency the respect it deserves, sir."

"I understand," Mason replied. "Now let's go to that office."

As the group began to exit the room, "Lieutenant" Borden, who had guarded the East Room door, positioned himself behind them, following five steps to the rear.

Gabriel handed the new President a package and said, "When you can, read these books. I think that it might contain some of the answers to questions that will come your way."

"Thanks, Gabe," Mason said, taking the package from his friend. The newly sworn President, Norene, and the family led the detail through the corridors toward the Oval Office.

When the informal procession reached the elevators that led to the private quarters, Norene gave her husband a big hug and whispered in his ear, "Hurry home."

Mason smiled and whispered back, "I won't be too long. But it will be a while before either of us is really *home* again. For us, this stately house represents 'temporary quarters.' I'll be up shortly," he said to Norene and the remainder of his family. "Please wait up for me."

With General Borden following, the men continued down the hall toward the Oval Office. When the doors opened, the men who were Operation Annuit Coeptis realized the significance of what they had done and where they were standing.

"This is sacred ground," Mason said, inviting his friends to have a seat on the sofas and chairs opposite the massive wood-carved desk. "I've only been here twice, but I know that this office is a seat of power and honor. Unfortunately, it has also been a harbor of deception and betrayal."

"Especially during the past two years," Morley said.

"It is my intent to return it to the status it enjoyed when Abraham Lincoln, Teddy Roosevelt, Harry Truman, and Ronald Regan sat behind that desk." Mason pointed to the desk across the room. "Don't get me wrong. I'm not trying to insinuate that I'm in their league, the men whose names I just mentioned."

"Don't say that, Mr. President," General Purcell said, "Many men have entered this office with those feelings and have been shaped by the office into great leaders."

"I will never delude myself into believing that I am anyone other than who I am, who I have always been. Nevertheless, we have a job to do and we are going to use Reagan's and Kennedy's policies as an initial framework to shape our own. These are different times, but many of President Reagan's and President Kennedy's policies should work as well today as they did back when, even though America is dealing with different kinds of enemies, foreign and domestic.

"The first thing we have to do is to regain the trust of the American people. That was the intention of the remarks I delivered to the world just minutes ago," Mason said. "We must move quickly to fulfill the promises I made out there, put in place people of responsibility to fill the vacancies created by the recent resignations. And I'm going to need you guys every step of the way. You got me into this. Now I'm going to need you to stay with me until I can pass the baton to General Purcell."

"We'll be with you, Mr. President, and him afterwards," Dale said.

"Do you know how strange that sounds? *Mr. President.*" Mason asked. "Do you really realize what we have bitten off here?"

General Purcell was quick to answer, "Mr. President, if a country lawyer from Illinois, a haberdasher from Missouri, and an actor from California could change the course of history, just imagine what a doctor with a law degree can do."

"Yeah, especially one who breeds and trains horses," Morley added, jokingly.

"Operation Annuit Coeptis has not yet accomplished its mission. We have a lot of work left to do and only nineteen months to complete the task. Fellows," Mason said, "I am going to keep all of you as close to my side as possible. Will you serve in the capacity I need you to serve?"

"I'm in," Raley Stovall answered.

"Count me in, too," Dale said.

"I was hoping you'd ask," Gabriel added.

"Brother," Morley said, "this could be fun."

"You know my answer, Mr. President," General Purcell replied.

"If behind the scenes is where I can be of the most help, it is in behind the scenes I shall remain," Daren stated.

"Then I've got the makings of an All-American team," Mason replied. "We kick it off tomorrow morning here in this office at seven o'clock. I'll have plenty of coffee and protein bars brought in. We're not going to serve donuts and cookies in this White House. We're going to set a good example and tackle this healthcare issue from inside out. That's what I originally came to this town to do."

"Does that mean that you want us to jog into work every morning, Mr. President and do sit-ups and push-ups between appointments?" Raley asked, trying to interject a bit of levity into an otherwise mind-boggling situation.

"No, I don't think that will be necessary, but I do want to issue a presidential order that elevators are off limits for anyone who can scale a flight of stairs.

"Here's my plan", Mason said. "General Purcell, as I indicated during my address to the nation earlier this afternoon, with your permission I would like to place your name into nomination for the office of Vice President."

"I'd be honored," the General replied, "though like yours, it is not an office I ever intended to seek."

"Dale, I plan to nominate you as the new Intelligence Director. Raley, I am going to nominate you as my Attorney General. Gabriel, I want you to be my Director of the CIA. And Morley, you will serve as my Chief of Staff and Special Adviser to the President. Daren, I am going to ask that General Purcell recommend you as a special adviser to the new Chairman of the Joint Chiefs, who will replace him. That way, you will have access to all military operations and still be able to keep out of the limelight. Is everyone willing to serve in the capacity I suggested, assuming that Congress confirms my nominations?"

Each man nodded affirmatively.

"You will interview the people in each of the sections of government that you will oversee. I will leave it up to you to decide who are worthy of the jobs they are holding down and who should be replaced. We are going to cut the fat out of Washington, literally. I want the best people available, regardless of where they are from, who are their parents, party affiliations, or who they supported in the last elections. We are going to try to take the politics and 'political correctness' out of government and run it unlike the business it is, a humongous, out-of-control business that is on the verge of collapse and still acting as though profits are rolling in."

The President added, "Now, one thing we should have learned from history. We need a plan steeped in logic. We need to have a clearly defined objective that we can relay to the American people, one based on sound business and moral principles, one with which they can easily identify. We will never lie to the people. If the press misprints or misstates my remarks or intentions, we will move quickly to see that the people hear the truth."

"And, how do we overcome the biased reporting that the people will hear from the press," Dale asked.

"We are going to be proactive and go on the offensive with keeping the American people duly informed. Unless it is a matter of national security, we will tell the truth, no matter what the consequences. If I have to, I'll address the nation every week. I want to reestablish trust in government, something that has long been missing. *Change* was the mantra of the last Administration. Ours will be the word *chance*. We will stress what I said in my address to the people, that we have a chance of a lifetime to follow the lead of the Founding Fathers, sacrifice individual agendas for the well-being of all."

"I like it," Gabriel interjected. "It's what all of us bought into when we served in the military and on teams of any kind."

"Our first mission is to convince the people that we are capable of looking after their business," Mason continued. "We will gather the best minds in the country to help write what I hope to be a reorganization plan that will turn the tide toward hope and prosperity. I don't want career politicians making policy. I want *professionals* doing the people's business."

"That will be a refreshing kind of 'change'." Raley said, sarcastically.

"The people in the trenches must become involved in their government. We are going to stop talking *to* Americans and begin talking *with* them," Mason said. His juices were flowing; and he was on a roll. It was almost as though he had suddenly risen to the task at hand.

"We'll need to review how Winston Churchill rallied Britain during some of its darkest days. He was not only a masterful communicator, he was a master strategist," Morley added. "I've read everything ever written about Churchill."

"Then, you come up with the 'Churchill Plan for America," Mason said. "We will learn the lessons of history, embracing those that succeeded, while avoiding those that failed. Once we establish the kind of government that this country needs, not only for the times at hand, but those to follow, we will create a succession plan that includes responsible people from all parties and try to educate the people on the errors of partisan politics."

"Good luck on that," Raley Stovall interrupted. "People in both parties have been brainwashed to believe that theirs is good and the other is bad."

"I am fully aware of that fact," Mason replied. "That's where the Tea Party participants come in. They are building the Independent base, one that will hold both parties accountable. I didn't say it was going to be easy. The 'Entitlement Generation' is trying to discredit their movement with trumped-up charges of racism. Some people seem to thrive on playing the good conscience of the people they hate. I want to be known as the President of Independent America, meaning an America that is independent from government and all kinds of prejudice."

"Do you mean that you are going to resign for the Republican Party and declare yourself as an Independent?" Gabriel asked

"No, I don't intend to resign from anything. I want to join and lead the people who feel that a free and independent citizenry is America's last hope. I said that we are going to demonstrate the self-destructive consequences of illogical partisanship, the kind of blind allegiance that Chauvin's followers exhibited in the eighteen hundreds."

"The National Organization of Women and the New Black Panthers might take exception to your definition of chauvinism," Dale chimed in.

"N.O.W has taken a broad-based term and hung it around the necks of men like a yoke. The Panthers are one of the most racist organizations in America. It will not be our intent to offend or alienate anyone or any well-meaning organization," Mason replied. "However, we will not waltz around the facts. Evil needs to be offended. The American people are ready for straight talk and truth. I think they are fed up with lies, hollow promises and misrepresentations."

"I couldn't agree with you more," General Purcell added.

"General, in your new capacity as Vice President," Mason responded, "I intend to have you take the lead on a number of issues, especially those to rebuild our military and regain our status in the world. Securing our borders and defending this nation will be a top priority. You will not be a 'behind-the-scenes' Vice President. The American people will know that you are involved in policy and the execution thereof. I want the people to begin thinking of you as their next President. This nation needs another General, like its *first* President. We are in a war for our very survival. It's time that we had warrior at the helm again. And I intend to see that America gets it, if it's the last thing I do."

"Yeah," Gabriel chimed in, "It will be comforting to see someone at the helm who has actually stared evil in the face and beaten it into the ground."

"That's why the General is the best choice to become America's next President," Mason added. "When he moves into that office, Daren should remain in the Pentagon to be our eyes and ears."

"Hopefully, I can help convince Congress and your new Secretary of Defense to take even better care of our reserve forces and national guard retirees," Daren Borden said. "In years to come, they are going to be an even more important asset of our domestic defense forces.

"During these next nineteen months," Mason told the group, "not only will we assemble a team of competent men and women for him to lead into the battle for the hearts and minds of the American people, but someone who can take care of today's needs and challenges. We will be putting a winning team in place that can make the next ten years a renaissance of American values. And, it is my hope that I can count on all of you to see that the plan succeeds."

"If we can do this," Raley added, "the next decade will be reminiscent of the nineteen eighties. America will be that shining city on the hill that the rest of the world will have no choice but to look up to."

Morley said, "We should consider reviving a 'Contract With America-like' theme and have each candidate for office in upcoming elections sign an oath to look after the people's business in a thoughtful and prudent manner. It worked well for Newt Gingrich and company. They tried to be too conciliatory to the opposing party who played on Gingrich's trust in the goodness of man and lost the clout that the people gave them."

The newly sworn President reached into his back pocket and took out a small notebook, the edges of which were worn. From it he retrieved a one-dollar bill. Then he reached into his left pocket and pulled out his wallet, from which he retrieved five additional one-dollar bills. He handed a bill to the five men in his presence and said, "The bill I hold in my right hand was given to me by my grandmother when I was thirteen years old. She told me that America's foundation was inscribed on this piece of currency, as an indicator of the nation's sovereignty.

"Look on the back of the bill that I have given to each of you," he added. "There, you will see two circles surrounding symbols. Together, they comprise the great seal of the United States.

"The First Continental Congress requested that Benjamin Franklin and a group of men come up with a seal. It took the first Congress four years to accomplish this task and another two years to get it approved."

Mason asked, looking at the faces of his colleagues, "Do all of you know the story of the dollar bill?"

"A lot of it," Morley answered, "but let us hear where you are going with this."

Mason continued, 'If you look at the left-hand circle, you will see a pyramid. Notice the face of the pyramid is lighted, and the western side is dark. At the time the faces of this bill were created, this country was just beginning. There were a lot of unknowns in the West."

"Yeah and there still is," Raley said.

"At the time that the dollar bill was designed, early Americans had not begun to explore that part of our country, nor did the Founders know what the country they were creating would do for Western civilization. The pyramid—the most stable of geometric designs—is uncapped, signifying that we were not even close to being finished. Inside the capstone you have the all-seeing eye, an ancient symbol for divinity. It was Franklin's belief that one man couldn't do it alone, but a group of men, with the favor and help of God, could do anything."

"I didn't know that Franklin said those things. However, I think that Operation Annuit Coeptis just verified his remarks," Dale interjected.

"Now, look at the Latin words around the pyramid, 'ANNUIT COEPTIS,'" Mason said. "As you know by now, these words are interpreted as 'Providence (God) has favored our undertaking.' The Latin *below* the pyramid, 'NOVUS ORDO SECLORUM,' means, 'a new order has begun.'"

"That sounds a bit ominous," Raley chimed in, "especially considering what the Order of the Illuminati has up its sleeve."

"We'll get to that," Mason replied and continued, "At the base of the pyramid is the Roman numeral for 1776 (MDCCLXXVI). Also note that the phrase, 'IN GOD WE TRUST,' is inscribed on this currency. This was inscribed there to send a message to the disciples of God's enemy, Lucifer."

"If the previous Administration had remained in office for another six years, you can bet that phrase would be eliminated from everything in America," Dale added.

"Now, if you look at the right-hand circle, and check it carefully, you will see what is on every national cemetery in the United States. It is also on the Parade of Flags Walkway at the Bushnell, Florida National Cemetery, and is the centerpiece of monuments to most heroes. Slightly modified, it is the seal of the President of the United States, and it is always visible whenever a President speaks, yet very few people know what the symbols on the seal mean. I wonder if some of our Presidents have known."

"Or cared," Gabriel interjected.

"The bald eagle was selected as a symbol for victory for two reasons," Mason added. "First, he is not afraid of a storm or great heights; he is strong and smart enough to soar above stormy times. Secondly, the eagle wears no material crown. America had just broken from the King of England and his Lucifer-worshiping overlords when the plates for this currency were struck."

Again Gabriel interrupted, "Now a new set of self anointed kings—or gods, as they believe themselves to be—wants to make us their subjects."

"Right," Mason responded. "Notice the shield in front of the eagle is unsupported, indicating that this country is intended to stand on its own. At the top of that shield you will see a white bar, signifying Congress, a unifying factor. In 1776, we were coming together as one nation. In the eagle's beak you will see the phrase: 'E PLURIBUS UNUM,' meaning 'one from many.' And, nowhere on the dollar bill does the hyphen appear. The founding fathers would have charged anyone who used a hyphen in front of 'American' with treason."

"Yeah, a 'melting pot' means that previous ties are melted into one mixture. The people supporting illegal immigration have a different interpretation of 'one from many,' Dale added. "They seem to favor, instead, the policy of 'many from many.'"

"And, that's in direct conflict with the Founding Fathers' intentions," Mason answered. "Above the eagle, you will find the thirteen stars, representing the thirteen original colonies, and any clouds of misunderstanding rolling away. Again, America was coming together as one nation, under God. Notice what the eagle holds in his talons. He holds an olive branch and arrows, signifying that this country wants peace, but we will never apologize for defending ourselves or be afraid to fight to preserve peace. The eagle always wants to face the olive branch, but in time of war, his gaze turns towards the arrows."

"Today, the eagle must have a crick in its neck. Though we are at war, it has been forced to look the other way for the past two years," Raley said sarcastically.

"We're going to change that," General Purcell injected into the conversation. "A sleeping giant eagle is about to be aroused."

Mason continued with his story. "Some people contend that the number thirteen is an unlucky number. This is almost a worldwide belief. The most credible origin of this myth comes from the thirteen hundreds, when, threatened by power of the Knights Templar—and eager to acquire their wealth—King Philip secretly ordered the mass arrest and assassination of all the Knights in France on Friday, October 13, 1307-*Friday the 13th*. Though we don't know if the Founding Fathers had any direct links to the Knights Templar, many were Freemasons, a group thought to be committed to carrying some of the traditions of the Knights Templar forward. And the Illuminati's Rothschild Family had ties with France's former King Philip, a connection that faced the founding fathers and us today. The dollar bill sends that message, too, to all who are sworn to protect this nation against its enemies.'"

"How do you know all this stuff?" Raley Stovall asked.

"I've long been interested in connecting the dots between the past, present, and future," Mason replied. "In the next few months, I want to try and open the eyes of Americans so that they can begin to do so, as well. But let me continue with the story of the dollar bill that I learned from my grandmother.

"Though the number thirteen was embraced by America's Founders, you will usually never see a room numbered thirteen, or any hotels or motels with a thirteenth floor. But think about this from the perspective of a group of men not unlike us who were stepping into the unknown. The number thirteen was probably a message to the Rothschilds and the twelve other powerful families with whom they associated that 'we intend to establish an open empire to counter the one you rule from the shadows.' You see, each of the Illuminati's thirteen ruling families has a Council of Thirteen as well. The number thirteen has great significance to them. They know that there are twelve types of energies that pass through the ten aspects—or dimensions—of the God-mind. The totality of the twelve energies equals a thirteenth energy. Having experienced the twelve ascending spheres of knowledge, the spirit is ready for the final realm of enlightenment—the thirteenth one—known in the science of Kaballah as Adam Kadmon; thus the name the thirteen families adopted for themselves: "The Illuminated Ones' or 'Illuminati.'"

"That's where their name comes from," Dale blurted out. "I've always wondered about its origin."

"After you've read the book I gave to you after your swearing in ceremony, you will understand all of this even better," Gabriel said to Mason.

Mason nodded, and continued, "The Founding Fathers knew all these things and set out to forestall the Illuminati's plan to take over the world, at least their emerging part of the world. The Illuminati also refer to themselves as 'a supranational sovereignty.' At least that's the term used by the former American member, David Rockefeller. His and the other twelve families have always known that there are really thirteen Zodiac signs, not twelve as most people think. The families have kept the thirteenth sign—sign of the Dragon—hidden for centuries. They keep the qualities and traits of Lucifer's and the Annunaki's sign secret to avoid giving away clues to the reptilian mind-pattern of thriving off the blood of its captives."

Morley commented, "I never totally understood what role the Illuminati played in the founding of America. I had considered that they were the enemies of America from the get go."

"It's an enigma," Mason replied. "From what I have learned about *the Illuminati* and from its 'Protocol of the Elders of Zion,' once they witnessed the formation of this nation they moved in rather quickly to counter the measures that the Founding Fathers were instilling in the Constitution to keep them from gaining control of this side of the Atlantic—and by using the Illuminati's own secret code, they were sending a message to the Inner Circle. That's the only explanation that I have, now, to explain the use of the number thirteen by America's Founding Fathers. It is interesting though that at the time of the Declaration of Independence, there were:

> thirteen original colonies,
> thirteen signers of the Declaration,
> thirteen stripes on our flag,
> thirteen steps on the Pyramid,
> thirteen letters in Annuit Coeptis,
> thirteen letters in E Pluribus Unum,
> thirteen stars above the eagle,
> thirteen bars on the shield,
> thirteen leaves on the olive branch,
> thirteen fruits and, if you look closely,
> thirteen arrows.

And finally, if you notice the arrangement of the thirteen stars in the right-hand circle, you will see that they are arranged as a Star of David. Keep in mind that some of the original thirteen families were of Jewish origin. Imprinting the Star of David on the dollar bill was ordered by George Washington who, when he asked a wealthy Philadelphian named Hayim Solomon what he would like as a personal reward for his services to the Continental Army, Solomon said he wanted nothing for himself but that he would like something for his people that would indicate their role in founding a nation that, hopefully, God would look favorably on. The Star of David was the result. Few people know that it was Solomon's fortune, or that of those he fronted for, that funded the Continental Army. Mr. Solomon saw the new world as a 'new Jerusalem—the shining city on the hill'—alluded to in the prophesies and immediately became a true patriot. He gave everything to that vision in which he believed and died a pauper."

"Knowing that the Illuminati generally finance both sides of wars, do you think that Hayim Solomon could have been an Illuminist?" Dale asked.

"Not if he died a pauper," Mason replied.

General Borden added, "And, like Hayim Solomon, too many veterans have invested too much to ever let the messages inscribed on the one-dollar bill fade into oblivion. In recent years, too many veterans remember coming home to an America that didn't seem to care. And far too many veterans never came home at all."

"The message of the dollar bill will be the civics' lesson and agenda of my Administration," Mason stated. "I want every member of my Cabinet and every government employee to know the story. I want every school in America to teach the lesson of the dollar bill and the chance *to earn one*. If I have to, I will visit the schools and tell the story myself. Or, maybe, I'll use the Presidential Saturday morning address to the nation to teach the story."

"That's a clever idea," Gabriel said. "I like it."

"I'd like to think of the project as one to repatriate our schools and institutions of higher learning, to have them return—at least in principle—to the mindset of our founding fathers. If we can build upon the ashes of treachery and deceit that caused the edifice, called America, to implode, perhaps a new America—one free of the Hidden Hand of the Illuminati—can rise from its own ashes."

"Changing the mindset of liberal-minded teachers won't be easy," Daren said.

"I didn't mean to imply that it would be easy," the President said, "Nothing that our OAC team has accomplished has been easy. Nevertheless, I want to take America back to the basics, to her beginning, so that we can not only understand our roots, but understand the sacrifices that were made by freedom-loving men and women who gave their all so that a new country could be born. And I want each of you to pledge that you will help me carry this message forward."

"Though I know that you've denied the obvious, it sounds as though you have been preparing to be President for a very long time. I will help you carry your message to the people, Mr. President," General Purcell said immediately.

The others pledged to do their part as well.

"I didn't intend to give a speech here today. I only wanted to share my thoughts and see if each of you is in agreement," Mason said.

"We are with you," Gabriel replied, enthusiastically. The others followed with the same answer.

"We'll have to be creative with what we name the contract that we intend to have the candidates' sign who agree to run for Congress in the next election. I don't want to call it the same as the nineteen eighties group named it. Use something that includes the term 'oath.'

"And this time," Mason added, "we will put people in positions of power who will not lose their way, cannot be bought by power or money, and keep a hand on the throttle, not just for the short term, but for decades to come. If we can do these things, Khrushchev's promise will not come to pass. If there's any burying to be done, it will be us—*the U.S.*—who will be doing the burying."

"What about the term, *'Project Thirteen'*? Gabriel asked.

"Yeah," Dale replied, "in recognition of the repetition of the number thirteen on the dollar bill."

"And the biblical repetitions of the number twelve, plus *the One* omnipotent being responsible for all that is," Daren interjected.

"I like it," Raley added.

"Me, too," Morley said.

"What about you, Mr. President?" General Purcell asked. "It's your plan."

"Project Thirteen," Mason said. "I like its ring. Is there enough money from the recovered assets to distribute at least twelve thousand dollars to Americans who deserve it?"

"Twelve thousand and *one* dollars," Morley interjected. "We'll give each of the recipients *one* to keep on themselves as a reminder of the messages on the dollar bill."

Raley pulled out his calculator and punched numbers. "There is enough money," he said, "If we recover all that was stolen by the previous Administration and their comrades."

"That's perfect," Mason replied, "a dozen thousand dollars, plus one. Now, let's move on securing the nation's future," he added, turning his attention to General Purcell.

"Mr. President," the General said, "to get America back on track we have to look at the challenges before us as a war that we have no alternative but to win, as did the founders when they broke away from the grips of British imperialism. Unless we look at a new declaration, freeing the people from the mounting vice of socialistic policies, we will go the way of other failed civilizations. What do you have *us* do, Mr. President?"

"Do what you do best," Mason answered, rising up out of his chair. "Be bold. Be brave. Be Americans. Be the custodians of the people's trust. Present the facts. Tell the truth and let an informed people decide for themselves the kind of destiny they want to create. I for one trust the hearts and souls of the American people. If we put the fate of the nation back into their hands, America should be all right."

"We'll follow your lead," General Purcell said, glancing at the others in the room for affirmation.

In unison, all agreed.

"Then, let's all get to work. Each of you knows what to do. For me, I'm going to start by drafting the remarks I intend to make in my final address to the nation as its President."

"But you still have almost two years left in this term," Morley protested.

"Yes, I do," Mason replied, "However, if I start now, I'll know what all I have to accomplish *before* I step aside."

As the meeting began to break up, Mason approached General Purcell and asked," Harold, can you stay behind for a few minutes? I want to ask you something."

"Absolutely," the General replied.

The others said their goodbyes and exited.

"General, do you remember the first day we met, when you told me that your great grandfather had been a sharecropper near Prideville?" Mason inquired.

"Yes, I do," the General replied. "I told you that he had been a slave, but was set free and ended up there."

"You know that I chose the name for Operation Annuit Coeptis. When I suggested it, you seemed to be a bit stunned. Prior to that time, did the words, 'God has blessed our work' mean anything special to you?"

"They sure did," General Purcell replied. "They have been passed down through my family for several generations."

"What was your great grandfather's name?" Mason asked.

"Harold Henderson," the General replied. "I was named after him. Why do you ask?"

"General, you aren't going to believe this. My great grandmother knew your great grandfather and great grandmother well. They worked on her farm after they were set free."

"It was your great grandmother who gave them the horse and wagon, wasn't it?"

"It was," Mason replied. "And, she wrote the words, 'God has blessed our work' on the bottom of the letter of recommendation she wrote for him. What a small world it is."

"You know, Dr. Edmonds, my grandmother used to play with your grandmother. Wasn't her name Laney?"

"It was." Mason replied. "The notebook from which I retrieved the dollar bill earlier contains a virtual library of wisdom that I learned from her and some others along the way."

"My grandmother was Mary, Harold and Hattie's oldest daughter. I'm so glad to meet a descendent of the lady who took my ancestors in and gave them a chance when they had nothing but hope and the willingness to work," General Purcell said. "Someday, I would like to talk to you about the wisdom that Miss Laney—that's what my grandmother called her—shared with you."

"I'd like that," the President replied.

"And I'll tell you about the things that my grandmother, Mary, told me," General Purcell added. "I suspect that there'll be a lot of similarity. She said that Miss Laney taught her how to read and write and that they talked a lot. They were like sisters. Your people gave my people a chance to better themselves."

"And, they did. Times were hard in those days for everybody. Obviously, a chance was what your family needed. Just look at how far you and your ancestors have come," Mason said to the General. "God has, indeed, blessed the hard work of you and your family."

"Those of us who put our faith first and worked to make life better have done all right. Just like your family did," General Purcell added. "We'll make a good team, Mr. President."

"I think it's time that you called me Mason," the doctor responded.

"And for you to call me Harold," the General said.

"And one last thing," President Edmonds said. "Would you look into a trip made by General Moon to Russia within the past couple of years? I understand that President Padgett sent him there to cut a deal with the Russians to send troops to the U.S. in case civil war breaks out here."

The look on General Purcell's face spoke volumes. "Did President Padgett do this?" the General asked. "That bastard! He really is out to destroy America. I would bet that Padgett surveyed U.S. Soldiers, Sailors, and Marines and found out that they wouldn't take up arms against fellow Americans. So, he decided to cut a deal with the Russians to do it for him."

The President answered, "We also have to assume that the massive influx of Muslims into the U.S. plays into his plan too."

"All he'd have to have done was to arm them with weapons," the General said.

"Or refuse to secure America's borders and let them bring them with them," Mason added.

"We've got a mess on our hands," General Purcell said. "If you don't need me any more today, I need to get to work on this."

The two men first shook hands and then, with a mannish hug, renewed a bond that had been established between their families more than one hundred and fifty years before, at a time in history when such things were uncommon. But it was more. The handshake and hug sealed a pledge to bring Americans together.

As Harold Purcell was leaving the office, he turned to Mason and said, "I should have picked up on the connection when you chose 'Annuit Coeptis' as the name of our undertaking."

CHAPTER 21

"God help us," President Edmonds sighed, dropping the final Operation Annuit Coeptis report on the desk before him. "Those sons of bitches truly believe that they are the descendents of the ancient Annunaki. This time, however, they have not only defied the laws of God but those of man. They have lied and conned their way into untold wealth and power." The twisted trail of treachery and deceit was farther-reaching than even he had imagined.

Though the report contained mostly bad news, at least one promising conclusion had been reached by *OAC*:

> *"It is our conclusion that America's best days lie behind her. However, a 1770's colonial-like revolution could reset the Cycle of Democracy, free Americans from bondage, and give the U.S. new life for generations to come."*

With mind churning, Mason returned to the list of high-ranking government officials who were owned by the Order of the Illuminati.

"The entire group ought to be hanged on the fifty-yard line during half time at the Super Bowl," the new President said to himself. "How could people who despise America have ascended to power right before our eyes? And, once in office, how could they have maneuvered legislation through Congress that clearly was designed to break the backs of a loyal and unsuspecting people?"

For a non-elected President, especially when the polls showed that a vast majority of Americans distrusted Washington, winning back the people's confidence would not be easy.

Still pondering the most recent opus of revelations, Mason backed away from the presidential desk, turning as he approached the windows at the south end of the Oval Office. As he moved closer to the partially frosted glass, a blanket of shadows could be seen stretching across the White House lawn. Above the Washington cityscape, a full moon hung softly in the evening skies. As if anticipating some miraculous sign to appear, Mason's weary eyes scanned the heavens.

"Somewhere out there are the souls of men and women who paid the ultimate sacrifice for their country," Mason said to whatever spirits might be listening. "How will their spirits respond to the revelation that members of their own government were engaged in a game of international monopoly, bargaining for real estate of a global board with their lives? What would *they* want me to say on their behalf, to Congress, to the world? More than likely they'd want me to tell America to wake up and come to their senses. Otherwise the ghosts of soldiers past will haunt us until we do." Clinching his teeth, he could feel the muscles in his jaws bulge in response to the thought of what the previous Administration had done.

The President had good reason to be both angry and concerned. The grip of what *OAC* called the "*Hidden Hand, the Invisible Empire, Moriah Conquering Wind, Bilderbergers,* and a *Shadow Government*" permeated so deeply into American culture that it was hard to know whom to trust. The Illuminati were everywhere. Historical records showed that the Inner Circle would not hesitate to destroy anyone or anything that got in their way. And President Edmonds, the former physician, congressman, and HHS Secretary was moving quickly into the line of fire.

Mason was keenly aware of the consequences of the options at his disposal. He also had to face the fact that he, too, had placed his right hand on the Bible and swore to protect and defend "the Great American Dream" against all enemies, foreign and domestic. The ghosts of soldiers past might be waiting and watching. And he wanted them on his side.

If America had any hope of being spared from subjugation to an oppressive worldwide government, time was short and resources were shorter. He had to act, resolutely. Because of the policies of the previous Administration, the nation was on the verge of financial collapse.

Clearly, a lot was riding on the new President's shoulders. Hopefully, *this* revolution that he intended to lead would be fought at the ballot boxes throughout America. But unless he and his staff could pull off such a miracle, not only would the U.S. be doomed, human rights the world over could be doomed forever. George Orwell's *1984* would become a book of fact, not fiction.

Before he could finish the ghastly thought of an Orwellian-like government controlling the United States of America, a shooting star streaked across the heavens, moving upward from left to right, burning out almost as quickly as it appeared. "Could this be a sign?" Mason said to himself. "If it is an omen, there must be a message. Perhaps, just perhaps, a miracle is possible."

Leaving the window and moving across the room toward the dying flames in the fireplace, Mason looked for an answer. None was forthcoming.

"Could the shooting star be just a flash in the sky and not an omen?" Mason asked, sensing the warmth of the embers on his body, drawing him closer. He lifted the poker from its hook and skillfully stoked what remained of the fire. Immediately, vibrant flames reappeared. The advantage of stoking a seemingly dying fire was just one of many lessons learned at community peanut boilings and as a Boy Scout in the 1950s.

"I wonder what kind of world we'd have today if scouting were taught in America's schools and if it were a prerequisite for holding public office," Mason said as he watched the fiery flames dance to the rhythm of the crackling sounds generated from within. And, then the answer he'd been waiting for leaped into his head.

"I have to find a way to stoke whatever embers still burn in the minds and spirits of the American people and rekindle the commitment to God and country so boldly demonstrated by America's Founding Fathers. Though I addressed these matters to the people following my swearing in ceremony, I have to repeat it clearly and often. Instead of the usual political rhetoric that Presidents put forth, I'll use my first State of the Union speech to reveal what I have learned to be fact. Then I'll publish OAC's findings as a Presidential Commission's Report."

Mason returned to the *Resolute* desk to make an entry into his pocket notebook. Searching for a pen, he opened the cabinet door to the left of the knee hole. Like other parts of the gifted heirloom, it had been carved from the recovered remains of a sunken British ship, the *HMS Resolute*. In 1880, Queen Victoria presented the desk to then President Rutherford B. Hayes. Ever since, it served as a reminder to each Commander-in-Chief that though he may find himself engulfed by a sea of troubles, in one form or another, resoluteness endures.

Behind the desk's cabinet like doors were paired stacks of drawers in which non-classified articles were often stored. Mason tugged on the top drawer of the left hand stack, hoping to locate a pen or pencil. The drawer would open to a third of its length only. Though he found nothing with which to write, the spine of *Let Us Make Man* was clearly visible. It was one of two books that were contained in the package presented to Mason by Gabriel Shade immediately following the presidential oath of office ceremony.

One section of *Let Us Make Man* had immediately caught the President's attention when he opened the package and thumbed through the book, the one that dealt with the seemingly never-ending battle between good and evil, in heaven and on earth.

The package given to Mason by his long-time friend also contained a book that was co-authored by the same author and a colleague in North Carolina that expounded on the theme. The matters facing America and its new President fit right into an ongoing cosmic conflict, the one originally described in Genesis and later Isaiah, when Lucifer and the Angels of Darkness were banished from heaven after an unsuccessful coup d'état and when the Annunaki "sons of god," with the encouragement of

Lucifer, their leader, intermarried with the daughters of Adam and Eve.

As a result of the unauthorized mixing of genes, a hybrid tribe of beings possessing supernatural powers began to multiply and exercise their influence over early mankind. It was the Annunaki's goal to show God that the race He created would rather follow the defiant sons of God led by Lucifer rather than God Himself. Perhaps reviewing the author's previously written thoughts on the subject might provide insight for the President's upcoming address.

Dueling with the unforgiving drawer Mason pulled even harder on the handle. The book he was attempting to retrieve didn't seem to be the problem. Upon closer examination, Mason identified the problem, the edge of a piece of white paper that had somehow become lodged between the drawer and the track on which the drawer was intended to slide.

As luck would have it, the paper was just out of finger's reach. Mason looked around for a retrieving device. He found what he needed on the credenza behind him, the symbolic Presidential letter opener.

With problem solved and paper finally in hand, Mason's eyes were drawn to the upper left hand corner of the crinkled 5x7-inch sheet. An unfamiliar facsimile representing the all-seeing-eye had been embossed in the upper left hand corner. Inscribed immediately below it were the words: NOVUS, NOVUS ORDO SECLORUM. From college Latin, Mason knew that the words meant: A *New,* New World Order. The phrase closely matched the one found on the U.S. dollar bill, only a second "NOVUS" had been added.

Mason proceeded to read the handwritten note that had been inscribed farther down on the battered sheet of paper:

> "President Padgett,
> As directed, the amount of $10 million U.S. was deposited in your personal account on April 13, 2009, in

AIG Private Bank, Zurich, Switzerland (more to come).

Your continued assistance is crucial to The Order's cause.

Solomon"

New questions abounded. "Is there no shame? Who is Solomon? Could 'The Order' refer to the Order of the Illuminati? Could Solomon be George Soros? Could he be a descendent of the ancient Annunaki? Could President Padgett be one too? How could the former President have been so careless as to leave this trail of evidence behind? I didn't know that AIG had a bank in Switzerland. No wonder AIG was bailed out by President Padgett's Administration. *Ten million dollars!* How many such transfers were made to Padgett and members of his Cabinet or to members of Congress?" Mason thought to himself.

"This has to be where some of the unaccounted-for stimulus money went, to private bank accounts in Switzerland." Mason's mind was racing. "The conspiracy might go deeper than even OAC realized. I'm sure Padgett meant to clean out this desk and leave no trace of such activities behind. I guess it shows that in times of duress, even the most cunning of scoundrels becomes careless. This might be the smoking gun we've been looking for."

Though Mason never got around to making the entry he had intended to make in the notebook that he called *Laney's Book of Wisdom*, the President carefully parted the pages. In the dead center of the notebook, he inserted the recently discovered piece of paper.

. . . .

That evening, pressing a button on the phone that connected his office with that of the presidential secretary, Mason heard a familiar voice reply, "Yes, Mr. President."

Mason leaned forward. Peering through the partially closed door, he could see Martha Shores, his trusty assistant, who appeared to be searching for something under her desk while answering her phone. Having worked with Dr. Edmonds throughout his many careers, she had become a master at multitasking.

"Martha, I didn't know you were still here. Why haven't you gone home?" the President asked, speaking into the phone. "I expected to have a member of the night staff answer. What time is it?"

"It's eight thirty, Mr. President. I left earlier, but I had to come back to get a package for my granddaughter. I forgot to take it with me this afternoon. Tomorrow is her birthday and I wanted to give it to her before I came to work. What do you need me to do?"

"If you don't mind, I would like for you to reach a doctor for me," the President replied.

"Are you alright," Martha asked, displaying concern in her voice.

"Oh yes. I'm sorry. I didn't mean to cause alarm," the President said. "I have the doctor's book here on my desk and wanted to ask him about it. It has his name and city of residence on the back inside cover."

"I'll be right there," Martha acknowledged.

Approaching the President's desk, Martha handed him a telephone message. "I found this on my desk when I returned this evening. It was taken by one of the night staff. I thought that it might be important" She passed the note to the President as he handed *Let Us Make Man* to her.

The message read, "Mr. Solomon called from the American Embassy in Brussels, Belgium, and asked that you contact him. His number is [44] (0)29 2078-6633. It is a matter of extreme importance."

"Now they are running the show from the American Embassy in Brussels. If those bastards think that I can be bought, they have another thought coming," Mason said, wadding the note and slamming it into the trashcan under his desk.

Martha stood motionless. She had never seen her boss react in such a manner, at least not to a telephone message. "Do you still want me to make the call to the doctor in Alabama?" she asked.

"Yes, I'm sorry. We'll deal with the other matter tomorrow."

Without further adieu, the President's assistant returned to her desk. In less than a minute she buzzed the President's intercom and announced, "I have the doctor on the line."

....

The conversation was cordial but direct. After getting the answer he had hoped for, the President hung up the phone. He walked back across the room and assumed a familiar pose in front of the fireplace. It was where he did some of his best thinking. With his left hand resting on the mantle, Mason stared again into the flames, pondering the revelations of the evening, especially the phone message from Brussels. He had read that Michel de Nostradamus often stared into candle light, looking for visions of things to come. It was worth a try. He could use all the help he could muster.

"If I am to deal with what is happening today and plan for what tomorrow may bring, I will need to revisit the past. I have to know that what I am doing is the right way to approach what America is up against. History is known to repeat. So, I start at the beginning, begin with the first time that Americans freed themselves from a House of Overlords, in 1776," the President said aloud, as though he intended for the walls of Oval Office to capture his words for posterity. "From there, I may be able to trace a series of connected—but perhaps overlooked—events," Mason surmised, suddenly realizing that the hour was late and he was growing tired.

Again Mason used the poker to control the fire before him. This time he carefully spread the remaining fragments of logs apart allowing the flames to die a natural death.

"That's how they extinguished the fires of patriotism," the President said to himself. "They separated us from the 'one from many' rule."

Once he made sure that the protective screen on the hearth was secure, Mason extinguished the lights in the

Oval Office and headed upstairs to the residential quarters of the White House.

"It has been a long day," he said to himself, mounting the flight of stairs. "The things I've learned seem more like fiction than fact. And because of the nature of what has been revealed, I will surely become a target of the Rothschild Formula."

"What is the Rothschild Formula?" Norene asked, standing at the top of the spiral staircase, who had heard his words to himself. "I was on my way down to get you. It's late and you need some sleep."

"Oh, an old remedy to stop the spread of truth," Mason answered, not wanting to upset his wife.

"Put that mind of yours in neutral," Norene said. "Let's go to bed." Taking her husband's hand in hers, she added, "Come with me. I'll give you a back rub and you'll fall right off to sleep."

CHAPTER 22

It was a short and restless night. Mason had been awake since 3:00 a.m., weaving thoughts of the previous day into a first run at his upcoming State of the Union address. At precisely 7:00 a.m., and with draft in hand, he arrived at the Oval Office. Morley Bronkston, Raley Stovall, Dale Jackson, Gabriel Shade, Daren Borden and Harold Purcell, his partners in OAC, were waiting outside for their regularly scheduled morning meeting with the President.

"Here's what I intend to tell Congress and the American people in my State of the Union address next week," Mason began, handing each of the men a copy of a document that he had spent most of the night drafting, before the men could take their seats on the matching sofas that flanked a now lifeless fireplace. "A lot of what I am going to say and you have before you is a restatement of things that we have discussed on several occasions, but this is the first time that I have put it all together in a story that the American people need to hear. First, I want to run this draft of my upcoming State of the Union address past you guys and make sure that I am not overstating the facts."

Standing before the *Resolute* desk, the President read from pages drafted on a personal computer that he kept upstairs in the residential quarters. As he read aloud, his OAC colleagues occasionally glanced down at the papers that he had given them.

"My fellow Americans, tonight I intend to speak to you, not only as your President, but as one of you, an American who is deeply concerned about the state of this nation.

"When I decided to run for political office in my home state of Alabama, I swore an oath to those whose trust I solicited that I would never lie to them or any other American. Tonight, I intend to keep that promise.

"What you are about to hear will be disturbing, for I am going to reveal for the first time in these honorable chambers a formula for destroying America, however the formula itself is not new. In fact, all or portions of it have been used since this great nation was first founded. Some will find the revelations of the next few minutes unbelievable. I expect there to be an outcry from the architects of the sinister plan that I am about to reveal, elitists who have assumed the roles of gods and conspired to dominate humanity and bring down the United States of America so that it can be folded into a World Government of their own making.

"How could such a thing happen? The answer is simple. Reverse the role of the individual and government. Substitute dependence on *self* for dependence on government.

"It has been said that a democracy cannot exist as a permanent form of government. It can only exist until the voters discover they can vote themselves prosperity from the public treasury. From that moment on, the majority always votes for the candidates promising them the most benefits from the public treasury, with the result that a democracy always collapses over loose fiscal policy, always followed by a dictatorship. After dictatorship comes revolution. What kind of revolution ensues has always been determined by the people.

"The average age of the world's greatest civilizations has been 200 years. Some might find it surprising that the

United States of America has already passed its life expectancy as a democracy. And yet, it is still holding on, though barely. That a wounded America still has a heartbeat is troubling to a group of intellectual elites and world bankers. The reason that our nation is hanging on is because they underestimated the resilient American spirit.

"Research conducted during the past several months revealed a series of unconscionable acts perpetrated on you, the American people, each of which was intended to see that the Cycle of Democracy plays out quickly and that you are taken through the final cycle: from independence to bondage."

The President stopped reading from the pages he held in his hand and spoke directly to his advisers.

"I know that the experts say that a speech should appeal to an eighth-grade graduate, but I think the American people have been underestimated. They need to be reminded of what has happened to other democracies. And this message not only needs to reach Americans, but America's enemies. Do you agree?"

The men sitting on the couches nodded in the affirmative, anxiously waiting to hear the rest of what the President intended to say.

The President returned to his prepared remarks:

"Tonight, I intend to show you how you have been manipulated and lied to for too long. You deserve to know the truth about the state of this Union and how it came to be.

"The investigation that I, along with a group of American patriots, initiated was named in honor of a Latin phrase imprinted on the face of our dollar bill, Annuit Coeptis. The Founding Fathers placed it there for two reasons: as a pledge and a prayer. Annuit Coeptis means 'May the Guiding Power of the universe' look favorably upon our undertakings.'

"Operation Annuit Coeptis, or O.A.C. for short, revealed that America has been under siege for a very long time, in fact since the very birth of this nation.

"In 1776 while American colonies were breaking away from an oppressive European monarchy, a never-before-revealed secret confederacy was being established in Bavaria by a German-born law professor named Adam Weishaupt. He and his hand-picked group of powerful European families were in the throes of creating an ambitious plan designed to take over the world.

"Though insiders and skeptics avow that no connection exists between Professor Weishaupt's Order of the Illuminati, the document named *Protocols of the Elders of Zion,* and America's current problems, history suggested otherwise."

"Have you actually read *The Protocols* in their entirety?" Gabriel interrupted.

"I have," President Edmonds answered. "I pulled the entire document up on the internet last night. What I read made my blood boil. Those arrogant sons of bitches have set themselves up as gods and plan to recreate the world in their own image." The President returned to the script:

"Since the motives of this small group of conspirators were clandestine in nature, the Illuminati organizers needed a shield of respectability. They infiltrated the Freemasons on both sides of the Atlantic, taking on many Masonic rituals, signs, and symbols and using them not to honor God, but God's enemy, Lucifer. Eventually and unfairly, their actions unduly brought the credibility of Freemasonry itself into question.

"Having successfully gained influence with governing bodies throughout Europe, in the nineteenth century the conspirators turned their attention westward and focused on the newly formed United States of America. To create the kind of unrest and internal strife they needed to stake out a claim in the new world, they instituted a previously proven tactic—the Rothschild Formula—the same deceptive campaign that caused the people to turn against their king and queen and launch the French Revolution. Surely, Professor Weishaupt's co-conspirators concluded, yet another revolution could be instigated. And so was born the United States Civil War."

"You have done your homework," Daren Borden observed. "You won't read any of this in traditional history books. And remember what I've always told you, as military officers we are taught that there are no coincidences."

"Exactly," the President rejoined. "That's been part of the problem. Until Operation Annuit Coeptis, no one has collected and put all the pieces of this ugly global puzzle together."

Returning to the draft of his upcoming speech the President said:

"In 1861, with the shot fired on Fort Sumter, the United States was successfully split, geographically and ideologically, much more so than existed prior to the incident off the shores of Charleston, South Carolina. Tens of thousands of men died in a conflict that was billed as

"The War Between the States," when, in reality, it was a war between ideologies, whether people should be the master of their own minds and actions, or whether they are to mind their master. The war was conceived and orchestrated by outsiders, based far from our shores: in Europe.

"In order to achieve their objectives, the draconian gods of an emerging Invisible Empire pitted Americans against Americans, financing both sides of the war. By doing so, they could ensure that *they*—the financiers—emerged victoriously. It was a premeditated holocaust in which the Illuminati watched from the sidelines as brother massacred brother.

"When the carnage ended, bondage simply took on a different face. Prewar slave masters were replaced by new ones, wearing the cloak of a seemingly omnipotent government, not just in Southern states, but throughout the nation.

"Thirteen powerful European patriarchs who made up the Illuminati's Inner Circle had done what they set out to do, gain an even stronger foothold in the new world.

"When the Civil War ended, and with the death of states' rights, the Illuminati had a forever divided nation in their grasp, never to release the grip. President Lincoln saw what was happening and set out to right a greater wrong. Because the Rothschild Formula was invoked, he never got that chance."

"Pardon me, Mr. President," General Purcell interjected. "You and I know what you say to be true, but a lot of Americans with black skin have been led to believe a different version of Civil War history. They'll be told, and many will believe, that you are the one rewriting history. You need to be prepared to respond to their charges."

"I know, General, and I will," the President replied. "My grandmother warned me about lumping people of any color, religion, or creed into one batch. Ever since that day, I have refused to do so. And it's high time that people from all walks of life know the truth about those who want to divide and enslave us all by using the various colors of propaganda. We can't rebuild America on lies or half-truths. Every faction of our nation will have to put aside the things that divide us and focus on the things that unite us, beginning with a factual account of America's history."

While the General nodded in agreement, the President returned to his prepared remarks:

"OAC also discovered that at the turn of the twentieth century, a seat on the Illuminati's Inner Circle was assigned to the head of America's Rockefeller Family. Years later his son inherited the patriarch's seat, referring to his *Bilderberger* colleagues in a speech he delivered to them as a 'supranational sovereignty of intellectual elites and world bankers.' The younger Rockefeller went on to describe the group's 'one world order' concept of governance as 'preferable to national auto-determination practiced in past centuries.' Then he thanked the American media for its help in creating a world order of the Invisible Empire's making saying, 'We are grateful to the Washington Post, the New York Times, Time Magazine and other great publications whose directors have attended our meetings and (we have) respected their promises of discretion for almost forty years.' Rockefeller concluded his remarks to the 1991 Inner Circle meeting by stating, 'It would have been impossible for us to develop our plan for the world if we had been subjected to the lights of publicity during those years.' That's how American's mainstream media played a role in one of the most cleverly conceived False Flag Operations and cover-ups of all time. Though they knew the facts, they hid them from a trusting nation."

"Sorry to interrupt again," General Purcell said, "but do you think it is a reach for the American people to know what a False Flag Operation is?"

"It may be, Harold," Mason answered, "but some of our enemies will be listening to my remarks too and I want them to know that we are on to them."

"If that's your intent, I think it is fine to leave it in," the General replied.

The President continued:

> "Convinced that the world is theirs to rule, the 'supranational sovereignty' determine where, and what kinds of, chaos best serve their purpose. They wave the flag of America, but pledge allegiance to a flag of another empire."

President Edmonds paused and glanced at General Purcell, who smiled and nodded in agreement with the President's explanation, and read on:

> "The Invisible Empire that is America's archenemy seems to know who will win *before* conflict breaks out or votes are cast." Through their environmental minions, they create disasters that lead to more regulation. They set forest fires and cause chemical spills. They create so-called accidents at nuclear power plants and commit acts of terror inciting oil spills. Each havoc-reeking environmental

disaster is orchestrated so that they can gain greater control of the populace through government regulation, in the name of protecting the planet that they are destroying."

"With all due respect," Raley Stovall said, calmly interrupting the President. "Are you sure that you are ready to take on both the press and the environmentalists? You know how ruthless they both can be. It's early in your presidency and it might be better to gain a foothold with the people and then go after the press with both barrels blazing. And, are you sure that now is the time to expose some of the acts of terrorism to which you just eluded?"

"Raley, my friend, I know that you know that. And the Invisible Empire knows about the acts of domestic terrorism that they are promoting in our country. That reference is for them and the cable networks. Let's see how they pick up on it. Tomorrow is not early enough to expose the mother of all cover-ups," the President answered and read on:

"From historical documents, it appears that not only were the French Revolution and U.S. Civil War engineered by the Illuminati, but World Wars I and II, the failed League of Nations, its successor (the United Nations), Global Warming, and the global economic crisis of 2009. In each case, the Order engineered the sacrifice of fellow human beings, fortunes, national wonders, and, sometimes, nations to restructure a world to their liking.

"One World advocates also expand their spheres of influence by employing a gentler style of warfare, a tried and true weapon of mass destruction known as progressive liberalism, or 'gradual reform.'

"Until I received OAC's final report, I had never read books written by Karl Marx and Vladimir Lenin. However, I know that they were the fathers of progressive liberalism and its reform objective: communism. However, because of the circumstances that we are facing today, I had to familiarize myself with the thought processes of two of capitalism's most notorious enemies. What I learned is that the tactic of conquest known as progressive liberalism and its cousin, socialism, are both based on evolution rather than revolution. Revolution is reserved for the rapid overthrow of government, usually by force.

"During its investigation OAC discovered that the protocols that guide the Illuminatists' actions describe clever ways to kill the human spirit worldwide—and, in turn, abolish human rights, thereby subjugating the masses to a small group of self-anointed overlords. In truth, the Illuminati intend to bring about the exact opposite of the stated goals of their False Flag propaganda campaigns on human rights.

"When pieces of the puzzle are aligned, a recognizable image begins to emerge: a single World Government created of the Illuminati, by the Illuminati, and for the Illuminati, with a single purpose in mind: world domination."

The President paused and glanced at Gabriel Shade, who nodded, indicating that he was convinced that Mason had read the fine print and references of the OAC report as well as the body of the text. Moving on through the draft of what would become the bones of his State of the Union speech, the President asked a rhetorical question:

"How could a few brazen men and women acquire such arrogance and gain such power? The answer is simple: money—to be exact, debt. They control the purse strings of much of the world.

> They finance wars and the conflicts that *they* create. In the world of the Illuminati, the lender is the master of the debtor; and in the world of wealth and power, to owe is to be owned. To be owned is to be enslaved. So, bondage by any other name is still bondage, regardless of the social disguise in which it is dressed or flag that flies above its seat of government."

Once again, the President paused to read the face of General Purcell, who, as his other colleague had previously gestured, nodded in agreement.

> "One of the tactics used successfully by the Illuminati against capitalism is named after two left-wing professors at New York's Columbia University. *The Cloward-Piven Strategy* explains how it is possible to bring about the fall of capitalism by intentionally creating debt and its accomplice, premeditated poverty."

"*The Cloward-Piven Strategy* was not in the OAC report," Dale Jackson muttered under his breath. The President heard his friend's remark and stopped reading.

"No," the President said, "but it should be added. I learned about it last night, right after I reread *The Protocols of the Elders of Zion.*"

He returned to the prepared text:

> "First, governments with one-world intentions assume the role of caretaker, providing entitlements to targeted portions of the population. Then people at both ends of the social spectrum are encouraged to accumulate more debt than they can ever hope to repay. When hope seems lost, Big Brother comes to the rescue, redistributing money from the public coffers. With each

handout and bailout, additional caveats of subordination are required of the receivers, until there is no more wealth to redistribute. The economy collapses. And a dictator, in this case the Illuminati, moves in to pick up the scattered pieces.

"Over the years, all manner of emissaries have assimilated into America's culture to do the Illuminati's bidding. Others were recruited from within and organized into political action groups and civil liberties unions. As was done in Hitler's Germany, the youth were targeted and turned against the very form of government that gave them the right to voice their opposition.

"Regardless of age or place of origin, the organizers' instructions were to *change* the U.S. from a capitalistic system to one based on socialistic principles, more specifically Illuminati principles. They began infiltrating America's educational systems, rewriting history, making heroes of fellow Illuminati emissaries, changing textbooks and curricula, indoctrinating our children into viewing their parents, government, and the world from an *anti-*capitalist point of view. In rewriting history books that children read, they followed an ancient Annunaki principle: 'The living can make the dead do any trick that the living feels necessary.'

"Lucifer's Illuminati created animosity among religions and races and by holding evil's heroes up to the emerging youth of the world, are able to redirect the moral compass of generations to come to the Illuminati's way of thinking.

"Cleverly, God's and our archenemy encouraged Americans to split loyalties by inserting a hyphen between the term

'American' and the name of some country in which distant ancestors might have lived. They fostered class warfare, further dividing Americans along income lines and social standing. America's successful entrepreneurs were fair game. Hard-working men and women were ridiculed and taxed, while the superrich Illuminati watched from the sidelines, padding their already inflated bank accounts and portfolios.

"America's, and God's, enemies have successfully used every conceivable faction of the age old war tactic: 'divide and conquer.' And, because Americans were not properly forewarned by a complicit press, the Illuminati's plan was and is working to perfection.

"Backed by the self-anointed gods of the New World Order, Illuminati disciples gained positions of leadership and influence in America's primary seats of power: Washington, New York, Chicago, and Hollywood. The reason: centralized seats of power are easier for an aggressor to surround and seize. From these centers of influence Illuminatists were able to change both how Americans viewed themselves as well as the manner in which the world sees us."

Out of the corners of his eyes, the President could see each of the men sitting before him slowly nodding in agreement as he spoke.

"By using high profile entertainers as mouthpieces, the Illuminati set out to deceive the people into believing that capitalism and conservatism—not Marxism or totalitarianism—were the greatest threats to a utopian world.

"From a variety of platforms, Illuminati disciples challenged venerable institutions, fostered dissention, altered laws, instilled 'political correctness,' applauded immorality, rewarded incompetence, denounced God, emasculated worldwide intelligence gathering operations and, with the mainstream media's assistance, swayed public opinion from 'father knows best' to a 'government knows all' way of thinking.

"The formula for America's near-death experience has been working ... and for a very long time. In the 1940s, under President Franklin Delano Roosevelt—and to add to the kind of debt they needed to impose on Americans—Illuminatists completed a plan that had been initiated a decade earlier. They made sure that the previously unmatched U.S. gold reserves were depleted. Then, they defrauded the American people into believing that a Social Security Trust Fund would ensure prosperity in retirement years, though they raided the fund each year to finance other social programs, each designed to win the allegiance of the non-working class at the expense of working people.

"It was no coincidence that in the 1960s progressives began to make the U.S. dependent on foreign oil and gas, while the drug-soaked hip generation demonstrated for making love instead of war, intended to stop the spread of communism. Illuminati disciples in the White House and Congress installed far-reaching social entitlement programs intended to drain the treasuries of individuals and institutions alike.

"The U.S. has been pressured into abandoning nuclear energy. In breakneck fashion, however, other countries around the world built nuclear plants. It was 'unfair,' we were told, for the U.S. to be the nuclear superpower of the world. It has always been the Invisible Empire's goal to orchestrate the destruction of every arbitrary power that could threaten its own.

"All across America, Illuminati-supported political action groups demonstrated in the streets, at airports, and to lawmakers, and were successful in preventing the U.S. from becoming an energy-independent nation. Today, as planned, we are heavily reliant on oil from nations that don't particularly like us. And nations with whom we've had major disagreements in the past—China and Japan to be exact—now own our debt. As lenders, they are in a position to influence U.S. policy. We only need to look at the past to see what our future may hold.

"Imagine being under the oppressive thumbs of terrorist supported countries. While some of America's leaders have pandered to these countries, the most ardent enemies of human rights on the globe have one mission in mind—to own us in order to destroy our way of life.

"Although the U.S. built the only transoceanic connection within the Americas with taxpayer money, the Panama Canal was given in the 1970's to Panama during the Carter Administration. The canal is now controlled by China. Historians will look back and ask, 'What were the Americans thinking?'"

At this point in the session, the President's advisers seemed to have settled into the message he was intent on delivering. Each sat quietly and listened.

"The formula to ensure America's demise goes even farther back. The Great Depression of the 1920s and 1930s achieved one of the Illuminati's goals.

Though the 1920 depression took place during the presidency of one of their globalist emissaries, President Woodrow Wilson, history has been kind to him. Progressive historians continue to celebrate his failed League of Nations, the intended precursor of a World Government. It is no accident that the intended role of the League of Nations has now been assumed by the United Nations.

"Economic recessions and depressions are the work of the Illuminati. Both American depressions drove independent banks all across the U.S. out of business. As intended, the people and their government were then forced to borrow money from banks that the Illuminati controlled, many of which existed in countries that were not traditional allies of the U.S.

"Another result of America's two great depressions, as well as with the great oil embargo of the 1970s and the recession of 2009, was an evolutionary shifting of influence, power, and wealth, the vast majority *away* from the people, toward global businesses, bigger government, and then to a 'new*er* world order.' one created and manipulated by the Order of the Illuminati.

"Now, let's look at the events of 2008 that led to the recession of 2009. It is also not a coincidence that at the direction of an insistent Congress, lenders threw away the keys to subprime lending locks and that shortly thereafter credit suddenly tightened. Fannie Mae and Freddie Mac were left holding a virtual sea of uncollectable debt. Banks stopped lending money, worldwide. While Wall Street and many banks went upside down, a few 'sacred cows' made billions and parked their fortunes offshore in secret bank accounts, including members of Congress and the previous Administration's Cabinet.

"As the Illuminati intended, the economy tanked, not just in the U.S., but globally. That's how recessions are created by the Illuminati, allowing 'world bankers and intellectual elites' to instill more regulations while they accumulate valuable assets at fire-sale prices and at the expense of American taxpayers."

Morley was the first to break the group's prolonged silence, asking, "What about calling some of those 'sacred cows' and 'fire sale vultures' by name?"

"I thought about it," the President replied, "but since we have reopened the investigations, I decided against it. However, here's what I intend to tell the people about some of the unholy connections between big business and government:

"What you, my fellow Americans, need to know is that there is not now, nor has there ever been, a shortage of oil, nor money. The Illuminati, acting in concert with the then all-too-cooperative Administrations in Washington, the oil companies, and OPEC, periodically decided to cut off the pipelines, preventing oil from entering U.S. ports and lending institutions from lending. Originally, this was done to drive independent oil companies and locally owned gas stations out of business. Then, the ploy spilled over into the financial sector. The result was that companies controlled by the Illuminati eliminated competition. Though monopolies were clearly dealing cards from the bottom of the deck, the Federal Trade Commission and the mainstream media remained silent.

"The same is the case with nuclear energy. Since pressures were brought to bear by environmental groups, who have always been Illuminati puppets, oil exploration in the U.S. has been curtailed. Who benefits from the international oil conspiracy or domestic oil spills of the manmade kind on this side of the Atlantic? Who benefits from a ban on building nuclear power plants? Who benefits from federal mandates restricting domestic drilling of oil and natural gas? Certainly, it *is not* the American people who benefit from such decisions. It was and is the large oil and gas magnates, their OPEC allies, and international bankers, who continue to transfer wealth out of America. These are the gods of new world order, the framers of America's formula for failure, architects of a One World Government. And it is *they* who always seem to profit from chaos. While they do, the mainstream media bow to their gods and remain silent."

The President paused once more to see if anyone had anything to add to the energy conspiracies to which he had eluded. Though eyebrows were still raised from his last statement, no one spoke, so he continued:

"As we enter the second decade of the twenty-first century, we are facing another Illuminati-contrived crisis. In the fall of 2009, what remained of the levies around responsible government was overrun. Madness and imprudence flooded Washington. In breakneck fashion, Congress and the previous Administration set about nationalizing everything in sight, throwing reason to the wind. Americans were led to believe that the government could spend its way into prosperity and needed to do it as quickly as possible. People who had never run as much as a lemonade stand were put in charge of solving the country's multitrillion-dollar financial woes. Not surprisingly, some of those responsible for creating the financial crisis were charged with resolving it. That's the way the Illuminati works. At the pleasure of the White House, professed anti-capitalists or communists were appointed to serve in oversight positions. And as the shackles of bondage tightened, the mainstream media remained silent. Talking about the fox guarding the henhouse...

"Banks, the automobile industry, carbon emissions, and healthcare were brought under the control of the federal government that, in turn, answered to a worldwide sovereignty of intellectual elites and bankers. Presidentially appointed "czars," not Congress, were put in place to see that retribution and wealth redistribution policies were carried out. Spending spun out of control and the national debt rose to unprecedented levels. As intended, a hole was dug for future generations of Americans, out of which they are never expected to climb. The formula for America's demise was working: shackles of bondage tighten; the mainstre*am* media honor their oath of 'discretion' and remain silent.

"And although it was discovered that Illuminati-supported scientists had cooked the data on global warming, governments at home and abroad initiated legislation and moved toward treaties to further regulate free enterprise by limiting 'carbon emissions.' At the same time that the previous Administration—acting on behalf of the Illuminati—was bending arms to push carbon emission legislation through Congress, the gusher in the Gulf of Mexico was spewing immeasurable amounts of raw carbon into the waters, destroying life and a way of life for the inhabitants of the Gulf Coast. Rather than dealing with the gusher as a national emergency—insisting that the rupture is immediately plugged and the oil already polluting the Gulf is collected, the Administration turned away offers from experts at home and abroad who had solutions. Instead, it used the crisis for photo ops and a chance to initiate further regulation, but only after shaking down British Petroleum to the tune of twenty billion dollars, much of which is unaccounted for.

"The champion of the Illuminati's globalization movement is none other than a former Vice President of these United States, a Nobel Prize recipient who stands to make billions from the newly created 'cap and trade' industry. Is he an Illuminus? I'll leave that for you to decide."

"VOX News will have a hay day with this. They'll be glad to broadcast your State of the Union address," Morley let fall laughingly.

Mason simply smiled, and moved forward:

"As part of globalization efforts, monies collected from 'cap and trade' tariffs were promised to third world countries, ostensibly to assist them in complying with the new United Nations emission standards. The wheels of World Government are turning at an unprecedented speed.

"Not surprisingly, the billions collected from industrialized countries (like the U.S.) are slated to be deposited in none other than the World Bank or International Monetary Fund, both of which are controlled by the Illuminati. And, as the shackles of bondage are tightened, the mainstream media continues to be silent.

"The so-called Swine Flu Pandemic of 2009 is yet another example in which premeditated chaos was used to test the waters of government-controlled healthcare. There is absolutely no data that the flu season of 2009-2010 was any worse than previous years, or that the vaccine forced on many people, the world over, made one shred of difference. In many cases, complications from mass vaccination exceeded any good intended. The only people who benefitted from the swine flu scare were companies that produced and/or distributed the vaccine. Companies controlled by none other than, you guessed it, the Illuminati. And, the mainstream media reverently remained silent."

"Do you know that the flu pandemic was a hoax?" Raley Stovall asked the President, who responded, "The evidence is there. You've seen it. In fact, you helped gather it."

"I did, but I'm not a doctor and I wanted to know your take on the data," Raley said.

"I think what you discovered is valid," the President responded. "Along with many of the other *created* crises that I plan to reveal, the Swine Flu Crisis was an example of the 'Problem-Reaction-Solution Paradigm, and moved on:

> "*Change* had been promised to the people of the world and *change* we got, more change than any of us outside the Inner Circle expected. Truly a New World Order has been in charge—the Order of the Illuminati—a draconian global government *by* the Illuminati and *for* The Illuminati.
>
> "As were the characters in the children's story, *The Emperor's New Clothes,* honorable members of Congress in this chamber and the American people were duped. The only 'hope' Americans experienced was that the previous White House and this Congress would come to their senses.
>
> "Every public opinion poll indicated that you, the people, wanted your government to act responsibly: secure its borders, stop giving citizens' rights to noncitizens, and refrain from spending money it didn't have. The people want its government to stop mortgaging your children's and grandchildren's futures and put the long-term interest of America first. And, while America bleeds, the complicit mainstream media remains silent.
>
> "In keeping with a tradition of selective reporting, major networks and newspapers failed to point out that the kind of 'transparency' and 'change' the previous Administration promised during the presidential campaign of 2008 was simply nonexistent. In contrast to the Watergate scandal of the 1970's, investigative reporters in the mainstream press seem more focused on finding fault *with* Tea Party participants than reporting on the reasons *why* Tea Party participants have come out of their homes and places of business to make their voices heard.

"Clearly, the United States has been under siege, and for a very long time. Beginning in 1993 and extending until 2001, America's military and intelligence operations were summarily emasculated by a President who was a product of the hip generation and stated that he 'loathed' the military. And, you, the people, knew not. Although you had the right to know what those who aspired to occupy the White House said about America, the mainstream media chose not to reveal the truth.

"With New World Order gods gaining ground and assuming more positions of influence and power over the past century, the U.S. has been falling behind in the culture war."

Morley cleared his throat, trying to get the President's attention. Mason paused and said, "I assume you have something to add."

"Nothing to add, but I've been watching the time. You've already exceeded the longest State of the Union speech ever delivered. How much more do you have?"

"Not much. I'm almost done," Mason answered, returning his attention to the notes from which he was reading:

"America is beginning to resemble an embryonic Oceania, George Orwell's futuristic totalitarian society. Throughout the land, Illuminati-owned politicians, lawmakers, judges, and financiers confiscate freedoms from 'the people and relegate them to the Federal Government. Treaties and legislation are being drafted to circumvent the Second Amendment of the Constitution and take guns away from law-abiding citizens. History shows that this was done in Nazi Germany, prior to World War II and the Holocaust that cost more than ten million innocent people their lives.

"Gun control is not about public safety. To the contrary, it is an Illuminati ploy designed to ensure that the people can't organize a militia and fight back against the mounting control of a totalitarian form of government.

"The America we see around us today is indeed a changed nation from the one that the Constitutional framers founded. But the question that each of has to ask is this: is today's *changed* America a *better* America?

"Today's America is a product of both genetics and environment. We are a nation of immigrants, who came here to build a life based upon religious principles—to make a good country great and contribute to that objective. Today, in contrast, well-meaning religion is under attack by The Changers and illegal immigrants seem more interested in taking than contributing. We are also becoming immune to the very existence of the evil forces that seem committed to controlling everything in our environment.

"To paint the United States in the worst possible light in the eyes of the rest of the world, the entertainment industry glorifies the worst of American culture, turning out programs and movies depicting violence, drugs, and explicit sexual acts, in which human beings act more like animals than lovers. And the mainstream media remains silent, except when they routinely attack conservative citizens who peacefully and truthfully expose anti-American propaganda and actions. It is how the Rothschild Formula works. Discredit and destroy those who do not agree with the Invisible Empire's agenda.

"This is where Operation Annuit Coeptis entered the picture. What I have presented to you tonight are the facts as Operation Annuit Coeptis found them to exist in the first decade of the twenty-first century. OAC took a good long look at 'change' and what they saw was terrifying. It concluded that though this world change was later in coming than originally predicted, George Orwell's book, *1984,* was beginning to look more like fact than fiction. World bankers, intelligent elites, the mainstream media, and politicians are all 'Big Brothers' controlled by a single overbearing patriarch: the invisible Order of the Illuminati. This power-driven band of falsely enlightened individuals live by a different set of rules than it expects the rest of us to live by.

"Because of OAC's findings, I became convinced that America was at a crossroads. I stand before you tonight realizing that I am risking everything to let you, the people and the people's representatives, know the truth about the shaky and disturbing State of our Union, the individuals and forces responsible for our nation's decline and the challenges that lie before us.

"What happens next cannot be forecast with any degree of certainty. America's destiny now lies in *your* hands, an informed electorate, and the people you send to Washington to do your bidding. However, if the past is any indication of the future, I predict that the mainstream media will not remain silent after this address. I expect them to paint me as an 'out-of-touch and misguided conspiracy theorist.' And those of you who agree with me and OAC's findings will be, as well. One way to bring complicit media around is to turn away from their channels, beginning immediately after I have finished my remarks. With your own ears, you have heard what I have said and the truths I speak. You don't need some biased pundit with a list of talking points handed to them by handlers to tell you what I said.

"Stop buying or reading publications of media outlets that refuse to tell you the truth, the whole truth, and nothing but the truth. Boycott liberal and left wing websites. All media survive by ratings and the advertising revenues that high ratings command. Drive the all-powerful ratings of those who refuse to report the truth down and cut off their life blood, in this case advertising dollars. That's a peaceful way to bring them to their knees and hold them accountable to you, the people.

"Conversely, support those who are unafraid to share the truth with you. Those of us who believe that self-determination can take America back without ever pulling a trigger, without reaching for a club, without launching a missile. We do so by turning out on Election Day—every single Election Day—and replacing the sponsors of imprudence with those who exercise prudence."

Clearing his throat once more, Morley said, "With all due respect, five minutes ago you said that you were almost done. Are you?"

"I did get a bit carried away, didn't I?" the President replied. "I'm now at the call to action portion:

"My fellow Americans, my wish is that what I have revealed to you this evening is no more than a series of unrelated coincidences and that the picture I have presented to you proves to be no more than a theory. But to call what I have shared with you a theory would be telling you yet another lie. And, you have been fed lies for far too long.

"The gods of the invisible Global Empire known to us as the Illuminati and a complicit press do not believe that you are smart enough or committed enough to put the pieces of the puzzle together. They think that you have grown soft, no longer care, or are afraid to offend anyone, even though they may be stealing your freedom and/or confiscating your hard-earned resources. Frankly, I think they have misjudged you. And, I hope that you will rise up, throw off the shackles of bondage, and stand with me in the light of truth. Together, we will show the Shadow Government that it has underestimated the American spirit that burns within our hearts.

"As your President, I pledge to you that I will gather the best minds that exist within proven patriots and work untiringly with them to come up with a plan of action that gives us the best chance to re-found America and hit the re-set button on the Cycle of Democracy. Let us begin again, at the beginning. Let us move forward from bondage to spiritual faith; from spiritual faith to great courage; from courage to liberty; and from liberty to abundance. Let us prove the formula for America's destruction wrong. This is the only way I know to save our nation from those who would take it from us.

"In the days and months ahead, I will ask for your prayers and unwavering support.

"Good night. And, as the Founding Fathers asked, let us all pray that God will favor our undertakings and that He will bless the United States of America."

With that, Mason laid the draft of his speech on his desk and looked into the eyes of his OAC allies. "Now that you've heard the entire draft, what do you think?"

"I think you are going to get all of us killed," Raley answered. "You've called out a lot of powerful people. You are right in assuming that they will label you a conspiracy theorist.

"It's a bold and risky move. The networks might pull the plug right in the middle of your speech. No one has ever used their media to expose their own cover-ups," Dale added.

"It's long overdue," Morley said, "I really like the part about Dr. Alexander Tyler's Cycle of Democracy. That's powerful stuff."

CIA Director, Gabriel Shade, offered his thoughts. "What you've done is essentially reveal to the people much of the findings of our OAC investigation. Although the speech is factual, it is far too long. It will have to be edited down to about forty minutes. Anything beyond that will lose the attention of those whom you are trying to reach. Nevertheless, what you intend to tell the people is precisely what they've needed to hear. You might want to consider hitting the high points in the State of the Union address and using some of your Saturday morning radio addresses to delve deeper into the meat of your message? I'd bet the public would be glued to their radios every Saturday."

"I hadn't thought about that," Mason replied, "but it is a good idea. After I've been through the lessons of the dollar bill, I could move into these matters."

"Are you planning to give a copy of your remarks to the members of Congress and the press beforehand?" Gabriel asked. "You know it's been a long-standing tradition."

"No, this time we will break from that tradition. We can't give them any reason to attack me beforehand. Afterwards, they can have at it."

"I like the way you wove George Orwell's novel and the story about the emperor's nonexistent clothes into the speech," Daren said. "I think both will resonate with the people. And, I liked, how did you say it, the formula for America's demise? You know that you are going to be pressured to divulge all your sources, don't you? Just make sure that you don't mention my name."

"I don't intend to mention anyone's name," the President responded. "As far as the press is concerned, none of you were part of Operation Annuit Coeptis.

"I am intrigued at how you wove in the emasculation of our intelligence agencies and military during the Clinton years. Not very many people know about his hatred for the very military that Bill Clinton came to command when he became President. I certainly do. Moral was almost as low as it is today, especially after the Padgett Administration completed the mission that the Clintons were instructed to start," General Purcell said.

"Those Hippies and their global financiers never stopped campaigning against a strong and independent America," Gabriel interjected. "The shabby-looking demonstrators simply cleaned up, put on new clothes and took on different names as they prepared to take the next step in ushering in their vision of an emasculated military and—in turn—a vulnerable nation. With The Illuminati's assistance and blessings, the 'make love—not war' generation moved from the streets into the once-hallowed halls of government."

"Yeah, a lot of those Hippies and Weathermen have found their way to Washington, D.C.," Daren said. "It seems that some of them are still smoking pot, popping psychedelic drugs and blowing up American institutions. When it comes to making the kinds of decisions that will protect America from its enemies, they seem to favor the enemy."

Gabriel interrupted. "When the Clintons and Padgetts were in the White House, soldiers in the field, in the air and on the seas knew that we were fighting with one arm tied behind our back and without the full support of our government. We risked our lives so that the 'Hip and Hope Generations' could exercise the free speech they needed to damn us and the Constitution that gave them the right to do it."

"Gabe is right," General Purcell added. "I was a helicopter pilot in Viet Nam when the Clintons staged their anti-war march in Moscow and Jane Fonda, the former wife of CNN mogul, Ted Turner, playfully pandered to the Army that was killing American soldiers. When I close my eyes at night, I can still see the series of photographs taken of her sitting in the seat of a Viet Cong anti-aircraft gun—holding onto the controls and aiming it at the sky as though she was about to shoot us down."

"I'd like to know when America intends to fight a war that it actually intends to win," Daren said. "Ever since World War II, we have not committed the resources we have in our arsenal to defeat the enemy. It's as though we do just enough to keep from losing."

"That's an Illuminati Principle," Gabriel interjected. "The self-designated 'supranational sovereignty of intellectual elites and world bankers' try to level the playing fields—or should I say battle fields—so that no one nation becomes a superpower. They are masters at financing both sides of wars and conflicts. It's the old *Problem-Reaction-Solution Paradigm.* World bankers are all about balance and keeping the fighting going—by all means necessary; and they are masters at using intellectuals and elitists to help them promote their agenda. It doesn't take a rocket scientist to see that if America wanted to crush the third world countries that we've been at war with over the past seventy years, we could do it. In spite of the Left, we have the greatest fighting force in the history of the world. If the politicians and financiers would get out of our way, we'd end the conflicts in Iraq and Afghanistan within twelve months."

"That's a bold statement," Morley, who had simply been listening to the discussion taking place, said.

"It's true," Gabriel replied. "The reality as I assess it is that except for the Reagan and the Bush Administrations, the goal never was *to win.* It is though

Left Wing President's agendas were drafted right out of the *Protocols of the Learned Elders of Zion*—the *original* Emasculation Proclamation. To win would perpetuate the United States into a position of leadership and exceptionality. And, that does not fit the Illuminati's agenda, which is to create a global government—a totalitarian state which requires that America be collapsed and its wealth liquidated to finance the globalization of power."

Morley interrupted the conversation. "Since Daren and I the only ones here of Jewish ancestry, I feel the need to interject something. Anti-Semites have long used *The Protocols of Zion* to cast aspersions on Jewish people around the world. While some the document's authors and Illuminati founders were born Jews, I can tell you that the men who drafted *The Protocols* and any of those with traditionally Jewish names who sit on the Illuminati's Inner Circle do not speak for Judaism nor for any of the Jewish people I know. What about you, Daren?"

"Morley is right," Daren said. "Both he and I served in Viet Nam along with a lot of other Jews. If anyone questions our people's commitment to America's cause, all they have to do is to walk around Arlington National Cemetery and see the Star of David alongside the Christian crosses imbued on the headstones there. Since the birth of the United States, Jews have proudly and bravely fought against the Illuminati's agenda, part of which now appears to be to deliver both Israel and the U.S. into the hands of their enemies."

"Thank you both for pointing that out," Mason said. "While those of us in this sacred chamber understand that the Illuminati profess no religion and answer only to Lucifer, it will be up to me to make sure that freedom-loving people everywhere understand it."

"You've got a lot to tell the people of the world," Dale said, "and time is short. If we're going to get through this draft of your State of the Union address, we'd better move on. You are meeting with the rest of the Cabinet down the hall in twenty minutes."

"We have a huge task ahead of us," the President said. "The decision of how to prosecute the War on

Terror now falls on my shoulders. History will judge our Administration by what *we* do and not by what we say. In the next two weeks, I plan to have Vice President Purcell bring in the best minds in our military so that we can explore the options."

"I'm sure that America's enemies expect you to do just that," Daren said.

"That's what frightens them. Would you consider calling back General McKaskil," Daren asked.

"I want the best minds available," Mason replied. "If General McKaskil is one of them, I want him on my team."

"Then, you'll want McKaskil," General Purcell interjected. "He is a Counter Insurgency expert. That's why he was given the command to head up Afghan and Pakistani theatres of operations in the first place. He is a savvy warrior. He knew exactly what he was doing when he let the reporter in. He knew that what the reporter discovered would bring attention to how the men and women in the field and those who commanded them truly felt about the former President and Vice President's lack of commitment to winning. They seemed more interested in meeting the date they promised to withdraw than finishing the job. General McKaskil sacrificed himself in order to bring attention to what he and his troops were up against"

"I wish I could participate in what promises to be the first strategy session aimed at winning a war in a long time," Daren said, "but I'd better remain behind the scenes. Perhaps, I could pose again as a lieutenant standing guard, like I did during Mason's inauguration," he suggested.

"I think that's a fine idea," General Purcell said. "I'd like to get your take on the discussions after the fact."

"And, I wish that I could repeat what you guys have offered during the past several minutes," President Edmonds said. "Americans need to know about the obstacles that our military face on the civilian side."

The Vice President said, "As much as you may want to divulge these things in your State of the Union speech, you will have to wait for another opportunity. Just know that if you repeat some of the facts that we've discussed here today, your speech would be viewed by the Illuminati as a declaration of war, or should I say an appropriate and timely *response* to an already declared war on The U.S. Constitution, one in which I stand committed to fighting with you."

"Thanks, guys," Mason said. "I appreciate your initial thoughts. I'm scheduled to deliver the commencement address at Capstone University, my alma mater, on Sunday. I'd like to have your additional comments on the speech before I leave. That way, I can review them on the trip. I'm also trying to schedule a meeting with a colleague, the one I've asked to write what some may call my memoirs, and I'd like to give him a copy of the speech as well."

As his trusted colleagues and advisers began to leave the Oval Office, Mason asked Gabriel Shade, the former Army intelligence specialist, to remain behind.

"Check the U.S. Embassy in Brussels and see if we have someone by the name of Solomon working there in any capacity," the President said.

"I'll get right on it," Gabriel answered. "Is there anything in particular that I want to know about him or her, if they're there?"

"Yeah, I need to know *everything!*" the President replied. "Where he or she was born, went to school, family, friends, flavors of ice cream liked. *Everything.* This individual might be one of the Illuminati's top-level operatives.

"On your way out, will you ask Martha to step in here?" the President asked.

"You got it," Gabriel said, exiting the west door of the office. Realizing what he had said, Gabriel paused and said, "I'm sorry. I mean yes, Mr. President."

Mason replied, "Get out of here, Gabe. That's not necessary."

"Yes, it is, sir," Gabriel replied, "You are the President and *no one*—not even your best friends—should forget it."

"I know that you're right," Mason replied, "but, I'm really having a hard time adjusting to the formality of this office."

Gabriel answered, "Yes, Mr. President," and went about his work.

. . . .

When he was alone, Mason mused. "It's been a good start to a new day, and, hopefully, a new day for America," he thought, gazing out the southernmost window at the rising sun, peaking over the trees on the eastern border of the Rose Garden. He was relieved that his trusted friends and OAC allies hadn't shot too many holes in the draft of his proposed address. Gabriel was right. The speech had to be shortened. However, he would have to wait until he received their written comments before making any revisions. Then he would turn it over to the professional speechwriters for the finishing touches.

"I may only have one chance to say the things that I want to say while looking into the eyes of the American people. And I intend to make the most of it. Life sometimes makes once-in-a-lifetime demands on us," Mason said to himself. "It is our decision whether to do nothing, retreat, or rise to the occasion. For America's sake, I have to take seize this one moment in time."

He recalled the lyrics of a popular song of the 1980's in which singer/songwriter Dan Fogelberg described the thoughts of a young horse as it prepared to run in the Kentucky Derby, known in thoroughbred riding circles as the 'Run for the Roses.' Like the promising young thoroughbred in Fogelberg's song, Mason was facing the race of his life. He had entered "the chance of a lifetime in a lifetime of chance." And, the race was on.

Having made his decision, Mason bowed his head and prayed silently, "Heavenly Father, guide me through this murky track and the slippery turns I will face. Let me run a good race. Grant me the serenity to accept the things I cannot change, the courage to change the things I can, and the wisdom to know the difference." It was a prayer he had learned as a child, long before he became aware that the prayer was used by organizations that cater to individuals suffering from afflictions of dependency. Like so many other pearls of wisdom, Mason had transcribed the prayer into a little black notebook that he still carried in his right hip pocket, the same one in which he had placed the smoking-gun document he'd recently discovered in the Resolute desk.

CHAPTER 23

One hundred days after Mason Edmonds took the oath of the presidency every active-duty service man and woman, every person serving in the reserves, National Guard, or Coast Guard, and every retired and disabled veteran, and every taxpayer received an envelope that came from the United States Treasury. When the envelope was opened, recipients discovered a single new dollar bill and a check made out to them in the amount of twelve thousand U.S. dollars. The note accompanying the check and non-circulated dollar bill read:

> My fellow Americans,
> Please accept this bonus as part of a "stimulus package" that was originally intended to get America moving again. We are sorry that some of the stimulus money was misplaced for a while, but has been recovered. Though overdue, a rightful share is being returned to its rightful owners; those of you who have helped build this great nation and defend it against its enemies, adversaries of the American way, those who are already among us and those who scheme to be.
> I have also included in this mailing a brand new commemorative dollar bill, just printed by the U.S. Mint. Take time to study the words, drawings, and markings on it, as well as the enclosed pamphlet that explains the words and symbols on the front and back of the bill.
> You will find not only a portrait of this nation's first President, but messages that were displayed there at the direction of the Founding Fathers.
> Do not spend the dollar bill. Keep it with you always as a remembrance of the vision and wisdom of the Founding Fathers. And know

that this certificate was intended not only to be a show of strength to America's enemies, but an enduring contract between a people and its government, a contract that is in jeopardy of being replaced with one in which a single world government will erase nations' ability to self-rule.

And, as you see the world changing around you, never lose site of the fact that the dollar bill signifies the oath that exists between the citizens of this Republic and the Godly principles upon which it was founded.

Thank you for your devotion and service to your country.

May God bless you; and may God bless America.

Mason Owen Edmonds
President of the United States of America

. . . .

One of the letters containing a twelve-thousand-dollar check and a freshly minted dollar bill was mailed into the hands of Mrs. Horace Jacoby. The ninety-one-year-old widow opened the official-looking letter. The sight of a check and dollar bill raised a lot of questions.

She began to read. When she came to the signature and personalized note at the bottom of the letter, tears began to well. In his own handwriting, the President had written:

PS. Mrs. Jacoby, I hope you are well. Please find enclosed a token of America's appreciation for your husband's and sons' service. It was my honor to have known them—and you. Use this check to do something special for yourself.

As the wife and mother of America's finest, you too are owed your country's appreciation.
Affectionately,
Mason

Mrs. Jacoby took the one-dollar bill into the light of the window in her kitchen. She read the document explaining the meaning of the words and symbols on the bill. Because her eyesight was not as good as it once was, she opened a drawer below the countertop she used as an in-home office and retrieved a magnifying glass. With it, she could read the words and emblems printed on the bill. The serial number of the bill began with the letter G, followed by the numbers 1776.

The capital letter that is traditionally displayed within the two concentric circles identifying the Federal Reserve Bank of issue was replaced with a tiny Caduceus, the sign of healing.

As she scanned the other emblems and words on the bill, her eyes were naturally drawn to the eye atop the pyramid. Strangely, it seemed to be staring into her soul.

Though unable to translate the Latin phrases imprinted on the bill, Mrs. Jacoby knew that if Mason was behind asking Americans to proudly carry the commemorative bill upon which they were printed, these mysterious words must portray an allegiant message.

. . . .

Two weeks after the mass mailing was sent, Morley delivered to President Edmonds a handwritten note. "We've received hundreds of thousands of 'thank you' notes from people all over America, but this one was addressed simply to 'Mason Edmonds, The White House, Washington, D.C." It seemed to have a more personal touch than the others and I thought that you might want to see it."

Mason took the letter from his friend and adviser. He leaned back in the chair behind the presidential desk and read the words, obviously written with a somewhat shaky hand.

"My Dear Mason,

Thank you for you kind note and the unexpected surprise of twelve thousand <u>and one</u> dollars. The check could not have arrived at a better time.

I know that Horace and my two sons are looking down from Heaven and thanking you, too. They were proud to be Americans and to fight for their country. I'm sure that when you became President, all the angels in heaven and earth celebrated.

Even though you sent along a letter of explanation, I still haven't been able to translate all those foreign words on the dollar bill, but as you asked, I keep it with me, in a medicine locket on a chain around my neck. It's the necklace that Horace gave to me on our first wedding anniversary. I'm sorry that I had to fold the bill up so tightly to get it to fit, but it's the only way I could be sure that I could keep it with me day and night.

I've asked my daughters-in-law to make sure that I'm buried with that dollar bill around my neck. As you suggested, I intend to keep with me always.

The twelve thousand dollars were used to catch up with my house payments. I was three months behind and the bank was threatening to take my house.

You once told me that I reminded you of your grandmother. That's interesting because when you and your wife came for dinner that Sunday, you reminded me so much of my oldest son, the first one killed in Vietnam. My youngest son was killed in action the following year. They were proud to wear the uniform of an American warrior and fight for what they believed in. I miss them terribly, but know that they died fighting for what they believed in...

If you're ever back in the Ashton area, I'd love to cook dinner for you again.

Love,
Grace Jacoby

. . . .

Holding back tears, Mason carefully folded the letter and put it in a worn notebook that he had retrieved from his right hip pocket.

"Wouldn't you prefer that I put that away for safekeeping until you write your memoirs?" Morley asked.

"No thanks. I'm going to keep this letter with me always, right next to the dollar bill given to me by my grandmother and the first bill off the press when the U.S. Mint printed the commemorative series of bills that we included with the *stimulus* checks," Mason replied.

"What is the name of that little book you carry with you?" Morley asked.

"It's named *Laney's Book of Wisdom*." Mason answered.

"I've never heard of that book," Morley said. "Is it a recent publication?"

"No, in fact it's a classic," Mason replied. "Next to the Bible, it's the one that that I refer to most often."

"It must be special, then," Morley said.

"It is," Mason responded.

"Is there anything else I can do for you, Bro?" Morley asked.

"As a matter of fact, there is. Aren't I scheduled to deliver the commencement address at Capstone University next month?"

"Let me check," Morley said, pulling his pocket computer from its case. "Yes, on the twelfth."

"Ashton is only about an hour away from the university's campus," the President said. "Make arrangements to drive me over to Ashton after I deliver my address. I don't want the press to know that I am going there. So do whatever you have to do to keep it quiet and make sure that the Secret Service detail is as small as the law allows so that we will not attract too much attention."

"Why, for God's sake, are we going to Ashton?" Morley asked. "Have you made the final changes to your State of the Union address? Earlier this week, you asked the OAC group to review the draft and make suggestions. We've all been working diligently to tighten the speech up so that you can deliver it in no more than thirty minutes. You haven't forgotten, have you?"

"Absolutely not. The State of the Union address that I will deliver to Congress and the American people on this coming Wednesday evening is the most important task before me. It is a message that the American people must hear. I'll review the suggestions that you, Dale, Gabriel, Raley, and Harold have made. And, by the way, I'd like for Daren to have some input as well. Will you get a copy to him? I'll review all your suggestions on the way back to Washington after I have dinner with a friend in Ashton," the President answered, "a grand lady and great American."

"Do I dare ask her name?" Mason's brother-in-law asked.

"You may. It's Grace, Grace Jacoby. And, before the rumor mill cranks up, she is ninety-one years young," the President replied. "Now, first thing in the morning we'll get her on the phone so that I can tell her that Norene and I are coming to dinner."

"Was there any other mail of note?" Mason asked.

"The usual letters from quacks, you know, death threats and such," Morley answered. "However, there is one that is different from the rest," he added, handing a 5x7-inch piece of paper to Mason. In the upper left hand corner of which was a symbol that Mason had seen before. It was a rather unique drawing of the all-seeing eye, underneath which the words *NOVUS, NOVUS ORDO SECLORUM* were inscribed.

Mason took the piece of paper from Morley and read the handwritten note:

"President Edmonds,

Consider this a final warning. You are a trouble-maker and an obstructionist to our plan.

Cease and desist or cease to exist. What will it be?

Solomon"

Mason reached for the little black notebook in his right hip pocket, where he had placed the piece of paper retrieved from the *Resolute* desk shortly after taking office. The paper, logo, and handwriting appeared to be identical matches.

Morley could tell by Mason's facial expressions that *this* death threat was different from the rest and that the President took it seriously.

"What is it?" Morley asked. "Do we need to do anything about this crackpot?"

"This one is not from a crackpot," Mason answered. "It is a message straight from the master of the Illuminati's Inner Circle and the earthly ruler of the sons of God."

"The who?" Morley asked. Mason handed both notes to Morley. "The crinkled one was stuck between a drawer and the slide in the desk. I had to fish it out with a letter opener."

Morley took the note and read:

"President Padgett,

As directed, the amount of $2.5 million U.S. was deposited in your personal account on April 13, 2009, in AIG Private Bank, Zurich, Switzerland.

Your continued assistance is crucial to the Order's cause.

Solomon"

"My God, Mason, why haven't you told me about this?" asked Morley. "This could be the smoking gun we need to convince the world that Padgett was dirty."

"I've had a lot on my mind. The nation is in trouble. I felt that we could deal with this in due time," Mason answered.

"Well, due time is now," Morley replied. "Whoever this Solomon is, this draconian son of a bitch must wield a lot of power. Where have I heard that name before?"

The President replied, "In the 18th Century, a man named Hayim Solomon was involved in creating the artwork that appears on the face of the dollar bill. We talked about him earlier today. But I don't think that there is any connection. I suspect this is Hungarian-born Gyargy Schwartz, a man who most of the workd knows as George Soros. He has been known to use the code name 'Soloman'."

"What should we do?" Morley inquired.

"It's eight-thirty," Mason said glancing at his watch. "Let's go up and spend a few minutes with the family before we turn in. We'll deal with it tomorrow."

Exiting the Oval Office, Mason turned and stared at the massive wood-carved desk sitting in front of the window. "Do you realize what we have undertaken?" he asked Morley. "A lot of presidents have sat behind that desk and the decisions made within the curved walls of this office have changed the course of history. Now, the future of the United States and the free world could rest on our ability to convince the American people that we are at a crossroads in history, again."

"The people have heard so many politicians utter those words that I'm not sure they will believe us," Morley said. "They have been desensitized to political rhetoric."

"We have to make them believe us. By our actions, we will prove to them that we are not politicians. We, the members of OAC, are like the Founding Fathers, interested only in what is good for the nation. We will shoot straight with the people even if we have to tell them what they don't want to hear. We won't govern by the results of polls. I'm not out to get reelected. I've already told them so."

"The best way to rebound America is to run the country like a business," Morley added.

"Precisely, and that's what I intend to do. We'll cut the waste, demand excellence in every branch of government, and replace incompetence with competence," Mason said.

"I'm not sure that the entitlement generation will know how to handle this new approach. Aren't you afraid of instigators and rioters, like in the nineteen sixties?" Morley asked.

"That's one of the reasons we are in the mess we're in now. Sometimes, you have to do the right thing, not the popular thing. America is held hostage by those we are afraid to offend. It's time to stand strong," the new President replied, his voice rising to express the passion within.

"Even if it requires mobilizing the National Guard, Reserves, and stateside active duty forces to maintain the peace?" Morley asked.

"I pray that won't be necessary," Mason replied. "In my first address to the nation next week, I intend to reveal my intentions. Hopefully, anyone planning to create unrest will see that we mean business."

"Man, are you going to tick off a lot of people. I read over the draft of your speech again earlier this morning. You do realize the risk you're taking, don't you?"

"I do. Life is all about risks. As a physician, I look at it this way. My country is dying, bleeding to death from self-inflicted wounds, or those strategically placed by powers that know exactly where and when to strike. Nevertheless, somebody has to stop the hemorrhaging. Before I deliver my State of the Union address, I plan to have a meeting with top congressional and special interest leaders to tell them of my plans. Hopefully, they will see that we mean business," Mason answered. "I intend to see who is with us and who is with the enemy. I'll call out the names of those who aren't on board, if necessary. I took an oath to defend this nation against all enemies, foreign and domestic. I will tell congressional leaders that, as our Constitution ensures, we welcome nonviolent expression of opinions. However, I will also make it clear that I have sworn to protect citizens and their property."

"Have you thought about a show of force?" Morley asked.

"I intend to put the new Vice President, General Purcell, in charge of setting the strategic plan to do so. I intend for him to serve two roles, Vice President and head of Homeland Security, which includes protecting Americans against those who call themselves Americans, but engage in anti-American activities. I want the people to realize that General Purcell is a seasoned warrior and is being groomed to be their next President."

"Do you think that the fact that he is a black man will make a difference to those who will encourage their constituents to take to the streets?" Morley asked.

"The color of Harold Purcell's skin has made no difference to this point. I certainly don't intend to exploit it now. I chose him because he is the man for the job," Mason responded defiantly. "I'm sick of how race is being used in America, to divide us."

"Calm down, Bro. I'm on your side. It's my job to raise such issues," Morley replied. "You are going to make some bold moves. I just want you have thought out all the ramifications."

"I know about ramifications and how the political left has tried to exploit race as a way to create chaos in America. I look on Harold Purcell as a man, not a black man," Mason stressed. "Many will find it hard to believe that fact. I was born into a segregated South and witnessed the Civil Rights movement first hand. Most of the unrest that I witnessed was staged by busloads of so-called Freedom Fighters from Northern states who were paid to create unrest. Southerners, black and white alike, mostly stood on the sidelines and observed the production. The mainstream media packaged the footage they shot to paint the South in the worst possible light. It was all staged."

"I recall you telling me that George Wallace told you how his "Stand in the Schoolhouse Door" was scripted and rehearsed beforehand," Morley remembered.

"Yeah, and a prominent black college president, Dr. Anthony Bishop, confirmed what Wallace said. Dr. Bishop told me that Wallace met with black leaders and told them of what he was about to do. Wallace told them, 'I can do more for your Civil Rights movement by opposing you than I could ever do for you by supporting you.' Dr. Bishop also told me to look at the record. In every election thereafter, Wallace carried the black vote. Just before he died, George Wallace was given a prestigious award by America's second largest black organization, the Southern Christian Leadership Conference. As often stated, politics does create strange bedfellows."

"For too long, opportunity has been more about form than substance. That's been a major part of America's problem. In his "I Have a Dream" speech, Martin Luther King said that he dreamed of a day when a man would be judged by the content of his character and not by the color of his skin. Well, at least in this Administration, King's dream has become a reality. Bringing Harold Purcell onto my team had nothing to do with skin color, quotas or political correctness. I looked at his character. I chose the man, not a symbol."

Clearly, Mason was exorcised about the thought of race entering his choice for a successor.

"We are going to cut out double-speak and tell it like it is," he said passionately. "I want the American people to know the truth about their country and those who have been running it. More than that, I want them to know who we are and what we stand for."

"That won't be easy. As it is, the mainstream media is not very happy with us. They liked the previous Administration," Morley said. "The press is in bed with the Illuminati. The facts have been glossed over for too long. Take war for example. The people need to know that more Americans are murdered by Americans in Washington, Chicago, Detroit, and other major cities throughout our nation than have been killed in either the Iraqi or Afghan wars. For too long, we have let those committed to America's destruction have their way ... and their say, without being held accountable. And, I can't think of anyone better to change the policies of apology and surrender than a general in the United States Army.

"You know that the drug lords, ACORN, and community organizers are going to raise holy hell, don't you? A lot of very powerful people are getting rich by breaking the laws or making them up as they go." Morley added.

"Isn't that what Operation Annuit Coeptis identified and corrected?" the President asked. "We're simply going to expand that operation into every phase of American life. We may only have one last chance to save this nation and, in turn, the world. America is the world's last hope. Today, we are a divided people, driven by the kind of distrust and uncertainty that has been strategically instilled in our people, beginning in kindergarten. The teachers' unions are under the Illuminati's thumbs. They are teaching our children a different version of history than we learned. For the sake of not embarrassing children who fail, standards have been lowered to the point that America is lagging behind the world in academic achievement. Though *officially* undeclared, we are surely at war: good against evil, honor against betrayal, mediocrity against excellence, selfishness against selflessness, responsibility against irresponsibility, American against American."

"As you know," Morley said, "I am a student of the Civil War. You are beginning to raise the same kind of issues that led to the firing of the first shot at Fort Sumter. And you know what followed."

"Well, my first shot will be aimed at eliminating the hyphen from the way any American describes himself or herself. Being the sports enthusiast that you are, I know that you remember the baseball phrase, 'no one ever arrived safely at second base until he or she broke from first base with no intention of looking back,'" Mason said.

"Sure, I do. That's a good analogy."

"Or a metaphor," Mason noted. "That's what my grandmother taught me almost fifty years ago. Like the founders of this country, the re-founders of America must have a total and undivided commitment to *this* country and its' Constitution. America has become two countries, one that believes that government is the solution; another that believes that government is the problem."

"In many respects, it is like the War Between the States—American versus American," Morley declared. "I just hope that when the bloodshed begins, patriots will rally."

"In every generation, they have," Mason replied. "Let's hope that this one is no different."

As the two men approached the portrait of President John F. Kennedy hanging on the wall of the West Wing, Mason stopped and looked up at painting. "I've always wondered if JFK saw this coming," Mason said. "He, too, was a student of history. He must have known about the natural progression of democracies. During his presidency, it was becoming clear that the United States was approaching the stage in which some citizens were being taught by organizers that the power of the vote could empower them to take from those who had worked and saved. When, in his inaugural speech, President Kennedy said, 'Ask *not* what your country can do for you; ask what you can do for your country,'" he must have stepped on the toes of social reconstructionists and reparationists. More than any others, that one statement may have sealed JFK's death warrant, as well as that of his brother Robert."

Morley was thoughtful. "Now that I hear what you are saying, it is possible that rather than killing the next brother in line for the presidency, they felt he could be of greater value to their cause *alive* than dead. It is possible the Chappaquiddick incidence was staged to kill his chances of being elected President; however, if he were a Senator, committed to a social democracy in which government controls the means of production and distribution, he would be useful for generations to come."

"Whether that was the plan for Teddy, it is surely the result. And the agenda that he promoted is consistent with how some have described socialism." Mason replied.

"Yeah, it is. In Marxist doctrine, socialism is a bridge between the capitalist stage and the communist stage, in which private ownership is phased out. The difference is that communists believe in the quick and bloody method of takeover, whereas socialists work more slowly and methodically, so that the target never realizes what hit it. Slow steps, not giant leaps," Morley said. "Like boiling a frog?"

"Man, does that sound familiar. In looking at this Administration's first two years in office it seems as though they are following the play book of Marx and Lenin," Mason proclaimed.

"The other part of building a bridge between capitalism and communism is to create a champion of the cause," Morley expanded on history. "From a long-term historical perspective, the assassination of President Kennedy will be viewed as a major step in creating a socialist champion."

"I think I know where you are going, but flesh it out."

"With both Jack and Bobby out of the way, Teddy was the perfect choice," Morley added. "From a purely political point of view, the significance of Chappaquiddick has been overlooked. Ted Kennedy may well have traded *life* for servitude. This may explain why the bills and programs some called the 'Lion of the Senate' spearheaded during the forty years he served there moved America closer toward a social democracy."

"Forty years. That's a long time. He could spearhead a lot of social change and block attempts to curtail a progressive, socialist agenda," Mason said.

"Yeah, like torpedoing the Supreme Court nomination of conservative judge Robert Bork," Morley said, nodding. "He came close to blocking Judge Clarence Thomas from the high court. As well as one of the early versions of the healthcare reform bill that carried his name.

"I've always wondered what kind of America we would have, today, had Jack Kennedy not been assassinated," Mason said.

"Unfortunately, we'll never know," Mason answered, glancing up at the slain President's portrait. "But one thing is certain. The people who play monopoly with the world wanted their own kind of America. By killing JFK, they killed America's best hope to save it from the enemies within."

Leaving President Kennedy's portrait and moving toward the stairwell, Morley asked, "What do you call the medical condition in which the human body does itself in?"

"Autoimmune diseases," Mason answered. "The body attacks its own cells, making the host ill."

"What causes this to happen?"

"Some experts believe that infections—viruses or bacteria—may trigger the problem," Mason answered

"And, how do you treat these infections."

"Aggressively, with high powered anti-inflammatory drugs, antibiotics and antiviral medications," the doctor answered, pausing to see Morley's line of thinking. "I see the connection. Neutralize the enemies *within*, and America will heal itself."

"With full force," Morley emphasized.

"Sometimes you lawyers actually can be part of the solution," Mason said, slapping his brother-in-law on the back. "I might just have just the remedy for what ails this nation."

"Will it come from your medical training or your legal training?" Morley asked.

"A healthy elixir of both," Mason answered as the two mean reached the top of the stairwell leading to residential quarters.

"I can't get the Solomon note off my mind," Morley said.

"I said that we'd address that tomorrow," Mason replied, as the two men entered the hallway lounging area in the residents' quarters.

"Well," Norene said, handing her husband a cup of his favorite brew of coffee, "did you guys solve all the world's problems?"

Putting his arm around his wife and walking toward the remainder of the family and friends gathered to celebrate the events of the day, Mason replied. "Not just yet, but I think we know where to begin."

CHAPTER 24

Try as he may, the President could not fall asleep. His mind was still spinning. He couldn't get the Illuminati and their formula for America's demise out of his mind. What were they thinking about him being the President? He certainly wasn't chosen by them.

Mason got out of bed as though he were going for a drink of water and went down the hall to the newly revamped private study on the second floor of the White House. His computer had been installed on a smaller wood-carved desk shortly after the inauguration ceremony that took place in the East Room downstairs.

Mason activated the computer and clicked on the icon along the bottom of the screen to pull up *The Protocols of the Meetings of the Learned Elders of Zion,* a document that he and his OAC colleagues had come to believe was the Illuminati's policies and procedures manual. It was not the first time that he had read the document. In fact, he had incorporated some of the findings in the draft of his State of the Union address.

While rereading *The Protocols,* Mason couldn't help but note several additional links in the sidebar of the website. For some reason he hadn't noticed them before. One of the links referenced the Annunaki, thought to be a species of giant beings referenced in Genesis 6:4 as the "sons of God." But, for now, he had to focus on the words imbued in *The Protocols* and how they applied to the dilemmas he faced. He scrolled through the sections of the document until he reached the part that addressed how this 'supranational sovereignty' chose presidents and the people who surround them. Certain sentences and phrases caught his eye. The words he read were chilling:

"...We shall establish the responsibility of presidents and matters for which our impersonal puppet will be responsible. We shall arrange elections in favor of such presidents as have in their past some dark, undiscovered stain ... then they will be trustworthy agents for the accomplishment of our plans out of fear of revelations and from the natural desire of everyone who has attained power, namely, the retention of the privileges, advantages, and honor connected with the office of president ... deputies will provide cover for, will protect, will elect presidents, but we shall take from them the right to propose new, or make changes in existing laws, for this right will be given by us to the responsible president, a puppet in our hands. Naturally, the authority of the presidents will then become a target for every possible form of attack, but we shall provide him with a means of self-defense in the right of an appeal to the people, for the decision of the people over the heads of their representatives, that is to say, an appeal to that some blind slave of ours—the majority of the mob. Independently of this we shall invest the president with the right of declaring a state of war. We shall justify this last right on the ground that the president as chief of the whole army of the country must have it at his disposal, in case of need for the defense of the new republican constitution, the right to defend which will belong to him as the responsible representative of this constitution ... no one outside ourselves will any longer direct the force of legislation ... on the pretext of preserving political secrecy ... Upon the president will depend the appointment of presidents and vice presidents of the chamber (house) and the senate. Instead of constant sessions ... we shall reduce their sittings to a few months ... by use of the president, we shall instigate ministers and other officials ... about the president to evade his dispositions by taking measures of their own, for doing which they will be made the scapegoats in his place ... This part we especially recommend to be given to be played by the senate ... The president will, at our discretion, interpret the sense of such of the existing laws ... he will further annul (veto) them when we indicate to him the necessity to do so. Besides this, he will have the right to propose temporary laws and even new departures in the government constitutional working, the pretext both for the one and the other being the requirements for the supreme welfare of the state ... we shall obtain the power of destroying little by little, step by step, all that at the outset when we enter on our rights we are compelled to introduce into the constitutions of states to prepare for the transition to an imperceptible abolition of every kind of constitution, and then the time is come to turn every form of government into our despotism ('a system of government in which the ruler has unlimited power') ... The recognition of our despot (power) may also come before the destruction of the constitution; the moment for this recognition will come when the peoples, utterly wearied by the irregularities and incompetence—a matter which we shall arrange for—of their rulers, will clamor: '*Away with them and give us one king over all the earth who will unite us and annihilate the causes of disorders— frontiers, nationalities, religions, state debts—who will give us peace and quiet*

> which we cannot find under our rulers and representatives.' ... To produce the possibility of the expression of such wishes by all the nations, it is indispensable to trouble in all countries the people's relations with their governments so as to utterly exhaust humanity with dissension, hatred, struggle, envy, and even by the use of torture, by starvation, by the inoculation of diseases, by want, so that they see no other issue than to take refuge in our complete sovereignty in money and in all else ... But, if we give the nations of the world a breathing space the moment we long for is hardly likely ever to arrive."

Shaking his head in disbelief, Mason minimized the document along the bar at the bottom of his computer screen. Were *The Protocols* the work of some radical anti-Zionist or Nazi who was out to promote hatred in order to promote his own self-serving cause or was the document what it claimed to be: *The Protocols* of the meetings of the elders? The Illuminati?

In any respect, the document now had a *personal* meaning; for the "president" to which the document referred included his predecessor and himself. He remembered the words of Henry Ford, the father of the American automobile, when asked about the veracity of *The Protocols:*

> "The only statement I care to make about *The Protocols* ... is that they fit in with what is going on. They are sixteen years old, and they have fitted the world situation up to this time. They fit it now."

"And Ford's statement was made almost a hundred years ago," Mason said to himself. "Is it possible that they 'fit' today," he pondered, "or is it just coincidence, the behavior of man repeating itself in instinctive fashion?

Even in an unorganized fashion, greed, money, and power have always driven men to do the unthinkable to others. I wonder if it is because Ford spoke out against the document penned by the Elders of Zion, that the Illuminati employed gray propaganda and straddled him with the yoke of anti-Semitism?" Mason asked himself. "That's one of the ways they apply the Rothschild Formula."

The last thing Mason wanted was to be in the office of the presidency and come across as an out-of-touch conspiracy theorist. One of the early lessons he learned from his grandmother was the familiar phrase: "Where there's smoke, there is fire." Was there enough smoke here to seek the source of the fire? It was a question that deserved an answer. And, if there was any element of truth in *The Protocols,* as Commander-in-Chief he would be foolish to ignore them, not only for the sake of his own life, but for that of his country.

As Henry Ford had surmised, events of the past few decades clearly "fit" the plan outlined in *The Protocols.* And, with that in mind, decisions made during previous Administrations made more sense. Except for Kennedy, Nixon, and Reagan, the other former Presidents appeared to be "puppets," agents who *someone* or some *group* advised and orchestrated their words and actions. Could that group be the self-anointed overlords, who would now expect *him* to fall in line or be assassinated, either politically—as were Nixon and George W. Bush—or by bullets, as were Lincoln and Kennedy? Would he be as lucky as Ronald Reagan and Gerald Ford, who narrowly escaped the deadly sting of would-be assassins' bullets?

Did Ford know too much? Before becoming President, he had served on the Warren Commission, the commission that collected all the evidence about Kennedy's assassination, and *buried* it ... for the sake of "national security" or rather to keep the fact that an American President, who America's archenemy felt was a threat to their plans, was eliminated.

Walking back to the bedroom, Mason looked in himself for the usual signs of fear that should follow such revelations. However, none was present. He didn't know whether to be relieved of that fact or to be concerned that the things he had just learned hadn't quite sunk in. Did he know too much? Perhaps it was all too much to put in the proper perspective at such at late hour of a very long day.

"In any respect," he thought to himself, "like Scarlett O'Hara said in the final scene of *Gone with the Wind*, 'Tomorrow is another day.'"

Wending his way back to the left side of the presidential king-size bed that he had abandoned an hour earlier, Mason whispered, "I'll get to the bottom of this tomorrow."

"What did you say?" Norene asked.

"Oh, nothing, just talking to myself," Mason replied.

"What have you been doing? It's midnight." Norene realized that she had fallen asleep while waiting for Mason to come back to bed.

"Just doing a bit of homework. You know I'm giving the State of the Union address next Wednesday. I'm just reviewing some research that I used to draft portions of it. Good night, *First Lady*." He added, leaning over to kiss Norene on the cheek.

"You know I don't yet know how to respond to that title."

"Well, you might as well get used to it ... at least for the next eighteen months."

"Good night. And, sweet dreams," Norene uttered, her words falling off as she drifted back to sleep.

"I hope that I can dream," Mason thought. "Tomorrow is a big day, a very big day. It's my first press conference, so I'd better get some rest so that I don't come across as a weary President the first time I face the White House press corps."

Before he laid down again, he reached for the little notebook that he kept by his bedside—when it was not in his right hip pocket—and wrote in big bold letters: ***THE PROTOCOLS OF THE MEETINGS OF THE LEARNED ELDERS OF ZION—CONSIDER ALL IMPLICATIONS.***

CHAPTER 25

In a dark hour of the morning, Mason reached for the ringing phone stationed on the table next to his side of the presidential bed.

"Hello," he answered, clearing his throat.

"Mason, its Morley. I'm sorry to call you at this hour, but it is my responsibility to do such things."

"What time is it?"

"It's 4:30 a.m."

"This better be important," Mason said, struggling to gain his faculties.

"It is. I just received a call from a reporter at the *Washington Post*. There's been a plane crash over the Atlantic, killing all aboard," Morley said.

"A commercial flight?"

"No, a private plane."

"Go on," Mason urged.

"The plane was carrying former President Padgett, the former Vice President, and all of the Cabinet members who resigned prior to your taking office," Morley informed him.

At these unbelievable words, Mason sat straight up in the bed. "What else can you tell me?"

"Only that the group was returning from a meeting in Belgium. They had been vacationing at a private chateau in the country, outside Brussels," Morley said.

"Did anyone—staff or crew—survive?"

"No one," Morley responded. "Trans-Atlantic flight control said that they were talking with the crew when they heard what sounded to be an explosion or crash. At that same moment, the plane suddenly disappeared off the radar screen. All attempts to reach the crew were to no avail. They can only surmise that there was malfunction in the plane's engines causing it to fall into the ocean. A Navy submarine has been dispatched to the area to recover the plane's black box. We should have it in a day or so."

"I know that accidents happen, but this is all very strange," Mason said.

Hearing these words, Norene turned on the lamp next to her side of the bed and sat straight up. She did not speak, but listened intently to her husband's words.

"The Illuminati are headquartered in Belgium. The Grand Master of the draconian is said to live in a private chateau in the countryside on the outskirts of Brussels. You remember what Daren has always said, that there are no coincidences. This is too close to the perfect crime and too timely. All perpetrators and witnesses to the treasonous acts uncovered by OAC were eliminated. That such an accident killed most of the people who were implicated in the Illuminati's conspiracy is too much of a coincidence. First thing tomorrow morning, we'll get OAC on this. We have to get to the bottom of this incident, and fast. At first blush, it appears that the Rothschild Formula was invoked. Call me back if you have any additional information, otherwise we will discuss this at our usual morning meeting," the President instructed.

"Will do," Morley replied. "Sorry to awaken you, but I thought it was crucial for you to know about the incident as soon as possible."

"You did the right thing, Morley. Good night."

"What has happened?" Norene asked her husband.

"A tragedy, a terrible tragedy, but it was no accident. President Padgett and most of his former Cabinet were killed in a plane crash," Mason replied.

"Oh, my God," Norene said. "Will those people stop at nothing?"

"At nothing," Mason answered, "at nothing. Go back to sleep—if you can."

Norene knew her husband well and did not ask any further questions. In time, he would share his thoughts with her, but now he needed to debate his options with his alter ego.

Mulling over the news about the crash and its worldwide implications, Mason's mind continued to churn for the next half hour. He could envision how Solomon and the Inner Circle summoned President Padgett and his coconspirators to Belgium with the promise of additional payoffs and United Nations appointments, though the real purpose was surely to find out what, if anything, any of them had revealed to outsiders. Once Illuminati leaders had the information they needed, all witnesses were conveniently eliminated in what would be recorded by their comrades in the mainstream media as a tragic "accident."

Or could the whole thing be a hoax? His followers and supporters had touted President Padgett as a Messiah. Those who disagreed with his policies feared that he might be the Antichrist. If somehow, Padgett were to have sustained a mortal head wound and survived this fatal crash, his role in biblical prophecy would become crystal clear and the countdown to Armageddon begun.

. . . .

Mason never fell back asleep. His mind was racing, exploring the possibilities. At 5:30 a.m. Mason got out of bed, threw on the clothes he had worn the previous day, and went downstairs. When he entered the Oval Office, he went straight to the *Resolute* desk, where first edition copies of the *Washington Post* and *New York Times* were traditionally placed by the night shift of White House staff. In that regard, this morning was like the others.

He lifted the papers off the desk. As he had expected, and in oversized bold typeface, *the Washington Post* headlines read: **Former President and his Cabinet Die in Accident.** The *New York Times* headlines were similar: **Crash Kills Former President & Staff.** Both papers told of how the private 727 jet's navigation system failed, causing the pilots to lose their bearings and crash into the ocean near Greenland, killing all twenty aboard. No mention was made of the possible explosion that Morley had reported just hours before.

"How could the *Post* know that the navigation system failed?" Mason asked, rhetorically. "According to the intelligence given to Morley last night and this morning, no cause has been determined and none of those ostensibly aboard have been accounted for. It's as though the article was written in advance of the incident. It's like all assassinations throughout history. So much for believing the news; the press is part of the cover-up. Unless I get to the bottom of this and tell the people the truth, they will never know the truth."

Having learned how the mainstream press was spinning the crash, the President went back upstairs to dress for the tasks of the day.

With the reality of a mass assassination and, perhaps, the greatest cover-up in history looming, Mason felt as though, once again, America had been violated, snatching from her the ability to judge and discipline those who had wronged her. With no defendants and no witnesses, there could be no trial, unless one takes place in the absence of the defendant (*absente reo.*) When JFK was assassinated, the patsy murderer was killed by a Mafia family member already dying of cancer, before the President's alleged assassin could be questioned in a court of law. Knowing who was likely behind the fatal crash that ostensibly killed President Padgett and his Cabinet, Mason knew that they, too, would never be brought to justice, at least not on in this earthly realm.

"Damn you," Mason said in defiance, directing his anger at a ghostly presence he knew only by mysterious names: *The Order of the Illuminati, Moriah Conquering Wind, Hidden Hand, Invisible Empire,* or *Shadow Government.* "Is nothing beyond you? When your emissaries become a liability, you eliminate them and, with the assistance of a complicit press, cover up the act. This must not stand. Operation Annuit Coeptis will get to the bottom of this, too, if it's the last thing I accomplish."

. . . .

When Morley Bronkston, Raley Stovall, Dale Jackson, Gabriel Shade, Daren Borden, and Harold Purcell entered the Oval Office for their morning meeting, Mason was loaded for bear. He told his OAC partners that the crash over the Atlantic was to be investigated to the fullest extent. No stone was to be left unturned.

"As each of you know, there was no love lost between President Padgett, his Cabinet, and me; however, as the sitting President, I feel that it is my responsibility to see that the circumstances surrounding their deaths is properly investigated. Conversely, if this thing has been staged for more sinister purposes, we must know that as well. Either way, this is a national security matter. Get me the plane's manifest as soon as possible. I want to know the names and profiles of everyone on board, including the crew and any guests."

As the President spoke, he could see his colleagues frantically taking notes so that nothing he said could be misunderstood. On the other hand, his OAC colleagues saw an emerging leader. Mason paused for a moment and said, "In case any of you feel that you aren't getting all of this down, everything said here is being documented by the newly installed Oval Office recording system."

Mason could see the looks of surprise on the faces of his colleagues. "Yes, I know the problems that such a system has caused in the past," he said, "but we have nothing to hide today and will not have anything to hide as long as I'm in this office. What is important is that what goes on in this office can never be misrepresented—by anyone!"

Having disclosed the presence of the previously unknown documentation system, the President continued, "The plane's black box must be recovered. Gabriel, as Director of the CIA, and Dale, Intelligence Director, I want the two of you to work with the heads of the other 15 elements that make up the Intelligence Community. Collectively, the 17 of you will make up my Commission on Espionage and Terrorism. Stress to each of them that I want this incident involving the former President at the top of their list of priorities. In each of those organizations we have people who specialize in such crimes, and I want the best assigned to this project. And I want cooperation between each of these intelligence gathering organizations. We are not concerned about one-upmanship here. I want everyone at the airport where the plane departed questioned, anyone who had access to the plane, or anything that went on it. If anyone tampered with the control systems and engines of that plane, we must know the names of that person or persons and who he or they worked for."

Expressing the "take charge" part of his personality, the President said, "I also want the proper aviation authorities to be present when the in-flight conversations are heard for the first time—*in this very office*," the President ordered. "And, if anyone in any of the intelligence organizations of aviation community seems to be dragging his feet or trying to obstruct this investigation, I want to know it. That person will be immediately taken off the project and subjected to investigation. The people behind this crash have friends in every segment of government and defense. We are going to flush them out. Unlike the Commission appointed by President Lyndon Johnson, the Warren Commission, I intend for the Commission on Espionage and Terrorism to gather, analyze, and release the facts, not destroy or hide them. If the Shadow Government can get away with this mass assassination, they can get away with anything. We can't allow that to happen. Are there any questions?"

"Not a question," Gabriel said. "But I was just thinking back over the last few years of similar events: Marilyn Monroe, Vince Foster, Ron Brown—all knew enough to expose people in high places. It cost them their lives. And now this."

"Do *we* know too much?" Raley Stovall asked.

"Not as much as we must know," Harold Purcell insisted. "We are warriors—each of us in our own way—and we are at war. We have been for a very long time. We just weren't sure who the enemy was. They are masters of deceit, creating skirmishes to distract us and drain our resources, wearing the people down with the thought and cost of war—and now this. Now that we know who we are fighting, we can focus our efforts on exposing and defeating them."

"Thank you for that, General," Mason said, in a demeanor that was more presidential than his colleagues had previously witnessed. Although he was among friends, the President made no bones about his resolve to solve the atrocity that had been committed, or discover if a hoax was being pulled over the eyes of the world.

Having heard no further question or comments, Mason said, "Let's get to work."

When the door closed behind his fellow OAC members, Mason leaned back and closed his eyes.

"What men do, what they knowingly do, knowing not what they do," he said. "The world is becoming more evil with every passing day. Dear God, give me the strength to rise to the task that is before me and the wisdom to lead this nation into battle against the Dragon at our gate.

CHAPTER 26

The day for Mason to deliver the commencement address at his alma mater arrived. Before dawn, Mason, Norene, and Morley boarded Marine One and headed for Andrews Air Force Base where Air Force One awaited.

As the helicopter lifted off the White House pad, Morley handed Mason an envelope.

"Put this in your pocket and read what's inside later," Morley said.

"What is it?" Mason asked.

"An article about reviving America," Morley replied. "It was written by Gary Hubbell and published in the *Aspen Times*. Do you know Hubbell?"

"No, I don't think so. Perhaps, I met him somewhere along the line."

"Well, it seems that he might be someone that we'd want to know," Morley said. "I like his style. He could be an asset to Operation Annuit Coeptis."

"If you insist, I'll read what the man wrote. When did you say that he wrote this?" the President asked, placing the envelope into the inner pocket of his jacket.

"Just before Easter, in 2010," Morley answered. "Just read it. You'll see that the country was ready for someone like you to take the reins, restore confidence in the American way and bring reason back to Washington."

. . . .

On Air Force One, after making sure that Norene and Morley were settled in the parlor area Mason excused himself and went straight into the small office prepared for the President. He wanted to review the speech he intended to deliver later that day.

Leaning back in his chair, Mason retrieved the envelope from his jacket pocket. He removed the newspaper article from the envelope. The date of the article's publication was of particular interest, March 30, 2010, just months before Mason took the oath of office and long before the President's plane ostensibly went down.

After reading the first paragraph, Mason realized that he had seen the article. It was a shocker, outlining Gary Hubble's views on how the previous Administration's arrogance was beginning to awaken the sleeping giant that is America. He had a few minutes and decided to review what Hubble had written.

"I hope that Hubbell is right." Having read the article, Mason folded it and replaced it in his jacket pocket. "No, I *pray* that he is right. America can't stand for a violent revolution. It has to take place at the ballot box. Now that I am President, my job is to make sure that every American is armed with the knowledge needed and the commitment to do their part in re-founding America."

....

A massive crowd welcomed President Edmonds to his alma mater. Not since the death of the university's beloved coach in the 1980s had so many people turned out to pay tribute to one of their heroes.

President Edmonds delivered the much anticipated graduation commencement address to a packed coliseum and received a standing ovation. He told them of the story behind the dollar bill and challenged each of those present to bring America back to its once-famed glory. The President's message resonated with old and young alike.

Except for the more liberal-leaning members of the university's faculty, the listeners were on their feet chanting "Thirteen...Thirteen... Thirteen." The President's story of how the number thirteen was chosen by the Founding Fathers to send a message to those who would choose to be its enemies particularly resonated with young people, who had been convinced by mainstream media reports that their futures looked bleak.

....

Exiting the politically charged auditorium, Mason, Norene, and Morley slipped into a window-tinted, black SUV parked in a loading area inside the building. Identical vehicles, occupied by armed Secret Service agents, were parked in front of and behind the President's SUV.

"It was your best speech ever," Norene said.

"Thanks, Honey, I had a good story to tell and I drew energy from the faces of those concerned young people in the audience. They've been so drenched in false hope and negativism that they seemed hungry to hear about a future that they could help build, and how to go about doing it."

"Well, you gave them what they wanted," Norene said. "I'm proud of you."

The overhead door opened and the caravan of vehicles exited the building, immediately falling in behind a parade of police motorcycles, which strategically began a choreographic maneuver placing motorcycles in front of, to the sides of, and behind the President's SUV. The motorcade's intended destination was the local airport, where Air Force One was waiting. However, as the motorcade entered a tunnel, under a railway trestle, all vehicles came to a crawl. The President's SUV pulled out of the line and was replaced with an identical vehicle that had been secretly waiting in the shadows of the trestle. Sitting in the rear seats of the replacement vehicle were the President's and First Lady's doubles. In times of heightened security such measures were often used.

The driver of the President's vehicle waited until the motorcade was well out of view. Then, as directed by the Commander-in-Chief, he did a one-eighty heading in the direction from which they had originally come.

When the motorcycle-escorted motorcade arrived at the airport, the black SUV's were directed into a private hangar. The huge hangar doors closed securely behind as the last vehicle entered the structure. Special Agent Wyndall Morian went directly to the center vehicle and opened the door. He was shocked to see the President's and First Lady's doubles sitting in the middle row.

"What the hell?" Morian asked Justin Landry, the agent sitting in the right front seat.

"You'll know soon enough," Landry replied. "Agent Goodrich will call you shortly."

Visibly disturbed that he had not been forewarned about the switch, Morian stormed away from the vehicle and stole away to a distant corner of the hangar. Agent Landry watched as Morian retrieved a cell phone from its belt holster and placed an outgoing call.

"Who could he be calling?" Landry said to the agent behind the wheel. "Don't you find it strange that he would be using a cell phone rather than our secure radio system?"

"It is a bit unusual," the driver replied. "I'll keep an eye on him."

. . . .

In the car with the presidential couple, Agent Goodrich asked, "Mr. President, can you tell me where are we going?"

"We're going to a town called Ashton," Morley replied on the President's behalf, leaning forward and handing Agent Sean Goodrich the GPS coordinates and address.

"That's an hour and ten minutes away," Agent Goodrich commented.

"We know," Morley said. "The President has been there before. Just make sure that you obey the speed limit and all traffic signs. We don't want to get pulled over and blow our cover."

"What is the purpose of this secret mission?"

"You'll know when we get there," Morley replied. "Don't worry. It's nothing of a risky nature."

"With all due respect, Mr. Bronkston, anything that exposes the President is risky. It's my job, and that of the other agents in this detail, to protect him. Please don't make our job more difficult."

"We're going to visit one of the President's old friends, the ninety-year-old widow of a World War II veteran. She has invited him and the First Lady to an early dinner," Morley said. "Anyway, everyone in the world except us thinks that the President is in the SUV that should be in a secure hangar at the airport. His and the First Lady's doubles have been ordered not to exit the vehicle until we arrive. The press will be told that the President is meeting with old friends and teammates from his college days."

Mason and Norene, riding in the middle seats of the SUV, simply listened to the verbal exchanges.

"Who else knows about this?" Agent Goodrich asked.

"Just Mrs. Jacoby and us," the President interjected.

"Are you sure, Mr. President?"

"Well, as sure as anybody can be," the President replied.

"I don't like it, sir," the agent answered. "Out here by ourselves, we are sitting ducks. I think we should go back NOW."

"Your recommendation has been noted," President Edmonds replied. "I think the decoy SUV and doubles for the First Lady and me should keep everyone occupied at the airport until our return, including anyone who might have sinister motives."

"Yes, Mr. President," Goodrich replied "if you insist."

"I insist," the President replied.

Holding his radio phone next to his lips, Goodrich said, "Agent One calling Agent Three. Come in, please."

"This is Three. Come in," came the reply over the radio phone. The voice was that of another member of the President's Secret Service detail, Agent Wyndall Morian.

"The Eagle is delayed. Hold all other birds in the nest until further notified," Goodrich ordered.

"I know that the Eagle has been delayed," Morian replied in a sharp tone. "Why wasn't I informed that the winds had changed?"

"Sometimes storms blow in unexpectedly—and from unfavorable directions," Goodrich answered. "Just keep the other birds in the nest until I can get there. Understood?

"Understood," Morian answered. "What's your ETA and 10/84?"

"Fifty minutes, Eight hundred, Veteran's Trace in Ashton," Goodrich answered.

"Got it," Morian replied in a tone that seemed hurried.

"What's the hurry?" Goodrich asked.

"Uh, no hurry; just thought you were done."

Having finished the conversation with Goodrich, Morian made his way back to the distant corner from which he had made his previous call. On his cell phone, he dialed a number.

. . . .

In the President's SUV, with the eyes of a hawk Agent Goodrich scanned the road ahead, behind, and on all sides. "Open the internal cover of the moon roof," he said to Daniel Thoms, the Secret Service agent who was driving the vehicle. "I thought I heard the sound of a helicopter pass over. With the moon-roof cover retracted, I can see if *anything* flies overhead or at least hear it better than if the top window is closed. You keep your eyes peeled on the road ahead and let me know if you detect any suspicious behavior from cars or trucks along the way. And Mr. Bronkston, would you keep an eye out the rear of the vehicle and let me know if you see anything?"

"Yes, sir," both Thoms and Morley answered, following Goodrich's orders.

The President, First Lady, and Morley engaged in small talk, reviewing the message that President Edmonds had delivered to those who attended the commencement. All the time, Morley, who was in the third row seat of the SUV, was looking over his shoulder at the road behind.

"I can't stop thinking about what you told the graduating seniors," Norene said to her husband. "Though most of them have only read about President Kennedy, they seemed to react favorably when you repeated the challenge he made to Americans about asking themselves what they could do for America rather than the other way around."

"Yeah," Morley voiced. "I liked the part about how the Jewish star ended up on the one-dollar bill. Also, I saw several professors smile when you told the story about the student, the teacher, and the butterfly that one of your medical school professors told your graduating class."

"I'm not sure that some of the professors in the audience were very happy with my remarks, especially the one sitting on the front row right in front of the lectern. For most of the time I was talking I could see him squirming. The bulk of college professors lean far left. Many of them have bought into the Illuminati's propaganda. That's one of the challenges we have yet to overcome. I'm not sure how we do it, though," the President remarked.

"Yeah, it took fifty years for social deconstructionists to get their people planted into the schools. They created a whole generation of "Indigo Children," Norene interjected.

Both Mason and Morley turned to look at Norene. "That's a term that I hadn't heard," Mason said.

"It is one of those so-called 'New Age' things that grew out of the 'flower children' movement from the 1960s, which eventually developed a negative connotation. A product of that movement, a parapsychologist, claimed the she saw an indigo colored aura around some of the troubled children that she treated. While many of them appeared to have special abilities, many suffer from challenging conditions such as autism," Norene explained.

"Sounds like someone is taking a bit of science and using it to promote a socio-political agenda," Morley interjected.

"It's an old Illuminati tactic," Mason said.

"From what I've heard you two guys discuss in the past, the effect would fit that mold. My understanding is that it was confiscated and promoted by the progressive movement to further anti-war and environmental agendas. They claim a new generation of 'Indigo Children' will change the world into one in which war will not exist. To achieve this end—they espouse—misbehavior should not be disciplined, rather good people should have empathy for evil and destructive behavior," Norene answered.

"I can see how the Illuminati would want liberal-leaning teachers to buy into this agenda," Morley said. "It's time that the trustees and regents of America's colleges see what is happening."

"I wish I had known about this indigo thing before my speech. I would have mentioned it. Maybe, I'll weave it into my State of the Union speech," Mason said. "What our country needs is to replace pseudo-science ideologists in our schools with instructors who are dedicated *to teaching* rather than *indoctrinating*," the President added.

"Agent One, come in," the voice on the other end of the radio phone said. It belonged to Agent Morian.

"This is One. Go ahead," Goodrich replied.

"What is your ETA?" Agent Morian asked.

"Ten minutes," Goodrich answered.

"Keep me posted," Morian requested.

"Will do. One out," Goodrich replied, glancing over at Thoms and asking, "Why is Morian so interested in our estimated time of arrival?"

. . . .

"Ashton hasn't changed in the past forty years," Mason said to Norene as their vehicle passed through the town district.

"I remember that bank there on the corner and the post office across the street. There are a lot of empty buildings," she acknowledged.

"I'm sorry to say that the same thing has happened to small towns all across America. Downtowns are becoming ghost towns," Mason replied.

"Some things change and some things remain the same. It's the people who simply pass through. The things we build begin to decay the moment they are completed," Norene said.

"That's why it is important *to* maintain if one hopes to sustain." Interrupting himself, the President directed, "Turn left at the first road outside town."

. . . .

"This is it," President Edmonds said, as the SUV approached the entrance to the Jacoby place.

"Pull over here," Agent Goodrich said to Thoms. "I want to get out and look around before we enter the driveway. This place is more secluded than I thought."

. . . .

Returning to the vehicle, Goodrich said to Thoms, "I don't like how the place is surrounded by a forest that we haven't combed."

"Let's go in," President Edmonds said to Goodrich.

"Are you asking my opinion, Mr. President, or giving me an order?"

"Consider it an order."

Goodrich nodded to Thoms to do as the President said.

The dirt driveway leading to the house was several hundred yards in length, and a rail fence completely surrounded the house. The small wood-framed house sat in the center of an open pasture, which was surrounded by planted pines and thick underbrush. Two cows and a single black horse were grazing in the front pasture.

"Is there a garage attached to the house?" Goodrich asked the President.

"The last time I was here, there was no garage," President Edmonds answered.

"Pull up as closely as you can to the front porch," Goodrich said to Agent Thoms. The driver did as directed.

"Mr. President, there is no way that I can adequately protect you as we move from this vehicle to the front door. And because of the rail fence, we can't drive any closer than this. It's at least fifty feet to the house's entrance. Are you okay with that?" Goodrich asked, "Or should I remove some of the fencing and have Agent Thoms drive us to the front door?"

"You worry too much, Goodrich," the President said. "No one lives within a mile or so of this place."

"It's not the residents that concern me, Mr. President," the agent replied.

Goodrich went alone to the front door alone and knocked.

To the woman who answered, the agent said, "Ma'am, I'm Special Agent Goodrich, assigned to President Edmonds' detail. Are you Mrs. Jacoby?"

"I am," she replied.

"The President is here to meet with you."

"My word," Mrs. Jacoby responded. "Dr. Edmonds *is* a man of his word. He did come. I'm so honored. I can't wait to see him. It's been years."

Though tinted glass prevented Grace Jacoby from seeing the individuals inside the SUV, she nevertheless waved just in case the President was looking her way.

"If you will remain inside, I'll bring President Edmonds and his party in," Goodrich said.

"Who else came with you?" Mrs. Jacoby asked.

"The First Lady and her brother," Goodrich answered. "And the agent who is driving the vehicle."

"That's great. I have cooked enough for an army. I haven't met Norene's brother, but I remember her as a caring, beautiful lady," Mrs. Jacoby recalled.

"Yes, Ma'am." Under his breath Goodrich said, "And I do wish we had an army with us." Goodrich said under his breath.

"Did you say something?"

"I said that the First Lady truly is a caring, beautifully lady," Goodrich lied. "Is anyone else in the house or on your property?"

"Oh no," she answered. "I'm all alone. This is a private dinner, just for the President, and of course his guests."

"If you don't mind, may I walk through your house before we bring the President's party inside?"

"Absolutely," Grace Jacoby replied. "Make yourself at home."

Having been satisfied that no one else was inside, Goodrich went out the back door, surveying the surrounding areas from the back porch. Then, he circled the house, returned to the SUV, and said, "Mr. Bronkston, you go first. When you are safely inside, Thoms and I will escort the First Lady in. Then we will return for the President. If anyone comes into the house or you see anything unusual, alert me right away. Will you, please?"

"Sounds like a plan to me," Morley responded, somewhat flippantly, but did as directed.

With Morley safely inside, Agents Goodrich and Thoms flanked the First Lady and escorted her up the steps, onto the porch, and through the front door.

"Come in, dear," Mrs. Jacoby said to Norene. "It's been a long time. And you are every bit as beautiful as I remembered."

"Thank you for having us in your home, Mrs. Jacoby. You are a special friend to my husband. He thought so much of your husband and your sons. Please know how much we appreciate their service. We mourned for you when they passed away."

"My boys were killed in action. Both were decorated heroes," Grace Jacoby said, proudly.

"I know. And, the President is aware that they were, too," Norene acknowledged.

"Have a seat on the sofa. Can I get you some iced tea?" Grace asked Norene.

"That sounds great. And, I'm sure that Mason will want some, too. If you have a slice of pineapple could you put a piece in each of our glasses?"

"You even remembered how I serve ice tea, Norene. I'm impressed. I learned that from my sister. She lives in Gaspar, about two hours from here. I'll be right back," Grace said, making her way into the kitchen.

. . . .

Surveying the grounds and surrounding areas on his way back to the vehicle, Goodrich said to Thoms, "I'll be glad when we get the President onto Air Force One. This whole situation gives me the creeps."

Thoms opened the rear door to the SUV and Goodrich said to the remaining passenger, "Okay, Mr. President, when you are ready."

"I'm ready," President Edmonds said. "I've been ready."

The President got out of the vehicle and strategically positioned himself between the two Secret Service agents, as he had been trained to do. The only difference was that on this occasion another two agents, who usually walked in front of and behind the President, were absent. Walking in lock step with Goodrich and Thoms, the President approached the front porch. To his protector's dismay, the absence of the other members of the detail was not the only security protocol that had been violated. In fact, there were many violations. And that there were, gave reason for concern. Security measures were instilled for a purpose, to protect the President, at least as much as was humanly possible.

The fifty feet to the house seemed like fifty miles. Will we ever get there? Should we run? Are we overreacting? Who knows that we are here, anyway? Though on the outside everyone appeared calm, questions of concern were whirling around in the heads of the President *and* his men.

At long last, the party reached the steps leading to the front porch. One step, two steps, three steps were scaled. As the agents changed positions, one moving in front of and the other behind the President, a sharp *crack* was heard behind them. Goodrich and Thoms immediately recognized the sound. It was that of a high-powered rifle being fired. Each of the agents whirled around to see a small cloud of smoke coming from the woods to their right. Goodrich quickly checked the President, who was still standing. Thoms pulled a gun from his shoulder holster and returned fire in the direction from which the bullet came. After pushing the President through the front door, Goodrich and Thoms emptied the cases of their SIG P-229s, firing into the woods.

No shots were returned. During the commotion, President Edmonds had gone on ahead and was safely seated on the sofa in the living room, or so it seemed.

"Are you okay, sir?" Goodrich asked.

"I've been hit," the President replied, lying down on the sofa.

"Where, sir?" Goodrich asked.

"Under my right shoulder blade."

"Oh, my God," Norene cried out.

"Stay calm, Honey," Mason said to his wife.

Goodrich said to Thoms, "Call Morian and tell him what has happened and to get a Black Hawk Medevac chopper from the Army base here, *now*!

"Mrs. Jacoby, what is your address?" agent Thoms asked.

Visibly shaken, Grace fumbled for the correct answer, and after what seemed a lifetime, blurted out, "1800 Veteran's Trace."

"And, tell him to dispatch one of the standby details from the military base to comb the woods." Having issued the order, Goodrich ran into the living room where the President was now lying on Mrs. Jacoby's sofa. "Talk to me, Mr. President." Goodrich pled.

"It burns deep inside my chest. That's all I can tell you now," the President replied.

"What can I do?" Mrs. Jacoby asked.

"How are you, Grace?" Mason asked the elderly lady, who was frantic about what had occurred at her home.

"It's my fault. I shouldn't have invited you here. We've got to get you to a hospital," Mrs. Jacoby said. "Can I call Dr. Smith? He lives just down the road, in Laneville? He can be here in fifteen minutes. I know he can."

"Ma'am, with all due respect, I need you to go into the next room and get us some towels, ice, and a pan of water. Then, let us handle this," Agent Thoms said to Mrs. Jacoby.

"What can I do?" Norene asked.

"I'm not sure, just yet, Ma'am," Goodrich replied, ripping off the President's jacket and shirt. He rolled President Edmonds onto his left side so that he and Thoms could examine the wound.

Blood was gushing from the bullet hole in the President's back. Goodrich grabbed the shirt he had ripped off the President, wadded it up and said to Agent Thoms, "Hold this over the wound. Press down as firmly as you can to see if we can stop some of the bleeding." Then Goodrich pressed the talk button on his radio and said, "This is Agent One, come in Three."

"Three here, what is the situation there?" Agent Morian replied.

"The President is down. I repeat, the President is down. One shot, to the right rear chest. Did you reach the Medevac Black Hawk?" Goodrich asked.

"I'm on it. Should be there in ten minutes," Morian replied. "It'll be deployed from the military base close by."

"And, the search detail?" Goodrich asked.

"I'm on it, too," Morian replied.

"Call ahead and alert the university hospital in Steelton. Tell them that we are bringing the President there. And have them call in a team of the top chest surgeons on their staff. I don't know how severe the wound is, yet," Goodrich said.

"Copy that. Is the President stable?" Morian asked.

"Got to go. I'll follow up shortly. Stay in touch with the Medevac unit."

"Ten-four," Morian replied.

"Mr. President, how do you feel?" Goodrich asked, looking at the blood-soaked shirt. From the amount of blood it had absorbed, the agent knew that the President was bleeding internally and profusely.

"Not so good," the President answered. "I can tell that my blood pressure is dropping and my pulse is speeding up. I feel a bit dizzy. Put me on the floor. Lift my legs up on the sofa. That will keep blood flowing to my brain rather than away from it."

"I don't know if that's such a good idea, Mr. President," Agent Goodrich responded.

"Do as I say, Goodrich," the President said. "Remember that I'm also a doctor."

"Yes, Mr. President. Forgive me," Goodrich replied while following the President's command. Turning to Thoms, Goodrich said, "Get Morian back on the radio and find out where that damned chopper is."

"This is Three, Go ahead," came the reply.

"Where is the chopper?" Thoms asked.

"It should be there," Morian replied. "I sent it to 1800 Veteran's Plaza."

"Veteran's Plaza!" Agent Goodrich exclaimed. "Mrs. Jacoby," he called out to the woman he had asked to wait in the adjoining room, "where is Veteran's Plaza?"

"Oh my goodness," she replied. "It's all the way across town. That's a shopping center. It's about five miles east of here."

"Three, its 1800 Veteran's *Trace*—one, eight, zero, zero Veteran's Trace. That's T as in Tango, R as in Romeo. Do you have it?"

"Yes, I've got it," Morian responded. "Sorry for the misunderstanding."

"Misunderstanding, man!" Goodrich exclaimed. "Why the hell didn't you confirm the address using GPS? We're trying to save the President's life. What are you doing?"

"I'm trying to do my job," Morian replied

Clicking the mute button on his radio, Goodrich said to Thoms, "This is not like Morian. He has never made such a blatant error, especially not under pressure. I wonder who he is doing a job *for*."

Goodrich released the mute button on his radio and ordered, "Tell the chopper to fly due west. I'll see if I can set fire to something to create some smoke to help the chopper identify the house," Goodrich said, and turned again to Mrs. Jacoby. "Ma'am I need something to burn, something that will create a lot of smoke. What do you have?"

"There are three bales of pine straw on the back porch. I was going to put straw in my flower beds before the President came, but didn't get around to it," Grace Jacoby answered.

Goodrich looked at Thoms. Not a word was spoken, yet Thoms knew what he was to do. "I'm on it," he replied and went straight away to the back porch. Lifting a bale of straw in each arm, Thoms ran into a bare spot at the edge of the yard where he set fire to them with his cigarette lighter. As expected, a dark cloud of smoke rose toward the sun of midday sky.

Tending the wounded leader, "How are you, Mr. President," Goodrich asked.

"I wish I could tell you what you want to hear," the President answered. "But the truth is I'm losing a lot of blood and having difficulty breathing. I suspect that my right lung has collapsed and that I have a hemothorax. So far, my heart seems to be holding up fine. Is the chopper close?"

"Very close, sir," Goodrich replied. "It will be here any minute with a medical team aboard."

The agent barely got the words out of his mouth when the familiar sound of a helicopter was heard above the roof. Within seconds a team of medics jumped out of the chopper and rushed into the room, where they sprang into action.

"What's my blood pressure?" President Edmonds asked the medic who was checking it.

"It's 80/50, Mr. President," she answered.

"That's not good, soldier," the President replied, his voice weakening.

The medical crew went about their work with precision and efficiency, placing an oxygen mask over the President's mouth and nose, starting an IV, and hanging a bag of Lactated Ringers solution.

"Do you have a large intracath with you?" the President asked.

"Yes, sir," one of the corpsmen answered.

"Take the guard off the needle and hand it to me," the President ordered and took the needle in his right hand. Using his left hand he felt the lower edge of his right twelfth rib, counted up four spaces and stuck the needle into his chest cavity. Immediately, blood began to gush from the open end of the catheter.

"This should drain some of the blood that is accumulated in my chest and collapsing parts of my lung that wasn't hit by the bullet. If I pass out or when the blood stops pouring, cap off the open of the catheter, understood?" the President ordered.

"Yes, sir," the corpsman answered.

Quickly, an IV was started in the President's left arm. The fluid from a sterile bag would replace some of the blood volume that he had lost. And oxygen being administered with a nasal mask would help make the remaining blood in his system more effective in keeping vital organs functioning.

"Let's get him in the chopper and to the hospital," the leader of the medical team, a Colonel, ordered.

The President was lifted onto an evacuation stretcher and carried toward the helicopter.

"I'm coming with you," Norene said.

"Ma'am," the Colonel said, "I don't think that's a good idea."

"I want her with me," the President demanded.

"Yes, sir," the Colonel answered.

"Goodbye, Morley," Mason said. "Thanks for all you have done. Stay the course. There's work left to do. General Purcell will need you."

Morley, trying to appear confident, replied, "You got it, Bro. I'll see you at the hospital."

The President motioned for Mrs. Jacoby to come closer. "I'm sorry to have this happen at your home. We had so much to talk about."

Holding back the tears, Grace Jacoby just nodded.

"Agent Thoms," President Edmonds said, "thanks for your service and loyalty."

"It has been an honor to serve you, Mr. President."

The first Black Hawk lifted off as Agent Thoms and Morley boarded another that had arrived on the scene. Its' occupants watching for additional threats, the second helicopter followed closely behind the one in which the President, the First Lady, and Agent Goodrich were riding.

As the two choppers were heading toward the hospital, a third Blackhawk landed and a detail of eight soldiers jumped out and ran toward the nearby woods in search of the shooter.

....

Though it was difficult to hear over the sounds of the helicopter's engine and spinning blades, Mason said to Norene, "Honey, this doesn't look very good. I'm not going to make it. I want..."

Norene interrupted him, "You *are* going to make it. You have to," she added, struggling to control her emotions.

"If I could *will* the bleeding in my chest to stop, I would, Honey. The facts are the facts. The bullet hit a major vessel, prob*ably my vena cava. I don't have long. And I need you to listen closely to what I have* to say. Lean down here so that I can talk to you," Mason said, his voice weakening with each word.

Norene clasped her husband's hand and looked into his eyes. "I love you," she said. "I always have. I always will."

"I love you, too," Mason replied. "You have stood by me every step of the way. We have been a good team. Though we didn't finish what we set out to do, I'd like to think that we made a good start. I don't have any regrets and I don't want you to, either. I did what I had to do."

"How can I go on without you?" Norene asked.

"You have to. Now, it's up to you to carry the message we have tried to get across to the American people. Be my voice. Find a way to republish the report on Operation Annuit Coeptis and let the people know the truth. Call the doctor who has agreed to write my memoirs. He can help," Mason said, struggling to breathe and speak. Tell him everything."

"I will," Norene said. "I promise."

"Take *Laney's Little Book of Wisdom* out of my right hip pocket and have someone transcribe the notes I wrote in it. Then give each of our children and grandchildren a copy. I promised my grandmother that I would pass her words of wisdom to my children. Tell them to stick together, like families should."

"They will treasure a copy of the notebook that has meant so much to you. I am sure."

"And, Honey, please get a copy of those same notes to Harold Purcell. He once told me that he'd like to have them. Make sure to tell him to pursue the notation I made about *Protocols* and to consider their implications and those of a piece of paper that I folded and placed between the pages. He has a draft of the State of the Union address that I intended to give next week. Tell him I want him to give it in my absence if he is inclined to do so. Will you do that?"

"Yes, I will," Norene answered, in response to her husband's dying concerns about America's future.

"Tell Morley to pursue the Solomon note. And, tell Mrs. Jacoby how sorry I am for all the trouble we caused her."

With words steadily becoming less audible, the President requested, "Tell these young men and women in uniform—the Medevac crew—that I appreciate and respect what they are trying to do. Let them know what I know, that the inevitable is not their fault and some things are beyond a caregiver's control." He added, "Is Goodrich in here?"

"Goodrich," the President said. "This is not your fault. You warned me. And I didn't listen. I take full responsibility and I hope you can forgive me for having this happen on your watch. You did your job. Somebody very close to you—and me—is responsible. Though I have no proof, I have long suspected him. Though he tried to hide it, his eyes spoke volumes. For the sake of the American people, find out who owns Agent Morian. Tell Gabriel Slade that I said, 'Don't let them get away with this, not like they did when President Kennedy was shot.' Understood?"

"Understood, Mr. President. I'm so sorry. I should have picked up on Morian in time."

"Morian is good at what he does, very good. That's why they wanted him. But he's only the tip of the iceberg. Follow the money. Follow the power. Follow the people who hate the America that we were in the process of reviving. Follow the incident with President Padgett's plane. That's where you'll find the guilty parties."

"Yes sir, Mr. President, you have my word."

"That's good enough for me, Goodrich," Mason said and motioned for Norene to come closer.

"If I could choose a place to die and in whose presence it would be, it would be with you and a group of American soldiers. I just wish I had the opportunity to say goodbye to our children and grandchildren. Do that for me. Will you?"

"I will, Darling," Norene said, "I will tell them how much you loved them."

Growing ever weaker, Dr. Edmonds said, "Though I never rode in one until I became President, as a boy I watched helicopters fly overhead and wondered what it was like to be in one. Tell General Purcell that I said a Black Hawk is as good a place as any to end my portion of our journey and that the mission is now in his hands. And, Darling, believe me when I tell you that his are capable hands. But tell Harold that unless he exposes and brings to justice the people behind this, he will be next. And without him, the America of our dreams will go by the wayside."

The pulse oxymeter indicated that the President's oxygen concentration in what blood remained within his cardiovascular system was dropping to a dangerously low level. As she was trained to do, the medic replaced the oxygen mask over the President's mouth and nose and said, "Mr. President, take a couple of deep breaths, if you can, sir."

Try as he might, Mason's lungs would not expand. Blood continued to pour from the catheter he had inserted between his ribs. He coughed twice, bringing up blood each time. His chest cavities and lungs were filled with blood. "Take the mask off, please," he said to the medic, and she complied with the President's wishes.

Trying to muster all the strength that remained in his failing body, Mason looked into the eyes of his wife and said, "When the cardiac monitor goes to a straight line, remember my wishes. Do not allow them to initiate a resuscitative code. Promise?"

"I promise," Norene replied.

And, with his last shallow breath, Mason Edmonds whispered to his wife, "I'll miss you most of all. Just know that we'll be together again, someday ... somewhere special, where Evil is not allowed to exist."

With those words, the EKG pattern on the cardiac monitor converted to a straight line and the alarm sounded. The medic who had been monitoring the President's vital signs looked up at the First Lady for direction. Norene shook her head from side to side, indicating that no further resuscitative measures be conducted, as her husband's advance directive specified.

Realizing that her husband was gone, she threw herself across his lifeless body and sobbed. "I love you. I'm so sorry," she said.

For more than five minutes, not a word was spoken in the Black Hawk. Then, trying to console the First Lady, Agent Goodrich said, "America has lost a patriot and a fearless warrior."

"One of the best, ever," Norene replied. "He truly loved this country and what it once meant to mankind's search for purpose."

When the chopper landed at the heliport atop the hospital in Steelton, Agent Goodrich was the first to exit. He was met by Agent Wyndall Morian, a medical team, and the chief of the university's police force.

Goodrich walked straight to Morian, slowly reached inside his jacket for his SIG P-229 and poked it into Morian's ribs. "Agent Wyndall Morian, don't make a move. You are under arrest for the murder of the President of the United States of America." Placing cuffs on the hands of a man who had violated the oath he took to protect the President, Goodrich read Agent Morian his Miranda Rights: "You have the right to remain silent. You have the right to ..."

"Chief," Agent Goodrich said to the head of the university's police force when Morian's rights had been completely spoken, as required by law, "would you assist me in taking this traitor to the nearest jail? Find the darkest cell in the safest place possible. Do not allow anyone to visit him. I don't want anything to happen to him until we can extract what we need to know."

"Gladly," the chief replied and began to lead Agent Morian away.

As the two men approached the door leading to the elevator, a man dressed in a white lab coat retrieved a pistol from the coat's pocket and pointed it at Morian. Goodrich, with his gun still in his hand, had been watching as the chief and Morian approached the mysterious bystander. Instinctively, Goodrich raised his firearm and hit the would-be assassin in his heart with a barrage of bullets from his SIG P-229. The man dropped to the ground, without having had a chance to fire a shot.

With the shooter lying dead, the crowd of hospital officials and staff on the roof, who had fallen onto the heliport's surface as a measure of protection, began to rise to their feet.

Once he was assured that the shooter was dead and that Morian was safely on his way to jail, Goodrich went to the Black Hawk in which the First Lady and President's body had remained during the attempted assassination of one of the perpetrators of the President's death. Explaining the need for her to be transported to the airport where Air Force one waited, Goodrich said, "Ma'am, I'm so sorry about this."

"You have done your job, Agent Goodrich," Norene said. "And, you did it well. Thank you. Clearly, there is an evil conspiracy at work here. Now we have to bring the other people behind this heinous act to justice."

"Yes, Ma'am," Goodrich replied. "That is precisely what I intend to do. I have no choice. I gave my word to the President."

With Morian safely in a cell of the hospital's basement jail, the elevator was sent back to the roof. The Black Hawk lifted off the hospital's roof and headed east toward the Steelton airport. Walking through the parted path created by observers, Agent Goodrich approached the open door, where a deputy sheriff had taken over the elevator's controls.

As the door began to close, Agent Goodrich took a final glance at the Black Hawk in which lay his fallen

President, a man who only wanted to see his nation be well again and become a beacon to the world.

Deputy Marsha Allen pressed "G" for ground. On the way down, Deputy Allen said to Agent Goodrich, "I knew the President. I worked with him on a project to catch and punish people forging prescriptions and selling drugs to children. He was a good man. I think I speak for all patriotic Americans when I tell you that Dr. Edmonds made a difference. History will remember him favorably."

Agent Goodrich replied, "Sometime in the future, I would like for you to tell me about it, the sting operation that you and he worked on? I'd like to pass the story on to the First Lady."

"It would be my honor," the deputy replied. "It would truly be an honor."

When the elevator reached the ground floor, Agent Goodrich walked through the hospital lobby, filled with Americans who stood reverently to pay respects for the fallen President.

After making sure that Agent Morian was safely shackled and locked away in the hospital's jail cell, he climbed into a black SUV with heavily tinted windows and drove away toward the municipal airport at Steelton. There, the First Lady, crew and secret service agents waited aboard Air Force One. From the window of the 747, she watched while the body of her slain husband, the forty-fifth President of the United States of America, was taken aboard.

Air Force One climbed effortlessly and reverently into the western sky, where the sun was hanging on the horizon. Wiping the streaming tears from her cheeks and peering through the window of the jumbo jet at the majestic sunset, Norene Edmonds remembered how she and Mason loved viewing the masterpieces that as evening approached embellished the western sky. The daily ritual represented the end of one day and the hopes that another would follow on the morrow.

As in previous days, the sky was full of color and artistry. Norene could only hope that the mosaic masterpiece in the western sky was a sign of beautiful things to come. She could only pray that the day's end was a good omen—that the time of one patriotic President was ending and that of another would begin when the life-sustaining light reappeared on the dawn to follow.

"That," she surmised, "would be the fulfillment of her late husband's dream, one for which he paid the ultimate sacrifice."

CHAPTER 27

Following the telecast being viewed from a sprawling country chateau located just outside Brussels, Belgium, a red telephone was lifted from its receiver. Instantly, another red phone rang in an office of CIA Headquarters in Langley, Virginia.

"Yes, Grand Master," Spartacus said, lifting the phone to his ear.

"It is time to bring Padgett back from the dead," Solomon uttered in a calm, quiet voice.

"Yes, Grand Master, I understand. I'll initiate the plan immediately," Spartacus answered. "As described in their Bibles, when it appears that President Padgett survived the crash and a seemingly mortal head wound, enough people will be convinced that he is the promised Messiah. He will be reelected by a landslide," Spartacus said. "I'll set the wheels in motion and notify our friends in the press."

On the following morning, the New York Times, Washington Post and other mainstream media outlets published the Illuminati's pre-packaged story, as it was written:

Padgett Lives

"Miracles indeed do happen. Former President Padgett escaped death. Defying all natural phenomena, he survived the crash of the private plane in which he, his wife, and members of his Cabinet were returning from Europe.

"A lone nighttime fisherman in the waters off Greenland saw the plane dive into the water and went to investigate. Arriving on the scene, he found a single lifeless body floating on the back and bleeding profusely from a scalp wound.

"The fisherman didn't recognize the former President and presumed him dead. Nevertheless, he loaded President Padgett's body in his boat. Along the way, and although he appeared lifeless, the former President suddenly coughed water from his lungs and began to breathe.

"Having no hospital in the small fishing village, the fisherman took the rescued passenger to his austere cabin. There he cared for the unconscious survivor.

"Three days later, the former President miraculously awakened from a death defying experience and revealed his identity to his caretaker. Immediately, the fisherman went into his village and notified the authorities.

"President Padgett was airlifted from Greenland late last evening and taken to Walter Reed Army Hospital for further studies and evaluations. Having returned from the dead, the former President is expected to make a full recovery. The bodies of the crew and other passengers aboard the plane were never recovered."

"It is done. The people have their Messiah. And after all these centuries, we have their world," the man who liked to be called Solomon uttered, as he dropped his copy of the New York Times in his lap, rocked back in his chair and propped his feet up on a hand-carved desk from ancient Samaria.

The symbolic Ark of the Annunaki Covenant desk was made of gopher wood timbers recovered from the remains of a large wooden ship discovered on Mount Ararat by Samarian explorers. Generation by generation, the desk and its contents were passed down to the Order's next patriarch.

Locked away in a small vault hidden in the bottom left hand drawer is the original copy of the *Protocols of the Learned Elders of Zion*, a list of laws and a secret oath. Both were reportedly written in blood on skin from the back of a human being.

It is said that the laws and oath are inscribed in a no-longer-spoken language and that the blood used to write the sinister documents was from Abel, slain brother of Cain. The much heralded biblical murder was orchestrated and witnessed by the Annunaki. A secret additive was used to prevent the container filled with Abel's blood from clotting. It is this oath and the laws that it references to which Annunaki descendants and their earthly converts swear upon being confirmed as Illuminists.

While in a secret chateau in Belgium Solomon was relishing in Lucifer's apparent victory, on the opposite side of the Atlantic President Purcell and the remaining members of Operation Annuit Coeptis were sitting down for an emergency session with the Israeli Prime Minister and the Director of Mossad, the Israeli Institute for Intelligence and Special Tasks.

"We have won but the first round in this battle," President Purcell said.

"Agreed," the Israeli Prime Minister said. "We thought we knew who our mutual enemies were, but it appears that we only knew the identities of their puppets."

"Their god is the eternal archenemy of ours," the Director of Mossad added.

"Well, if I were a betting man, I'd put everything I have on the God that favored the creation of our two nations," the Israeli Prime Minister added.

"If we are to save the world from the forces of evil and the battle of Armageddon, that's what is it going to take," President Purcell said, "everything we have *and* Divine intervention."

EPILOGUE:

Excerpts from a prepublication interview with former First Lady Norene Bronkston Edmonds

To be asked to write the life story of the late Dr. Mason L. Edmonds, former President of the United States of America, is a singular and distinctive honor. Though it is an overused cliché, this man truly was bigger than life? Was he truly the embodiment of the American spirit that resides in all of us? Time will tell. However, after learning about the man and his mission, I understand why America's enemies would have been threatened by the things he knew and advocated.

If I was going to do justice to the late President, I needed to know as much as anyone could about him. The person who was most qualified to tell me about him was his widow, Norene Edmonds. I chose to republish the First Lady's comments as they were shared with me and with minimal editing.

A lot has happened in the world since I first interviewed the former First Lady. After months of research and writing, I completed the late President's biography. I chose to entitle the book *The Oath*. Now that you have read it, you will understand why the title I chose seemed appropriate.

When the media learned that I had conducted in-depth interviews with the late President's widow, a plethora of questions and rumors about her surfaced. Like President Edmonds, the First Lady was a wealth of information, some of which made a lot of people uneasy. Many in the mainstream media asked how she spends her time and what are her own ambitions in the political arena?

What I learned is that *this* former First Lady is different from others who held the title. In fact, with what I have been able to ascertain, every one of the former First

Ladies had had different interests and ambitions. Some have remained in the limelight, making millions giving speeches around the world, accompanied by teams of Secret Service men and women who were paid with America's taxpayer money. Others have retreated from the public's view.

I can tell you that when Air Force Two landed at the Naval Air Base just a few miles east of Fountainhead Ranch, with her, Norene Edmonds dismissed as many of the Secret Service detail as the law allowed. She insisted, however, that the one assigned to her have a medical background and be prepared to assist with volunteer service in VA hospitals, as her late husband had planned to do after leaving office. In short, *this* former First Lady chose not to retreat. She continued with her chosen mission, advancing her late husband's passion for the Oath of Thirteen project.

I had to experience this "mission" for myself. So I made a trip to Fountainhead Ranch and arranged for a series of interviews with the former First Lady.

On the first morning, I sat with Norene Edmonds on the veranda of her home at Fountainhead Ranch, where the President and his closest advisers had gathered to discuss national security issues. Between sips of coffee, she directed my attention to the herd of horses grazing in the pasture behind the house, pointing to each one, calling him or her by name.

"Mason loved to sit here and watch the horses," She said. "Sometimes, we sat for hours without speaking watching them do what is bred into their genes."

The two young colts playing "chase" caught her eye. "Now, that's a picture," she said. "I wish there was a way to package whatever it is that those two young colts have and give it to some of the residents we saw today in the senior care facility. It is a sad thing to see anything or anyone who was once strong and vibrant begin to fade."

I replied, "Remember, I've read the report published by the healthcare commission that your late husband appointed, Ma'am. When you talk about that which was once strong and vibrant, are you referring to the patients in the senior care facility or to the United States?"

"You are a perceptive man," she answered. "My husband often told me, 'It is one thing to see the natural progression of aging and infirmity. It is another to see others engineer the demise of that which you love.' He often quoted C.S. Elliot, who said, 'Of all tyrannies, a tyranny sincerely exercised for the good of its victims may be the most oppressive.' Mason said that there was a medical condition which illustrated Elliot's observation. It is called Munchausen's Syndrome by proxy."

"Could you spell that," I asked.

"Gladly," she said, complying with my request.

"People suffering from this disorder intentionally create conditions in someone they are supposed to care for—one of their children or dependents," she added. "Instead of nurturing the person entrusted in their care, they impose unhealthy conditions on them, causing the child or dependent to suffer, often resulting in multiple unnecessary operations or hospitalizations."

"Why in the world would a parent or guardian do such a thing?" I asked.

"That's the mystery of the disorder. Mason believed it was all about manipulation and control," Mrs. Edmonds replied.

"That's the message that he was trying to get across in having the Edmonds' Commission's Report, **OPERATION ANNUIT COEPTIS,** published, isn't it, Ma'am?"

"Precisely," she responded. "As a physician, he knew that people and nations acted—and reacted—in similar manners. I heard him say that the human body was designed to last at least one hundred and twenty years and that the natural lifespan of a democracy was a little more than twice that of the human body. It is the things people do to our bodies and nations—and what others do to us— that shorten life spans and cause us to wear down and die prematurely. That's why it was so hard for him to accept what some of the leaders who were exposed by Operation Annuit Coeptis were doing—intentionally bleeding America to the brink of death—for their own benefit, like Munchausen's Syndrome by proxy."

"President Edmonds had a unique perspective on the role of government in people's lives, didn't he?" I asked, inviting his widow to reveal a side of her late husband that only she could know.

"He did," the former First Lady answered. "The oath that you and he took when you graduated from medical school, the one he took when he, later, graduated from law school, the one he took when he became a U.S. congressman, and the one he took when he assumed the office of the presidency swore him to protect and defend a way of life based upon the laws of man and God. He believed that people, individually and collectively, behave in compliance with how other human beings and nations behaved in the past."

"Is that why he was so intrigued with the writings of Dr. Albert Schweitzer?" I asked. "I heard him mention Dr. Schweitzer in a speech he gave to the American College of Surgeons while he was in Congress."

"My husband liked to say that this is the set of rules on which Albert Schweitzer based his Nobel Prize-winning philosophy known as 'Reverence for Life,' an oath that every human being can take, a simple one that is rooted in the Scriptures. When given the opportunity to do so, my husband reminded people of the 'Golden Rule': 'Do unto others as you would have them do unto you.' By doing so, the doer would exhibit a reverence for life that would speak volumes about whose values the doer of such acts had adopted. You see, my husband believed that the Creators intended for us to be our brothers' and sisters' keepers.

"If we weren't put on this planet to look after each other, then why are we here?" the former First Lady asked.

"Did I understand you to say Creators, plural?" I asked.

"You did. I was under the impression that you were the author of a book entitled *Let Us Make Man*. Mason read your book and agreed with your conclusion that Genesis 1:26 affirms that although none was needed, an omnipotent God asked for assistance when it came to making man."

"I'm honored to know that the late President had read my book and that he agreed with some of my conclusions," I said.

"He found your approach to creation and evolution well-founded in both theology and science," the First Lady said.

"Speaking of being our brothers' and sisters' keepers," I interjected, "may I ask you what happened to the letters your late husband kept in the safety deposit boxes—you know, the ones that he called 'insurance'—if in fact they ever existed? Rumors of their existence have been floating around Washington ever since he met with the man whom he replaced in the Oval Office."

"It's hard to keep a secret in Washington," Norene Edmonds replied. "Yes, they did exist. Mason believed that he was a threat to the individuals that Operation Annuit Coeptis eventually exposed. He wrote their names and misdoings in a document that he put away in case he was killed. Then the crash with everyone aboard occurred—at least that is what the press has led everyone to believe. Miraculously, and after my husband was assassinated, President Padgett surfaced. Back from the dead, or so they say.

The commission my husband appointed to look into the matter is still gathering information. Mason also believed that it was possible that none of the perpetrators and their families and friends were aboard. I guess, in time, we will know."

"Where are the documents that your husband had locked away now? Do you intend to release them?"

"Let me take your first question first," She responded. "On the trip to New York for the rerelease of **OPERATION ANNUIT COEPTIS**, I followed the plan that Mason had given to me years before. I took a circuitous route in the private plane provided by the publisher. Leaving Fountainhead, the plane turned west to Independence Missouri. There, I made a visit to the Truman National Bank. Next, the plane flew northeastward to Gettysburg, Pennsylvania, where I visited the Lincoln National Bank. Finally we flew into Alexandria, Virginia, where I visited the Robert E. Lee

National Bank, which is located very close to Arlington, the Confederate General's former plantation. I'm sure you know that Arlington is the home of the cemetery of America's fallen heroes. It bears the name of the plantation once owned by Robert E. Lee before the Civil War. It is also where the Tomb of the Unknown Soldier is located ... and, of course, my husband's burial site."

"It's sad to learn that some of the graves and headstones were not treated with the kind of respect that the men and women buried in and below them deserved," I said.

"That's bureaucracy," the First Lady answered. "When people who never fought for the freedoms they enjoy are put in charge, bad things happen."

"Sorry to interrupt," I said. "What did you after leaving Virginia?"

"After leaving Alexandria, I boarded the plane and flew into a private airport just outside New York City. I put the envelopes that I had collected from the safety boxes in each of the cities I visited in a duffle bag."

"Where is the bag now?" I asked the former First Lady.

"In my cedar closet."

"Does anyone else know that you have them?"

"Not until now," she answered. "Just you."

"What do you intend to do with the letters," I asked.

"Well," Mrs. Edmonds said, "I'm going to keep three of the originals in a safer place and give one copy of each to you. Two VOX hosts have a copy, as well. I want you to use the contents of the safety deposit boxes in the book you are writing. The information they contained will help you inform the American people about the events leading up to my husband's death. But, just in case something happens to you—or me—I want the letters to find their way into the hands of those who will reveal the truth. I'm not going to tell you, just now, who that will be. I think that many of us underestimated the resolve and power of those Operation Annuit Coeptis brought down."

"May I ask you a sensitive question, Mrs. Edmonds?"

"Anything," she responded. "I've agreed to meet with you so that you can tell my husband's story, the one based on facts."

"Do you hold a grudge against those who assassinated your husband?"

The answer I received might surprise you.

She said, "I won't lie to you. Sure, I feel hard toward those who plotted against and gunned down a good man in cold blood because they didn't agree with his vision for America. I feel sorry for our country and its people. The fact that there are those who would conspire to do whatever is necessary to take the freedoms we have enjoyed from us is what should make every American rise up against those kinds of people and let the voices of reason be heard."

"Do you think that the American people will do that—rise up against the Illuminati?" I asked.

"As the wife of a physician I learned that it is possible to mask an infection or cancer for a while, but that which is destructive eventually reveals itself. My husband did his part. He exposed the cause of the diseases eating away at the United States. Now it is up to you and me to do our part, to help President Purcell capture and bring the Illuminati and their emissaries to justice. Those behind the sinister plan that Operation Annuit Coeptis uncovered and my husband's death must answer to the American people, and then to God. I don't envy them having to answer to either, much less both," she said, expecting the interview to end there.

"If you will indulge me, Ma'am, there is one question that I've always wanted to ask a former First Lady or President. Do you mind if I pose it to you?" I said.

The former First Lady graciously nodded,

"What would you say was the most valuable lesson you learned during your stint in Washington?" I asked.

The former First Lady replied, "I learned a lot. It was there that I came to see how a government, unchecked, can become an entity unto itself. Did you ever see the movie *2001: A Space Odyssey?*"

"Sure," I responded.

"Then, you'll understand my answer," Mrs. Edmonds replied. "You'll recall that in the movie, HAL, the super computer, eventually took on a personality of its own, independent of the one its programmers had instilled."

"Yes. I remember."

"That's Washington. It's HAL, embodied. It is no longer the people's government. It is an entity unto itself, self-perpetuating and self-preserving, or so it thinks. The problem is that the majority of the people who are in high places are controlled by the intellectual elites and world bankers that run the world. The existing government has become a monster, consuming everything in sight, including the people's freedoms and assets. The massive, self-perpetuating bureaucracy that has been allowed to confiscate our nation's capitol needs to be dismantled and rebuilt, like HAL was in the movie. Don't get me wrong. There were a few good people in government who were there for the right reasons, but the good ones were overshadowed by those who were there for the wrong reasons. If Americans could tour the buildings that their money built and see first-hand the incompetence that exists among the people who are making decisions *for those of us who pay their salaries*, they would be outraged.

"My husband was fond of repeating the lessons learned in nursery rhymes and children's stories. He said that they contained wisdom often forgotten when we become adults. After being in Washington for a few months, he once told me that the nation's capitol reminded him of Oz in the story *The Wizard of Oz.*"

"How so?" I asked.

She replied, "You remember that the people of Oz had been led to believe that wizard was all-powerful and all-knowing. The people of Oz held him in awe until it was discovered that the wizard was merely an ordinary man hiding behind an imposing facade with an amplified speaker that had been designed to add authority to his voice.

"Well, that's what 'government' is. When people speak of 'the Government,' they are not referring to an living, breathing entity, but an onerous image, created by politicians and bureaucrats who are hiding behind the façade they create and perpetuate. Many of the decision-makers are less well informed and less educated than the vast majority of the people whose lives they hold in the palms of their hands. Too many of them have never worked for a living, met a payroll, or been forced to work within a budget."

Clearly, I had struck a nerve. The former First Lady went on, unprompted.

"As a whole, the Washington that I saw when my husband and I went there was not the real world, but a fictitious kingdom, like Oz. And like Oz, it is controlled by a closed clique of people whose egos generally outweigh their credentials, a fraternity of politicians and aides who look at power as an aphrodisiac, a body of wasteful individuals who are quick to give everyone else's money away, but unwilling to part with their own, or with the extraordinary benefits of the offices they hold, a society of career leeches living off the republic they seem bent on destroying, a community of self-indulgent cowards who are afraid to stand for what is right and just, for fear of *offending* those whose sensitivities are used for personal and political gain. In short, Washington is a society of the most inept group of individuals that I had ever encountered. That's the Washington that existed when Mason and I went there. "

"You don't seem to have a very high opinion of some of the people who are turning the wheels of government," I added.

"I lived there. We dealt with them, firsthand. I saw what my husband had to do to try and get even simple, no-brainer things done. Inefficiencies seemed to be built into the system. Look at the crisis in the Gulf of Mexico. While the beautiful life-filled waters along the coast were being bathed in oil, bureaucrats were checking with the environmentalist, animal rights proponents, and other single-purposed organizations, being careful not to erode their political base. Meanwhile, the very environment that some of these organizations claim to be concerned about was drowning in oil.

"Washington is more concerned over political correctness, affirmative action, and getting re-elected than moral correctness and efficient action. Jobs are created to put people on the government's payroll to do essentially nothing but occupy a chair and a desk, work twenty minutes out of an hour, and draw a check," the former First Lady said. "That's the Washington we discovered when we got there."

"What did Washington look like when you left?"

"Like a wolf dressed up in sheep's clothing. The promising difference is that there is a new sheriff in town. My husband rocked the ship of state, but it needed to be capsized. Fortunately, a like-minded individual occupies the Oval Office today. President Purcell is as tough as they come. Starting with my husband's Administration, a few of the political gangsters were replaced with the kind of people that the Founding Fathers envisioned running the government, but the old guard was simply lying low. Like bears when the snow comes and cold winds blow, they are hibernating. Their quest for power, and the people who pull their strings, will not allow them to go away, at least not for very long. They are already working their way back in."

"What indicators suggest that those exposed by Operation Annuit Coeptis are regaining a foothold?" I asked.

"The first indication that they are doing so was when they contacted virtually every publishing house in the world and blacklisted *OPERATION ANNUIT COEPTIS: A Presidential Commission's Report*. Do you know," the First Lady said, "this is the first time in the history of this country that a presidentially appointed commission's report was removed from the shelves of book stores and warehouses?"

"I'm sorry to say that it hadn't occurred to me," I admitted.

"With all due respect, that's one of the problems facing this country. People don't read or listen *between the lines*. The report of the commission that my late husband appointed revealed the facts, facts that the American people deserved to know about their government and the people who were stealing them blind. That's why those it exposed went to work and got it blacklisted. That's why the same people are already working to keep the book that you are currently writing from being published. In their world, they have to suppress the truth and silence those who speak it. They will be back if the American people let them."

"What can be done to keep America strong?" I asked.

The former First Lady seemed to be poised for the question. "I'll tell you what my late husband believed. He believed that the advice of President John F. Kennedy is the answer. You will recall that President Kennedy said, 'Ask not what your country can do for you. Ask what you can do for your country.' Mason repeated those words in a commencement address on the day he was shot. But he added a phrase to President Kennedy's statement: 'Don't just ask, *do* what you can do for your country.'"

The First Lady realized that she was beginning to let her emotions show through. She collected herself and continued, "My husband believed that this generation of Americans seems to have gotten it backwards. Today, too many are asking what their country can do for them. Just look at the tax dollars handed out in the so-called stimulus packages and bailouts of 2009. Do you think that the people and businesses receiving the money considered what they were doing for their country or for themselves? Do you think that they considered what it cost other Americans to have them continue in the style to which they had become accustomed, or felt they deserved? Did they care? My husband was so encouraged by the response that he received from the graduating seniors following the commencement address at his alma mater. They seemed to be moved by his no-nonsense revelations about the state of this country and their own roles in returning it to reason. For the first time, many of them realized that their futures were mortgaged in order to fund a World Government agenda who would continue to *take from them* until there was nothing left to take. They understood the message he conveyed, that throughout history, survivors have seen to it that good times follow bad. He was convinced that those who heard his words would join the grass-roots ballot-box revolution and, once again, bring order out of chaos."

"It is clear that you truly understood your husband's vision and mission," I said to Norene Edmonds. "I'm impressed that you recall so much of what he said."

"Mason and I were married for 45 years. We shared everything. I was with him when he worked his way through medical school and developed his philosophies. I went with him during the years that he made medical speeches and gave lectures. I was on the campaign trail with him when he ran for Congress. We talked a lot about his vision for America before he agreed to come back from leave and assume the position of Secretary of Health and Human Services, gaining him the Presidency under the most unusual of circumstances. Yes, I knew my husband. I loved my husband. And I believe as strongly as ever in the American way of life that he was desperately trying to revive."

"If I may be so bold, did he have any final instructions for you before he died?"

"As he lay dying in that helicopter, he asked me to help you tell his story, to carry his message forward. That is all I am trying to do. This interview and the book that it will lead to is not at all about me, it is about a shining example of the American way, an example personified in the life of my late husband."

"You seem so calm when you talk about him and the circumstances that led to this interview," I said to Mrs. Edmonds.

"Don't be fooled by outward appearances. Inside, my gut is wrenching. It is hard to balance the hurt and passion I feel with the diplomacy and resoluteness that is necessary to convince people that I am telling the truth," she replied.

"I think you are doing an admirable job of balancing them all."

"Mason's hope was that the American people will take a hard look at the individuals and organizations that are committed to shaping the destiny of the United States the way *they* want it to be. His Commission on Education and Ethics is supposed to look at what our children are being taught and who is teaching them. He felt that the reason why America was losing its way was that America's adversaries have worked themselves in positions of authority and influence. He hoped that fair-minded people in every corner of this great nation will wake up, to let their voices be heard and take the country back from those who would change it in a way that undermines the intent of the Founding Fathers," she added. "His dying wish was that people from all walks of life will support President Purcell in his efforts to 'create a more perfect union.' one that emerges from requiring everyone we send to Washington to pledge an oath to God and country, and abide by it."

"That wouldn't make the atheists very happy—or the ACLU," I said.

"Mason was not about making everyone happy, especially America's enemies. He was about making whatever is *wrong*, right. He hoped that every American child would come to know about the message behind the Oath of Thirteen before graduating from kindergarten, that they are encouraged to carry a dollar bill with them at all times, and that they are reminded of the capitalistic institutions it represents every time they transfer a dollar from their hands to another human being. This was my husband's hope. And, I hope that you will explain what the Oath of Thirteen means in the book you are writing."

"You can bet on it," I answered, then asked the former First Lady if there was anything else she wished for.

She replied, "Yes, there is one more thing that my husband believed would be good for America. The press is often referred to as the "Fourth Estate of Government." That being the case, every graduate from schools of journalism or every media employee should be required to take an oath, swearing them to report the truth, the whole truth and nothing but the truth. The oath, to which they should swear, would have them put their personal agendas aside and refrain from trying to change the world with the manner in which they report the news. My husband felt that this kind of change would begin to correct many of America's, and the world's ills. That was the *unstated* message in the book entitled *OPERATION ANNUIT COEPTIS*. And, that is why the report was blacklisted."

Somewhat taken aback by such a revolutionary suggestion, I paused for a moment to collect my thoughts. The only thing I could think to ask was, "Is there anything else that *you* intend to do?"

The former First Lady answered. "Yes, with your help, I intend to continue being my husband's voice. Together, we will speak through the book that you are writing. He once wrote an op-ed that the newspapers wouldn't print. He wanted to remind the American people that pulling the strings of many of the politicians who they have entrusted to control their destiny is a powerful and relentless group of overlords that see America as the next plum in their attempt to enslave the world to *their* self-serving ways. I think I have a copy of it over here in his desk drawer."

Opening the bottom right drawer of a walnut-stained oak desk, the former First Lady retrieved a packet of papers from a file. "Here it is," she said. "My husband wrote:

> '*That these shadowy overlords exist is hidden from the public eye by the media they control. If their False Flag agendas were known to the average citizen, there would be a grass-roots revolution that would make the one in 1776 pale in comparison.*'

"No wonder they wouldn't publish the article," I declared. "They feared the grass-roots revolution to which he referred."

"Here is the oath signed by the founding members of Operation Annuit Coeptis," she said, retrieving another document from the file and handing it to me.

I read the words written on the printed page and noted with interest the signatures of the men who had signed it. Now that much of their mission had been accomplished, the pledge they took on that day in 2009 was more meaningful than words can express. Each of the men had boldly inscribed their names on a declaration of a different kind, one that stated:

> 'We, the founding members of *Operation Annuit Coeptis,* do solemnly swear and avow to use all means necessary to protect and defend the United States of America against individuals, organizations, or governments that engage in, or support, activities intended to undermine or undo the Declarations and Constitution crafted by the Republic's Founding Fathers. Furthermore, we pledge to expose and bring to justice all who participate in acts of deceit and/or treason against the Republic and its lawful citizens. And, as we go forth to fulfill the terms and conditions of this oath, we pray that God will look favorably upon our undertakings.'

I read the last sentence of the document with a new appreciation for the resolve of five brave patriots who were willing to sign their names to such a declaration.

"Surely," I said to the former First Lady, "God looked upon their undertakings favorably. And the United States of America was given a second chance."

"Let us hope so," she answered. "There's still a lot of work to be done and a lot of powerful people who would like to see President Purcell fail or be removed from their path, as was my husband. Just keep in mind that retreat does not always mean surrender. Sometimes the enemy returns to camp in order to come again with a new plan, new leaders, and new weapons."

"May I ask you about something that I saw as I glanced over the op-ed piece that your husband wrote?" I asked.

"Sure, anything," she replied.

"I noticed the term 'False Flag.' The only other time that I've heard the term is on the night the President called me from the Oval Office. Do you know what it means?" I asked.

"All I know is what I heard him and Morley talking about one night as we sat on our veranda," She said. "It is a military term used for deception. In order for an aggressor to slip up on his prey, he flies the flag of the prey, making him believe that he is one of them. Before the prey realizes what has happened—it is too late to react."

"Do you think that this is a tactic used by your husband's predecessor?" I asked.

"I know that Mason believed it was. I heard him say that President Padgett seemed to be more committed to America's enemies than the country he was sworn to lead. In the beginning, he refused to wear the traditional Presidential lapel flag pen. He refused to place his right hand over his heart and repeat the pledge of allegiance to the flag of the United States of America. He claimed to be a Christian, yet seemed to follow Muslim teachings. Yeah, a lot of people questioned whose flag he flew in his soul," the First Lady added.

"May I follow up on your statement about his Muslim traditions?" I asked.

"Absolutely," she replied.

"I noticed that whenever President Padgett traveled to Muslim nations that his wife didn't go with him. Was there a reason for that?"

"I can only tell you what I heard Morley tell my husband when he asked the same question," she answered. "If the purpose of a trip has political implications, the wife of a Muslim man may not accompany him into countries that adhere to Sharia law. They pointed out many indications that the former President was beholding to his Muslim upbringing, including bowing to the King of Saudi Arabia, demonstrating to the Muslim where his heart still lies."

"Do you think that this had anything to do with his Administration's stand on the terrorists' trials from Guantanamo Bay," I asked.

"Again, I can tell you what my husband believed," she replied. "It is prohibited for a Muslim to contribute to the death of another Muslim; and if a military court found the terrorists guilty, the President of the United States would have to sign off on their execution. If they were tried in civilian courts, the President would not have to do so."

"You have just answered a lot of questions for me—and I'm sure a lot of people who may read the book that I am writing," I said.

Taking advantage of her continued willingness to talk openly about a lot of sensitive issues, I asked Mrs. Edmonds if she had evidence that the sinister plan to bury America as we know it was a reality or a conspiratorial myth. She replied, emphatically, "It's a fact. Take healthcare for example. My husband had discovered that the government's interest in the healthcare arena had nothing to do with *taking care* of people. Electronic medical records had nothing to do with efficiency. It was yet another way for some government employee or officer to gain access to personal information about patients and those who cared for them" Mason said, 'The electronic medical record is yet another tool of Big Brother that allows government to monitor and control the lives of the people it intends to enslave.' In a nutshell, the healthcare charade was simply the next step in the overlords' plan to take charge of people's lives cradle to grave.

She continued, "I would suggest that the American people familiarize themselves with George Orwell's classic *1984*. It and the Public Broadcasting System's documentary entitled *Nietzsche and the Nazis* exposed the real agenda behind the previous Administration's healthcare reform. When some people heard my husband point out such things they called him a fatalist and conspiracists. He was anything but a fatalist. He was also not a conspiracists. Mason Edmonds was a realist. Look around you and you will see that every American lives with the kind of chaos created by those who are out to enforce the formula of America's demise. In order to promote *their* agenda, the Shadow Government killed my husband and severely wounded me, at least in spirit. They attempted to kill one of those acting as an informant in my husband's assassination on the day my husband died, knowing that the assassin's shooter would also be killed in the act. That's how they work. They cover their tracks. Mason was convinced that the Illuminati truly believe that they are descendants of superhuman beings and chosen to be the masters of the world and the rest of us were created to be their loyal subjects."

"Subjects or slaves?" I interjected.

"What's the difference," she replied, "Based on the research that Mason had conducted, he was convinced that the overlords use egotists like George Soros, who are vying to win a seat on the Illuminati's Inner Circle to do their bidding in the open. Atheist, anti-Americans have long been indoctrinating our children to their way of thinking, through schools, textbooks, and television programs. They took a verse from the Bible and adapted it to their way of indoctrination. Their version of Proverbs 22:6 would read: *"Train up a child in the way we think it should go; and even when he or she is old, he or she will not depart from it."* It is in response to this kind of indoctrination that so many parents take their children out of public schools and place them, instead, in private or parochial schools.

"Have you ever considered that this could also be part of the socialists' plan, to drive out the people who they may not be able to indoctrinate?" I asked. "By doing so, no one could debate the socialists' version of truth in the classroom. Such a plan would create a captive audience—their version of 'Indigo Children,' especially in public schools, an audience that is growing daily, by leaps and bounds?"

"Mason believed that every generation viewed the present as well as the future through the eyes of their teachers," the First Lady said. "That's why he felt so strongly that parents hold teachers and the schools in which they teach accountable for what children hear and read."

"What did your husband think about the growing population of Muslims in America?"

"From reading the Muslim's own policy documents, he was convinced that they were out to control the world by both aggression and by repopulating democratic nations with people committed only to Islam. I don't know if he had considered the possibility, but both scenarios could explain why God and prayer have been excluded from the schools and why textbooks are written to drum down America and its Founding Fathers," she replied, then added, "My husband also believed that Muslims were being used by the powerful order of intellectuals and bankers who were out to create a One World Government. Operation Annuit Coeptis discovered documents that affirmed his suspicions that America's enemies chip away at our thoughts and ideals not only through schools, but through movies, documentaries, and advertisements. Pay close attention to how television commercials dumb down some segments of our society and paint others in a positive light. They believe that if they control our attitudes towards issues and people, they can control our actions. Those out to create a One World Government truly believe that they know better than we do what is best for us."

"Who do *you* believe the Shadow Government you mentioned represent?" I asked the former First Lady.

"My husband's research, through Operation Annuit Coeptis, revealed that thirteen powerful families rule the world and that they use the biblical Book of Deuteronomy as a basis for their agendas and protocols. The report that was blacklisted concluded that the United Nations is their workshop. The World Bank is their hammer. Global warming is their vice. Oil is the driving force. The press is their helper. And the United States of America is the next nail that they are building in freedom's coffin. OAC documented how they've been pounding on us for years, trying to beat us down so that they could instill an Orwellian-styled' government worldwide."

Once again, the former First Lady got up out of her chair and went to her late husband's desk. She opened the file drawer and retrieved a copy of notes that the Commission on Espionage and Terrorism had used to compile its report. She handed me a sheet of paper. "This is what convinced Mason that America was in danger."

I took the sheet from the former First Lady and began to read.

The former First Lady got up from her chair and said, "It's going to take you a few minutes to read that document. I'm going to make some coffee. Would you like a cup?"

"I sure would, "I answered.

"How do you take it?" she asked.

"Black, thank you," I replied.

As she exited the room, my eyes returned to the document that she had handed to me.

> "Down through the ages there have been many secret societies and conspiratorial movements that had as their goals absolute rule of the world, overthrow of all existing governments, and the final destruction of all religion.
>
> "It was a professor of canon law at the University of Ingolstadt (Bavaria, Germany) who established a continuing organizational structure to direct the worldwide attach on religion and monarchy, and which organizational structure would eventually rule the world. His name was Adam Weishaupt and the organization he founded on May 1, 1776, was called the Order of the Illuminati (the same year as America declared its independence from British rule.)
>
> "As Weishaupt stated, 'we must do our utmost to procure the advancement of Illuminati into all important civil offices.' An Illuminist was required to take an oath which binds his every thought, action, and his fate to the administration of his superiors in the Order. An elaborate spy network was set up so that all members

would constantly be checking on the loyalty of each other.

"The secret police of the Order killed anyone who tried to inform the authorities about the (Illuminati's) conspiracy. This (policing) band was known as the 'Insinuating Brethren' and had as its insignia an all-seeing eye.

"The structure of the Order was pyramidal with Weishaupt at the top (of the pyramid). In reward for selling himself totally to the Order, the top-level Illuminatus was granted all the material and sensual benefits that could possibly be obtained. Weishaupt intended that "Money, services, honor, goods and blood must be expended for the fully proved Brethren." The original writings of the Order contained detailed instructions on how hatred and bloodshed might be created between different racial, religious, ethnic, and even sexual groups. The idea of promoting hatred between children and their parents was introduced.

"Even the kinds of buildings to be burned in urban insurrections were outlined. In short, virtually every subversive act one sees in the twentieth (and twenty-first) century was planned and written down by Adam Weishaupt over two hundred years ago. An examination of his (Weishaupt's) writings will fully substantiate this claim.

"It was not until the summer of 1782 (six years after the founding of the Order), that it really began to grow in power and influence, infiltrating (honorable societies and fraternities, such as) the freemasonic bodies of Western Europe and then taking control of them.

"By 1815, however, Weishaupt's ambassadors had begun to spread the conspiracy into many parts of the world beyond Bavaria and France. Two branches of the Illuminati formed the source that became the Communist League in 1848.

"The United States had been established as a Constitutional Republic in 1789, the same year the Illuminati's devastation of France (The French Revolution) began. (As it had done in France) Illuminists began organizing insurrectionary and secessionist movements to destroy the American republic as early as 1794. Their efforts were delayed by widespread public exposure (especially high-ranking Illuminists'—the Rothschild Family's—role in the slave trade).

"American branches of the Illuminati's European network (Young America and the Knights of the Golden Circle) finally established the secession movements that produced ... the Civil War of 1861-1865, and their agents assassinated President Abraham Lincoln after he defeated their plans to destroy the Union (by rallying the Union Army with the Emancipation Proclamation). Among the subversive and revolutionary nineteenth and early twentieth-century movements created by the Illuminati ... were the Marxian and 'utopian' socialist movements, anarchism, Fabian Socialism and Leninist Bolshevism. (To the Illuminati, chaos, war, and insurrection represent a means to an end.) Illuminist influence in the governments of Germany, Italy, France, Russia, Great Britain, and the United States combined to trigger ... World War I in 1914 for the purpose of justifying a world government structure (the unsuccessful League of Nations) after the war. The strategy was repeated again with another world war in 1939 (World War II) and the framework for a world government structure was created in 1945 as the United Nations."

"While the Order of the Illuminati began in Europe, it appeared that the United States had become a 'must-have' target; for the Order cannot create *a "one world government" without the United States.*"

At the bottom of the sheet the following words were written in Dr. Edmond's own handwriting: "*Conspiracy has many faces. A conspiracy to fabricate a conspiracy is as reprehensible as the act of actually conducting one, and just as deserving of exposure and remedy.*"

I had become so engrossed in the words I was reading that I had failed to notice that Norene Edmonds had reentered the room.

"I'm so sorry. I didn't see you come in."

"No problem," she replied. "Your coffee is on the table before you."

As I reached for the cup, I said to Mrs. Edmonds, "Who wrote this document?"

"A man named William McIlhaney. A summary of his findings were published in the September 1996 edition of *The New American.*"

"How did your husband know if McIlhaney's information was authentic?" I asked.

She answered, "Based on historical documentation and current events, the commission concluded that an Illuminati-like Order existed and that it appeared to be behind much of the chaos that existed within America and around the world.

"These revelations are disturbing," I said. "No wonder President Edmonds was considered a threat to a One World Government. He was onto their plan."

"The people behind this 'Order of the Illuminati' will let nothing stand in their way," the former First Lady answered. "They believe that it is their destiny to control all the peoples of the world. And Mason believed that a strong, independent, and self-sufficient United States of America was capitalism's last best hope. To him, it was that simple. And yet so many are blinded by the rhetoric and giveaway agendas the overlords promote, buying the masses' favor with other people's money. And, as their plan states, making them slaves to 'the Chosen,' the descendants of the lost tribe of the Annunaki. You're going to have to look that one up. It's too complicated for me to tell you about today."

"Thank you. I will," I replied, and continued with trying to get a full answer to the previous question.

"By 'other people's money' do you mean the American taxpayer?"

"Precisely," the First Lady replied. "No one should believe—for one moment—that the Illuminati will use any of their own money to promote their agenda. I think it was former British Prime Minister Margaret Thatcher who said, 'The problem with socialism is that eventually you run out of other people's money.' You need to put that in your book."

"I will," I replied.

"Mason was a fan of both Mrs. Thatcher and Ronald Reagan, two people whom he attributes to bringing down the Iron Curtain."

"With all you know, would you ever consider running for office?" I asked Norene Edmonds.

"No," she replied. "Long ago, I learned from my husband that each of us has to find our place in this world. I think I have found mine, to tell *his* story. That's the best way I know to promote the American way and the dreams he had for the nation that harbors it."

"Do you think that the people are ready to listen to the message?"

"Having grown up in rural America and around farms, my husband liked the ago-old truism: 'You can lead a horse to water, but you can't make it drink.' He also used to say that a doctor can't help a patient who doesn't want to be helped. In political terms, both truisms translated to leaders can't help a people until they choose to help themselves. I can only hope that Americans have come to realize what is at stake and are willing to stand up against all acts of tyranny, even those who work in the shadows. Too many of us have become the product of what we have been fed; and far too many have believed that they are helpless against an overbearing government."

"Your husband didn't believe that."

"Thank God that he didn't," Norene answered. "And thank God that the Founding Fathers and the brave people who drove the British imperialists out in the 1700s didn't give in, or give up, either. It was my husband's hope that patriotic Americans will once again come together and throw the newer versions of overlords out, declare independence from their oppressive ways and rebuild our government from the ground up. That's the only way we can keep the United States from going the way of Rome and Greece."

"Mrs. Edmonds," I said, "You truly have a grasp of the challenges facing our nation. I hope that you will not remain silent."

"I don't intend to," she replied. "I promised my husband that I would tell anyone who would listen what he wanted the world to hear. After reading one of your previous books, Mason commented on a statement you made on the inside flap of its dust jacket. He wrote it down in the little notebook he carried with him, the one he asked me to have printed. I know that he would want you to have a copy." She opened the drawer of the end table adjacent to the sofa. "Your statement is tabbed under 'L.'"

I took the booklet that she handed to me. It was entitled *Laney's Little Book of Wisdom*. Under the "L tab" I saw the quote from *Let Us Make Man*. It read: "Fear not the truth, but those who would suppress, distort, or ignore it."

The quote wasn't recorded exactly as I had previously written it, but the message was there. Until I interviewed the former First Lady, I didn't know that President Edmonds had read *Let Us Make Man*. On the night he called to ask me to help him tell his story, he only said that he had been given a copy by a mutual friend, Gabriel Shade. As busy as Presidents are, I hadn't expected him to have read the book. Who knows, perhaps it did play a role in the former President's asking me to write his memoirs. But that is another question to which we shall never know the answer. I looked up at Norene Edmonds, whose regal frame was patiently waiting for my next inquiry. When none came, she said, "You are not afraid of the truth, are you? You are not afraid of those who would try to suppress, distort, or ignore it, are you?"

"I think you already know the answer to your question," I replied. "But if you need to hear it spoken, No, I have no reservations about writing your husband's story. In fact, I consider it an honor to do so."

"I just wanted to hear you say it," Norene said. "Do you have everything you need?" indicating that it was time to wrap things up.

As she rose from her seat, she extended her hand in the manner that one would expect of a First Lady of the United States of America, saying "I have done the best I can, the very best I know how to share with you the thoughts, fears, and dreams of Mason Edmonds. In his efforts to combat the cancers eating away at this country, he came to realize that to those possessed by evil, truth is an insufferable rival. He and I have dealt with evil's emissaries. We have called to task those bent on enslaving us all. That we did, cost him his life. Though they have killed the man, they will never be able to kill the man's spirit. I will see to it. I have experienced hell and the ways of its angels, neither of which are pretty sights. I can only hope that somewhere in this vast universe Mason is making the case for God to intercede in the direction that this world seems to be heading, before mankind destroys itself."

Walking toward her front door, I asked, "Do you fear for your life?"

Without hesitation, Norene Edmonds answered, "No, why should I? If I'm here, I will be completing my husband's work. If his assassins kill me, I will join him, and we will work from another realm."

"I think we need you here for a while longer," I said. "Things are in disarray. Are there any leaders left?"

"Oh, yes," she replied. "They're out there. They just need to be encouraged to step forward. I think it was Glenn Beck who first suggested that what America needs is a group of re-founding fathers who would be as committed as the first. The only thing I would add is that this time around the re-founding fathers will be embraced by a group of re-founding mothers. You know, mothers have an inbred passion for protecting their young. And it is our children and our children's children who need us to exercise that inbred passion."

"Hopefully, in publishing Mason's story we can contribute to arousing the giants and humankind's inbred passion, both male and female," I added. "Perhaps your husband's story will encourage others to take up the mantle and lead."

"Let's hope so," the former First Lady replied. "Let me add just one more thing for your notes."

"Do you mind if I turn my tape recorder back on?" I asked.

She nodded, indicating that it was okay and began to speak. "I want to assure all who read the book that you plan to write that General Purcell is the right man for the times. When my husband became President, you will remember that he chose General Purcell as his Vice President and, from day one, was grooming the General to replace him in the Oval Office. My husband believed that General Purcell had the experience and character to be President in these times and would surround himself with able-bodied people dedicated to making America strong and vibrant once again. However, President Purcell needs the people's help and support for the challenges he faces."

"Do you want to add anything else to what has been said?"

"I have no more to offer at this time other than to say that I have told the truth. My husband wanted the people to know that the members of the previous administration were puppets to the group that calls themselves the Illuminati. Together, they came close to burying the America that had long nurtured and exported human rights around the globe. As you know, my husband studied history in order to understand the present and see the future. He was convinced that when the United States took down Saddam Hussein and brought a democracy into the Middle East, the Illuminati viewed the move as a step forward for freedom and human rights in that part of the world. Therefore, they demonized the Iraqi war and everyone who supported it. In concert with a complicit press, they poisoned the minds of the American people and looked for a President who would carry out their wishes to remove American troops from Iraq. They knew that if American Armed Forces were not there, in time the Illuminati would again take control of the country, its resources, and its ability to control the flow of ships, filled with oil, in and out of the Straits of Hormuz. They needed a President who would do what they needed. They found him in President Padgett."

"What do you think about President Padgett's miraculous return from the dead?"

"I am confident that the Commission on Espionage and Terrorism will get to the bottom of that question," she answered. "At this time, I'd rather not say more on the subject."

"I understand," I answered. "What do you expect the future to hold—for the United States, for the world?"

"If, and when," she said, "the United States loses its position as the leader of the free world, human rights advocates can say goodbye to human rights. As the children's fables teach, they will have truly killed the goose that laid golden eggs and/or followed the Pied Piper into the ocean, and to their own demise, as well as the cause for which they were naively committed."

"Will you allow one more question?" I inquired.

"Absolutely," she replied. "I know that you are here to learn about my late husband. He wanted you to tell his story, and me to help you do it."

"Did the President believe in reincarnation?" I didn't know if she would be willing to discuss such a matter.

"It's strange that you ask that question," the former First Lady answered. "Many times Mason and I talked about how he seemed to intuitively *know* things, things that one could only know if he or she had experienced them in another time and place.

"I remember his telling me about flashbacks of a time when he was an Indian chief somewhere in the Great Northwest. He believed that each life prepares the soul for lives to come, until we either get it right or demonstrate that we are not worthy of additional chances. Mason didn't talk about these matters to many people, especially after he began to put the pieces of the Illuminati's One World Government conspiracy together. His enemies and critics would have had a field day with such things.

"I know that he was enjoying reading one of your books, the one based on verses in Genesis suggesting that angels participated in the creation of and continued oversight of mankind. He was looking forward to talking with you about the things you wrote. He felt that you and he had a lot in common. That's why he chose you to be his storyteller.

"While there are many questions yet to be answered about creation, evolution, and reincarnation, I am convinced that Mason Edmonds was an old soul." She added, "A very old soul that gave to the world more than it took."

"Thank you Mrs. Edmonds," I said, turning off the recorder for the final time. "You have been gracious to spend so much time with me over the past few days. I will do my very best to tell your husband's story the way that you and he would want it told."

"How long do you intend to stay in the area?" the former First Lady asked.

"I'm not sure. It will take several days for me to read some of the materials you have given me. If it's okay, I'd like to come back and talk some more afterwards."

"I'll look forward to your visit," Norene Edmonds said, graciously.

As I drove out of the long, tree-lined driveway of Fountainhead Ranch, I glanced into my rear view mirror at the country home that Mason Edmonds had built for his wife and himself. I wondered how it must have felt to be President and have such a gracious and stately First Lady at my side. How does one deal with all the pomp, ceremony, and risks that surrounded the office, I asked myself, and still remain true to the people and principles that took him or her there?

Perhaps, in writing President Edmonds' story, I will discover the answer to that question and share it with the world.

I did return to talk with Norene Edmonds. We hashed out the details of her late husband's story so that I could paint his picture as accurately as possible to you, the reader.

As I write the last paragraphs of this manuscript, additional questions come to mind. Sometimes they awaken me in the middle of the night, haunting my psyche for answers.

Was Mason Edmonds a modern-day Don Quixote, haplessly jousting windmills, or the boy in the fable who cried "wolf" once too often? Could he have been a visionary, a champion of reason, a speaker of truth, a man who had put all the pieces of the puzzle together, exposing the false gods of the New World Order for what they are, an evil Invisible empire that threatens us all.

Part of my question was answered when I attended a town hall meeting conducted by President Purcell, during his "Awakening America" tour. During the question-and-answer portion of the meeting, I raised a hand and was recognized. I rose from my chair and asked the General about his predecessor and the Shadow Government's attempts to discredit the Edmonds' Commissions' Reports.

Answering the question, the General smiled and said, "Dr. Edmonds was a principled man who was true to each and every oath he had taken. He was not afraid of the truth, nor did he want the rest of us to be.

"I am convinced," the General who became President said, "that when historians look back at life of

President Edmonds, the time he occupied the Oval Office will be viewed as one in which America began to awaken from a state of apathy, a time when this great nation returned from a near-death experience. They will see the Edmonds' time as a new beginning in which fearless patriots took their country back from its enemies, both foreign and domestic. I have simply taken up where President Edmonds left off and intend to move the same agenda forward.

"His was a life well spent. Though it was cut short by an assassin's bullet, President Edmonds' shining example of fearless patriotism will not go unnoticed. Fair-minded scribes who record events and decisions will remember him as a man who helped shape the world for the better.

"The movement set in motion by President Edmonds will endure because we—people like those of us gathered here tonight—will see that it does. His memory and the values for which he stood cannot and will not be buried with the body lying beneath the shrine erected in his honor at Arlington. Like the eternal flame over his resting place, the spirit of Mason Edmonds lives on in each of us. And, because it does, we the people are his living legacy. Tell that to your children and your children's children. For if you don't tell them the truth, they may not know it.

"Thank you for asking the question," President Purcell added, glancing my way. "Did I answer it?"

"Yes, Mr. President. And if I might follow up?"

"Go ahead," President Purcell replied.

"Did President Edmonds leave behind notes that are currently in your possession addressing The Protocols of the Learned Elders of Zion?" I asked.

President Purcell hesitated in thoughtful contemplation before he answered.

"Let me respond to your question by saying that President Edmonds was an intuitive man, who felt it his responsibility to look at every potential threat to America's security. He considered the implications of all stated intentions to rob Americans of life, liberty, and the pursuit of happiness. From notes that he kept close to him, some of which have been passed on to me, I also know that he was fully aware of The Protocols to which you referred. The State of the Union speech that he intended to deliver, the same one that I delivered on President Edmonds' behalf, addressed extensive minutes of meetings held by a group that referred to themselves as 'The Learned Elders of Zion.' These documents were discovered by Operation Annuit Coeptis during its investigation and printed in the report that was later pulled from the shelves by its publisher."

President Purcell paused and looked into my eyes. "Did I sufficiently address your follow-up question?" he asked.

The best response I could muster was, "Absolutely and extraordinarily. Thank you, Mr. President."

Now that I have time to reflect on the President Purcell's answers, I am glad that, once again, my trusty tape recorder was rolling and that I can share his words with you, precisely and as they were spoken. I only wish you could have seen the gleam in President Purcell's eyes as he spoke about his predecessor, the man whose torch he proudly carries.

Rumor has it that in President Purcell's right hip pocket is a reproduction of a notebook entitled *Laney's Little Book of Wisdom*. Some day, I hope to get the chance to ask him if the rumor is true.

I wish I had asked President Purcell about another rumor, the one that former President Padgett, the man many believed fits the description of antichrist, was gearing up to launch a bid for the Presidency in the next election cycle, perhaps the last ever.

When this book hits the shelves, I have to wonder how former President Padgett and those who pull his strings will respond to its revelations. But, that is another story for another time.

END

Your Next Read

If you enjoyed *The Oath,* you will want to read the sequel: *The Annunaki Enigma: Armageddon 2012,* a novel by Dr. E. Gaylon McCollough and Dr. Symm Hawes McCord

Intro

Much has been written lately about a prophetic period in the future of our planet that is being referred to as "End Times". It is predicted to run collaterally with the formation of a one world government or what some may call a "One World Order", and climax with a great war in Israel over a mound known as 'har Megiddo' where the forces of good and evil clash in a battle that will end in the forces of evil being stopped and the leader, Satan, being thrown into an abyss for a thousand years.

Current geopolitical events are seemingly moving in such a pattern. Are these Biblical prophecies actually about to take place? Have leaders in our past believed the Bible's predictions and actually prepared for such a global disaster. *The Annunaki Enigma: Armageddon 2012* looks at current events and the attitudes of today's leaders and sees a parallel with the prognostications of the early writers of the Bible.

If this comes true, how will our Creator respond? Will He join forces with those on Earth to defeat such an enemy? Has He already set up a scenario for the defense of His creations at some point earlier in our history?

Also in the series:

The Annunaki Enigma: Creation

by

Dr. Symm H. McCord

Order from your favorite bookstore or from

www.a-argusbooks.com

Enjoy

Made in the USA
Charleston, SC
20 September 2010